THE EASTERN STORIES

SO-AAZ-884

Joseph Conrad

Edited by Ban Kah Choon

PENGUIN BOOKS

Penguin Books India (P) Ltd., 11 Community Centre, Panchsheel Park, New Delhi 110 017, India
Penguin Books Ltd., 27 Wrights Lane, London W8 5TZ, UK
Penguin Putnam Inc., 375 Hudson Street, New York, NY 10014, USA
Penguin Books Australia Ltd., Ringwood, Victoria, Australia
Penguin Books Canada Ltd., 10 Alcorn Avenue, Suite 300, Toronto, Ontario M4V 3B2, Canada
Penguin Books (NZ) Ltd., Cnr Rosedale & Airborne Roads, Albany, Auckland, New Zealand

First published by Penguin Books India 2000

This anthology copyright © Penguin Books India 2000
Introduction copyright © Ban Kah Choon 2000

Typeset in Sabon by Digital Technologies and Printing Solutions, New Delhi

Printed at Chaman Offset Printers, New Delhi

PENGUIN BOOKS
THE EASTERN STORIES

Joseph Conrad was born on 3 December 1857 in a part of Poland then occupied by Russia. He turned to the sea for a living and spent twenty years sailing to some of the remotest corners of the world, such as the West Indies, Australia, the Belgian Congo and Southeast Asia, which provided him with many extraordinary experiences that inspired his stories.

Conrad lived in Britain for many years and revolutionized modern English literature with his great novels *Lord Jim*, *Heart of Darkness*, *Nostromo* and *The Secret Agent*.

He died in 1924.

*

Ban Kah Choon has worked extensively in the ideological narratives of colonial Southeast Asia. He has recently edited a special issue of *Commentary on Materialism* and *The City of Forgetting: The Stories of Gopal Baratham*. A major study of the Special Branch in British Malaya, entitled *Absent History*, will be published shortly.

He teaches modernism and post-war Chinese literature at the National University of Singapore.

Contents

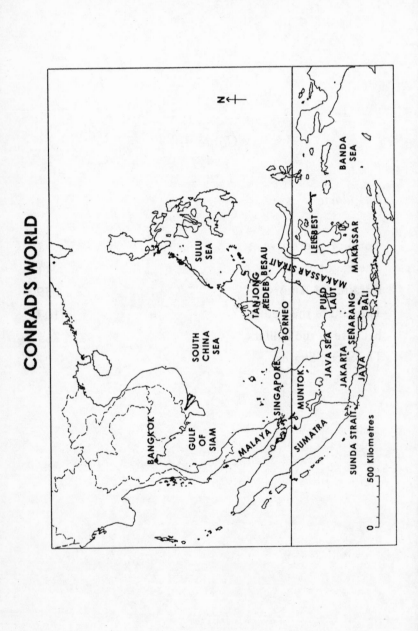

CONRAD'S WORLD

Introduction

Joseph Conrad is one of the few writers whose life was as compelling as the fiction he wrote. He was born Jozef Teodor Konrad Korzeniowski in 1857, in Berdyczow, Ukraine, a part of present-day Poland annexed by the Russians. His father, Apollo, was active both as a writer and a member of the underground resistance against the Russian Tsarist government. In 1862, after a summary trial for his clandestine activities, Apollo was exiled to Vologda, 300 miles to the north-east of Moscow. His family followed him into exile. This banishment to the equivalent of the Stalinist gulag affected Conrad's health severely. Throughout his childhood, as in his later life, Conrad suffered from the effects of the trauma, experiencing frequent nervous fits, epileptic bouts and migraine.

Yet his frail health fired, rather than weakened, his desire to be a sailor and traveller. The sea, uncharted territories and strange lands beckoned irresistibly to the young Conrad who was lured by their romanticism and freedom. Therefore, in October 1874, he travelled to Marseilles, the cosmopolitan Mediterranean port in southern France, determined to carry out his dream of becoming a sailor. This was the first of his many 'standing jumps', as he put it, which would take him far away from his familiar Polish surroundings and associations.

The following year, Conrad sailed as a ship's boy for the Caribbean.

However, it was his momentous decision to join the British Merchant Service that decisively shaped his career, both at sea and as a writer. In 1878, Conrad arrived in Lowestoft, England, where he signed up as an ordinary seaman on the *Skimmer of the Seas*, a small coastal vessel. England was then at the height of her imperial power and her ships could be found in the remotest corners of the world. The opportunity to travel further afield, to the outer reaches of the British empire, soon presented itself. In the years that followed, Conrad was to sail to Australia, India, the Malayan Archipelago, Singapore, Bangkok and the Congo.

Conrad's first voyage to the East was dogged by misfortune, underlining the dangers that confronted sailors in those days. In 1882, he signed on as second mate in the *Palestine*, a barque carrying coal from Falmouth to Bangkok. He was twenty-four and was soon to experience at first hand the economics of profit and greed that motivated the British presence in the East. The 425-ton *Palestine* was an old and unreliable ship, built in 1857, at Sutherland. According to Conrad's uncle, who took a dim view of subsequent events, the owner was only interested in 'blackguardly profit' and did not hesitate to expose his crew to danger if he could turn a profit.

In fact, the ship had such an unsavoury reputation that, after several fitful attempts to get the voyage under way, some of the crew left the ship. In the eight months that followed, the *Palestine* was docked at Falmouth to undergo repairs and await a new crew. Then, as if to tempt fate, the *Palestine* sailed for Bangkok on 17 September 1882, with a crew of thirteen men, among them Conrad. Unknown to them, the unscrupulous irresponsibility of the owner had turned the barque into a floating firebomb. Soon after clearing Java

Head along the southern tip of eastern Sumatra, spontaneous combustion led to a fire in the hull, followed soon after by a coal gas explosion that engulfed the barque in fire. On 14 March 1883, the crew abandoned ship and made for the small port of Muntok on Bangka Island in boats.

Conrad's first view of the East was, therefore, less than propitious. Yet it says much for the fascination the region exerted on him that, in writing of the experience years later, he would endow it with a sense of enchantment. Looking back, the episode must have been reminiscent of the mythic quality of a rites of passage, the moment when one crosses over from youth to maturity, innocence to experience. In 'Youth', written five years later, Conrad reworked many of these experiences, although he changed the ship's name to the *Judea* and introduced Marlow as the narrator. In other ways though, the circumstances were strikingly similar: from the troubles the ship faced on her journey to Bangkok, to the coal catching fire, the explosion and then the crew taking to the boats. However, instead of the thirteen-and-a-half hours Conrad took to reach Muntok, the story had the crew steering for many days. Whatever it was, the first sight of land and the East was clearly unforgettable.

> And this is how I see the East. I have seen its secret places and have looked into its very soul; but now I see it always always from a small boat, a high outline of mountains, blue and afar in the morning; like faint mist at noon; a jagged wall of purple at sunset. I have the feel of the oar in my hand, the vision of a scorching blue sea in my eyes . . . We drag at oars with aching arms, and suddenly a puff of wind, a puff faint and tepid and laden with strange odours of blossoms, of aromatic wood, comes out of the still night—the first sight of the East on my face. That I

can never forget. It was impalpable and enslaving, like a whispered promise of mysterious delight.

—'Youth'

Of course this is purplish and romantic, but it would be a mistake to dismiss it on these grounds. Behind the expressive gestures are intense feelings for the moment that heighten our awareness of the unique qualities of the land. 'Youth' has long been regarded as one of the finest stories of its kind ever written despite the occasional criticism of a tendency to overdramatize events.

The trajectory of Conrad's life and the stories he was to write confirm that the East exercised an impalpably enslaving effect upon his sensibilities. The region was for Conrad a theatre of images, sounds, smells, landscapes, scenes and, above all, the colourful people that he met and the lives they lived. What is most striking is how he used the sharpness and clarity of particular events or scenes to work upon our sensibilities. Conrad's imaginative genius evokes the powerful immediacy that makes us 'see', as he would have said. Open the book to any page and his words transport us, through their hypnotic rhythm, into scenes where even the smell takes on a different evocation.

Sunshine gleams between the lines of those short paragraphs—sunshine and the glitter of the sea. A strange name wakes up memories; the printed words scent the smoky atmosphere of today faintly, with the subtle and penetrating perfume as of land breezes breathing through the starlight of bygone nights; a signal fire gleams like a jewel on the high brow of a sombre cliff; great trees, the advanced sentries of immense forests, stand watchful and still over sleeping stretches of open water; a line of white

surf thunders on an empty beach, the shallow water
foams on the reefs; and green islets scattered through
the calm of noonday lie upon the level of a polished
sea, like a handful of emeralds on a buckler of steel.
—'Karain: A Memory'

Conrad has no hesitation writing poetry into his prose using
the full resources of words to appeal to our senses. Through
the pressure of this imaginative suggestiveness he is
constantly inviting his readers to make the mental leaps and
associations that carry our minds outwards to these unique
lands. The experience is always real, not just through the
words but through an awareness that there is a lived moment
behind the stories.

There is no better description of the Malayan land and
sea than stories like 'Karain' or 'The Lagoon'. Reading them,
we feel the heat of the midday sun, smell the scent of the
spice-filled air, and hear the whispering of waves as they
break lazily over distant reefs. However, he does not stop at
the physical geography, the external wrapping of the
landscape. Conrad takes us into the jubilation of discovering
a safe haven after days at sea, the frustrations of being
becalmed in the middle of the Gulf of Siam, the dangers of
hidden reefs and shoals and the fear evoked by a tropical
typhoon. Each of his stories is a masterful amalgamation of
sensations, feelings and judgement—reminders of how
constant human emotions are, even when set in the most
exotic of places.

In addition to making his readers see, Conrad also seeks
to make us think. He confronts his readers with the dilemmas
of existence—loyalty, betrayal, greed, the perverse impulses
of the heart and other moral issues. He is unashamedly moral
in the way that all great writers touch upon the moral and the
tragic through the questions they raise and the answers they

demand. For, what Conrad struggles with in his stories is the meaning of existence. In particular, he deals with the confrontations, often tragic, between differing ways of life and expectations as European culture comes into collision with indigenous Malay life. Conrad also explores the effects of loneliness upon man, the strange perversions of behaviour that isolation gives rise to, and the moral challenges these present. The stories draw attention to the enigma that the variety and complexity of life often confronts us with, drawing out the underlying psychological and spiritual tensions that always lie beneath the apparent placidity and normalcy of everyday life. They trigger off the impulses, anxieties and fears that come at unexpected moments to question us about our identity, achievements and fraternity. Style for Conrad is, therefore, never mere imaginative colouring, never a substitute for meaning but an invitation to the motives and the darkness of the human heart.

Many of these characteristics sprang from his Malayan experiences of ways of life that were facing rapid changes. When Conrad saw the East for the first time in 1883, Britain was well on its way to becoming the paramount power in the Malay Peninsula. However, many of the border regions continued to remain turbulent, thereby posing considerable challenges to British rule. Pirates, gangsters and bandits were always ready to take advantage of the instability, creating all manner of unrest and lawlessness whenever opportunities presented themselves. Rioting, random acts of criminal attacks, extortion and murders filled the pages of the local newspapers. Conrad was well aware of the underlying currents of violence that lay beneath the deceptive peace of British rule in the ports that he visited. In fact, the collision between European imperialism and the indigenous nations raised all kinds of questions that he was to explore in his writing.

Not surprisingly, the five years that Conrad spent in the Malay archipelago between 1883 and 1889, sailing in 'that part of the Eastern Seas from which I have carried away into my writing life the greatest number of suggestions,' were indeed memorable ones. Among other things, it was also in Southeast Asia that he obtained his first command as captain of the *Otago*. The account of that first command and his initiation into the responsibility of bringing the ship safely from Bangkok down the east coast of the Malayan peninsula to Singapore is conveyed in 'The Shadow Line'.

These years also coincided with momentous changes in the political and social life of the region. For, it was during this period that the transformation to the present-day political boundaries took place. European expansion had been at its height, making rapid inroads into the various lands, redrawing borders and altering geography. The founding of Singapore in 1819 by Stamford Raffles had strengthened British presence in the Malay peninsula. Together with Penang and Malacca, the British then controlled the entire Malacca Straits through which poured ships from Europe and India en route to the East. The European imperialist rivals also tried to carve out their various spheres of influence. The Anglo-Dutch Treaty of 1824 saw the two hitherto contending powers agreeing to their respective areas of dominance. It was understood that the Dutch were to retain control of the Indonesian archipelago while the British had a free hand in Malaya.

However it was not all entirely smooth sailing. Considerable ambiguity remained in regions like the Borneo territories where Dutch claims to establish suzerainty over the island were vigorously disputed by the British. Many of Conrad's stories touch upon the adventures of British gunrunners and blockade-runners who traded clandestinely in the Dutch-controlled Celebes. Playing hide-and-seek with

Dutch gunboats, these traders had also to dodge the many pirates that preyed upon ships. Conrad's stories also reflect the highly unsettled times as these islands plunged into factional warfare and anarchy. One undesirable side effect of the hegemony of British and Dutch rule was that traditional trade routes and ports lost their importance. As revenues plunged, the indigenous people, who had been dependent on commerce for their wealth, turned to piracy and war to bolster their dwindling revenue.

Even though much of the dangers facing Europeans in the early years of the century eventually passed, the risks of sailing in Southeast Asian waters were always present. The fate of women travellers who had the misfortune to fall into the hands of pirates, was particularly savage. John Thomson who served as a surveyor in Malaya and Singapore between 1839-1853 recalled a mutiny that took place on board the *Fawn*, a barque engaged in coastal trade between Singapore and Penang. The three English officers were murdered in their sleep while the captain's wife and her sister were subjected, in Thomson's word, to 'Satanic' abuses by the mutineers.

Whether by mutineers or pirates, random brutality was often practised. In an infamous case in north-eastern Borneo, the area into which Conrad was to sail, *Maria Frederika*, a Dutch schooner, was seized by a raiding war party after being becalmed. Both the captain and mate met particularly gruesome ends. They were carried ashore, buried to their waists in the sand and finally decapitated. Not even armed guards could offer adequate protection in the wilderness where trading posts were often sited. In 1878, a group of gangsters attacked the home of Superintendent Lloyd in Pangkor Island. Captain Lloyd was killed while his wife had her skull fractured with a hatchet. The lucky person in all this was her visitor, Isabella Bird, who was knocked unconscious with severe cuts to her head. The police guard that was provided for Captain Lloyd had little effect in deterring the attackers. Conrad was well aware of such attacks and the constant dangers posed to settlers as well as traders. In his novel, *Lord Jim*, he referred to the savage attack on James Birch, the British Resident of Perak who was speared to death in 1875 in Lower Perak while having a bath.

The landscapes, people and experiences that he encountered in these faraway ports and trading settlements were to provide Conrad with the material as well as the insights of his greatest works. While 'An Outpost of Progress' and *Heart of Darkness* are profound explorations of the flaws of colonialism in Africa, it was the East that held Conrad's affection. Many of his most memorable works are built around the encounters and experiences of Europeans in Southeast Asia. For Conrad, the East was shaped by his own voyages among the many islands, river settlements and ports. The area stretched from the Mae Nam Chao Phraya that flowed through Bangkok to Makassar and the Celebes Islands in the south. To the west, the Bangka Straits that separated the island of Bangka from Sumatra formed one end of the region. The island of Borneo (today, East Malaysia and Kalimantan) formed the other end. The range and comprehensive detail of Conrad's references to these places underline the powerful fascination they exerted on his imagination.

The Malay trilogy—*An Outcast of the Islands*, *Almayer's Folly* and *The Rescue*—recounts the exploits of Tom Lingard, the *rajah laut* or king of the seas in the Makassar Strait between Borneo and present-day Sulawesi. Conrad created a historical context that is richly authentic. Lingard organizes and supports a native uprising against the Dutch in Wajo (Sulawesi), stumbles upon a secret passage up the Pantai River and founds a trading settlement at Sambir, dreaming of the diamonds he would find in the interior of

Borneo. These events parallel the savage rivalry between the Dutch and the English, the indigenous uprisings and the mad scramble for wealth that brought traders like Lingard into the wildest parts of the region.

This region, bordering the Makassar Sea, featured in many of Conrad's prominent stories including 'Karain' and 'The Lagoon'. Unnamed narrators tell both stories. In the first, a trio of gunrunners, including Hollis, Jackson and the narrator, recounts their friendship with Karain, a native chief engaged in the territorial wars of the Bugis people. While the story is substantially about how Karain came to be haunted by the ghost of his friend Matara whom he killed in order to save the girl for whom he had developed an obsession, the context is wider. 'Karain' is also about interracial conflict and love as well as the erosion of indigenous values under the onslaught of European culture. 'The Lagoon' is a story within a story in which the European narrator listens to a tale of forbidden love, remorse and revenge by Arsat who had run off with his ruler's servant girl. Written within the conventions of the typical adventure stories of the period, both managed to go beyond their genre to the larger meanings of their themes of fidelity, courage and love.

Truth is stranger than fiction in this case. Conrad's inspiration for his characters often came from real-life persons. Their traces are scattered in the various towns and ports of Southeast Asia, a reminder of the not too distant past. In the midst of the rapidly changing cities where bits of the past disappear every day at alarming speed, we can still find reminders of these characters, their presence extending beyond the pages. Tom Lingard is based upon a real-life English adventurer, William Lingard, who was, not surprisingly, known as the *rajah laut*. Among other things, his fame as the king of the seas came from his many clashes with pirates as well as the discovery of a safe passage up the Pantai

River at the mouth of which he founded the trading settlement of Berau.

Lingard returned home to England leaving behind Charles Olmeijer, his relative by marriage, to look after Berau. Conrad was to base his striking character of Kaspar Almayer on Charles whom he got to know quite well. Olmeijer's final resting place, the grave of the *orang belanda* or Dutchman can be found in an abandoned cemetery in Surabaya, Java.

There were other famous incidents and characters from this period that found their way into Conrad's narratives. Conrad's famous novel, *Lord Jim*, is based on a real-life scandal of the eastern seas, in which Augustine Podmore Williams, the first mate, abandoned the *Jeddah* on August 1880. The *Jeddah* was carrying a full load of 953 pilgrims bound for Mecca when it apparently struck an underwater obstacle and developed a leak.

The *Jeddah* incident attracted much attention among sailing circles in the East. Williams, who was severely reprimanded by the subsequent court of inquiry, had to live down the widespread whisperings of cowardice and irresponsibility. Yet he chose not to run away. Rather, in an act of redemption and personal quest, he stayed on in Singapore throughout the rest of his life, re-establishing a solid reputation for himself there. He died in 1916 and was buried in Bidadari Cemetery, on the north-eastern outskirts of Singapore City. Conrad would have been fascinated by this story of erratic behaviour, courage and moral rebirth that became the talk of the city.

In that same year, another scandal, this time involving the famous sailing clipper, the *Cutty Sark* rocked even worldly-wise sailors. In the spring of 1880, the *Cutty Sark* was carrying a load of Welsh steam coal out to American navy ships in the Pacific. Bad feelings among the crew led to a fight in which Sydney Smith, the mate, broke the skull of one of the crew with an iron capstan bar, killing him. The drama and tragedy continued as Smith convinced Wallace, the ship's captain, to allow him to flee the ship. When the *Cutty Sark* reached Anjer, a little port in Java Head, Smith escaped to a nearby American ship, the *Colorado*, bound for Saigon. Although he was subsequently apprehended and charged with murder, Captain Wallace was overtaken by remorse and, while sailing up from Java, committed suicide by jumping over the side. Those familiar with *Lord Jim* would know that Conrad used this incident in his depiction of Captain Brierly. By a strange coincidence of fate, the *Cutty Sark* limped into Singapore harbour after its tragic journey three days after Augustine Williams' return to Singapore after the court of inquiry had convened at Aden to look into the sinking of the *Jeddah*.

The *Cutty Sark* incident would, as did Conrad's first command in the Otago, find expression in one of his most famous stories, 'The Secret Sharer'. Narrated by the young captain, the story recounts his rescue and concealment of Leggatt, the first mate of the *Sephola*, who was trying to flee after killing an insolent seaman in a moment of anger. As the voyage proceeded southwards from Bangkok to Singapore, Leggatt became transformed into the captain's doppelganger. Yet the fugitive would also be the key to the captain's redemption, for he was to become the means by which the novice captain would gain the respect of his crew. In an effort to help Leggatt, the captain had taken his ship perilously close to the eastern coastline of Malaya with its treacherous shoals and uncertain waters. Although Leggatt managed to get away unnoticed, the ship drifted dangerously close to the shore, forcing the captain to shift helm suddenly. This decisive act gained him the respect of his crew. Such a summary can only hint at the multiple levels of the story. However it does suggest something of the interweaving of self-recognition, temptation and coming of age that threw an ambivalent shading over one of his most remarkable stories.

Conrad reminds us that we should not rush to judgement. True understanding comes when we begin to wrestle with, and acknowledge, the ambivalence that we are often forced to face in our everyday existence. The typical Conradian protagonist lives on the margins of life, where his faith and beliefs are constantly challenged. Each faces a series of tests and temptations. Some succumb and must pay the price for their indiscretions as they struggle to reclaim their morality. Others are thrown into situations which invite them to compromise their ideals. All are, however, required to live with the consequences of their choices. This moral perspective is what makes Conrad a great writer, as he makes us aware of the strange paradoxes and contradictions of the human heart.

Conrad's best stories deal with this dual nature of existence where life choices have to be made even if it is recognized that only a thin margin separates good from bad, redemption from temptation. Such is the nature of life that, even if we sometimes want to be good, events often make this impossible. In 'Because of the Dollars', Conrad contrasts the efforts of Captain Davidson, 'a *really* good man' as the story stresses, to help Laughing Anne, with unexpected consequences. Out of his innate kindliness, Captain Davidson calls at the barren and poverty-stricken Mirrah settlement where Anne and her son are forced to live with Bamtz, a rattan trader. Anne saves Davidson telling him that Bamtz and a trio of villains are going to rob his ship. Realizing however that they have been betrayed, the crooks bludgeon Anne to death before escaping. Grateful for her help, Davidson takes Anne's son back with him. However, his wife refuses to believe his story, assuming that with Anne's reputation, the child could only be Davidson's. While the story turns on this contrast between actual goodness against superficial hypocrisy, the full impact of the story comes from the careful interweaving of recognizable types, situations and contexts that have been carefully worked into the narrative.

More than the scenes and events, it is Conrad's characters that hold our attention in all their bewildering certainties and hesitations, obsessions and fidelities, exuberance and dejection. They pass before us, a veritable parade of some of the most memorable heroes, villains, saints, fallen women, conmen, gunrunners, responsible captains and impulsive sailors in fiction. Despite his skill at depicting the landscape and the dexterity of his events, Conrad remains the pre-eminent creator of characters. His stories are full of personalities that remain in our minds long after we have put down the books: Karain, Hollis, Arsat, Jim, Brierly, Whalley, Laughing Anne, Leggatt, Falk, Axel Heyst, Marlow, Schomberg, among others. Each reflects a part of the East, its atmosphere and the enigma of existence with which it confronted men.

Conrad knew many settlements, ports and hidden places in the East. However, the one town and place that he was most familiar with and which featured most prominently in his writing is Singapore. To him, Singapore is that 'great Eastern port' or more usually, that 'eastern port', a multi-textured and multi-layered meeting place for all manner of men, ships and adventures. During his time in the East, Conrad got to know Singapore well. After the *Palestine* caught fire, the crew was taken to Singapore where an inquiry was held. In 1887, Conrad recuperated in Singapore after a falling spar on board the *Highland Forest* injured his back. He rested in the General Hospital before signing on as first mate in the *Vidar*. On this ship owned by the Syed Mohsin bin Salleh Al Jooffree Steamship Company of Singapore, Conrad made four trading trips between the island and the Dutch East Indies. His voyages took him to the remote settlements of Banjarmasin, Donggala, Berau and Tanjong Redap, many of which feature in his works.

However, it was Singapore that held the strongest fascination for him. Since its founding in 1819, the port had attracted many new settlers, so that by the time of Conrad's arrival, it was a bustling, cosmopolitan town with 170,000 people. It was the place where Almayer would send Nina for a 'white education'. Jim would become a water clerk after his disgrace on the *Patna* and the young narrator would obtain his first command from Captain Ellis, the Harbour Master. What is remarkable is the clarity and accuracy with which Conrad depicted the commercial centre of the port. Even today, it is still possible to trace the routes that his characters had taken as they went about their business, combining for the interested reader a fascinating physical journey evocative of history, literature and the day-to-day bustle of the sea front in that not too distant age.

Conrad's most sustained description of the port is found in 'The End of the Tether'. But by piecing together other references in stories such as 'The Shadow Line' and 'The Rescue', an even more comprehensive picture of the waterfront in the 1880s is obtained. In the main though, it is possible to use 'The End of the Tether' as a key index to the composite picture that emerges of the port of Singapore in those days. However, the story is not just about landscape, as it deals with universal issues like growing old and the spirit of generosity as well as with the hauntingly contemporary one of displacement.

'Tether' begins with Captain Whalley nursing the coastal steamer *Sofala* across the sand bar at Batu Berau along the Sumatran coast. Although he had been sailing in the East for forty years, Whalley, who was going blind, needed the help of his *serang* or mate to handle the ship. The narrative then shifts back in time in the next four and a half chapters, to the events that had led the captain to the *Sofala* before taking up the story again. It appears that the old captain had been forced to sell his 'retirement home', the small ship *Fair Maid*, in order to help his daughter make a living in Australia. Reluctantly he had accepted the post as master of the *Sofala*, investing whatever funds he had left in the ship. It was during this flashback that Whalley is shown walking along the sea front. When the story resumes, we discover that Massy, the chief engineer and owner of the ship, had decided to wreck the ship so that he could claim the insurance. In the event, an underwater shoal tore a hole in the hull and with water pouring into its holds, Whalley decided to go down with his ship.

It is clear that the story has more to offer than just a convincing description of the seafront. Yet there is no denying that part of its power comes from that very precise evocation of time and place. Whalley began his walk from the steps of 'one of the most important post offices of the East.' This was the General Post Office, housed at what is today the Fullerton Hotel although Conrad would more likely have known it as Fort Fullerton. The post office had moved to Fort Fullerton in 1874 from across the Singapore River, near Empress Place. Going down the steps of Fort Fullerton, Whalley would have entered the 'opened and untidy' thoroughfare that ran just in front of the building next to the sea.

From the steps, Whalley would have had a clear view of the western side of the Singapore waterfront in the late 1880s. He would have walked down onto a recently opened and 'untidy thoroughfare' with its row of 'slummy' Chinese shops on one side. To his right, the street continued past Johnston Pier on to the Consolidated Docks Company where the present-day container port is situated. In 1933, Johnston Pier was replaced by the modern Clifford Pier. Jungle and foliage came down to the edges of the docks and the place was shunned after dark because of the prowling tigers that did not hesitate to attack the careless passer-by.

Whalley turned left, walking past the Harbour Office and crossing Cavenagh Bridge onto Empress Place and the Esplanade. Named after the last Governor of the Straits Settlements, Colonel Orfeur Cavenagh, the bridge was manufactured in Scotland and assembled in 1869 by Indian convicts. Before the bridge was built, Whalley would have had to take the ferry, paying the obligatory ¼ cent charge for each trip. Although he was perhaps too preoccupied with his problems to take much notice, Whalley would have been aware that Empress Place was the civic and administrative centre of Singapore. Cavenagh Bridge led straight to the Empress Place Building built between 1864 and 1865. In that building were situated the Government Secretariat, Treasury, Education Department, Medical Services Department and the Attorney General's chambers. Whalley would not have paid too much attention either to the magnificent Town Hall to the left that was completed in 1862. Later extensions were added to the Town Hall, forming what is today the Victoria Theatre and Memorial Hall.

Whalley continued his walk along the Esplanade, the terraced shore along which he would have watched the hundreds of ships and boats in the roadstead. It was evening and a succession of stately open carriages would have been making their way along the seafront. From five in the evening till dusk, the ladies and their escorts would have been taking their exercise and walks, gossiping all the while about the community's most recent misconduct, scandal or impropriety. The Esplanade was soon to become known as Scandal Point. After the evening walk, a favourite place for tea would have been the fashionable Hotel de l'Europe, situated directly opposite the Esplanade, and the site of the present-day City Hall.

However, instead of going to the hotel for tea, Whalley continued walking, reaching St Andrew's Cathedral. Built by Indian convict labour in 1861, the early English Gothic style of the cathedral made it a prominent landmark. At that stage, instead of proceeding to the Officers' Sailor's Home where the present day Capitol building is, Whalley turned back, retracing his steps to the jetty where he called for a boat to take him back to his ship. One important monument that Conrad must have been aware of although we can understand why he did not mention it as he did not want to identify the location of the port, is the statue of Sir Stamford Raffles which was unveiled on 27 June 1887 by Sir Frederick Weld to coincide with the fiftieth anniversary of Queen Victoria's reign by the Governor. In those days, the statue was mounted at the far end of the Esplanade, close to the site of the present-day Singapore Recreation Club.

To read about Captain Whalley's walk in 'The End of the Tether' is to be transported irresistibly back to the Singapore of the 1880s, and have the scenes and life of that period recreated for us. It is still possible today, to take the same walk and identify the buildings and places, such as the Esplanade and Clifford's Pier, that Whalley saw. As we retrace the route, the years roll back and we step through a window into the past, becoming privileged observers of a Singapore that has remained unchanged amidst the rapid transformation of the landscape.

This selection brings together the most representative of Conrad's stories of the East. The settings range across most of what is known as Southeast Asia but which, more properly speaking at that period, would have been called the Malayan archipelago and peninsula. They take us to remote settlements far up muddy, dangerous rivers as well as to one of the greatest ports in the world. Conrad is a gentle and observant guide who provides some of the best introductions to these places.

Yet, as for all great writers, it is difficult to sum up finally the full extent of his achievements. Beyond the powerful evocations of the landscape and life, beyond the ambivalence that he sought to reveal and the fidelities he tried to present, something enigmatic always remains. Through a sudden glimmer of sunlight, a sailor's passing shadow or a snatch of a whisper, we are taken back to the tales told by Conrad. They remain the best witnesses of Conrad's achievements.

Singapore   *Ban Kah Choon*
November 2000

Youth: A Narrative

THIS could have occurred nowhere but in England, where men and sea interpenetrate, so to speak—the sea entering into the life of most men, and the men knowing something or everything about the sea, in the way of amusement, of travel, or of bread-winning.

We were sitting round a mahogany table that reflected the bottle, the claret-glasses, and our faces as we leaned on our elbows. There was a director of companies, an accountant, a lawyer, Marlow, and myself. The director had been a *Conway* boy, the accountant had served four years at sea, the lawyer—a fine crusted Tory, High Churchman, the best of old fellows, the soul of honour—had been chief officer in the P&O service in the good old days when mail-boats were square-rigged at least on two masts, and used to come down the China Sea before a fair monsoon with stunsails set alow and aloft. We all began life in the merchant service. Between the five of us there was the strong bond of the sea, and also the fellowship of the craft, which no amount of enthusiasm for yachting, cruising, and so on can give, since one is only the amusement of life and the other is life itself.

Marlow (at least I think that is how he spelt his name) told the story, or rather the chronicle, of a voyage:

'Yes, I have seen a little of the Eastern seas; but what I remember best is my first voyage there. You fellows know there are those voyages that seem ordered for the illustration of life, that might stand for a symbol of existence. You fight, work, sweat, nearly kill yourself, sometimes do kill yourself, trying to accomplish something—and you can't. Not from any fault of yours. You simply can do nothing, neither great nor little—not a thing in the world—not even marry an old maid, or get a wretched 600-ton cargo of coal to its port of destination.

'It was altogether a memorable affair. It was my first voyage to the East, and my first voyage as second mate; it was also my skipper's first command. You'll admit it was time. He was sixty if a day; a little man, with a broad, not very straight back, with bowed shoulders and one leg more bandy than the other, he had that queer twisted-about appearance you see so often in men who work in the fields. He had a nutcracker face, chin and nose trying to come together over a sunken mouth—and it was framed in iron-grey fluffy hair, that looked like a chinstrap of cottonwool sprinkled with coal dust. And he had blue eyes in that old face of his, which were amazingly like a boy's, with that candid expression some quite common men preserve to the end of their days by a rare internal gift of simplicity of heart and rectitude of soul. What induced him to accept me was a wonder. I had come out of a crack Australian clipper, where I had been third officer, and he seemed to have a prejudice against crack clippers as aristocratic and high-toned. He said to me, "You know, in this ship you will have to work." I said I had to work in every ship I had ever been in. "Ah, but this is different, and you gentlemen out of them big ships; . . . but there! I dare say you will do. Join tomorrow."

'I joined tomorrow. It was twenty-two years ago; and I was just twenty. How time passes! It was one of the happiest days of my life. Fancy! Second mate for the first time—a really responsible officer! I wouldn't have thrown up my new billet for a fortune. The mate looked me over carefully. He was also an old chap, but of another stamp. He had a Roman nose, a snow-white, long beard, and his name was Mahon, but he insisted that it should be pronounced Mann. He was well connected; yet there was something wrong with his luck, and he had never got on.

'As to the captain, he had been for years in coasters, then in the Mediterranean, and last in the West Indian trade. He had never been round the Capes. He could just write a kind of sketchy hand, and didn't care for writing at all. Both were thorough good seamen of course, and between those two old chaps I felt like a small boy between two grandfathers.

'The ship also was old. Her name was the *Judea*. Queer name, isn't it? She belonged to a man Wilmer, Wilcox—some name like that; but he has been bankrupt and dead these twenty years or more, and his name don't matter. She had been laid up in Shadwell basin for ever so long. You may imagine her state. She was all rust, dust, grime—soot aloft, dirt on deck. To me it was like coming out of a palace into a ruined cottage. She was about 400 tons, had a primitive windlass, wooden latches to the doors, not a bit of brass about her, and a big square stern. There was on it, below her name in big letters, a lot of scrollwork, with the gilt off, and some sort of a coat of arms, with the motto "Do or Die" underneath. I remember it took my fancy immensely. There was a touch of romance in it, something that made me love the old thing—something that appealed to my youth!

'We left London in ballast—sand ballast—to load a cargo of coal in a northern port for Bankok. Bankok! I thrilled. I had been six years at sea, but had only seen Melbourne and Sydney, very good places, charming places in their way—but Bankok!

'We worked out of the Thames under canvas, with a North Sea pilot on board. His name was Jermyn, and he dodged all day long about the galley drying his handkerchief before the stove. Apparently he never slept. He was a dismal man, with a perpetual tear sparkling at the end of his nose, who either had been in trouble, or was in trouble, or expected to be in trouble—couldn't be happy unless something went wrong. He mistrusted my youth, my commonsense, and my seamanship, and made a point of showing it in a hundred little ways. I dare say he was right. It seems to me I knew very little then, and I know not much more now; but I cherish a hate for that Jermyn to this day.

'We were a week working up as far as Yarmouth Roads, and then we got into a gale—the famous October gale of twenty-two years ago. It was wind, lightning, sleet, snow, and a terrific sea. We were flying light, and you may imagine how bad it was when I tell you we had smashed bulwarks and a flooded deck. On the second night she shifted her ballast into the lee bow, and by that time we had been blown off somewhere on the Dogger Bank. There was nothing for it but go below with shovels and try to right her, and there we were in that vast hold, gloomy like a cavern, the tallow dips stuck and flickering on the beams, the gale howling above, the ship tossing about like mad on her side; there we all were, Jermyn, the captain, everyone, hardly able to keep our feet, engaged on that gravedigger's work, and trying to toss shovelfuls of wet sand up to windward. At every tumble of the ship you could see vaguely in the dim light men falling down with a great flourish of shovels. One of the ship's boys (we had two), impressed by the weirdness of the scene, wept as if his heart would break. We could hear him blubbering somewhere in the shadows.

'On the third day the gale died out, and by and by a north-country tug picked us up. We took sixteen days in all to get from London to the Tyne! When we got into dock we had lost our turn for loading, and they hauled us off to a tier where we remained for a month. Mrs Beard (the captain's name was Beard) came from Colchester to see the old man. She lived on board. The crew of runners had left, and there remained only the officers, one boy, and the steward, a mulatto who answered to the name of Abraham. Mrs Beard was an old woman, with a face all wrinkled and ruddy like a winter apple, and the figure of a young girl. She caught sight of me once, sewing on a button, and insisted on having my shirts to repair. This was something different from the captains' wives I had known on board crack clippers. When I brought her the shirts, she said: "And the socks? They want mending, I am sure, and John's—Captain Beard's—things are all in order now. I would be glad of something to do." Bless the old woman. She overhauled my outfit for me, and meantime I read for the first time *Sartor Resartus* and Burnaby's *Ride to Khiva*. I didn't understand much of the first then; but I remember I preferred the soldier to the philosopher at the time; a preference which life has only confirmed. One was a man, and the other was either more—or less. However, they are both dead, and Mrs Beard is dead, and youth, strength, genius, thoughts, achievements, simple hearts—all die . . . No matter.

'They loaded us at last. We shipped a crew. Eight able seamen and two boys. We hauled off one evening to the buoys at the dock gates, ready to go out, and with a fair prospect of beginning the voyage next day. Mrs Beard was to start for home by a late train. When the ship was fast we went to tea. We sat rather silent through the meal—Mahon, the old couple, and I. I finished first, and slipped away for a smoke, my cabin being in a deckhouse just against the poop. It was high water, blowing fresh with a drizzle; the double dock gates were opened, and the steam colliers were going in and out in the darkness with their lights burning bright, a great plashing of propellers, rattling of winches, and a lot of hailing on the pierheads. I watched the procession of headlights gliding high, and of green lights gliding low in the night, when suddenly a red gleam flashed at me, vanished, came into view again, and remained. The fore end of a steamer loomed up close. I shouted down the cabin, "Come up, quick!" and then heard a startled voice saying afar in the dark, "Stop her, sir." A bell jingled. Another voice cried warningly, "We are going right into that barque, sir." The answer to this was a gruff "All right," and the next thing was a heavy crash as the steamer struck a glancing blow with the bluff of her bow about our fore-rigging. There was a moment of confusion, yelling, and running about. Steam roared. Then somebody was heard saying, "All clear, sir." . . . "Are you all right?" asked the gruff voice. I had jumped forward to see the damage, and hailed back, "I think so." "Easy astern," said the gruff voice. A bell jingled. "What steamer is that?" screamed Mahon. By that time she was no more to us than a bulky shadow manoeuvring a little way off. They shouted at us some name—a woman's name, Miranda or Melissa, or some such thing. "This means another month in this beastly hole," said Mahon to me, as we peered with lamps about the splintered bulwarks and broken braces. "But where's the captain?"

'We had not heard or seen anything of him all that time. We went aft to look. A doleful voice arose hailing somewhere in the middle of the dock, *"Judea* ahoy!" . . . How the devil did he get there? . . . "Hallo!" we shouted. "I am adrift in our boat without oars," he cried. A belated waterman offered his services, and Mahon struck a bargain with him for half a crown to tow our skipper alongside; but it was Mrs Beard that came up the ladder first. They had been floating about the dock in that mizzly cold rain for nearly an hour. I was never so surprised in my life.

'It appears that when he heard my shout "Come up", he understood at once what was the matter, caught up his wife, ran on deck, and across, and down into our boat, which was fast to the ladder. Not bad for a sixty-year-old. Just imagine that old fellow saving heroically in his arms that old woman—the woman of his life. He set her down on a thwart, and was ready to climb back on board when the painter came adrift somehow, and away they went together. Of course in the confusion we did not hear him shouting. He looked abashed. She said cheerfully, "I suppose it does not matter my losing the train now?" "No, Jenny—you go below and get warm," he growled. Then to us: "A sailor has no business with a wife—I say. There I was, out of the ship. Well, no harm done this time. Let's go and look at what that fool of a steamer smashed."

"It wasn't much, but it delayed us three weeks. At the end of that time, the captain being engaged with his agents, I carried Mrs Beard's bag to the railway station and put her all comfy into a third-class carriage. She lowered the window to say, "You are a good young man. If you see John—Captain Beard—without his muffler at night, just remind him from me to keep his throat well wrapped up." "Certainly, Mrs Beard," I said. "You are a good young man; I noticed how attentive you are to John—to Captain—" The train pulled out suddenly; I took my cap off to the old woman: I never saw her again . . . Pass the bottle.

'We went to sea next day. When we made that start for Bankok we had been already three months out of London. We had expected to be a fortnight or so—at the outside.

'It was January, and the weather was beautiful—the beautiful sunny winter weather that has more charm than in the summer time, because it is unexpected, and crisp, and you know it won't, it can't, last long. It's like a windfall, like a godsend, like an unexpected piece of luck.

'It lasted all down the North Sea, all down the Channel; and it lasted till we were three hundred miles or so to the westward of the Lizards: then the wind went round to the sou'west and began to pipe up. In two days it blew a gale. The *Judea*, hove to, wallowed on the Atlantic like an old candlebox. It blew day after day: it blew with spite, without interval, without mercy, without rest. The world was nothing but an immensity of great foaming waves rushing at us, under a sky low enough to touch with the hand and dirty like a smoked ceiling. In the stormy space surrounding us there was as much flying spray as air. Day after day and night after night there was nothing round the ship but the howl of the wind, the tumult of the sea, the noise of water pouring over her deck. There was no rest for her and no rest for us. She tossed, she pitched, she stood on her head, she sat on her tail, she rolled, she groaned, and we had to hold on while on deck and cling to our bunks when below, in a constant effort of body and worry of mind.

'One night Mahon spoke through the small window of my berth. It opened right into my very bed, and I was lying there sleepless, in my boots, feeling as though I had not slept for years, and could not if I tried. He said excitedly—"You got the sounding rod in here, Marlow? I can't get the pumps to suck. By God! it's no child's play."

'I gave him the sounding rod and lay down again, trying to think of various things—but I thought only of the pumps. When I came on deck they were still at it, and my watch relieved at the pumps. By the light of the lantern brought on deck to examine the sounding rod I caught a glimpse of their weary, serious faces. We pumped all the four hours. We pumped all night, all day, all the week—watch and watch. She was working herself loose, and leaked badly—not enough to drown us at once, but enough to kill us with the work at the pumps. And while we pumped the ship was going from us piecemeal: the bulwarks went, the stanchions were torn out, the ventilators smashed, the cabin door burst in. There was not a dry spot in the ship. She was being gutted bit by bit. The long boat changed, as if by magic, into matchwood where she stood in her gripes. I had lashed her myself, and was rather proud of my handiwork, which had withstood so long the malice of the sea. And we pumped. And there was no break in the weather. The sea was white like a sheet of foam, like a caldron of boiling milk; there was not a break in the clouds, no—not the size of a man's hand—no, not for so much as ten seconds. There was for us no sky, there were for us no stars, no sun, no universe—nothing but angry clouds and an infuriated sea. We pumped watch and watch, for dear life; and it seemed to last for months, for years, for all eternity, as though we had been dead and gone to a hell for sailors. We forgot the day of the week, the name of the month, what year it was, and whether we had ever been ashore. The sails blew away, she lay broadside on under a weather cloth, the ocean poured over her, and we did not care. We turned those handles, and had the eyes of idiots. As soon as we had crawled on deck I used to take a round turn with a rope about the men, the pumps, and the mainmast, and we turned, we turned incessantly, with the water to our waists, to our necks, over our heads. It was all one. We had forgotten how it felt to be dry.

'And there was somewhere in me the thought: By Jove! this is the deuce of an adventure—something you read about; and it is my first voyage as second mate—and I am only twenty—and here I am lasting it out as well as any of these men, and keeping my chaps up to the mark. I was pleased. I would not have given up the experience for worlds. I had moments of exultation. Whenever the old dismantled craft pitched heavily with her counter high in the air, she seemed to me to throw up, like an appeal, like a defiance, like a cry to the clouds without mercy, the words written on her stern: "*Judea*, London. Do or Die."

'Oh youth! The strength of it, the faith of it, the imagination of it! To me she was not an old rattletrap carting about the world a lot of coal for a freight—to me she was the endeavour, the test, the trial of life. I think of her with pleasure, with affection, with regret—as you would think of someone dead you have loved. I shall never forget her ... Pass the bottle.

'One night when tied to the mast, as I explained, we were pumping on, deafened with the wind, and without spirit enough in us to wish ourselves dead, a heavy sea crashed aboard and swept clean over us. As soon as I got my breath I shouted, as in duty bound, "Keep on, boys!" when suddenly I felt something hard floating on deck strike the calf of my leg. I made a grab at it and missed. It was so dark we could not see each other's faces within a foot—you understand.

'After that thump the ship kept quiet for a while, and the thing, whatever it was, struck my leg again. This time I caught it—and it was a saucepan. At first, being stupid with fatigue and thinking of nothing but the pumps, I did not understand what I had in my hand. Suddenly it dawned upon me, and I shouted, "Boys, the house on deck is gone. Leave this, and let's look for the cook."

'There was a deckhouse forward, which contained the galley, the cook's berth, and the quarters of the crew. As we had expected for days to see it swept away, the hands had been ordered to sleep in the cabin—the only safe place in the ship. The steward, Abraham, however, persisted in clinging to his berth, stupidly, like a mule—from sheer fright I believe, like an animal that won't leave a stable falling in an earthquake. So we went to look for him. It was chancing death, since once out of our lashings we were as exposed as if on a raft. But we went. The house was shattered as if a shell had exploded inside. Most of it had gone overboard—stove, men's quarters, and their property, all was gone; but two posts, holding a portion of the bulkhead to which Abraham's bunk was attached, remained as if by a miracle. We groped in the ruins and came upon this, and there he was, sitting in his bunk, surrounded by foam and wreckage, jabbering cheerfully to himself. He was out of his mind; completely and for ever mad, with this sudden shock coming upon the fag end of his endurance. We snatched him up, lugged him aft, and pitched him head-first down the cabin companion. You understand there was no time to carry him down with infinite precautions and wait to see how he got on. Those below would pick him up at the bottom of the stairs all right. We were in a hurry to go back to the pumps. That business could not wait. A bad leak is an inhuman thing.

'One would think that the sole purpose of that fiendish gale had been to make a lunatic of that poor devil of a mulatto. It eased before morning, and next day the sky cleared, and as the sea went down the leak took up. When it came to bending a fresh set of sails the crew demanded to put back—and really there was nothing else to do. Boats gone, decks swept clean, cabin gutted, men without a stitch but what they stood in, stores spoiled, ship strained. We put her head for home, and—would you believe it? The wind came east right in our teeth. It blew fresh, it blew continuously. We had to beat up every inch of the way, but she did not leak so badly, the water keeping comparatively smooth. Two hours' pumping in every four is no joke—but it kept her afloat as far as Falmouth.

'The good people there live on casualties of the sea, and no doubt were glad to see us. A hungry crowd of shipwrights sharpened their chisels at the sight of that carcass of a ship. And, by Jove! they had pretty pickings off us before they were done. I fancy the owner was already in a tight place. There were delays. Then it was decided to take part of the cargo out and caulk her topsides. This was done, the repairs finished, cargo reshipped; a new crew came on board, and we went out—for Bankok. At the end of a week we were back again. The crew said they weren't going to Bankok—a hundred and fifty days' passage—in a something hooker that wanted pumping eight hours out of the twenty-four; and the nautical papers inserted again the little paragraph: "*Judea.* Barque. Tyne to Bankok; coals; put back to Falmouth leaky and with crew refusing duty."

'There were more delays—more tinkering. The owner

13

came down for a day, and said she was as right as a little fiddle. Poor old Captain Beard looked like the ghost of a Geordie skipper—through the worry and humiliation of it. Remember he was sixty, and it was his first command. Mahon said it was a foolish business, and would end badly. I loved the ship more than ever, and wanted awfully to get to Bankok. To Bankok! Magic name, blessed name. Mesopotamia wasn't a patch on it. Remember I was twenty, and it was my first second-mate's billet, and the East was waiting for me.

'We went out and anchored in the outer roads with a fresh crew—the third. She leaked worse than ever. It was as if those confounded shipwrights had actually made a hole in her. This time we did not even go outside. The crew simply refused to man the windlass.

'They towed us back to the inner harbour, and we became a fixture, a feature, an institution of the place. People pointed us out to visitors as "That, 'ere barque that's going to Bankok—has been here six months—put back three times." On holidays the small boys pulling about in boats would hail, "*Judea*, ahoy!" and if a head showed above the rail shouted, "Where you bound to?—Bankok?" and jeered. We were only three on board. The poor old skipper mooned in the cabin. Mahon undertook the cooking, and unexpectedly developed all a Frenchman's genius for preparing nice little messes. I looked languidly after the rigging. We became citizens of Falmouth. Every shopkeeper knew us. At the barber's or tobacconist's, they asked familiarly, "Do you think you will ever get to Bankok?" Meantime the owner, the underwriters, and the charterers squabbled amongst themselves in London, and our pay went on . . . Pass the bottle.

'It was horrid. Morally it was worse than pumping for life. It seemed as though we had been forgotten by the world, belonged to nobody, would get nowhere; it seemed that, as if bewitched, we would have to live for ever and ever in that inner harbour, a derision and a byword to generations of longshore loafers and dishonest boatmen. I obtained three months' pay and five days' leave, and made a rush for London. It took me a day to get there and pretty well another to come back—but three months' pay went all the same. I don't know what I did with it. I went to a music hall, I believe, lunched, dined, and supped in a swell place in Regent Street, and was back to time, with nothing but a complete set of Byron's works and a new railway rug to show for three months' work. The boat-man who pulled me off to the ship said: "Hallo! I thought you had left the old thing. *She* will never get to Bankok." "That's all you know about it," I said, scornfully—but I didn't like that prophecy at all.

'Suddenly a man, some kind of agent to somebody, appeared with full powers. He had grog-blossoms all over his face, an indomitable energy, and was a jolly soul. We leaped into life again. A hulk came alongside, took our cargo, and then we went into dry dock to get our copper stripped. No wonder she leaked. The poor thing, strained beyond endurance by the gale, had, as if in disgust, spat out all the oakum of her lower seams. She was recaulked, new coppered, and made as tight as a bottle. We went back to the hulk and re-shipped our cargo.

'Then, on a fine moonlight night, all the rats left the ship.

'We had been infested with them. They had destroyed our sails, consumed more stores than the crew, affably shared our beds and our dangers, and now, when the ship was made seaworthy, concluded to clear out. I called Mahon to enjoy the spectacle. Rat after rat appeared on our rail, took a last look over his shoulder, and leaped with a hollow thud into the empty hulk. We tried to count them, but soon lost the tale. Mahon said: "Well, well! don't talk to me about the intelligence of rats. They ought to have left before, when we had that narrow squeak from foundering. There you have the proof how silly is the superstition about them. They leave a good ship for an old rotten hulk, where there is nothing to eat, too, the fools! . . . I don't believe they know what is safe or what is good for them, any more than you or I."

'And after some more talk we agreed that the wisdom of rats had been grossly overrated, being in fact no greater than that of men.

'The story of the ship was known, by this, all up the Channel from Land's End to the Forelands, and we could get no crew on the south coast. They sent us one all complete from Liverpool, and we left once more—for Bankok.

'We had fair breezes, smooth water right into the tropics, and the old *Judea* lumbered along in the sunshine. When she went eight knots everything cracked aloft, and we tied our caps to our heads; but mostly she strolled on at the rate of three miles an hour. What could you expect? She was tired—that old ship. Her youth was where mine is—where yours is—you fellows who listen to this yarn; and what friend would throw your years and your weariness in your face? We didn't grumble at her. To us aft, at least, it seemed as though we had been born in her, reared in her, had lived in her for ages, had never known any other ship. I would just as soon have abused the old village church at home for not being a cathedral.

'And for me there was also my youth to make me patient. There was all the East before me, and all life, and all the thought that I had been tried in that ship and had come out pretty well. And I thought of men of old who, centuries ago, went that road in ships that sailed no better, to the land of palms, and spices, and yellow sands, and of brown nations ruled by kings more cruel than Nero the Roman, and more splendid than Solomon the Jew. The old bark lumbered on, heavy with her age and the burden of her cargo, while I lived the life of youth in ignorance and hope. She lumbered on through an interminable procession of days; and the fresh gilding flashed back at the setting sun, seemed to cry out over the darkening sea the words painted on her stern, *"Judea,* London. Do or Die."

'Then we entered the Indian Ocean and steered northerly for Java Head. The winds were light. Weeks slipped by. She crawled on, do or die, and people at home began to think of posting us as overdue.

'One Saturday evening, I being off duty, the men asked me to give them an extra bucket of water or so—for washing clothes. As I did not wish to screw on the fresh-water pump so late, I went forward whistling and with a key in my hand to unlock the forepeak scuttle, intending to serve the water out of a spare tank we kept there.

'The smell down below was as unexpected as it was frightful. One would have thought hundreds of paraffin lamps had been flaring and smoking in that hole for days. I was glad to get out. The man with me coughed and said, "Funny smell, sir." I answered negligently, "It's good for the health they say," and walked aft.

'The first thing I did was to put my head down the square of the midship ventilator. As I lifted the lid a visible breath, something like a thin fog, a puff of faint haze, rose from the opening. The ascending air was hot, and had a heavy, sooty, paraffiny smell. I gave one sniff, and put down the lid gently. It was no use choking myself. The cargo was on fire.

'Next day she began to smoke in earnest. You see it was to be expected, for though the coal was of a safe kind, that cargo had been so handled, so broken up with handling, that it looked more like smithy coal than anything else. Then it had been wetted—more than once. It rained all the time we were taking it back from the hulk, and now with this long passage it got heated, and there was another case of spontaneous

17

combustion.

'The captain called us into the cabin. He had a chart spread on the table, and looked unhappy. He said, "The coast of West Australia is near, but I mean to proceed to our destination. It is the hurricane month too; but we will just keep her head for Bankok, and fight the fire. No more putting back anywhere, if we all get roasted. We will try first to stifle this 'ere damned combustion by want of air."

'We tried. We battened down everything, and still she smoked. The smoke kept coming out through imperceptible crevices; it forced itself through bulkheads and covers; it oozed here and there and everywhere in slender threads, in an invisible film, in an incomprehensible manner. It made its way into the cabin, into the forecastle; it poisoned the sheltered places on the deck, it could be sniffed as high as the mainyard. It was clear that if the smoke came out the air came in. This was disheartening. This combustion refused to be stifled.

'We resolved to try water, and took the hatches off. Enormous volumes of smoke, whitish, yellowish, thick, greasy, misty, choking, ascended as high as the trucks. All hands cleared out aft. Then the poisonous cloud blew away, and we went back to work in a smoke that was no thicker now than that of an ordinary factory chimney.

'We rigged the force pump, got the hose along, and by and by it burst. Well, it was as old as the ship—a prehistoric hose, and past repair. Then we pumped with the feeble head pump, drew water with buckets, and in this way managed in time to pour lots of Indian Ocean into the main hatch. The bright stream flashed in sunshine, fell into a layer of white crawling smoke, and vanished on the black surface of coal. Steam ascended mingling with the smoke. We poured salt water as into a barrel without a bottom. It was our fate to pump in that ship, to pump out of her, to pump into her; and after keeping water out of her to save ourselves from being drowned, we frantically poured water into her to save ourselves from being burnt.

'And she crawled on, do or die, in the serene weather. The sky was a miracle of purity, a miracle of azure. The sea was polished, was blue, was pellucid, was sparkling like a precious stone, extending on all sides, all round to the horizon—as if the whole terrestrial globe had been one jewel, one colossal sapphire, a single gem fashioned into a planet. And on the lustre of the great calm waters the *Judea* glided imperceptibly, enveloped in languid and unclean vapours, in a lazy cloud that drifted to leeward, light and slow; a pestiferous cloud defiling the splendour of sea and sky.

'All this time of course we saw no fire. The cargo smouldered at the bottom somewhere. Once Mahon, as we were working side by side, said to me with a queer smile: "Now, if she only would spring a tidy leak like that time when we first left the Channel—it would put a stopper on this fire. Wouldn't it?" I remarked irrelevantly, "Do you remember the rats?"

'We fought the fire and sailed the ship too as carefully as though nothing had been the matter. The steward cooked and attended on us. Of the other twelve men, eight worked while four rested. Everyone took his turn, captain included. There was equality, and if not exactly fraternity, then a deal of good feeling. Sometimes a man, as he dashed a bucketful of water down the hatchway, would yell out, "Hurrah for Bankok!" and the rest laughed. But generally we were taciturn and serious—and thirsty. Oh! how thirsty! And we had to be careful with the water. Strict allowance. The ship smoked, the sun blazed . . . Pass the bottle.

'We tried everything. We even made an attempt to dig down to the fire. No good, of course. No man could remain more than a minute below. Mahon, who went first, fainted there, and the man who went to fetch him out did likewise.

19

We lugged them out on deck. Then I leaped down to show how easily it could be done. They had learned wisdom by that time, and contented themselves by fishing for me with a chain hook tied to a broom handle, I believe. I did not offer to go and fetch up my shovel, which was left down below.

'Things began to look bad. We put the long boat into the water. The second boat was ready to swing out. We had also another, a fourteen-foot thing, on davits aft, where it was quite safe.

'Then, behold, the smoke suddenly decreased. We redoubled our efforts to flood the bottom of the ship. In two days there was no smoke at all. Everybody was on the broad grin. This was on a Friday. On Saturday no work, but sailing the ship of course, was done. The men washed their clothes and their faces for the first time in a fortnight, and had a special dinner given them. They spoke of spontaneous combustion with contempt, and implied *they* were the boys to put out combustions. Somehow we all felt as though we each had inherited a large fortune. But a beastly smell of burning hung about the ship. Captain Beard had hollow eyes and sunken cheeks. I had never noticed so much before how twisted and bowed he was. He and Mahon prowled soberly about hatches and ventilators, sniffing. It struck me suddenly poor Mahon was a very, very old chap. As to me, I was as pleased and proud as though I had helped to win a great naval battle. Oh youth!

'The night was fine. In the morning a homeward-bound ship passed us hull down—the first we had seen for months; but we were nearing the land at last, Java Head being about 190 miles off, and nearly due north.

'Next day it was my watch on deck from eight to twelve. At breakfast the captain observed, "It's wonderful how that smell hangs about the cabin." About ten, the mate being on the poop, I stepped down on the main deck for a moment. The carpenter's bench stood abaft the main mast: I leaned against it sucking at my pipe, and the carpenter, a young chap, came to talk to me. He remarked, "I think we have done very well, haven't we?" and then I perceived with annoyance the fool was trying to tilt the bench. I said curtly, "Don't, Chips," and immediately became aware a queer sensation, of an absurd delusion—I seemed somehow to be in the air. I heard all round me like a pent-up breath released—as if a thousand giants simultaneously had said Phoo!—and felt a dull concussion which made my ribs ache suddenly. No doubt about it—I was in the air, and my body was describing a short parabola. But short as it was, I had the time to think several thoughts in, as far as I can remember, the following order: "This can't be the carpenter—What is it?—Some accident—Submarine volcano?—Coals, gas!—By Jove! we are being blown up—Everybody's dead. I am falling into the after-hatch—I see fire in it."

'The coal dust suspended in the air of the hold had glowed dull red at the moment of the explosion. In the twinkling of an eye, in an infinitesimal fraction of a second since the first tilt of the bench, I was sprawling full length on the cargo. I picked myself up and scrambled out. It was quick like a rebound. The deck was a wilderness of smashed timber, lying crosswise like trees in a wood after a hurricane; an immense curtain of soiled rags waved gently before me—it was the main sail blown to strips. I thought, "The masts will be toppling over directly;" and to get out of the way bolted on all-fours towards the poop ladder. The first person I saw was Mahon, with eyes like saucers, his mouth open, and the long white hair standing straight on end round his head like a silver halo. He was just about to go down when the sight of the main deck stirring, heaving up, and changing into splinters before his eyes, petrified him on the top step. I stared at him in unbelief, and he stared at me with a queer kind of shocked curiosity. I did not know that I had no hair, no eyebrows, no eyelashes, that my young moustache was burnt off, that my face was black, one cheek laid open, my nose cut, and my chin bleeding. I had lost my cap, one of my slippers, and my shirt was torn to rags. Of all this I was not aware. I was amazed to see the ship still afloat, the poop deck whole—and, most of all, to see anybody alive. Also the peace of the sky and the serenity of the sea were distinctly surprising. I suppose I expected to see them convulsed with horror . . . Pass the bottle.

'There was a voice hailing the ship from somewhere—in the air, in the sky—I couldn't tell. Presently I saw the captain—and he was mad. He asked me eagerly, "Where's the cabin table?" and to hear such a question was a frightful shock. I had just been blown up, you understand, and vibrated with that experience, I wasn't quite sure whether I was alive. Mahon began to stamp with both feet and yelled at him. "Good God! don't you see the deck's blown out of her?" I found my voice, and stammered out as if conscious of some gross neglect of duty, "I don't know where the cabin table is." It was like an absurd dream.

'Do you know what he wanted next? Well, he wanted to trim the yards. Very placidly, and as if lost in thought, he insisted on having the foreyard squared, "I don't know if there's anybody alive," said Mahon, almost tearfully. "Surely," he said, gently, "there will be enough left to square the foreyard."

'The old chap, it seems, was in his own berth winding up the chronometers, when the shock sent him spinning. Immediately it occurred to him—as he said afterwards—that the ship had struck something, and ran out into the cabin. There, he saw, the cabin table had vanished somewhere. The deck being blown up, it had fallen down into the lazarette of course. Where we had our breakfast that morning he saw only a great hole in the floor. This appeared to him so awfully mysterious, and impressed him so immensely, that what he saw and heard after he got on deck were mere trifles in comparison. And, mark, he noticed directly the wheel deserted and his barque off her course—and his only thought was to get that miserable, stripped, undecked, smouldering shell of a ship back again with her head pointing at her port of destination. Bankok! That's what he was after. I tell you this quiet, bowed, bandy-legged, almost deformed little man was immense in the singleness of his idea and in his placid ignorance of our agitation. He motioned us forward with a commanding gesture; and went to take the wheel himself.

'Yes; that was the first thing we did—trim the yards of that wreck! No one was killed, or even disabled, but everyone was more or less hurt. You should have seen them! Some were in rags, with black faces, like coal heavers, like sweeps, and had bullet heads that seemed closely cropped, but were in fact singed to the skin. Others, of the watch below, awakened by being shot out from their collapsing bunks, shivered incessantly, and kept on groaning even as we went about our work. But they all worked. That crew of Liverpool hard cases had in them the right stuff. It's my experience they always have. It is the sea that gives it—the vastness, the loneliness surrounding their dark stolid souls. Ah! Well! we stumbled, we crept, we fell, we barked our shins on the wreckage, we hauled. The masts stood, but we did not know how much they might be charred down below. It was nearly calm, but a long swell ran from the west and made her roll. They might go at any moment. We looked at them with apprehension. One could not foresee which way they would fall.

'Then we retreated aft and looked about us. The deck was a tangle of planks on edge, of planks on end, of splinters, of ruined woodwork. The masts rose from that chaos like big trees above a matted undergrowth. The interstices of that

23

mass of wreckage were full of something whitish, sluggish; stirring—of something that was like a greasy fog. The smoke of the invisible fire was coming up again, was trailing, like a poisonous thick mist in some valley choked with dead wood. Already lazy wisps were beginning to curl upwards amongst the mass of splinters. Here and there a piece of timber, stuck upright, resembled a post. Half of a fife rail had been shot through the foresail, and the sky made a patch of glorious blue in the ignobly soiled canvas. A portion of several boards holding together had fallen across the rail, and one end protruded overboard, like a gangway leading upon nothing, like a gangway leading over the deep sea, leading to death—as if inviting us to walk the plank at once and be done with our ridiculous troubles. And still the air, the sky—a ghost, something invisible was hailing the ship.

'Someone had the sense to look over; and there was the helmsman, who had impulsively jumped overboard anxious to come back. He yelled and swam lustily like a merman, keeping up with the ship. We threw him a rope, and presently he stood amongst us, streaming with water and very crestfallen. The captain had surrendered the wheel, and stood apart, elbow on rail and chin in hand, gazing at the sea wistfully. We asked ourselves, What next? I thought, Now, this is something like. This is great. I wonder what will happen. Oh youth!

'Suddenly Mahon sighted a steamer far astern. Captain Beard said, "We may do something with her yet." We hoisted two flags, which said in the international language of the sea, "On fire. Want immediate assistance." The steamer grew bigger rapidly, and by and by spoke with two flags on her foremast, "I am coming to your assistance."

'In half an hour she was abreast, to windward, within hail, and rolling slightly, with her engines stopped. We lost our composure, and yelled all together with excitement,

"We've been blown up." A man in a white helmet, on the bridge, cried, "Yes! All right! All right!" and he nodded his head, and smiled, and made soothing motions with his hand as though at a lot of frightened children. One of the boats dropped in the water, and walked towards us upon the sea with her long oars. Four kalashes pulled a swinging stroke. This was my first sight of Malay seamen. I've known them since, but what struck me then was their unconcern: they came alongside, and even the bowman standing up and holding to our main chains with the boathook did not deign to lift his head for a glance. I thought people who had been blown up deserved more attention.

'A little man, dry like a chip and agile like a monkey clambered up. It was the mate of the steamer. He gave one look, and cried, "Oh boys—you had better quit."

'We were silent. He talked apart with the captain for a time—seemed to argue with him. Then they went away together to the steamer.

'When our skipper came back we learned that the steamer was the *Somerville,* Captain Nash, from West Australia to Singapore via Batavia with mails, and that the agreement was she should tow us to Anjer or Batavia, if possible, where we could extinguish the fire by scuttling, and then proceed on our voyage to Bankok! The old man seemed excited. "We will do it yet," he said to Mahon, fiercely. He shook his fist at the sky. Nobody else said a word.

'At noon the steamer began to tow. She went ahead, slim and high, and what was left of the *Judea* followed at the end of seventy fathom of tow rope—followed her swiftly like a cloud of smoke with mastheads protruding above. We went aloft to furl the sails. We coughed on the yards, and were careful about the bunts. Do you see the lot of us there, putting a neat furl on the sails of that ship doomed to arrive nowhere? There was not a man who didn't think that at any moment the masts would topple over. From aloft we could not see the ship for smoke, and they worked carefully, passing the gaskets with even turns. "Harbour furl—aloft there!" cried Mahon from below.

'You understand this? I don't think one of those chaps expected to get down in the usual way. When we did I heard them saying to each other, "Well, I thought we would come down overboard, in a lump—sticks and all—blame me if I didn't." "That's what I was thinking to myself," would answer wearily another battered and bandaged scarecrow. And, mind, these were men without the drilled-in habit of obedience. To an onlooker they would be a lot of profane scallywags without a redeeming point. What made them do it—what made them obey me when I, thinking consciously how fine it was, made them drop the bunt of the foresail twice to try and do it better? What? They had no professional reputation—no examples, no praise. It wasn't a sense of duty; they all knew well enough how to shirk, and laze, and dodge—when they had a mind to it—and mostly they had. Was it the two pounds ten a month that sent them there? They didn't think their pay half good enough. No; it was something in them, something inborn and subtle and everlasting. I don't say positively that the crew of a French or German merchantman wouldn't have done it, but I doubt whether it would have been done in the same way. There was a completeness in it, something solid like a principle; and masterful like an instinct—a disclosure of something secret—of that hidden something, that gift of good or evil that makes racial difference, that shapes the fate of nations.

'It was that night at ten that, for the first time since we had been fighting it, we saw the fire. The speed of the towing had fanned the smouldering destruction. A blue gleam appeared forward, shining below the wreck of the deck. It wavered in patches, it seemed to stir and creep like the light of a glow-worm. I saw it first, and told Mahon. "Then the game's up," he said. "We had better stop this towing, or she will burst out suddenly fore and aft before we can clear out." We set up a yell; rang bells to attract their attention; they towed on. At last Mahon and I had to crawl forward and cut the rope with an axe. There was no time to cast off the lashings: red tongues could be seen licking the wilderness of splinters under our feet as we made our way back to the poop.

'Of course they very soon found out in the steamer that the rope was gone. She gave a loud blast of her whistle, her lights were seen sweeping in a wide circle, she came up ranging close alongside; and stopped. We were all in a tight group on the poop looking at her. Every man had saved a little bundle or a bag. Suddenly a conical flame with a twisted top shot up forward and threw upon the black sea a circle of light, with the two vessels side by side and heaving gently in its centre. Captain Beard had been sitting on the gratings still and mute for hours, but now he rose slowly and advanced in front of us, to the mizzen shrouds. Captain Nash hailed: "Come along! Look sharp. I have mailbags on board. I will take you and your boats to Singapore."

'"Thank you! No!" said our skipper. "We must see the last of the ship."

'"I can't stand by any longer," shouted the other "Mails—you know."

'"Ay! ay! We are all right."

'"Very well! I'll report you in Singapore . . . Goodbye!"

'He waved his hand. Our men dropped their bundles quietly. The steamer moved ahead, and passing out of the circle of light, vanished at once from our sight, dazzled by the fire which burned fiercely. And then I knew that I would see the East first as commander of a small boat. I thought it fine; and the fidelity to the old ship was fine. We should see the last of her. Oh, the glamour of youth! Oh, the fire of it, more dazzling than the flames of the burning ship, throwing a magic light on the wide earth, leaping audaciously to the sky, presently to be quenched by time, more cruel, more pitiless, more bitter than the sea—and like the flames of the burning ship surrounded by an impenetrable night.'

*

'The old man warned us in his gentle and inflexible way that it was part of our duty to save for the underwriters as much as we could of the ship's gear. Accordingly we went to work aft, while she blazed forward to give us plenty of light. We lugged out a lot of rubbish. What didn't we save? An old barometer fixed with an absurd quantity of screws nearly cost me my life: a sudden rush of smoke came upon me, and I just got away in time. There were various stores, bolts of canvas, coils of rope; the poop looked like a marine bazaar, and the boats were lumbered to the gunwales. One would have thought the old man wanted to take as much as he could to his first command with him. He was very, very quiet, but off his balance evidently. Would you believe it? He wanted to take a length of old stream cable and a kedge anchor with him in the long boat. We said, "Ay, ay, sir," deferentially, and on the quiet let the things slip overboard. The heavy medicine chest went that way, two bags of green coffee, tins of paint—fancy, paint!—a whole lot of things. Then I was ordered with two hands into the boat to make a stowage and get them ready against the time it would be proper for us to leave the ship.

'We put everything straight, stepped the long boat's mast for our skipper, who was to take charge of her, and I was not sorry to sit down for a moment. My face felt raw, every limb ached as if broken, I was aware of all my ribs, and would have sworn to a twist in the backbone. The boats, fast astern, lay in a deep shadow, and all around I could see the circle of the sea lighted by the fire. A gigantic flame arose forward straight and clear. It flared fierce, with noises like the whirr of wings, with rumbles as of thunder. There were cracks, detonations, and from the cone of flame the sparks flew upwards, as man is born to trouble, to leaky ships, and to ships that burn.

'What bothered me was that the ship, lying broadside to the swell and to such wind as there was—a mere breath—the boats would not keep astern where they were safe, but persisted, in a pig-headed way boats have, in getting under the counter and then swinging alongside. They were knocking about dangerously and coming near the flame, while the ship rolled on them, and, of course, there was always the danger of the masts going over the side at any moment. I and my two boat-keepers kept them off as best we could, with oars and boathooks; but to be constantly at it became exasperating, since there was no reason why we should not leave at once. We could not see those on board, nor could we imagine what caused the delay. The boat-keepers were swearing feebly, and I had not only my share of the work but also had to keep at two men who showed a constant inclination to lay themselves down and let things slide.

'At last I hailed, "On deck there," and someone looked over. "We're ready here," I said. The head disappeared, and very soon popped up again. "The captain says, All right, sir, and to keep the boats well clear of the ship."

'Half an hour passed. Suddenly there was a frightful racket, rattle, clanking of chain, hiss of water, and millions of sparks flew up into the shivering column of smoke that stood leaning slightly above the ship. The catheads had burned away, and the two red-hot anchors had gone to the bottom, tearing out after them two hundred fathom of red-hot chain. The ship trembled, the mass of flame swayed as if ready to collapse, and the fore-topgallant-mast fell. It darted down like an arrow of fire, shot under, and instantly leaping up within an oar's-length of the boats, floated quietly, very black on the luminous sea. I hailed the deck again. After some time a man in an unexpectedly cheerful but also muffled tone, as though he had been trying to speak with his mouth shut, informed me, "Coming directly, sir," and vanished. For a long time I heard nothing but the whirr and roar of the fire. There were also whistling sounds. The boats jumped, tugged at the painters, ran at each other playfully, knocked their sides together, or, do what we would, swung in a bunch against the ship's side. I couldn't stand it any longer, and swarming up a rope, clambered aboard over the stern.

'It was as bright as day. Coming up like this, the sheet of fire facing me was a terrifying sight, and the heat seemed hardly bearable at first. On a settee cushion dragged out of the cabin, Captain Beard, his legs drawn up and one arm under his head, slept with the light playing on him. Do you know what the rest were busy about? They were sitting on deck right aft, round an open case, eating bread and cheese and drinking bottled stout.

'On the background of flames twisting in fierce tongues above their heads they seemed at home like salamanders, and looked like a band of desperate pirates, The fire sparkled in the whites of their eyes, gleamed on patches of white skin seen through the torn shirts. Each had the marks as of a battle about him—bandaged heads, tied-up arms, a strip of dirty rag round a knee—and each man had a bottle between his legs and a chunk of cheese in his hand. Mahon got up. With his handsome and disreputable head, his hooked profile, his long white beard, and with an uncorked bottle in his hand, he resembled one of those reckless sea robbers of old making merry amidst violence and disaster. "The last meal on board," he explained solemnly. "We've had nothing to eat all day, and it was no use leaving all this." He flourished the bottle and indicated the sleeping skipper. "He said he couldn't swallow anything, so I got him to lie down," he went on; and as I stared, "I don't know whether you are aware, young fellow, the man had no sleep to speak of for days—and there will be dam' little sleep in the boats." "There will be no boats by and by if you fool about much longer," I said, indignantly. I walked up to the skipper and shook him by the shoulder. At last he opened his eyes, but did not move. "Time to leave her, sir," I said, quietly.

'He got up painfully, looked at the flames, at the sea sparkling round the ship, and black, black as ink, further away; he looked at the stars shining dim through a thin veil of smoke in a sky black, black as Erebus.

'"Youngest first," he said.

'And the ordinary seaman, wiping his mouth with the back of his hand, got up, clambered over the taffrail, and vanished. Others followed. One, on the point of going over, stopped short to drain his bottle, and with a great swing of his arm flung it at the fire. "Take this!" he cried.

'The skipper lingered disconsolately, and we left him to commune alone for a while with his first command. Then I went up again and brought him away at last. It was time. The ironwork on the poop was hot to the touch.

'Then the painter of the long boat was cut, and the three boats, tied together, drifted clear of the ship. It was just sixteen hours after the explosion when we abandoned her. Mahon had charge of the second boat, and I had the smallest—the fourteen-foot thing. The long boat would have taken the lot of us; but the skipper said we must save as much property as we could—for the underwriters—and so I got my first command. I had two men with me, a bag of biscuits, a few tins of meat, and a beaker of water. I was ordered to keep close to the long boat, that in case of bad weather we might be taken into her.

'And do you know what I thought? I thought I would part company as soon as I could. I wanted to have my first command all to myself. I wasn't going to sail in a squadron if there were a chance for independent cruising. I would make land by myself. I would beat the other boats. Youth! All youth! The silly, charming, beautiful youth.

'But we did not make a start at once. We must see the last of the ship. And so the boats drifted about that night, heaving and setting on the swell. The men dozed, waked, sighed, groaned. I looked at the burning ship.

'Between the darkness of earth and heaven she was burning fiercely upon a disc of purple sea shot by the blood-red play of gleams; upon a disc of water glittering and sinister. A high, clear flame, an immense and lonely flame, ascended from the ocean, and from its summit the black smoke poured continuously at the sky. She burned furiously, mournful and imposing like a funeral pile kindled in the night, surrounded by the sea, watched over by the stars. A magnificent death had come like a grace, like a gift, like a reward to that old ship at the end of her laborious days. The surrender of her weary ghost to the keeping of stars and sea was stirring like the sight of a glorious triumph. The masts fell just before daybreak, and for a moment there was a burst and turmoil of sparks that seemed to fill with flying fire the night, patient and watchful, the vast night lying silent upon the sea. At daylight she was only a charred shell, floating still under a cloud of smoke and bearing a glowing mass of coal within.

'Then the oars were got out, and the boats forming in a line moved round her remains as if in procession—the long boat leading. As we pulled across her stern a slim dart of fire shot out viciously at us, and suddenly she went down, head first, in a great hiss of steam. The unconsumed stern was the last to sink; but the paint had gone, had cracked, had peeled off, and there were no letters, there was no word, no stubborn device that was like her soul, to flash at the rising sun her creed and her name.

'We made our way north. A breeze sprang up, and about noon all the boats came together for the last time. I had no mast or sail in mine, but I made a mast out of a spare oar and hoisted a boat awning for a sail, with a boathook for a yard. She was certainly over-masted. but I had the satisfaction of knowing that with the wind aft I could beat the other two. I had to wait for them. Then we all had a look at the captain's chart, and, after a sociable meal of hard bread and water, got our last instructions. These were simple: steer north, and keep together as much as possible. "Be careful with that jury-rig, Marlow," said the captain; and Mahon, as I sailed proudly past his boat, wrinkled his curved nose and hailed, "You will sail that ship of yours under water, if you don't look out, young fellow." He was a malicious old man—and may the deep sea where he sleeps now rock him gently, rock him tenderly to the end of time!

'Before sunset a thick rain squall passed over the two boats, which were far astern, and that was the last I saw of them for a time. Next day I sat steering my cockleshell—my first command—with nothing but water and sky around me. I did sight in the afternoon the upper sails of a ship far away, but said nothing, and my men did not notice her. You see, I was afraid she might be homeward bound, and I had no mind to turn back from the portals of the East. I was steering for Java—another blessed name—like Bankok, you know. I steered many days.

'I need not tell you what it is to be knocking about in an open boat. I remember nights and days of calm, when we pulled, we pulled, and the boat seemed to stand still, as if bewitched within the circle of the sea horizon. I remember the heat, the deluge of rain squalls that kept us baling for dear life (but filled our water cask), and I remember sixteen hours on end with a mouth dry as a cinder and a steering oar over the stern to keep my first command head on to a breaking sea. I did not know how good a man I was till then. I remember the drawn faces, the dejected figures of my two men, and I remember my youth and the feeling that will never come back any more—the feeling that I could last for ever, outlast the sea, the earth, and all men; the deceitful feeling that lures us on to joys, to perils, to love, to vain effort—to death; the triumphant conviction of strength, the heat of life in the handful of dust, the glow in the heart that with every year grows dim, grows cold, grows small and expires—and expires, too soon too soon—before life itself.

'And this is how I see the East. I have seen its secret places and have looked into its very soul; but now I see it always from a small boat, a high outline of mountains, blue and afar in the morning; like faint mist at noon; a jagged wall of purple at sunset. I have the feel of the oar in my hand, the vision of a scorching blue sea in my eyes. And I see a bay, a wide bay, smooth as glass and polished like ice, shimmering in the dark. A red light burns far off upon the gloom of the land, and the night is soft and warm. We drag at the oars with aching arms, and suddenly a puff of wind, a puff faint and tepid and laden with strange odours of blossoms, of aromatic wood, comes out of the still night—the first sigh of the East on my face. That I can never forget. It was impalpable and enslaving, like a charm, like a whispered promise of mysterious delight.

'We had been pulling this finishing spell for eleven hours. Two pulled, and he whose turn it was to rest sat at the tiller. We had made out the red light in that bay and steered for it, guessing it must mark some small coasting port. We passed two vessels, outlandish and high-sterned, sleeping at anchor, and, approaching the light, now very dim, ran the boat's nose against the end of a jutting wharf. We were blind with fatigue. My men dropped the oars and fell off the thwarts as if dead. I made fast to a pile. A current rippled softly. The scented obscurity of the shore was grouped into vast masses, a density of colossal clumps of vegetation, probably, mute and fantastic shapes. And at their foot the semicircle of a beach gleamed faintly, like an illusion. There was not a light, not a stir, not a sound. The mysterious East faced me, perfumed like a flower, silent like death, dark like a grave.

'And I sat weary beyond expression, exulting like a conqueror, sleepless and entranced as if before a profound, a fateful enigma.

'A splashing of oars, a measured dip reverberating on the level of water, intensified by the silence of the shore into loud claps, made me jump up. A boat, a European boat, was coming in. I invoked the name of the dead; I hailed: *Judea* ahoy! A thin shout answered.

'It was the captain. I had beaten the flagship by three hours, and I was glad to hear the old man's voice again, tremulous and tired: "Is it you, Marlow?" "Mind the end of that jetty, sir," I cried.

'He approached cautiously, and brought up with the deep-sea lead line which we had saved—for the underwriters. I eased my painter and fell alongside. He sat, a broken figure at the stern, wet with dew, his hands clasped in his lap. His men were asleep already. "I had a terrible time of it," he murmured. "Mahon is behind—not very far." We conversed in whispers, in low whispers, as if afraid to wake up the land. Guns, thunder, earthquakes would not have awakened the men just then.

'Looking round as we talked, I saw away at sea a bright light travelling in the night. "There's a steamer passing the bay," I said. She was not passing, she was entering, and she even came close and anchored. "I wish," said the old man, "you would find out whether she is English. Perhaps they could give us a passage somewhere." He seemed nervously anxious. So by dint of punching and kicking I started one of my men into a state of somnambulism, and giving him an oar, took another and pulled towards the lights of the steamer.

'There was a murmur of voices in her, metallic hollow clangs of the engine room, footsteps on the deck. Her ports shone, round like dilated eyes. Shapes moved about, and there was a shadowy man high up on the bridge. He heard my oars.

'And then, before I could open my lips, the East spoke to me, but it was in a Western voice. A torrent of words was poured into the enigmatical, the fateful silence; outlandish, angry words, mixed with words and even whole sentences of good English, less strange but even more surprising. The voice swore and cursed violently; it riddled the solemn peace of the bay by a volley of abuse. It began by calling me pig, and from that went crescendo into unmentionable adjectives—in English. The man up there raged aloud in two languages, and with a sincerity in his fury that almost convinced me I had, in some way, sinned against the harmony of the universe. I could hardly see him, but began to think he would work himself into a fit.

'Suddenly he ceased, and I could hear him snorting and blowing like a porpoise. I said—

'"What steamer is this, pray?"

'"Eh? What's this? And who are you?"

'"Castaway crew of an English barque burnt at sea. We came here tonight. I am the second mate. The captain is in the long boat, and wishes to know if you would give us a passage somewhere."

'"Oh, my goodness! I say . . . This is the *Celestial* from Singapore on her return trip. I'll arrange with your captain in the morning . . . and . . . I say . . . did you hear me just now?"

'"I should think the whole bay heard you."

'"I thought you were a shore boat. Now, look here—this infernal lazy scoundrel of a caretaker has gone to sleep again—curse him. The light is out, and I nearly ran foul of the end of this damned jetty. This is the third time he played me this trick. Now, I ask you, can anybody stand this kind of thing? It's enough to drive a man out of his mind. I'll report him . . . I'll get the Assistant Resident to give him the sack, by . . . ! See—there's no light. It's out, isn't it? I take you to witness the light's out. There should be a light, you know. A red light on the—"

'"There was a light," I said, mildly.

'"But it's out, man! What's the use of talking like this? You can see for yourself it's out—don't you? If you had to take a valuable steamer along this godforsaken coast you would want a light too. I'll kick him from end to end of his miserable wharf. You'll see if I don't. I will—"

'"So I may tell my captain you'll take us?" I broke in.

'"Yes, I'll take you. Good night," he said, brusquely.

'I pulled back, made fast again to the jetty, and then went to sleep at last. I had faced the silence of the East. I had heard some of its language. But when I opened my eyes again the silence was as complete as though it had never been broken. I was lying in a flood of light, and the sky had never looked so far, so high, before. I opened my eyes and lay without moving.

'And then I saw the men of the East—they were looking at me. The whole length of the jetty was full of people. I saw brown, bronze, yellow faces, the black eyes, the glitter, the colour of an Eastern crowd. And all these beings stared without a murmur, without a sigh, without a movement. They stared down at the boats, at the sleeping men who at night had come to them from the sea. Nothing moved. The fronds of palms stood still against the sky. Not a branch stirred along the shore, and the brown roofs of hidden houses peeped through the green foliage, through the big leaves that hung shining and still like leaves forged of heavy metal. This was the East of the ancient navigators, so old, so mysterious, resplendent and sombre, living and unchanged, full of danger and promise. And these were the men. I sat up suddenly. A wave of movement passed through the crowd from end to end, passed along the heads, swayed the bodies, ran along the jetty like a ripple on the water, like a breath of wind on a field—and all was still again. I see it now—the wide sweep of the bay, the glittering sands, the wealth of green infinite and varied, the sea blue like the sea of a dream, the crowd of attentive faces, the blaze of vivid colour—the water reflecting it all, the curve of the shore, the jetty, the high-sterned outlandish craft floating still, and the three boats with the tired men from the West sleeping, unconscious of the land and the people and of the violence of sunshine. They slept thrown across the thwarts, curled on bottom boards, in the careless attitudes of death. The head of the old skipper, leaning back in the stern of the long boat, had fallen on his breast, and he looked as though he would never wake. Farther out old Mahon's face was upturned to the sky, with the long white beard spread out on his breast, as though he had been shot where he sat at the tiller; and a man, all in a heap in the bows of the boat, slept with both arms embracing the stern head and with his cheek laid on the gunwale. The East looked at them without a sound.

'I have known its fascination since; I have seen the mysterious shores, the still water, the lands of brown nations, where a stealthy Nemesis lies in wait, pursues, overtakes so many of the conquering race, who are proud of their wisdom, of their knowledge, of their strength. But for me all the East is contained in that vision of my youth. It is all in that moment when I opened my young eyes on it. I came upon it from a tussle with the sea—and I was young—and I saw it looking at me. And this is all that is left of it! Only a moment; a moment of strength, of romance, of glamour—of youth! . . . a flick of sunshine upon a strange shore, the time to remember, the time for a sigh, and—goodbye!—Night!—Goodbye . . .!'

He drank.

'Ah! The good old time—the good old time. Youth and the sea. Glamour and the sea! The good, strong sea, the salt, bitter sea, that could whisper to you and roar at you and knock your breath out of you.'

He drank again.

'By all that's wonderful it is the sea, I believe, the sea itself—or is it youth alone? Who can tell? But you here—you all had something out of life: money, love—whatever one gets on shore—and, tell me, wasn't that the best time, that time when we were young at sea; young and had nothing, on the sea that gives nothing, except hard knocks—and sometimes a chance to feel your strength—that only—what you all regret?'

And we all nodded at him: the man of finance, the man of accounts, the man of law, we all nodded at him over the polished table that like a still sheet of brown water reflected our faces, lined, wrinkled; our faces marked by toil, by deceptions, by success, by love; our weary eyes looking still, looking always, looking anxiously for something out of life, that while it is expected is already gone—has passed unseen, in a sigh, in a flash—together with the youth, with the strength, with the romance of illusions.

The Lagoon

THE white man, leaning with both arms over the roof of the little house in the stern of the boat, said to the steersman—

'We will pass the night in Arsat's clearing. It is late.'

The Malay only grunted, and went on looking fixedly at the river. The white man rested his chin on his crossed arms and gazed at the wake of the boat. At the end of the straight avenue of forests cut by the intense glitter of the river, the sun appeared unclouded and dazzling, poised low over the water that shone smoothly like a band of metal. The forests, sombre and dull, stood motionless and silent on each side of the broad stream. At the foot of big, towering trees, trunkless nipa palms rose from the mud of the bank, in bunches of leaves enormous and heavy, that hung unstirring over the brown swirl of eddies. In the stillness of the air every tree, every leaf, every bough, every tendril of creeper and every petal of minute blossoms seemed to have been bewitched into an immobility perfect and final. Nothing moved on the river but the eight paddles that rose flashing regularly, dipped together with a single splash; while the steersman swept right and left with a periodic and sudden flourish of his blade describing a glinting semicircle above his head. The churned-up water frothed alongside with a confused murmur. And the white man's canoe, advancing upstream in the short-lived disturbance of its own making, seemed to enter the portals of a land from which the very memory of motion had forever departed.

The white man, turning his back upon the setting sun, looked along the empty and broad expanse of the sea reach. For the last three miles of its course the wandering, hesitating river, as if enticed irresistibly by the freedom of an open horizon, flows straight into the sea, flows straight to the east—to the east that harbours both light and darkness. Astern of the boat the repeated call of some bird, a cry

43

discordant and feeble, skipped along over the smooth water and lost itself, before it could reach the other shore, in the breathless silence of the world.

The steersman dug his paddle into the stream, and held hard with stiffened arms, his body thrown forward. The water gurgled aloud; and suddenly the long, straight reach seemed to pivot on its centre, the forests swung in a semicircle, and the slanting beams of sunset touched the broadside of the canoe with a fiery glow, throwing the slender and distorted shadows of its crew upon the streaked glitter of the river. The white man turned to look ahead. The course of the boat had been altered at right angles to the stream, and the carved dragon-head of its prow was pointing now at a gap in the fringing bushes of the bank. It glided through, brushing the overhanging twigs, and disappeared from the river like some slim and amphibious creature leaving the water for its lair in the forests.

The narrow creek was like a ditch: tortuous, fabulously deep; filled with gloom under the thin strip of pure and shining blue of the heaven. Immense trees soared up, invisible behind the festooned draperies of creepers. Here and there, near the glistening blackness of the water, a twisted root of some tall tree showed amongst the tracery of small ferns, black and dull, writhing and motionless, like an arrested snake. The short words of the paddlers reverberated loudly between the thick and sombre walls of vegetation. Darkness oozed out from between the trees, through the tangled maze of the creepers, from behind the great fantastic and unstirring leaves; the darkness, mysterious and invincible; the darkness scented and poisonous of impenetrable forests.

The men poled in the shoaling water. The creek broadened, opening out into a wide sweep of a stagnant lagoon. The forests receded from the marshy bank, leaving a level strip of bright green, reedy grass to frame the reflected blueness of the sky. A fleecy pink cloud drifted high above, trailing the delicate colouring of its image under the floating leaves and the silvery blossoms of the lotus. A little house, perched on high piles, appeared black in the distance. Near it, two tall nibong palms, that seemed to have come out of the forests in the background, leaned slightly over the ragged roof, with a suggestion of sad tenderness and care in the droop of their leafy and soaring heads.

The steersman, pointing with his paddle, said, 'Arsat is there. I see his canoe fast between the piles.'

The polers ran along the sides of the boat glancing over their shoulders at the end of the day's journey. They would have preferred to spend the night somewhere else than on this lagoon of weird aspect and ghostly reputation. Moreover, they disliked Arsat, first as a stranger, and also because he who repairs a ruined house, and dwells in it, proclaims that he is not afraid to live amongst the spirits that haunt the places abandoned by mankind. Such a man can disturb the course of fate by glances or words; while his familiar ghosts are not easy to propitiate by casual wayfarers upon whom they long to wreak the malice of their human master. White men care not for such things, being unbelievers and in league with the Father of Evil who leads them unharmed through the invisible dangers of this world. To the warnings of the righteous they oppose an offensive pretence of disbelief. What is there to be done?

So they thought, throwing their weight on the end of their long poles. The big canoe glided on swiftly, noiselessly, and smoothly, towards Arsat's clearing, till, in a great rattling of poles thrown down, and the loud murmurs of 'Allah be praised!' it came with a gentle knock against the crooked piles below the house.

The boatmen with uplifted faces shouted discordantly, 'Arsat! O Arsat!' Nobody came. The white man began to climb the rude ladder giving access to the bamboo platform before the house. The juragan of the boat said sulkily, 'We will cook in the sampan, and sleep on the water.'

'Pass my blankets and the basket,' said the white man, curtly.

He knelt on the edge of the platform to receive the bundle. Then the boat shoved off, and the white man, standing up, confronted Arsat, who had come out through the low door of his hut. He was a man young, powerful, with broad chest and muscular arms. He had nothing on but his sarong. His head was bare. His big, soft eyes stared eagerly at the white man, but his voice and demeanour were composed as he asked, without any words of greeting—

'Have you medicine, Tuan?'

'No,' said the visitor in a startled tone. 'No. Why? Is there sickness in the house?'

'Enter and see,' replied Arsat, in the same calm manner, and turning short round, passed again through the small doorway. The white man, dropping his bundles, followed.

In the dim light of the dwelling he made out on a couch of bamboos a woman stretched on her back under a broad sheet of red cotton cloth. She lay still, as if dead; but her big eyes, wide open, glittered in the gloom, staring upwards at the slender rafters, motionless and unseeing. She was in a high fever, and evidently unconscious. Her cheeks were sunk slightly, her lips were partly open, and on the young face there was the ominous and fixed expression—the absorbed, contemplating expression of the unconscious who are going to die. The two men stood looking down at her in silence.

'Has she been long ill?' asked the traveller.

'I have not slept for five nights,' answered the Malay, in a deliberate tone. 'At first she heard voices calling her from the water and struggled against me who held her. But since the sun of today rose she hears nothing—she hears not me. She sees nothing. She sees not me—me!'

He remained silent for a minute, then asked softly 'Tuan, will she die?'

'I fear so,' said the white man, sorrowfully. He had known Arsat years ago, in a far country in times of trouble and danger, when no friendship is to be despised. And since his Malay friend had come unexpectedly to dwell in the hut on the lagoon with a strange woman, he had slept many times there, in his journeys up and down the river. He liked the man who knew how to keep faith in council and how to fight without fear by the side of his white friend. He liked him—not so much perhaps as a man likes his favourite dog—but still he liked him well enough to help and ask no questions, to think sometimes vaguely and hazily in the midst of his own pursuits, about the lonely man and the long-haired woman with audacious face and triumphant eyes, who lived together hidden by the forests—alone and feared.

The white man came out of the hut in time to see the enormous conflagration of sunset put out by the swift and stealthy shadows that, rising like a black and impalpable vapour above the treetops, spread over the heaven, extinguishing the crimson glow of floating clouds and the red brilliance of departing daylight. In a few moments all the stars came out above the intense blackness of the earth and the great lagoon gleaming suddenly with reflected lights resembled an oval patch of night sky flung down into the hopeless and abysmal night of the wilderness. The white man had some supper out of the basket, then collecting a few sticks that lay about the platform, made up a small fire, not for warmth, but for the sake of the smoke, which would keep off the mosquitoes. He wrapped himself in the blankets and sat with his back against the reed wall of the house, smoking thoughtfully.

Arsat came through the doorway with noiseless steps and

squatted down by the fire. The white man moved his outstretched legs a little.

'She breathes,' said Arsat in a low voice, anticipating the expected question. 'She breathes and burns as if with a great fire. She speaks not; she hears not—and burns!'

He paused for a moment, then asked in a quiet, incurious tone 'Tuan . . . will she die?'

The white man moved his shoulders uneasily and muttered in a hesitating manner

'If such is her fate.'

'No, Tuan,' said Arsat, calmly. 'If such is my fate. I hear, I see, I wait. I remember . . . Tuan, do you remember the old days? Do you remember my brother?'

'Yes,' said the white man. The Malay rose suddenly and went in. The other, sitting still outside, could hear the voice in the hut. Arsat said: 'Hear me! Speak!' His words were succeeded by a complete silence. 'O Diamelen!' he cried, suddenly. After that cry there was a deep sigh. Arsat came out and sank down again in his old place.

They sat in silence before the fire. There was no sound within the house, there was no sound near them; but far away on the lagoon they could hear the voices of the boatmen ringing fitful and distinct on the calm water. The fire in the bows of the sampan shone faintly in the distance with a hazy red glow. Then it died out. The voices ceased. The land and the water slept invisible, unstirring and mute. It was as though there had been nothing left in the world but the glitter of stars streaming, ceaseless and vain, through the black stillness of the night.

The white man gazed straight before him into the darkness with wide-open eyes. The fear and fascination, the inspiration and the wonder of death—of death near, unavoidable, and unseen, soothed the unrest of his race and stirred the most indistinct, the most intimate of his thoughts.

The ever ready suspicion of evil, the gnawing suspicion that lurks in our hearts, flowed out into the stillness round him—into the stillness profound and dumb, and made it appear untrustworthy and infamous, like the placid and impenetrable mask of an unjustifiable violence. In that fleeting and powerful disturbance of his being the earth enfolded in the starlight peace became a shadowy country of inhuman strife, a battlefield of phantoms terrible and charming, august or ignoble, struggling ardently for the possession of our helpless hearts. An unquiet and mysterious country of inextinguishable desires and fears.

A plaintive murmur rose in the night; a murmur saddening and startling, as if the great solitudes of surrounding woods had tried to whisper into his ear the wisdom of their immense and lofty indifference. Sounds hesitating and vague floated in the air round him, shaped themselves slowly into words; and at last flowed on gently in a murmuring stream of soft and monotonous sentences He stirred like a man waking up and changed his position slightly. Arsat, motionless and shadowy, sitting with bowed head under the stars, was speaking in a low and dreamy tone—

'. . . for where can we lay down the heaviness of our trouble but in a friend's heart? A man must speak of war and of love. You, Tuan, know what war is, and you have seen me in time of danger seek death as other men seek life! A writing may be lost; a lie may be written; but what the eye has seen is truth and remains in the mind!'

'I remember,' said the white man, quietly. Arsat went on with mournful composure—

'Therefore I shall speak to you of love. Speak in the night. Speak before both night and love are gone—and the eye of day looks upon my sorrow and my shame; upon my blackened face; upon burnt-up heart.'

A sigh, short and faint, marked an almost imperceptible pause and then his words flowed on, without a stir, without a gesture.

'After the time of trouble and war was over and you went away from my country in the pursuit of your desires, which we, men of the islands, cannot understand, I and my brother became again, as we had been before, the sword-bearers of the Ruler. You know we were men of family, belonging to a ruling race, and more fit than any to carry on our right shoulder the emblem of power. And in the time of prosperity Si Dendring showed us favour, as we, in time of sorrow, had showed to him the faithfulness of our courage. It was a time of peace. A time of deer hunts and cockfights; of idle talks and foolish squabbles between men whose bellies are full and weapons are rusty. But the sower watched the young rice shoots grow up without fear, and the traders came and went, departed lean and returned fat into the river of peace. They brought news, too. Brought lies and truth mixed together, so that no man knew when to rejoice and when to be sorry. We heard from them about you also. They had seen you here and had seen you there. And I was glad to hear, for I remembered the stirring times, and I always remembered you, Tuan, till the time came when my eyes could see nothing in the past, because they had looked upon the one who is dying there—in the house.'

He stopped to exclaim in an intense whisper, 'O Mara bahia! O Calamity!' then went on speaking a little louder:

'There's no worse enemy and no better friend than a brother, Tuan, for one brother knows another, and in perfect knowledge is strength for good or evil. I loved my brother. I went to him and told him that I could see nothing but one face, hear nothing but one voice. He told me: "Open your heart so that she can see what is in it—and wait. Patience is wisdom. Inchi Midah may die or our Ruler may throw off his

fear of a woman!" . . . I waited! . . . You remember the lady
with the veiled face, Tuan, and the fear of our Ruler before her
cunning and temper. And if she wanted her servant, what
could I do? But I fed the hunger of my heart on short glances
and stealthy words. I loitered on the path to the bathhouses in
the daytime, and when the sun had fallen behind the forest I
crept along the jasmine hedges of the women's courtyard.
Unseeing, we spoke to one another through the scent of
flowers, through the veil of leaves, through the blades of long
grass that stood still before our lips; so great was our
prudence, so faint was the murmur of our great longing. The
time passed swiftly . . . and there were whispers amongst
women—and our enemies watched, my brother was gloomy,
and I began to think of killing and of a fierce death . . . We are
of a people who take what they want—like you whites. There
is a time when a man should forget loyalty and respect. Might
and authority are given to rulers, but to all men is given love
and strength and courage. My brother said, "You shall take
her from their midst. We are two who are like one." And I
answered, "Let it be soon, for I find no warmth in sunlight
that does not shine upon her." Our time came when the Ruler
and all the great people went to the mouth of the river to fish
by torchlight. There were hundreds of boats, and on the white
sand, between the water and the forests, dwellings of leaves
were built for the households of the Rajahs. The smoke of
cooking fires was like a blue mist of the evening, and many
voices rang in it joyfully. While they were making the boats
ready to beat up the fish, my brother came to me and said,
"Tonight!" I looked to my weapons and when the time came
our canoe took its place in the circle of boats carrying the
torches. The lights blazed on the water, but behind the boats
there was darkness. When the shouting began and the
excitement made them like mad, we dropped out. The water
swallowed our fire, and we floated back to the shore that was

dark with only here and there the glimmer of embers. We could hear the talk of slave girls amongst the sheds. Then we found a place deserted and silent. We waited there. She came. She came running along the shore, rapid and leaving no trace, like a leaf driven by the wind into the sea. My brother said gloomily, "Go and take her; carry her into our boat." I lifted her in my arms. She panted. Her heart was beating against my breast. I said, "I take you from those people. You came to the cry of my heart, but my arms take you into my boat against the will of the great!" "It is right," said my brother. "We are men who take what we want and can hold it against many. We should have taken her in daylight." I said, "Let us be off"; for since she was in my boat I began to think of our Ruler's many men. "Yes. Let us be off," said my brother. "We are cast out and this boat is our country now—and the sea is our refuge." He lingered with his foot on the shore, and I entreated him to hasten, for I remembered the strokes of her heart against my breast and thought that two men cannot withstand a hundred. We left, paddling downstream close to the bank; and as we passed by the creek where they were fishing, the great shouting had ceased, but the murmur of voices was loud like the humming of insects flying at noonday. The boats floated, clustered together, in the red light of torches, under a black roof of smoke; and men talked of their sport. Men that boasted, and praised, and jeered—men that would have been our friends in the morning, but on that night were already our enemies. We paddled swiftly past. We had no more friends in the country of our birth. She sat in the middle of the canoe with covered face; silent as she is now; unseeing as she is now—and I had no regret at what I was leaving because I could hear her breathing close to me—as I can hear her now.'

He paused, listened with his ear turned to the doorway, then shook his head and went on:

'My brother wanted to shout the cry of challenge—one cry only—to let the people know we were freeborn robbers who trusted our arms and the great sea. And again I begged him in the name of our love to be silent. Could I not hear her breathing close to me? I knew the pursuit would come quick enough. My brother loved me. He dipped his paddle without a splash. He only said, "There is half a man in you now—the other half is in that woman. I can wait. When you are a whole man again, you will come back with me here to shout defiance. We are sons of the same mother." I made no answer. All my strength and all my spirit were in my hands that held the paddle—for I longed to be with her in a safe place beyond the reach of men's anger and of women's spite. My love was so great, that I thought it could guide me to a country where death was unknown, if I could only escape from Inchi Midah's fury and from our Ruler's sword. We paddled with haste, breathing through our teeth. The blades bit deep into the smooth water. We passed out of the river; we flew in clear channels amongst the shallows. We skirted the black coast; we skirted the sand beaches where the sea speaks in whispers to the land; and the gleam of white sand flashed back past our boat, so swiftly she ran upon the water. We spoke not. Only once I said, "Sleep, Diamelen, for soon you may want all your strength." I heard the sweetness of her voice, but I never turned my head. The sun rose and still we went on. Water fell from my face like rain from a cloud. We flew in the light and heat. I never looked back, but I knew that my brother's eyes, behind me, were looking steadily ahead, for the boat went as straight as a bushman's dart, when it leaves the end of the sumpitan. There was no better paddler, no better steersman than my brother. Many times, together, we had won races in that canoe. But we never had put out our strength as we did then—then, when for the last time we paddled together! There was no braver or stronger man in our country than my

53

brother. I could not spare the strength to turn my head and look at him, but every moment I heard the hiss of his breath getting louder behind me. Still he did not speak. The sun was high. The heat clung to my back like a flame of fire. My ribs were ready to burst, but I could no longer get enough air into my chest. And then I felt I must cry out with my last breath, "Let us rest!" . . . "Good!" he answered; and his voice was firm. He was strong. He was brave. He knew not fear and no fatigue . . . My brother!'

A murmur powerful and gentle, a murmur vast and faint; the murmur of trembling leaves, of stirring boughs, ran through the tangled depths of the forests, ran over the starry smoothness of the lagoon, and the water between the piles lapped the slimy timber once with a sudden splash. A breath of warm air touched the two men's faces and passed on with a mournful sound—a breath loud and short like an uneasy sigh of the dreaming earth.

Arsat went on in an even, low voice.

'We ran our canoe on the white beach of a little bay close to a long tongue of land that seemed to bar our road; a long wooded cape going far into the sea. My brother knew that place. Beyond the cape a river has its entrance, and through the jungle of that land there is a narrow path. We made a fire and cooked rice. Then we lay down to sleep on the soft sand in the shade of our canoe, while she watched. No sooner had I closed my eyes than I heard her cry of alarm. We leaped up. The sun was halfway down the sky already, and coming in sight in the opening of the bay we saw a prau manned by many paddlers. We knew it at once; it was one of our Rajah's praus. They were watching the shore, and saw us. They beat the gong, and turned the head of the prau into the bay. I felt my heart become weak within my breast. Diamelen sat on the sand and covered her face. There was no escape by sea. My brother laughed. He had the gun you had given him, Tuan, before you went away, but there was only a handful of powder. He spoke to me quickly: "Run with her along the path. I shall keep them back, for they have no firearms, and landing in the face of a man with a gun is certain death for some. Run with her. On the other side of that wood there is a fisherman's house—and a canoe. When I have fired all the shots I will follow. I am a great runner, and before they can come up we shall be gone. I will hold out as long as I can, for she is but a woman—that can neither run nor fight, but she has your heart in her weak hands." He dropped behind the canoe. The prau was coming. She and I ran, and as we rushed along the path I heard shots. My brother fired—once—twice—and the booming of the gong ceased. There was silence behind us. That neck of land is narrow. Before I heard my brother fire the third shot I saw the shelving, shore, and I saw the water again; the mouth of a broad river. We crossed a grassy glade. We ran down to the water. I saw a low hut above the black mud, and a small canoe hauled up. I heard another shot behind me. I thought, "That is his last charge." We rushed down to the canoe; a man came running from the hut, but I leaped on him, and we rolled together in the mud. Then I got up, and he lay still at my feet. I don't know whether I had killed him or not. I and Diamelen pushed the canoe afloat. I heard yells behind me, and I saw my brother run across the glade. Many men were bounding after him, I took her in my arms and threw her into the boat, then leaped in myself. When I looked back I saw that my brother had fallen. He fell and was up again, but the men were closing round him. He shouted, "I am coming!" The men were close to him. I looked. Many men. Then I looked at her. Tuan, I pushed the canoe! I pushed it into deep water. She was kneeling forward looking at me, and I said, "Take your paddle," while I struck the water with mine. Tuan, I heard him cry. I heard him cry my name twice; and I heard voices shouting, "Kill! Strike!" I never turned back. I heard him calling my name again with a great shriek, as when life is going out together with the voice—and I never turned my head. My own name! . . . My brother! Three times he called—but I was not afraid of life. Was she not there in that canoe? And could I not with her find a country where death is forgotten—where death is unknown!'

The white man sat up. Arsat rose and stood, an indistinct and silent figure above the dying embers of the fire. Over the lagoon a mist drifting and low had crept, erasing slowly the glittering images of the stars. And now a great expanse of white vapour covered the land: it flowed cold and gray in the darkness, eddied in noiseless whirls round the tree trunks and about the platform of the house, which seemed to float upon a restless and impalpable illusion of a sea. Only far away the tops of the trees stood outlined on the twinkle of heaven, like a sombre and forbidding shore—a coast deceptive, pitiless and black.

Arsat's voice vibrated loudly in the profound peace.

'I had her there! I had her! To get her I would have faced all mankind. But I had her—and—'

His words went out ringing into the empty distances. He paused, and seemed to listen to them dying away very far—beyond help and beyond recall. Then he said quietly

'Tuan, I loved my brother.'

A breath of wind made him shiver. High above his head, high above the silent sea of mist the drooping leaves of the palms rattled together with a mournful and expiring sound. The white man stretched his legs. His chin rested on his chest, and he murmured sadly without lifting his head—

'We all love our brothers.'

Arsat burst out with an intense whispering violence

'What did I care who died? I wanted peace in my own heart.'

He seemed to hear a stir in the house—listened—then stepped in noiselessly. The white man stood up. A breeze was coming in fitful puffs. The stars shone paler as if they had retreated into the frozen depths of immense space. After a chill gust of wind there were a few seconds of perfect calm and absolute silence. Then from behind the black and wavy line of the forests a column of golden light shot up into the heavens and spread over the semicircle of the eastern horizon. The sun had risen. The mist lifted, broke into drifting patches, vanished into thin flying wreaths; and the unveiled lagoon lay, polished and black, in the heavy shadows at the foot of the wall of trees. A white eagle rose over it with a slanting and ponderous flight, reached the clear sunshine and appeared dazzlingly brilliant for a moment, then soaring higher, became a dark and motionless speck before it vanished into the blue as if it had left the earth forever. The white man, standing gazing upwards before the doorway, heard in the hut a confused and broken murmur of distracted words ending with a loud groan. Suddenly Arsat stumbled out with outstretched hands, shivered, and stood still for some time with fixed eyes. Then he said—

'She burns no more.'

Before his face the sun showed its edge above the tree-tops, rising steadily. The breeze freshened; a great brilliance burst upon the lagoon, sparkled on the rippling water. The forests came out of the clear shadows of the morning, became distinct, as if they had rushed nearer—to stop short in a great stir of leaves, of nodding boughs, of swaying branches. In the merciless sunshine the whisper of unconscious life grew louder, speaking in an incomprehensible voice round the dumb darkness of that human sorrow. Arsat's eyes wandered slowly, then stared at the rising sun.

'I can see nothing,' he said half aloud to himself.

'There is nothing,' said the white man, moving to the edge of the platform and waving his hand to his boat. A shout came faintly over the lagoon and the sampan began to glide towards the abode of the friend of ghosts.

'If you want to come with me, I will wait all the morning,' said the white man, looking away upon the water.

'No, Tuan,' said Arsat, softly. 'I shall not eat or sleep in this house, but I must first see my road. Now I can see nothing—see nothing! There is no light and no peace in the world; but there is death—death for many. We are sons of the same mother—and I left him in the midst of enemies; but I am going back now.'

He drew a long breath and went on in a dreamy tone:

'In a little while I shall see clear enough to strike—to strike. But she has died, and . . . now . . . darkness.'

He flung his arms wide open, let them fall along his body, then stood still with unmoved face and stony eyes, staring at the sun. The white man got down into his canoe. The polers ran smartly along the sides of the boat, looking over their shoulders at the beginning of a weary journey. High in the stern, his head muffled up in white rags, the juragan sat moody, letting his paddle trail in the water. The white man, leaning with both arms over the grass roof of the little cabin, looked back at the shining ripple of the boat's wake. Before the sampan passed out of the lagoon into the creek he lifted his eyes. Arsat had not moved. He stood lonely in the searching sunshine; and he looked beyond the great light of a cloudless day into the darkness of a world of illusions.

Karain: A Memory

*'Be it thy course to busy giddy minds
With foreign quarrels . . .'*
                              Shakespeare

We knew him in those unprotected days when we were content to hold in our hands our lives and our property. None of us, I believe, has any property now, and I hear that many, negligently, have lost their lives; but I am sure that the few who survive are not yet so dim-eyed as to miss in the befogged respectability of their newspapers the intelligence of various native risings in the Eastern Archipelago. Sunshine gleams between the lines of those short paragraphs—sunshine and the glitter of the sea. A strange name wakes up memories; the printed words scent the smoky atmosphere of today faintly, with the subtle and penetrating perfume as of land breezes breathing through the starlight of bygone nights; a signal fire gleams like a jewel on the high brow of a sombre cliff; great trees, the advanced sentries of immense forests, stand watchful and still over sleeping stretches of open water; a line of white surf thunders on an empty beach, the shallow water foams on the reefs; and green islets scattered through the calm of noonday lie upon the level of a polished sea, like a handful of emeralds on a buckler of steel.

There are faces too—faces dark, truculent, and smiling; the frank audacious faces of men barefooted, well armed and noiseless. They thronged the narrow length of our schooner's decks with their ornamented and barbarous crowd, with the variegated colours of checkered sarongs, red turbans, white jackets, embroideries; with the gleam of scabbards, gold rings, charms, armlets, lance blades, and jewelled handles of weapons. They had an independent bearing, resolute eyes, a restrained manner; and we seem yet to hear their soft voices speaking of battles, travels, and escapes; boasting with composure, joking quietly; sometimes in well-bred murmurs extolling their own valour, our generosity; or celebrating with loyal enthusiasm the virtues of their ruler. We remember the faces, the eyes, the voices, we see again the gleam of metal; the murmuring stir of that crowd, brilliant, festive, and martial; and we seem to feel the touch of friendly brown hands that, after one short grasp, return to rest on a chased hilt. They were Karain's people—a devoted following. Their movements hung on his lips; they read their thoughts in his eyes; he murmured to them nonchalantly of life and death, and they accepted his words humbly, like gifts of fate. They were all free men, and when speaking to him said, 'Your slave.' On his passage voices died out as though he had walked guarded by silence; awed whispers followed him. They called him their war-chief. He was the ruler of three villages on a narrow plain; the master of an insignificant foothold on the earth—of a conquered foothold that, shaped like a young moon, lay ignored between the hills and the sea.

From the deck of our schooner, anchored in the middle of the bay, he indicated by a theatrical sweep of his arm along the jagged outline of the hills the whole of his domain; and the ample movement seemed to drive back its limits, augmenting it suddenly into something so immense and vague that for a moment it appeared to be bounded only by the sky. And really, looking at that place, landlocked from the sea and shut off from the land by the precipitous slopes of mountains, it was difficult to believe in the existence of any neighbourhood. It was still, complete, unknown, and full of a life that went on stealthily with a troubling effect of solitude; of a life that seemed unaccountably empty of anything that would stir the thought, touch the heart, give a hint of the ominous sequence of days. It appeared to us a land without memories, regrets, and hopes; a land where nothing could survive the coming of the night, and where each sunrise, like a dazzling act of special creation, was disconnected from the eve and the morrow.

Karain swept his hand over it. 'All mine!' He struck the deck with his long staff; the gold head flashed like a falling star; very close behind him a silent old fellow in a richly embroidered black jacket alone of all the Malays around did not follow the masterful gesture with a look. He did not even lift his eyelids. He bowed his head behind his master, and without stirring held hilt up over his right shoulder a long blade in a silver scabbard. He was there on duty, but without curiosity, and seemed weary, not with age, but with the possession of a burdensome secret of existence. Karain, heavy and proud, had a lofty pose and breathed calmly. It was our first visit, and we looked about curiously.

The bay was like a bottomless pit of intense light. The circular sheet of water reflected a luminous sky, and the shores enclosing it made an opaque ring of earth floating in an emptiness of transparent blue. The hills, purple and arid, stood out heavily on the sky: their summits seemed to fade into a coloured tremble as of ascending vapour; their steep sides were streaked with the green of narrow ravines; at their foot lay ricefields, plantain-patches, yellow sands. A torrent wound about like a dropped thread. Clumps of fruit-trees marked the villages; slim palms put their nodding heads together above the low houses; dried palm-leaf roofs shone afar, like roofs of gold, behind the dark colonnades of tree-trunks; figures passed vivid and vanishing; the smoke of fires stood upright above the masses of flowering bushes; bamboo fences glittered, running away in broken lines between the fields. A sudden cry on the shore sounded plaintive in the distance, and ceased abruptly, as if stifled in the downpour of sunshine. A puff of breeze made a flash of darkness on the smooth water, touched our faces, and became forgotten. Nothing moved. The sun blazed down into a shadowless hollow of colours and stillness.

It was the stage where, dressed splendidly for his part, he strutted, incomparably dignified, made important by the power he had to awaken an absurd expectation of something heroic going to take place—a burst of action or song—upon the vibrating tone of a wonderful sunshine. He was ornate and disturbing, for one could not imagine what depth of horrible void such an elaborate front could be worthy to hide. He was not masked—there was too much life in him, and a mask is only a lifeless thing; but he presented himself essentially as an actor, as a human being aggressively disguised. His smallest acts were prepared and unexpected, his speeches grave, his sentences ominous like hints and complicated like arabesques. He was treated with a solemn respect accorded in the irreverent West only to the monarchs of the stage, and he accepted the profound homage with a sustained dignity seen nowhere else but behind the footlights and in the condensed falseness of some grossly tragic situation. It was almost impossible to remember who he was—only a petty chief of a conveniently isolated corner of Mindanao, where we could in comparative safety break the law against the traffic in firearms and ammunition with the natives. What would happen should one of the moribund Spanish gun-boats be suddenly galvanized into a flicker of active life did not trouble us, once we were inside the bay—so completely did it appear out of the reach of a meddling world; and besides, in those days we were imaginative enough to look with a kind of joyous equanimity on any chance there was of being quietly hanged somewhere out of the way of diplomatic remonstrance. As to Karain, nothing could happen to him unless what happens to all—failure and death; but his quality was to appear clothed in the illusion of unavoidable success. He seemed too effective, too necessary there, too much of an essential condition for the existence of his land and his people, to be destroyed by anything short of an earthquake. He summed up his race, his country, the elemental force of ardent life, of tropical nature. He had its luxuriant strength, its fascination; and, like it, he carried the seed of peril within.

In many successive visits we came to know his stage well—the purple semicircle of hills, the slim trees leaning over houses, the yellow sands, the streaming green of ravines. All that had the crude and blended colouring, the appropriateness almost excessive, the suspicious immobility of a painted scene; and it enclosed so perfectly the accomplished acting of his amazing pretences that the rest of the world seemed shut out forever from the gorgeous spectacle. There could be nothing outside. It was as if the earth had gone on spinning, and had left that crumb of its surface alone in space. He appeared utterly cut off from everything but the sunshine, and that even seemed to be made for him alone. Once when asked what was on the other side of the hills, he said, with a meaning smile, 'Friends and enemies—many enemies; else why should I buy your rifles and powder?' He was always like this—word-perfect in his part, playing up faithfully to the mysteries and certitudes of his surroundings. 'Friends and enemies'—nothing else. It was impalpable and vast. The earth had indeed rolled away from under his land, and he, with his handful of people, stood surrounded by a silent tumult as of contending shades. Certainly no sound came from outside. 'Friends and enemies!' He might have added, 'and memories,' at least as far as he himself was concerned; but he neglected to make that point then. It made itself later on, though; but it was after the daily performance—in the wings, so to speak, and with the lights out. Meantime he filled the stage with barbarous dignity. Some ten years ago he had led his people—a scratch lot of wandering Bugis—to the conquest of the bay, and now in his august care they had forgotten all the past, and had lost all concern for the future. He gave them wisdom, advice, reward, punishment, life or death, with the same serenity of attitude and voice. He understood irrigation and the art of war—the qualities of weapons and the craft of boat-building. He could conceal his heart; had more endurance; he could swim longer, and steer a canoe better than any of his people; he could shoot straighter, and negotiate more tortuously than any man of his race I knew. He was an adventurer of the sea, an outcast, a ruler—and my very good friend. I wish him a quick death in a stand-up fight, a death in sunshine; for he had known remorse and power, and no man can demand more from life. Day after day he appeared before us incomparably faithful to the illusions of the stage, and at sunset the night descended upon him quickly, like a falling curtain. The seamed hills became black shadows towering high upon a clear sky; above them the glittering confusion of stars resembled a mad turmoil stilled by a gesture; sounds ceased, men slept, forms vanished—and the reality of the universe alone remained—a marvellous thing of darkness and glimmers.

II

BUT it was at night that he talked openly, forgetting the exactions of his stage. In the daytime there were affairs to be discussed in state. There were at first between him and me his own splendour, my shabby suspicions, and the scenic landscape that intruded upon the reality of our lives by its motionless fantasy of outline and colour. His followers thronged round him; above his head the broad blades of their spears made a spiked halo of iron points, and they hedged him from humanity by the shimmer of silks, the gleam of weapons, the excited and respectful hum of eager voices. Before sunset he would take leave with ceremony, and go off sitting under a red umbrella, and escorted by a score of boats. All the paddle flashed and struck together with a mighty splash that reverberated loudly in the monumental amphitheatre of hills. A broad stream of dazzling foam trailed behind the flotilla. The canoes appeared very black on the white hiss of water; turbaned heads swayed back and forth; a multitude of arms in crimson and yellow rose and fell with one movement; the spearmen upright in the bows of canoes had variegated sarongs and gleaming shoulders like bronze statues; the muttered strophes of the paddlers' song ended periodically in a plaintive shout. They diminished in the distance; the song ceased; they swarmed on the beach in the long shadows of the western hills. The sunlight lingered on the purple crests, and we could see him leading the way to his stockade, a burly bareheaded figure walking far in advance of a straggling cortège, and swinging regularly an ebony staff taller than himself. The darkness deepened fast; torches gleamed fitfully, passing behind bushes; a long hail or two trailed in the silence of the evening; and at last the night stretched its smooth veil over the shore, the lights, and the voices.

Then, just as we were thinking of repose, the watchmen of the schooner would hail a splash of paddles away in the starlit gloom of the bay; a voice would respond in cautious tones, and our serang, putting his head down the open skylight, would inform us without surprise, 'That Rajah, he coming. He here now.' Karain appeared noiselessly in the doorway of the little cabin. He was simplicity itself then; all in white; muffled about his head; for arms only a kriss with a plain buffalo-horn handle, which he would politely conceal within a fold of his sarong before stepping over the threshold. The old sword-bearer's face, the worn-out and mournful face so covered with wrinkles that it seemed to look out through the meshes of a fine dark net, could be seen close above his shoulders. Karain never moved without that attendant, who stood or squatted close at his back. He had a dislike of an open space behind him. It was more than a dislike—it resembled fear, a nervous preoccupation of what went on where he could not see. This, in view of the evident and fierce loyalty that surrounded him, was inexplicable. He was there alone in the midst of devoted men; he was safe from neighbourly ambushes, from fraternal ambitions; and yet more than one of our visitors had assured us that their ruler could not bear to be alone. They said, 'Even when he eats and sleeps there is' always one on the watch near him who has strength and weapons.' There was indeed always one near him, though our informants had no conception of that watcher's strength and weapons, which were both shadowy and terrible. We knew, but only later on, when we had heard the story. Meantime we noticed that, even during the most important interviews, Karain would often give a start, and interrupting his discourse, would sweep his arm back with a sudden movement, to feel whether the old fellow was there. The old fellow, impenetrable and weary, was always there. He shared his food, his repose, and his thoughts; he knew his plans, guarded his secrets; and, impassive behind his master's agitation, without stirring the least bit, murmured above his head in a soothing tone some words difficult to catch.

It was only on board the schooner, when surrounded by white faces, by unfamiliar sights and sounds, that Karain seemed to forget the strange obsession that wound like a black thread through the gorgeous pomp of his public life. At night we treated him in a free and easy manner, which just stopped short of slapping him on the back, for there are liberties one must not take with a Malay. He said himself that on such occasions he was only a private gentleman coming to see other gentlemen whom he supposed as well born as himself. I fancy that to the last he believed us to be emissaries of Government, darkly official persons furthering by our illegal traffic some dark scheme of high statecraft. Our denials and protestations were unavailing. He only smiled with discreet politeness and inquired about the Queen. Every visit began with that inquiry; he was insatiable of details; he was fascinated by the holder of a sceptre the shadow of which, stretching from the westward over the earth and over the seas, passed far beyond his own hand's-breadth of conquered land. He multiplied questions; he could never know enough of the Monarch of whom he spoke with wonder and chivalrous respect—with a kind of affectionate awe! Afterwards, when we had learned that he was the son of a woman who had many years ago ruled a small Bugis state, we came to suspect that the memory of his mother (of whom he spoke with enthusiasm) mingled somehow in his mind with the image he tried to form for himself of the far-off Queen whom he called Great, Invincible, Pious, and Fortunate. We had to invent details at last to satisfy his craving curiosity; and our loyalty must be pardoned, for we tried to make them fit for his august and resplendent ideal. We talked. The night slipped over us, over the still schooner, over the sleeping land, and over the sleepless sea that thundered amongst the reefs outside the bay. His paddlers, two trustworthy men, slept in the canoe at the foot of our side-ladder. The old confidant, relieved from duty, dozed on his heels, with his back against the companion-doorway; and Karain sat squarely in the ship's wooden armchair, under the slight sway of the cabin lamp, a cheroot between his dark fingers, and a glass of lemonade before him. He was amused by the fizz of the thing, but after a sip or two would let it get flat, and with a courteous wave of his hand ask for a fresh bottle. He decimated our slender stock; but we did not begrudge it to him, for, when he began, he talked well. He must have been a great Bugis dandy in his time, for even then (and when we knew him he was no longer young) his splendour was spotlessly neat, and he dyed his hair a light shade of brown. The quiet dignity of his bearing transformed the dim-lit cuddy of the schooner into an audience-hall. He talked of inter-island politics with an ironic and melancholy shrewdness. He had travelled much, suffered not a little, intrigued, fought. He knew native Courts, European Settlements, the forests, the sea, and, as he said himself, had spoken in his time to many great men. He liked to talk with me because I had known some of these men: he seemed to think that I could understand him, and, with a fine confidence, assumed that I, at least, could appreciate how much greater he was himself. But he preferred to talk of his native country—a small Bugis state on the island of Celebes. I had visited it some time before, and he asked eagerly for news. As men's names came up in conversation he would say, 'We swam against one another when we were boys'; or, 'We had hunted the deer together—he could use the noose and the spear as well as I.' Now and then his big dreamy eyes would roll restlessly; he frowned or smiled, or he would become pensive, and, staring in silence, would nod slightly for a time at some regretted vision of the past.

His mother had been the ruler of a small semi-independent state on the sea-coast at the head of the Gulf of Boni. He spoke of her with pride. She had been a woman resolute in affairs of state and of her own heart. After the death of her first husband, undismayed by the turbulent opposition of the chiefs, she married a rich trader, a Korinchi man of no family. Karain was her son by that second marriage, but his unfortunate descent had apparently nothing to do with his exile. He said nothing as to its cause, though once he let slip with a sigh, 'Ha! my land will not feel any more the weight of my body.' But he related willingly the story of his wanderings, and told us all about the conquest of the bay. Alluding to the people beyond the hills, he would murmur gently, with a careless wave of the hand, 'They came over the hills once to fight us, but those who got away never came again.' He thought for a while, smiling to himself. 'Very few got away,' he added, with proud serenity. He cherished the recollections of his successes; he had an exulting eagerness for endeavour; when he talked, his aspect was warlike, chivalrous, and uplifting. No wonder his people admired him. We saw him once walking in daylight amongst the houses of the settlement. At the doors of huts groups of women turned to look after him, warbling softly, and with gleaming eyes; armed men stood out of the way, submissive and erect; others approached from the side, bending their backs to address him humbly; an old woman stretched out a draped lean arm—'Blessings on thy head!' she cried from a dark doorway; a fiery-eyed man showed above the low fence of a plantain-patch a streaming face, a bare breast scarred in two places, and bellowed out pantingly after him, 'God give victory to our master!' Karain walked fast, and with firm long strides; he answered greetings right and left by quick piercing glances. Children ran forward between the houses, peeped fearfully round corners; young boys kept up with him, gliding between bushes: their eyes gleamed through the dark leaves. The old sword-bearer, shouldering the silver scabbard, shuffled hastily at his heels with bowed head, and his eyes on the ground. And in the midst of a great stir they passed swift and absorbed, like two men hurrying through a great solitude.

In his council hall he was surrounded by the gravity of armed chiefs, while two long rows of old headmen dressed in cotton stuffs squatted on their heels, with idle arms hanging over their knees. Under the thatch roof supported by smooth columns, of which each one had cost the life of a straight-stemmed young palm, the scent of flowering hedges drifted in warm waves. The sun was sinking. In the open courtyard suppliants walked through the gate raising, when yet far off, their joined hands above bowed heads, and bending low in the bright stream of sunlight. Young girls, with flowers in their laps, sat under the wide-spreading boughs of a big tree. The blue smoke of wood fires spread in a thin mist above high-pitched roofs of houses that had glistening walls of woven reeds, and all round them rough wooden pillars under the sloping eaves. He dispensed justice in the shade; from a high seat he gave orders, advice, reproof. Now and then the hum of approbation rose louder, and idle spearmen that lounged listlessly against the posts, looking at the girls, would turn their heads slowly. To no man had been given the shelter of so much respect, confidence, and awe. Yet at times he would lean forward and appear to listen as for a far-off note of discord, as if expecting to hear some faint voice, the sound of light footsteps; or he would start half up in his seat, as though he had been familiarly touched on the shoulder. He glanced back with apprehension; his aged follower whispered inaudibly at his ear; the chiefs turned their eyes away in silence, for the old wizard, the man who could command ghosts and send evil spirits against enemies, was speaking low to their ruler. Around the short stillness of the open place the trees rustled faintly, the soft laughter of girls playing with the flowers rose in clear bursts of joyous sound. At the end of upright spear-shafts the long tufts of dyed horse-hair waved crimson and filmy in the gust of wind; and beyond the blaze of hedges the brook of limpid quick water ran invisible and loud under the drooping grass of the bank, with a great murmur, passionate and gentle.

After sunset, far across the fields and over the bay, clusters of torches could be seen burning under the high roofs of the council shed. Smoky red flames swayed on high poles, and the fiery blaze flickered over faces, clung to the smooth trunks of palm-trees, kindled bright sparks on the rims of metal dishes standing on fine floor-mats. That obscure adventurer feasted like a king. Small groups of men crouched in tight circles round the wooden platters; brown hands hovered over snowy heaps of rice. Sitting upon a rough couch apart from the others, he leaned on his elbow with inclined head; and near him a youth improvised in a high tone a song that celebrated his valour and wisdom. The singer rocked himself to and fro, rolling frenzied eyes; old women hobbled about with dishes, and men, squatting low, lifted their heads to listen gravely without ceasing to eat. The song of triumph vibrated in the night, and the stanzas rolled out mournful and fiery like the thoughts of a hermit. He silenced it with a sign, 'Enough!' An owl hooted far away, exulting in the delight of deep gloom in dense foliage; overhead lizards ran in the attap thatch, calling softly; the dry leaves of the roof rustled; the rumour of mingled voices grew louder suddenly. After a circular and startled glance, as of a man waking up abruptly to the sense of danger, he would throw himself back, and under the downward gaze of the old sorcerer take up, wide-eyed, the slender thread of his dream. They watched his moods; the swelling rumour of animated talk subsided like a wave on a sloping beach. The chief is pensive. And above the spreading whisper of lowered voices only a light rattle of weapons would be heard, a single louder word distinct and alone, or the grave ring of a big brass tray.

III

FOR two years at short intervals we visited him. We came to like him, to trust him, almost to admire him. He was plotting and preparing a war with patience, with foresight—with a fidelity to his purpose and with a steadfastness of which I would have thought him racially incapable. He seemed fearless of the future, and in his plans displayed a sagacity that was only limited by his profound ignorance of the rest of the world. We tried to enlighten him, but our attempts to make clear the irresistible nature of the forces which he desired to arrest failed to discourage his eagerness to strike a blow for his own primitive ideas. He did not understand us, and replied by arguments that almost drove one to desperation by their childish shrewdness. He was absurd and unanswerable. Sometimes we caught glimpses of a sombre, glowing fury within him—a brooding and vague sense of wrong, and a concentrated lust of violence which is dangerous in a native. He raved like one inspired. On one occasion, after we had been talking to him late in his campong, he jumped up. A great, clear fire blazed in the grove; lights and shadows danced together between the trees; in the still night bats flitted in and out of the boughs like fluttering flakes of denser darkness. He snatched the sword from the old man, whizzed it out of the scabbard, and thrust the point into the earth. Upon the thin, upright blade the silver hilt, released, swayed before him like something alive. He stepped back a pace, and in a deadened tone spoke fiercely to vibrating steel: 'If there is virtue in the fire, in the iron, in the hand that forged thee, in the words spoken over thee, in the desire of my heart, and in the wisdom of thy makers—then we shall be victorious together!' He drew it out, looked along the edge. 'Take,' he said over his shoulder to the old sword-bearer. The other, unmoved on his hams, wiped the point with a corner of his sarong, and returning the weapon to its scabbard, sat nursing it on his knees without a single look upwards. Karain, suddenly very calm, reseated himself with dignity. We gave up remonstrating after this, and let him go his way to an honourable disaster. All we could do for him was to see to it that the powder was good for the money and the rifles serviceable, if old.

But the game was becoming at last too dangerous; and if

we, who had faced it pretty often, thought little of the danger, it was decided for us by some very respectable people sitting safely in counting-houses that the risks were too great, and that only one more trip could be made. After giving in the usual way many misleading hints as to our destination, we slipped away quietly, and after a very quick passage entered the bay. It was early morning, and even before the anchor went to the bottom the schooner was surrounded by boats.

The first thing we heard was that Karain's mysterious sword-bearer had died a few days ago. We did not attach much importance to the news. It was certainly difficult to imagine Karain without his inseparable follower; but the fellow was old, he had never spoken to one of us, we hardly ever had heard the sound of his voice; and we had come to look upon him as upon something inanimate, as a part of our friend's trappings of state—like that sword he had carried, or the fringed red umbrella displayed during an official progress. Karain did not visit us in the afternoon as usual. A message of greeting and a present of fruit and vegetables came off for us before sunset. Our friend paid us like a banker, but treated us like a prince. We sat up for him till midnight. Under the stern awning bearded Jackson jingled an old guitar and sang, with an execrable accent, Spanish love songs; while young Hollis and I, sprawling on the deck, had a game of chess by the light of a cargo lantern. Karain did not appear. Next day we were busy unloading, and heard that the Rajah was unwell. The expected invitation to visit him ashore did not come. We sent friendly messages, but fearing to intrude upon some secret council, remained on board. Early on the third day we had landed all the powder and rifles, and also a six-pounder brass gun with its carriage which we had subscribed together for a present for our friend. The afternoon was sultry. Ragged edges of black clouds peeped over the hills, and invisible thunderstorms circled outside, growling like wild beasts. We got the schooner ready for sea, intending to leave next morning at daylight. All day a merciless sun blazed down into the bay, fierce and pale, as if at white heat. Nothing moved on the land. The beach was empty, the villages seemed deserted; the trees far off stood in unstirring clumps, as if painted; the white smoke of some invisible bush-fire spread itself low over the shores of the bay like a settling fog. Late in the day three of Karain's chief men, dressed in their best and armed to the teeth, came off in a canoe, bringing a case of dollars. They were gloomy and languid, and told us they had not seen their Rajah for five days. No one had seen him! We settled all accounts, and after shaking hands in turn and in profound silence, they descended one after another into their boat, and paddled to the shore, sitting close together, clad in vivid colours, with hanging heads: the gold embroideries of their jackets flashed dazzlingly as they went away gliding on the smooth water, and not one of them looked back once. Before sunset the growling clouds carried with a rush the ridge of hills, and came tumbling down the inner slopes. Everything disappeared; black whirling vapours filled the bay, and in the midst of them the schooner swung here and there in the shifting gusts of wind. A single clap of thunder detonated in the hollow with a violence that seemed capable of bursting into small pieces the ring of high land, and a warm deluge descended. The wind died out. We panted in the close cabin; our faces streamed; the bay outside hissed as if boiling; the water fell in perpendicular shafts as heavy as lead; it swished about the deck, poured off the spars, gurgled, sobbed, splashed, murmured in the blind night. Our lamp burned low. Hollis, stripped to the waist, lay stretched out on the lockers, with closed eyes and motionless like a despoiled corpse; at his head Jackson twanged the guitar, and gasped out in sighs a mournful dirge about hopeless love and eyes like stars. Then we heard startled voices on deck crying in the rain, hurried footsteps overhead, and suddenly Karain appeared in the doorway of the cabin. His bare breast and his face glistened in the light; his sarong, soaked, clung about his legs; he had his sheathed kriss in his left hand; and wisps of wet hair, escaping from under his red kerchief, stuck over his eyes and down his cheeks. He stepped in with a headlong stride and looking over his shoulder like a man pursued. Hollis turned on his side quickly and opened his eyes. Jackson clapped his big hand over the strings and the jingling vibration died suddenly. I stood up.

'We did not hear your boat's hail!' I exclaimed.

'Boat! The man's swum off,' drawled out Hollis from the locker. 'Look at him!'

He breathed heavily, wild-eyed, while we looked at him in silence. Water dripped from him, made a dark pool, and ran crookedly across the cabin floor. We could hear Jackson, who had gone out to drive away our Malay seamen from the doorway of the companion; he swore menacingly in the patter of a heavy shower, and there was a great commotion on deck. The watchmen, scared out of their wits by the glimpse of a shadowy figure leaping over the rail, straight out of the night as it were, had alarmed all hands.

Then Jackson, with glittering drops of water on his hair and beard, came back looking angry, and Hollis, who, being the youngest of us, assumed an indolent superiority, said without stirring, 'Give him a dry sarong—give him mine; it's hanging up in the bathroom.' Karain laid the kriss on the table, hilt inwards, and murmured a few words in a strangled voice.

'What's that?' asked Hollis, who had not heard.

'He apologizes for coming in with a weapon in his hand,' I said, dazedly.

'Ceremonious beggar. Tell him we forgive a friend . . . on such a night,' drawled out Hollis. 'What's wrong?'

Karain slipped the dry sarong over his head, dropped the wet one at his feet, and stepped out of it. I pointed to the wooden armchair—his armchair. He sat down very straight, said 'Ha!' in a strong voice; a short shiver shook his broad frame. He looked over his shoulder uneasily, turned as if to speak to us, but only stared in a curious blind manner, and again looked back. Jackson bellowed out, 'Watch well on deck there!' heard a faint answer from above, and reaching out with his foot slammed-to the cabin door.

'All right now,' he said.

Karain's lips moved slightly. A vivid flash of lightning made the two round sternports facing him glimmer like a pair of cruel and phosphorescent eyes. The flame of the lamp seemed to wither into brown dust for an instant, and the looking-glass over the little sideboard leaped out behind his back in a smooth sheet of livid light. The roll of thunder came near, crashed over us; the schooner trembled, and the great voice went on, threatening terribly, into the distance. For less than a minute a furious shower rattled on the decks. Karain looked slowly from face to face, and then the silence became so profound that we all could hear distinctly the two chronometers in my cabin ticking along with unflagging speed against one another.

And we three, strangely moved, could not take our eyes from him. He had become enigmatical and touching, in virtue of that mysterious cause that had driven him through the night and through the thunderstorm to the shelter of the schooner's cuddy. Not one of us doubted that we were looking at a fugitive, incredible as it appeared to us. He was haggard, as though he had not slept for weeks; he had become lean, as though he had not eaten for days. His cheeks were hollow, his eyes sunk, the muscles of his chest and arms twitched slightly as if after an exhausting contest. Of course it had been a long swim off to the schooner; but his face showed another kind of fatigue, the tormented weariness, the anger and the fear of a struggle against a thought, an idea—against something that cannot be grappled, that never rests—a shadow, a nothing, unconquerable and immortal, that preys upon life. We knew it as though he had shouted it at us. His chest expanded time after time, as if it could not contain the beating of his heart. For a moment he had the power of the possessed—the power to awaken in the beholders wonder, pain, pity, and a fearful near sense of things invisible, of things dark and mute, that surround the loneliness of mankind. His eyes roamed about aimlessly for a moment, then became still. He said with effort—

'I came here . . . I leaped out of my stockade as after a defeat. I ran in the night. The water was black. I left him calling on the edge of black water . . . I left him standing alone on the beach. I swam . . . he called out after me . . . I swam . . .'

He trembled from head to foot, sitting very upright and gazing straight before him. Left whom? Who called? We did not know. We could not understand. I said at all hazards—

'Be firm.'

The sound of my voice seemed to steady him into a sudden rigidity, but otherwise he took no notice. He seemed to listen, to expect something for a moment, then went on—

'He cannot come here—therefore I sought you. You men with white faces who despise the invisible voices. He cannot abide your unbelief and your strength.'

He was silent for a while, then exclaimed softly—

'Oh! the strength of unbelievers!'

'There's no one here but you—and we three,' said Hollis quietly. He reclined with his head supported on elbow and did not budge.

'I know,' said Karain. 'He has never followed me here. Was not the wise man ever by my side? But since the old wise man, who knew of my trouble, has died, I have heard the voice every night. I shut myself up—for many days—in the dark. I can hear sorrowful murmurs of women, the whisper of the wind, of the running waters; the clash of weapons in the hands of faithful men, their footsteps—and his voice! . . . Near . . . So! In my ear! I felt him near . . . His breath passed over my neck. I leaped out without a cry. All about me men slept quietly. I ran to the sea. He ran by my side without footsteps, whispering, whispering old words—whispering into my ear in his old voice. I ran into the sea; I swam off to you, with my kriss between my teeth. I, armed, I fled before a breath—to you. Take me away to your land. The wise old man has died, and with him is gone the power of his words and charms. And I can tell no one. No one. There is no one here faithful enough and wise enough to know. It is only near you, unbelievers, that my trouble fades like a mist under the eye of day.'

He turned to me.

'With you I go!' he cried in a contained voice. 'With you, who know so many of us. I want to leave this land—my people . . . and him—there!'

He pointed a shaking finger at random over his shoulder. It was hard for us to bear the intensity of that undisclosed distress. Hollis stared at him hard. I asked gently—

'Where is the danger?'

'Everywhere outside this place,' he answered, mournfully. 'In every place where I am. He waits for me on the paths, under the trees, in the place where I sleep—everywhere but here.'

He looked round the little cabin, at the painted beams, at the tarnished varnish of bulkheads; he looked round as if appealing to all its shabby strangeness, to the disorderly jumble of unfamiliar things that belong to an inconceivable life of stress, of power, of endeavour, of unbelief — to the strong life of white men, which rolls on irresistible and hard on the edge of outer darkness. He stretched out his arms as if to embrace it and us. We waited. The wind and rain had ceased, and the stillness of the night round the schooner was as dumb and complete as if a dead world had been laid to rest in a grave of clouds. We expected him to speak. The necessity within him tore at his lips. There are those who say that a native will not speak to a white man. Error. No man will speak to his master; but to a wanderer and a friend, to him who does not come to teach or to rule, to him who asks for nothing and accepts all things, words are spoken by the camp-fires, in the shared solitude of the sea, in riverside villages, in resting-places surrounded by forests — words are spoken that take no account of race or colour. One heart speaks — another one listens; and the earth, the sea, the sky, the passing wind and the stirring leaf, hear also the futile tale of the burden of life.

He spoke at last. It is impossible to convey the effect of his story. It is undying, it is but a memory, and its vividness cannot be made clear to another mind, any more than the vivid emotions of a dream. One must have seen his innate splendour, one must have known him before—looked at him then. The wavering gloom of the little cabin; the breathless stillness outside, through which only the lapping of water against the schooner's sides could be heard; Hollis's pale face, with steady dark eyes; the energetic head of Jackson held up between two big palms and with the long yellow hair of his beard flowing over the strings of the guitar lying on the table; Karain's upright and motionless pose, his tone—all this made an impression that cannot be forgotten. He faced us across the table. His dark head and bronze torso appeared above the tarnished slab of wood, gleaming and still as if cast in metal. Only his lips moved, and his eyes glowed, went out, blazed again, or stared mournfully. His expressions came straight from his tormented heart. His words sounded low, in a sad murmur as of running water; at times they rang loud like the

clash of a war-gong—or trailed slowly like weary
travellers—or rushed forward with the speed of fear.

IV

THIS IS, imperfectly, what he said—

'It was after the great trouble that broke the alliance of
the four states of Wajo. We fought amongst ourselves, and the
Dutch watched from afar till we were weary. Then the smoke
of their fire-ships was seen at the mouth of our rivers, and
their great men came in boats full of soldiers to talk to us of
protection and peace. We answered with caution and
wisdom, for our villages were burnt, our stockades weak, the
people weary, and the weapons blunt. They came and went;
there had been much talk, but after they went away
everything seemed to be as before, only their ships remained
in sight from our coast, and very soon their traders came
amongst us under a promise of safety. My brother was a
Ruler, and one of those who had given the promise. I was
young then, and had fought in the war, and Pata Matara had
fought by my side. We had shared hunger, danger, fatigue,
and victory. His eyes saw my danger quickly, and twice my
arm had preserved his life. It was his destiny. He was my
friend. And he was great amongst us—one of those who were
near my brother, the Ruler. He spoke in council, his courage
was great, he was the chief of many villages round the great
lake that is in the middle of our country as the heart is in the
middle of a man's body. When his sword was carried into a
campong in advance of his coming, the maidens whispered
wonderingly under the fruit-trees, the rich men consulted
together in the shade and a feast was made ready with
rejoicing and songs. He had the favour of the Ruler and the
affection of the poor. He loved war, deer hunts, and the
charms of women. He was the possessor of jewels, of lucky

weapons, and of men's devotion. He was a fierce man; and I had no other friend.

'I was the chief of a stockade at the mouth of the river, and collected tolls for my brother from the passing boats. One day I saw a Dutch trader go up the river. He went up with three boats, and no toll was demanded from him, because the smoke of Dutch warships stood out from the open sea, and we were too weak to forget treaties. He went up under the promise of safety, and my brother gave him protection. He said he came to trade. He listened to our voices, for we are men who speak openly and without fear, he counted the number of our spears, he examined the trees, the running waters, the grasses of the bank, the hills. He went up to Matara's country and obtained permission to build a house. He traded and planted. He despised our joys, our thoughts, and our sorrows. His face was red, his hair like flame, and his eyes pale, like a river mist; he moved heavily, and spoke with a deep voice; he laughed aloud like a fool, and knew no courtesy in his speech. He was a big, scornful man, who looked into women's faces and put his hand on the shoulders of free men as though he had been a noble-born chief. We bore with him. Time passed.

'Then Pata Matara's sister fled from the campong and went to live in the Dutchman's house. She was a great and wilful lady: I had seen her once carried high on slaves' shoulders amongst the people, with uncovered face, and I had heard all men say that her beauty was extreme, silencing the reason and ravishing the heart of the beholders. The people were dismayed; Matara's face was blackened with that disgrace, for she knew she had been promised to another man. Matara went to the Dutchman's house, and said, "Give her up to die—she is the daughter of chiefs." The white man refused and shut himself up, while his servants kept guard night and day with loaded guns. Matara raged. My brother called a council. But the Dutch ships were near, and watched our coast greedily. My brother said, "If he dies now our land will pay for his blood. Leave him alone till we grow stronger and the ships are gone." Matara was wise; he waited and watched. But the white man feared for her life and went away.

'He left his house, his plantations, and his goods! He departed, armed and menacing, and left all—for her! She had ravished his heart! From my stockade I saw him put out to sea in a big boat. Matara and I watched him from the fighting platform behind the pointed stakes. He sat cross-legged, with his gun in his hands, on the roof at the stern of his prau. The barrel of his rifle glinted aslant before his big red face. The broad river was stretched under him—level, smooth, shining, like a plain of silver; and his prau, looking very short and black from the shore, glided along the silver plain and over into the blue of the sea.

'Thrice Matara, standing by my side, called aloud her name with grief and imprecations. He stirred my heart. It leaped three times; and three times with the eye of my mind I saw in the gloom within the enclosed space of the prau a woman with streaming hair going away from her land and her people. I was angry—and sorry. Why? And then I also cried out insults and threats. Matara said, "Now they have left our land their lives are mine. I shall follow and strike—and, alone, pay the price of blood." A great wind was sweeping towards the setting sun over the empty river. I cried, "By your side I will go!" He lowered his head in sign of assent. It was his destiny. The sun had set, and the trees swayed their boughs with a great noise above our heads.

'On the third night we two left our land together in a trading prau.

'The sea met us—the sea, wide, pathless, and without voice. A sailing prau leaves no track. We went south. The moon was full; and, looking up, we said to one another,

"When the next moon shines as this one, we shall return and they will be dead." It was fifteen years ago. Many moons have grown full and withered and I have not seen my land since. We sailed south; we overtook many praus; we examined the creeks and the bays; we saw the end of our coast, of our island—a steep cape over a disturbed strait, where drift the shadows of shipwrecked praus and drowned men clamour in the night. The wide sea was all round us now. We saw a great mountain burning in the midst of water; we saw thousands of islets scattered like bits of iron fired from a big gun; we saw a long coast of mountain and lowlands stretching away in sunshine from west to east. It was Java. We said, "They are there; their time is near, and we shall return or die cleansed from dishonour."

'We landed. Is there anything good in that country? The paths run straight and hard and dusty. Stone campongs, full of white faces, are surrounded by fertile fields, but every man you meet is a slave. The rulers live under the edge of a foreign sword. We ascended mountains, we traversed valleys; at sunset we entered villages. We asked everyone, "Have you seen such a white man?" Some stared; others laughed; women gave us food, sometimes with fear and respect, as though we had been distracted by the visitation of God; but some did not understand our language, and some cursed us, or, yawning, asked with contempt the reason of our quest. Once, as we were going away, an old man called after us, "Desist!"

'We went on. Concealing our weapons, we stood humbly aside before the horsemen on the road; we bowed low in the courtyards of chiefs who were no better than slaves. We lost ourselves in the fields, in the jungle; and one night, in a tangled forest, we came upon a place where crumbling old walls had fallen amongst the trees, and where strange stone idols—carved images of devils with many arms and legs, with snakes twined round their bodies, with twenty heads and holding a hundred swords—seemed to live and threaten in the light of our camp fire. Nothing dismayed us. And on the road by every fire, in resting-places, we always talked of her and of him. Their time was near. We spoke of nothing else. No! not of hunger, thirst, weariness, and faltering hearts. No! we spoke of him and her! Of her! And we thought of them—of her! Matara brooded by the fire. I sat and thought and thought, till suddenly I could see again the image of a woman, beautiful, and young, and great and proud, and tender, going away from her land and her people. Matara said, "When we find them we shall kill her first to cleanse the dishonour—then the man must die." I would say, "It shall be so; it is your vengeance." He stared long at me with his big sunken eyes.

'We came back to the coast. Our feet were bleeding, our bodies thin. We slept in rags under the shadow of stone enclosures; we prowled, soiled and lean, about the gateways of white men's yards. Their hairy dogs barked at us, and their servants shouted from afar, "Begone!" Low-born wretches, that keep watch over the streets of stone campongs, asked us who we were. We lied, we cringed, we smiled with hate in our hearts, and we kept looking here, looking there for them—for the white man with hair like flame, and for her, for the woman who had broken faith, and therefore must die. We looked. At last in every woman's face I thought I could see hers. We ran swiftly. No! Sometimes Matara would whisper, "Here is the man," and we waited, crouching. He came near. It was not the man—those Dutchmen are all alike. We suffered the anguish of deception. In my sleep I saw her face, and was both joyful and sorry . . . Why? . . . I seemed to hear a whisper near me. I turned swiftly. She was not there! And as we trudged wearily from stone city to stone city I seemed to hear a light footstep near me. A time came when I heard it always, and I was glad. I thought, walking dizzy and weary in sunshine on the hard paths of white men—I thought, She is there—with us! . . . Matara was sombre. We were often hungry.

'We sold the carved sheaths of our krisses—ivory sheaths with golden ferules. We sold the jewelled hilts. But we kept the blades—for them. The blades that never touch but kill—we kept the blades for her . . . Why? She was always by our side . . . We starved. We begged. We left Java at last.

'We went West, we went East. We saw many lands, crowds of strange faces, men that live in trees and men who eat their old people. We cut rattans in the forest for a handful of rice, and for a living swept the decks of big ships and heard curses heaped upon our heads. We toiled in villages; we wandered upon the seas with the Bajow people, who have no country. We fought for pay; we hired ourselves to work for Goram men, and were cheated; and under the orders of rough white faces we dived for pearls in barren bays, dotted with black rocks, upon a coast of sand and desolation. And everywhere we watched, we listened, we asked. We asked traders, robbers, white men. We heard jeers, mockery, threats—words of wonder and words of contempt. We never knew rest; we never thought of home, for our work was not done. A year passed, then another. I ceased to count the number of nights, of moons, of years. I watched over Matara. He had my last handful of rice; if there was water enough for one he drank it; I covered him up when he shivered with cold; and when the hot sickness came upon him I sat sleepless through many nights and fanned his face. He was a fierce man, and my friend. He spoke of her with fury in the daytime, with sorrow in the dark; he remembered her in health, in sickness. I said nothing; but I saw her every day—always! At first I saw only her head, as of a woman walking in the low mist on a river bank. Then she sat by our fire. I saw her! I looked at her! She had tender eyes and a ravishing face. I murmured to her in the night. Matara said sleepily sometimes, "To whom are you talking? Who is there?" I answered quickly, "No one" ... It was a lie! She never left me. She shared the warmth of our fire, she sat on my couch of leaves, she swam on the sea to follow me ... I saw her! ... I tell you I saw her long black hair spread behind her upon the moonlit water as she struck out with bare arms by the side of a swift prau. She was beautiful, she was faithful, and in the silence of foreign countries she spoke to me very low in the language of my people. No one saw her; no one heard her; she was mine only! In daylight she moved with a swaying walk before me upon the weary paths; her figure was straight and flexible like the stem of a slender tree; the heels of her feet were round and polished like shells of eggs; with her round arm she made signs. At night she looked into my face. And she was sad! Her eyes were tender and frightened; her voice soft and pleading. Once I murmured to her, "You shall not die," and she smiled . . . ever after she smiled! . . . She gave me courage to bear weariness and hardships. Those were times of pain, and she soothed me. We wandered patient in our search. We knew deception, false hopes; we knew captivity, sickness, thirst, misery, despair . . . Enough! We found them! . . .'

He cried out the last words and paused. His face was impassive and he kept still like a man in a trance. Hollis sat up quickly, and spread his elbows on the table. Jackson made a brusque movement, and accidentally touched the guitar. A plaintive resonance filled the cabin with confused vibrations and died out slowly. Then Karain began to speak again. The restrained fierceness of his tone seemed to rise like a voice from outside, like a thing unspoken but heard; it filled the cabin and enveloped in its intense and deadened murmur the motionless figure in the chair.

'We were on our way to Atjeh, where there was war; but the vessel ran on a sandbank, and we had to land in Delli. We had earned a little money, and had bought a gun from some

Selangore traders; only one gun, which was fired by the spark of a stone: Matara carried it. We landed. Many white men lived there, planting tobacco on conquered plains, and Matara . . . But no matter. He saw him! . . . The Dutchman! . . . At last! . . . We crept and watched. Two nights and a day we watched. He had a house—a big house in a clearing in the midst of his fields; flowers and bushes grew around; there were narrow paths of yellow earth between the cut grass, and thick hedges to keep people out. The third night we came armed, and lay behind a hedge.

'A heavy dew seemed to soak through our flesh and made our very entrails cold. The grass, the twigs, the leaves, covered with drops of water, were gray in the moonlight. Matara, curled up in the grass shivered in his sleep. My teeth rattled in my head so loud that I was afraid the noise would wake up all the land. Afar, the watchmen of white men's houses struck wooden clappers and hooted in the darkness. And, as every night, I saw her by my side. She smiled no more! . . . The fire of anguish burned in my breast, and she whispered to me with compassion, with pity, softly—as women will; she soothed the pain of my mind; she bent her face over me—the face of a woman who ravishes the hearts and silences the reason of men. She was all mine, and no one could see her—no one of living mankind! Stars shone through her bosom, through her floating hair. I was overcome with regret, with tenderness, with sorrow. Matara slept . . . Had I slept? Matara was shaking me by the shoulder, and the fire of the sun was drying the grass, the bushes, the leaves. It was day. Shreds of white mist hung between the branches of trees.

'Was it night or day? I saw nothing again till I heard Matara breathe quickly where he lay, and then outside the house I saw her. I saw them both. They had come out. She sat on a bench under the wall, and twigs laden with flowers crept high above her head, hung over her hair. She had a box on her lap, and gazed into it, counting the increase of her pearls. The Dutchman stood by looking on; he smiled down at her; his white teeth flashed; the hair on his lip was like two twisted flames. He was big and fat, and joyous, and without fear. Matara tipped fresh priming from the hollow of his palm, scraped the flint with his thumb-nail, and gave the gun to me. To me! I took it . . . O fate!

'He whispered into my ear, lying on his stomach, "I shall creep close and then amok . . . let her die by my hand. You take aim at the fat swine there. Let him see me strike my shame off the face of the earth—and then . . . you are my friend—kill with a sure shot." I said nothing; there was no air in my chest—there was no air in the world. Matara had gone suddenly from my side. The grass nodded. Then a bush rustled. She lifted her head.

'I saw her! The consoler of sleepless nights, of weary days; the companion of troubled years! I saw her! She looked straight at the place where I crouched. She was there as I had seen her for years—a faithful wanderer by my side. She looked with sad eyes and had smiling lips; she looked at me . . . Smiling lips! Had I not promised that she should not die!

'She was far off and I felt her near. Her touch caressed me, and her voice murmured, whispered above me, around me, "Who shall be thy companion, who shall console thee if I die?" I saw a flowering thicket to the left of her stir a little . . . Matara was ready . . . I cried aloud—"Return!"

'She leaped up; the box fell; the pearls streamed at her feet. The big Dutchman by her side rolled menacing eyes through the still sunshine. The gun went up to my shoulder. I was kneeling and I was firm—firmer than the trees, the rocks, the mountains. But in front of the steady long barrel the fields, the house, the earth, the sky swayed to and fro like shadows in a forest on a windy day. Matara burst out of the thicket; before him the petals of torn flowers whirled high as if driven by a tempest. I heard her cry; I saw her spring with open arms in front of the white man. She was a woman of my country and of noble blood. I heard her shriek of anguish and fear—and all stood still! The fields, the house, the earth, the sky stood still—while Matara leaped at her with uplifted arm. I pulled the trigger, saw a spark, heard nothing; the smoke drove back into my face, and then I could see Matara roll over head first and lie with stretched arms at her feet. Ha! A sure shot! The sun shine fell on my back colder than the running water. A sure shot! I flung the gun after the shot. Those two stood over the dead man as though they had been bewitched by a charm. I shouted at her, "Live and remember!" Then for a time I stumbled about in a cold darkness.

'Behind me there were great shouts, the running of many feet; strange men surrounded me, cried meaningless words into my face, pushed me, dragged me, supported me . . . I stood before the big Dutchman: he stared as if bereft of his reason. He wanted to know, he talked fast, he spoke of gratitude, he offered me food, shelter, gold—he asked many questions. I laughed in his face. I said, "I am a Korinchi traveller from Perak over there, and know nothing of that dead man. I was passing along the path when I heard a shot, and your senseless people rushed out and dragged me here." He lifted his arms, he wondered, he could not believe, he could not understand, he clamoured in his own tongue! She had her arms clasped round his neck, and over her shoulder stared back at me with wide eyes. I smiled and looked at her; I smiled and waited to hear the sound of her voice. The white man asked her suddenly, "Do you know him?" I listened—my life was in my ears! She looked at me long, she looked at me with unflinching eyes, and said aloud, "No! I never saw him before." . . . What! Never before? Had she forgotten already? Was it possible? Forgotten already—after so many years—so many years of wandering, of companionship, of trouble, of tender words! Forgotten already! . . . I tore myself out from the hands that held me and went away without a word . . . They let me go.

'I was weary. Did I sleep? I do not know. I remember walking upon a broad path under a clear starlight; and that strange country seemed so big, the rice-fields so vast, that as I looked around, my head swam with the fear of space. Then I saw a forest. The joyous starlight was heavy upon me. I turned off the path and entered the forest, which was very sombre and very sad.'

V

KARAIN'S tone had been getting lower and lower, as though he had been going away from us, till the last words sounded faint but clear, as if shouted on a calm day from a very great distance. He moved not. He stared fixedly past the motionless head of Hollis, who faced him, as still as himself. Jackson had turned sideways, and with elbow on the table shaded his eyes with the palm of his hand. And I looked on, surprised and moved; I looked at that man loyal to a vision, betrayed by his dream, spurned by his illusion, and coming to us unbelievers for help—against a thought. The silence was profound; but it seemed full of noiseless phantoms, of things sorrowful, shadowy, and mute, in whose invisible presence the firm, pulsating beat of the two ships' chronometers ticking off steadily the seconds of Greenwich Time seemed to me a protection and a relief. Karain stared stonily; and looking at his rigid figure, I thought of his wanderings, of that obscure Odyssey of revenge, of all the men that wander amongst illusions; of the illusions as restless as men; of the illusions faithful, faithless; of the illusions that give joy, that give sorrow, that give pain, that give peace; of the invincible illusions that can make life and death appear serene, inspiring, tormented, or ignoble.

A murmur was heard; that voice from outside seemed to flow out of a dreaming world into the lamplight of the cabin. Karain was speaking.

'I lived in the forest.

'She came no more. Never! Never once! I lived alone. She had forgotten. It was well. I did not want her; I wanted no one. I found an abandoned house in an old clearing. Nobody came near. Sometimes I heard in the distance the voices of people going along a path. I slept; I rested; there was wild rice, water from a running stream—and peace! Every night I sat alone by my small fire before the hut. Many nights passed over my head.

'Then, one evening, as I sat by my fire after having eaten, I looked down on the ground and began to remember my wanderings. I lifted my head. I had heard no sound, no rustle, no footsteps—but I lifted my head. A man was coming towards me across the small clearing. I waited. He came up without a greeting and squatted down into the firelight. Then he turned his face to me. It was Matara. He stared at me fiercely with his big sunken eyes. The night was cold; the heat died suddenly out of the fire, and he stared at me. I rose and went away from there, leaving him by the fire that had no heat.

'I walked all that night, all next day, and in the evening made up a big blaze and sat down—to wait for him. He had not come into the light. I heard him in the bushes here and there, whispering, whispering. I understood at last—I had heard the words before, "You are my friend—kill with a sure shot."

'I bore it as long as I could—then leaped away, as on this very night I leaped from my stockade and swam to you. I ran—I ran crying like a child left alone and far from the houses. He ran by my side, without footsteps, whispering,

93

whispering—invisible and heard. I sought people—I wanted men around me! Men who had not died! And again we two wandered. I sought danger, violence, and death. I fought in the Atjeh war, and a brave people wondered at the valiance of a stranger. But we were two; he warded off the blows . . . Why? I wanted peace, not life. And no one could see him; no one knew—I dared tell no one. At times he would leave me, but not for long; then he would return and whisper or stare. My heart was torn with a strange fear, but could not die. Then I met an old man.

'You all knew him. People here called him my sorcerer, my servant and sword-bearer; but to me he was father, mother, protection, refuge and peace. When I met him he was returning from a pilgrimage, and I heard him intoning the prayer of sunset. He had gone to the holy place with his son, his son's wife, and a little child; and on their return, by the favour of the Most High, they all died: the strong man, the young mother, the little child—they died; and the old man reached his country alone. He was a pilgrim serene and pious, very wise and very lonely. I told him all. For a time we lived together. He said over me words of compassion, of wisdom, of prayer. He warded from me the shade of the dead. I begged him for a charm that would make me safe. For a long time he refused; but at last, with a sigh and a smile, he gave me one. Doubtless he could command a spirit stronger than the unrest of my dead friend, and again I had peace; but I had become restless, and a lover of turmoil and danger. The old man never left me. We travelled together. We were welcomed by the great; his wisdom and my courage are remembered where your strength, O white men, is forgotten! We served the Sultan of Sula. We fought the Spaniards. There were victories, hopes, defeats, sorrow, blood, women's tears . . . What for? . . . We fled. We collected wanderers of a warlike race and came here to fight again. The rest you know. I am the ruler of a conquered land, a lover of war and danger, a fighter and a plotter. But the old man has died, and I am again the slave of the dead. He is not here now to drive away the reproachful shade—to silence the lifeless voice! The power of his charm has died with him. And I know fear; and I hear the whisper, "Kill! kill! kill!" . . . Have I not killed enough? . . .'

For the first time that night a sudden convulsion of madness and rage passed over his face. His wavering glances darted here and there like scared birds in a thunderstorm. He jumped up, shouting—

'By the spirits that drink blood: by the spirits that cry in the night: by all the spirits of fury, misfortune, and death, I swear some day I will strike into every heart I meet—I . . .'

He looked so dangerous that we all three leaped to our feet, and Hollis, with the back of his hand, sent the kriss flying off the table. I believe we shouted together. It was a short scare, and the next moment he was again composed in his chair, with three white men standing over him in rather foolish attitudes. We felt a little ashamed of ourselves. Jackson picked up the kriss, and, after an inquiring glance at me, gave it to him. He received it with a stately inclination of the head and stuck it in the twist of his sarong, with punctilious care to give his weapon a pacific position. Then he looked up at us with an austere smile. We were abashed and reproved. Hollis sat sideways on the table and, holding his chin in his hand, scrutinized him in pensive silence. I said—

'You must abide with your people. They need you. And there is forgetfulness in life. Even the dead cease to speak in time.'

'Am I a woman, to forget long years before an eyelid has had the time to beat twice?' he exclaimed, with bitter resentment. He startled me. It was amazing. To him his life—that cruel mirage of love and peace—seemed as real, as undeniable, as theirs would be to any saint, philosopher, or fool of us all. Hollis muttered—

'You won't soothe him with your platitudes.' Karain spoke to me.

'You know us. You have lived with us. Why?—we cannot know; but you understand our sorrows and our thoughts. You have lived with my people, and you understand our desires and our fears. With you I will go. To your land—to your people. To your people who live in unbelief; to whom day is day, and night is night—nothing more, because you understand all things seen, and despise all else! To your land of unbelief, where the dead do not speak, where every man is wise, and alone—and at peace!'

'Capital description,' murmured Hollis, with the flicker of a smile.

Karain hung his head.

'I can toil, and fight—and be faithful,' he whispered, in a weary tone, 'but I cannot go back to him who waits for me on the shore. No! Take me with you . . . Or else give me some of your strength—of your unbelief . . . A charm! . . .'

He seemed utterly exhausted.

'Yes, take him home,' said Hollis, very low, as if debating with himself. 'That would be one way. The ghosts there are in society, and talk affably to ladies and gentlemen, but would scorn a naked human being—like our princely friend. . . . Naked . . . Flayed! I should say. I am sorry for him. Impossible—of course. The end of all this shall be,' he went on, looking up at us—'the end of this shall be, that some day he will run amuck amongst his faithful subjects and send *ad patres* ever so many of them before they make up their minds to the disloyalty of knocking him on the head.'

I nodded. I thought it more than probable that such would be the end of Karain. It was evident that he had been hunted by his thought along the very limit of human endurance, and very little more pressing was needed to make him swerve over into the form of madness peculiar to his race. The respite he had during the old man's life made the return of the torment unbearable. That much was clear.

He lifted his head suddenly; we had imagined for a moment that he had been dozing.

'Give me your protection—or your strength!' he cried. 'A charm . . . a weapon!'

Again his chin fell on his breast. We looked at him, then looked at one another with suspicious awe in our eyes, like men who come unexpectedly upon the scene of some mysterious disaster. He had given himself up to us; he had thrust into our hands his errors and his torment, his life and his peace; and we did not know what to do with that problem from the outer darkness. We three white men looking at the Malay, could not find one word to the purpose amongst us—if indeed there existed a word that could solve that problem. We pondered, and our hearts sank. We felt as though we three had been called to the very gate of Infernal Regions to judge, to decide the fate of a wanderer coming suddenly from a world of sunshine and illusions.

'By Jove, he seems to have a great idea of our power,' whispered Hollis, hopelessly. And then again there was a silence, the feeble plash of water, the steady tick of chronometers. Jackson, with bare arms crossed, leaned his shoulders against the bulkhead of the cabin.

He was bending his head under the deck beam; his fair beard spread out magnificently over his chest; he looked colossal, ineffectual, and mild. There was something lugubrious in the aspect of the cabin; the air in it seemed to become slowly charged with the cruel chill of helplessness, with the pitiless anger of egoism against the incomprehensible form of an intruding pain. We had no idea what to do; we began to resent bitterly the hard necessity to get rid of him.

Hollis mused, muttered suddenly with a short laugh,

'Strength . . . Protection . . . Charm.' He slipped off the table and left the cuddy without a look at us. It seemed a base desertion. Jackson and I exchanged indignant glances. We could hear him rummaging in his pigeon-hole of a cabin. Was the fellow actually going to bed? Karain sighed. It was intolerable!

Then Hollis reappeared, holding in both hands a small leather box. He put it down gently on the table and looked at us with a queer gasp, we thought, as though he had from some cause become speechless for a moment, or were ethically uncertain about producing that box. But in an instant the insolent and unerring wisdom of his youth gave him the needed courage. He said, as he unlocked the box with a very small key, 'Look as solemn as you can, you fellows.'

Probably we looked only surprised and stupid, for he glanced over his shoulder, and said angrily

'This is no play; I am going to do something for him. Look serious. Confound it! . . . Can't you lie a little . . . for a friend!' Karain seemed to take no notice of us, but when Hollis threw open the lid of the box his eyes flew to it—and so did ours. The quilted crimson satin of the inside put a violent patch of colour into the sombre atmosphere; it was something positive to look at—it was fascinating.

VI

HOLLIS looked smiling into the box. He had lately made a dash home through the Canal. He had been away six months, and only joined us again just in time for this last trip. We had never seen the box before. His hands hovered above it; and he talked to us ironically, but his face became as grave as though he were pronouncing a powerful incantation over the things inside.

'Every one of us,' he said, with pauses that somehow

were more offensive than his words—'every one of us, you'll admit, has been haunted by some woman . . . And . . . as to friends . . . dropped by the way . . . Well! . . . ask yourselves . . .'

He paused. Karain stared. A deep rumble was heard high up under the deck. Jackson spoke seriously—

'Don't be so beastly cynical.'

'Ah! You are without guile,' said Hollis, sadly. 'You will learn . . . Meantime this Malay has been our friend . . .'

He repeated several times thoughtfully, 'Friend . . . Malay. Friend, Malay,' as though weighing the words against one another, then went on more briskly—

'A good fellow—a gentleman in his way. We can't, so to speak, turn our backs on his confidence and belief in us. Those Malays are easily impressed—all nerves, you know—therefore . . .'

He turned to me sharply.

'You know him best,' he said, in a practical tone. 'Do you think he is fanatical—I mean very strict in his faith?'

I stammered in profound amazement that 'I did not think so.'

'It's on account of its being a likeness—an engraved image,' muttered Hollis, enigmatically, turning to the box. He plunged his fingers into it. Karain's lips were parted and his eyes shone. We looked into the box.

There were there a couple of reels of cotton, a packet of needles, a bit of silk ribbon, dark blue; a cabinet photograph, at which Hollis stole a glance before laying it on the table face downwards. A girl's portrait, I could see. There were, amongst a lot of various small objects, a bunch of flowers, a narrow white glove with many buttons, a slim packet of letters carefully tied up. Amulets of white men! Charms and talismans! Charms that keep them straight, that drive them crooked, that have the power to make a young man sigh, an old man smile. Potent things that procure dreams of joy, thoughts of regret; that soften hard hearts, and can temper a soft one to the hardness of steel. Gifts of heaven—things of earth . . . Hollis rummaged in the box.

And it seemed to me, during that moment of waiting, that the cabin of the schooner was becoming filled with a stir invisible and living as of subtle breaths. All the ghosts driven out of the unbelieving West by men who pretend to be wise and alone and at peace—all the homeless ghosts of an unbelieving world—appeared suddenly round the figure of Hollis bending over the box; all the exiled and charming shades of loved women; all the beautiful and tender ghosts of ideals, remembered, forgotten, cherished, execrated; all the cast-out and reproachful ghosts of friends admired, trusted, traduced, betrayed, left dead by the way—they all seemed to come from the inhospitable regions of the earth to crowd into the gloomy cabin, as though it had been a refuge and, in all the unbelieving world, the only place of avenging belief. . . . It lasted a second—all disappeared. Hollis was facing us alone with something small that glittered between his fingers. It looked like a coin.

'Ah! here it is,' he said.

He held it up. It was a sixpence—a Jubilee sixpence. It was gilt; it had a hole punched near the rim. Hollis looked towards Karain.

'A charm for our friend,' he said to us. 'The thing itself is of great power—money, you know—and his imagination is struck. A loyal vagabond; if only his puritanism doesn't shy at a likeness . . .'

We said nothing. We did not know whether to be scandalized, amused, or relieved. Hollis advanced towards Karain, who stood up as if startled, and then, holding the coin up, spoke in Malay.

'This is the image of the Great Queen, and the most powerful thing the white men know,' he said, solemnly.

Karain covered the handle of his kriss in sign of respect, and stared at the crowned head.

'The Invincible, the Pious,' he muttered.

'She is more powerful than Suleiman the Wise, who commanded the genii, as you know,' said Hollis, gravely. 'I shall give this to you.' He held the sixpence in the palm of his hand, and looking at it thoughtfully, spoke to us in English.

'She commands a spirit, too—the spirit of her nation; a masterful, conscientious, unscrupulous, unconquerable devil ... that does a lot of good—incidentally ... a lot of good ... at times—and wouldn't stand any fuss from the best ghost out for such a little thing as our friend's shot. Don't look thunderstruck, you fellows. Help me to make him believe—everything's in that.'

'His people will be shocked,' I murmured.

Hollis looked fixedly at Karain, who was the incarnation of the very essence of still excitement. He stood rigid, with head thrown back; his eyes rolled wildly, flashing; the dilated nostrils quivered.

'Hang it all!' said Hollis at last, 'he is a good fellow. I'll give him something that I shall really miss.'

He took the ribbon out of the box, smiled scornfully, then with a pair of scissors cut out a piece from the palm of the glove.

'I shall make him a thing like those Italian peasants wear, you know.'

He sewed the coin in the delicate leather, sewed the leather to the ribbon, tied the ends together. He worked with haste. Karain watched his fingers all the time.

'Now then,' he said—then stepped up to Karain. They looked close into one another's eyes. Those of Karain stared in a lost glance, but Hollis's seemed to grow darker and looked out masterful and compelling. They were in violent contrast together—one motionless and the colour of bronze, the other dazzling white and lifting his arms, where the powerful muscles rolled slightly under a skin that gleamed like satin. Jackson moved near with the air of a man closing up to a chum in a tight place. I said impressively, pointing to Hollis—

'He is young, but he is wise. Believe him!'

Karain bent his head: Hollis threw lightly over it the dark-blue ribbon and stepped back.

'Forget, and be at peace!' I cried.

Karain seemed to wake up from a dream. He said, 'Ha!' shook himself as if throwing off a burden. He looked round with assurance. Someone on deck dragged off the skylight cover, and a flood of light fell into the cabin. It was morning already.

'Time to go on deck,' said Jackson.

Hollis put on a coat, and we went up, Karain leading.

The sun had risen beyond the hills, and their long shadows stretched far over the bay in the pearly light. The air was clear, stainless, and cool. I pointed at the curved line of yellow sands.

'He is not there,' I said, emphatically, to Karain. 'He waits no more. He has departed forever.'

A shaft of bright hot rays darted into the bay between the summits of two hills, and the water all round broke out as if by magic into a dazzling sparkle.

'No! He is not there waiting,' said Karain, after a long look over the beach. 'I do not hear him,' he went on, slowly. 'No!'

He turned to us.

'He has departed again—forever!' he cried.

We assented vigorously, repeatedly, and without compunction. The great thing was to impress him powerfully; to suggest absolute safety—the end of all trouble. We did our best; and I hope we affirmed our faith in the power of Hollis's charm efficiently enough to put the matter beyond the shadow of a doubt. Our voices rang around him joyously in the still air, and above his head the sky, pellucid, pure, stainless, arched its tender blue from shore to shore and over the bay, as if to envelop the water, the earth, and the man in the caress of its light.

The anchor was up, the sails hung still, and half-a-dozen big boats were seen sweeping over the bay to give us a tow out. The paddlers in the first one that came alongside lifted their heads and saw their ruler standing amongst us. A low murmur of surprise arose—then a shout of greeting.

He left us, and seemed straightway to step into the glorious splendour of his stage, to wrap himself in the illusion of unavoidable success. For a moment he stood erect, one foot over the gangway, one hand on the hilt of his kriss, in a martial pose; and, relieved from the fear of outer darkness, he held his head high, he swept a serene look over his conquered foothold on the earth. The boats far off took up the cry of greeting; a great clamour rolled on the water; the hills echoed it, and seemed to toss back at him the words invoking long life and victories.

He descended into a canoe, and as soon as he was clear of the side we gave him three cheers. They sounded faint and orderly after the wild tumult of his loyal subjects, but it was the best we could do. He stood up in the boat, lifted up both his arms, then pointed to the infallible charm. We cheered again; and the Malays in the boats stared—very much puzzled and impressed. I wondered what they thought; what he thought; . . . what the reader thinks?

We towed out slowly. We saw him land and watch us from the beach. A figure approached him humbly but openly—not at all like a ghost with a grievance. We could see other men running towards him. Perhaps he had been missed? At any rate there was a great stir. A group formed itself rapidly near him, and he walked along the sands, followed by a growing cortège and kept nearly abreast of the schooner. With our glasses we could see the blue ribbon on his neck and a patch of white on his brown chest. The bay was waking up. The smokes of morning fires stood in faint spirals higher than the heads of palms; people moved between the houses; a herd of buffaloes galloped clumsily across a green slope; the slender figures of boys brandishing sticks appeared black and leaping in the long grass; a coloured line of women, with water bamboos on their heads, moved swaying through a thin grove of fruit-trees. Karain stopped in the midst of his men and waved his hand; then, detaching himself from the splendid group, walked alone to the water's edge and waved his hand again. The schooner passed out to sea between the steep headlands that shut in the bay, and at the same instant Karain passed out of our life forever.

But the memory remains. Some years afterwards I met Jackson, in the Strand. He was magnificent as ever. His head was high above the crowd. His beard was gold, his face red, his eyes blue; he had a wide-brimmed gray hat and no collar or waistcoat; he was inspiring; he had just come home—had landed that very day! Our meeting caused an eddy in the current of humanity. Hurried people would run against us, then walk round us, and turn back to look at that giant. We tried to compress seven years of life into seven exclamations; then, suddenly appeased, walked sedately along, giving one another the news of yesterday. Jackson gazed about him, like a man who looks for landmarks, then stopped before Bland's window. He always had a passion for firearms; so he stopped short and contemplated the row of weapons, perfect and severe, drawn up in a line behind the black-framed panes. I stood by his side. Suddenly he said—

'Do you remember Karain?' I nodded.

'The sight of all this made me think of him,' he went on,

with his face near the glass . . . and I could see another man, powerful and bearded, peering at him intently from amongst the dark and polished tubes that can cure so many illusions. 'Yes; it made me think of him,' he continued, slowly. 'I saw a paper this morning; they are fighting over there again. He's sure to be in it. He will make it hot for the caballeros. Well, good luck to him, poor devil! He was perfectly stunning.'

We walked on.

'I wonder whether the charm worked—you remember Hollis's charm, of course. If it did . . . never was a sixpence wasted to better advantage! Poor devil! I wonder whether he got rid of that friend of his. Hope so . . . Do you know, I sometimes think that—' I stood still and looked at him.

'Yes . . . I mean, whether the thing was so, you know . . . whether it really happened to him . . . What do you think?'

'My dear chap,' I cried, 'you have been too long away from home. What a question to ask! Only look at all this.'

A watery gleam of sunshine flashed from the west and went out between two long lines of walls; and then the broken confusion of roofs, the chimney-stacks, the gold letters sprawling over the fronts of houses, the sombre polish of windows, stood resigned and sullen under the falling gloom. The whole length of the street, deep as a well and narrow like a corridor, was full of a sombre and ceaseless stir. Our ears were filled by a headlong shuffle and beat of rapid footsteps and an underlying rumour—a rumour vast, faint, pulsating, as of panting breaths, of beating hearts, of gasping voices. Innumerable eyes stared straight in front, feet moved hurriedly, blank faces flowed, arms swung. Over all, a narrow ragged strip of smoky sky wound about between the high roofs, extended and motionless, like a soiled streamer flying above the rout of a mob.

'Ye-e-e-s,' said Jackson, meditatively.

The big wheels of hansoms turned slowly along the edge

of sidewalks; a pale-faced youth strolled, overcome by weariness, by the side of his stick and with the tails of his overcoat flapping gently near his heels; horses stepped gingerly on the greasy pavement, tossing their heads; two young girls passed by, talking vivaciously and with shining eyes; a fine old fellow strutted, red-faced, stroking a white moustache; and a line of yellow boards with blue letters on them approached us slowly, tossing on high behind one another like some queer wreckage adrift upon a river of hats.

'Ye-e-es,' repeated Jackson. His clear blue eyes looked about, contemptuous, amused and hard, like the eyes of a boy. A clumsy string of red, yellow, and green omnibuses rolled swaying, monstrous and gaudy; two shabby children ran across the road; a knot of dirty men with red neckerchiefs round their bare throats lurched along, discussing filthily; a ragged old man with a face of despair yelled horribly in the mud the name of a paper; while far off, amongst the tossing heads of horses, the dull flash of harnesses, the jumble of lustrous panels and roofs of carriages, we could see a policeman, helmeted and dark, stretching out a rigid arm at the crossing of the streets.

'Yes; I see it,' said Jackson, slowly. 'It is there; it pants, rolls; it rolls; is strong and alive; it would smash you if you didn't look out; but I'll be hanged if it is yet as real to me as . . . as the other thing . . . say, Karain's story.'

I think that, decidedly, he had been too long away from home.

The End of the Tether

CONRAD'S SINGAPORE

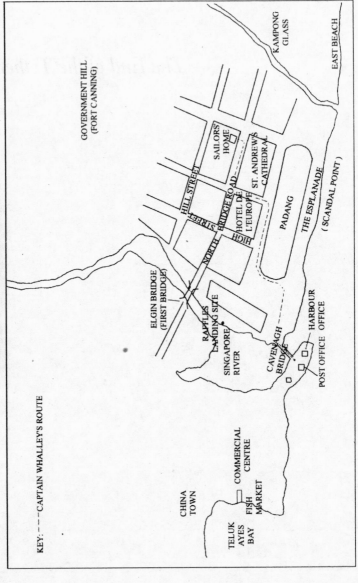

KEY: - - - CAPTAIN WHALLEY'S ROUTE

I

FOR a long time after the course of the steamer *Sofala* had been altered for the land, the low swampy coast had retained its appearance of a mere smudge of darkness beyond a belt of glitter. The sunrays fell violently upon the calm sea—seemed to shatter themselves upon an adamantine surface into sparkling dust, into a dazzling vapour of light that blinded the eye and wearied the brain with its unsteady brightness.

Captain Whalley did not look at it. When his Serang, approaching the roomy cane armchair which he filled capably, had informed him in a low voice that the course was to be altered, he had risen at once and had remained on his feet, face forward, while the head of his ship swung through a quarter of a circle. He had not uttered a single word, not even the word to steady the helm. It was the Serang, an elderly, alert, little Malay, with a very dark skin, who murmured the order to the helmsman. And then slowly Captain Whalley sat down again in the armchair on the bridge and fixed his eyes on the deck between his feet. He could not hope to see anything new upon this lane of the sea. He had been on these coasts for the last three years. From Low Cape to Malantan the distance was fifty miles, six hours' steaming for the old ship with the tide, or seven against. Then you steered straight for the land, and by and by three palms would appear on the sky, tall and slim and with their dishevelled heads in a bunch, as if in confidential criticism of the dark mangroves. The *Sofala* would be headed towards the sombre strip of the coast, which at a given moment, as the ship closed with it obliquely, would show several clean shining fractures—the brimful estuary of a river. Then on through a brown liquid, three parts water and one part black earth, on and on between the low shores, three parts black earth and one part brackish water, the *Sofala* would plough her way upstream, as she had done once every month for these seven years or more, long before he was aware of her existence, long before he had ever thought of having anything to do with her and her invariable voyages. The old ship ought to have known the road better than her men, who had not been kept so long at it without a change; better than the faithful Serang, whom he had brought over from his last ship to keep the captain's watch; better than he himself, who had been her captain for the last three years only. She could always be depended upon to make her courses. Her compasses were never out. She was no trouble at all to take about, as if her great age had given her knowledge, wisdom and steadiness. She made her landfalls to a degree of the bearing, and almost to a minute of her allowed time. At any moment, as he sat on the bridge without looking up, or lay sleepless in his bed, simply by reckoning the days and the hours he could tell where he was—the precise spot of the beat. He knew it well, too, this monotonous huckster's round, up and down the Straits; he knew its order and its sights and its people. Malacca to begin with, in at daylight and out at dusk, to cross over with a rigid phosphorescent wake this highway of the Far East. Darkness and gleams on the water, clear stars on a black sky, perhaps the lights of a home steamer keeping her unswerving course in the middle, or maybe the elusive shadow of a native craft with her mat sails flitting by silently—and low land on the other side in sight at daylight. At noon the three palms of the next place of call, up a sluggish river. The only white man residing there was a retired young sailor, with whom he had become friendly in the course of many voyages. Sixty miles farther on there was another place of call, a deep bay with only a couple of houses on the beach. And so on, in and out, picking up coastwise cargo here and there, and finishing with a hundred miles' steady steaming through the maze of an archipelago of small islands up to a large native town at the end of the beat. There was a three days' rest for the old ship before he started her again in inverse order, seeing the same shores from another bearing, hearing the same voices in the same places, back again to the *Sofala's* port of registry on the great highway to the East, where he would take up a berth nearly opposite the big stone pile of the harbour office till it was time to start again on the old round of 1,600 miles and thirty days. Not a very enterprising life, this, for Captain Whalley, Henry Whalley, otherwise Daredevil Harry Whalley, of the *Condor,* a famous clipper in her day. No. Not a very enterprising life for man who had served famous firms, who had sailed famous ships (more than one or two of them his own); who had made famous passages, had been the pioneer of new routes and new trades; who had steered across the unsurveyed tracts of the South Seas, and had seen the sun rise on uncharted islands. Fifty years at sea and forty out in the East ('a pretty thorough apprenticeship,' he used to remark smilingly), had made him honourably known to a generation of shipowners and merchants in all the ports from Bombay clear over to where East merges into the West upon the coast of the two Americas. His fame remained writ; not very large but plain enough, on the Admiralty charts. Was there not somewhere between Australia and China a Whalley Island and a Condor Reef? On that dangerous coral formation the celebrated clipper had hung stranded for three days, her captain and crew throwing her cargo overboard with one hand and with the other, as it were, keeping off her a flotilla of savage war canoes. At that time neither the island nor the reef had any official existence. Later the officers of Her Majesty's steam vessel *Fusilier,* despatched to make a survey of the route, recognized in the adoption of these two names the enterprise of the man and the solidity of the ship. Besides, as anyone who cares may see, the *General Directory*, vol. ii. p. 410, begins the description of the

'Malotuor Whalley Passage' with the words: 'This advantageous route, first discovered in 1850 by Captain Whalley in the ship *Condor,*' etc., and ends by recommending it warmly to sailing vessels leaving the China ports for the south in the months from December to April inclusive.

This was the clearest gain he had out of life. Nothing could rob him of this kind of fame. The piercing of the Isthmus of Suez, like the breaking of a dam, had let in upon the East a flood of new ships, new men, new methods of trade. It had changed the face of the Eastern seas and the very spirit of their life; so that his early experiences meant nothing whatever to the new generation of seamen.

In those bygone days he had handled many thousands of pounds of his employers' money and of his own; he had attended faithfully, as by law a shipmaster is expected to do, to the conflicting interests of owners, charterers, and underwriters. He had never lost a ship or consented to a shady transaction; and he had lasted well, outlasting in the end the conditions that had gone to the making of his name. He had buried his wife (in the Gulf of Petchili), had married off his daughter to the man of her unlucky choice, and had lost more than an ample competence in the crash of the notorious Travancore and Deccan Banking Corporation, whose downfall had shaken the East like an earthquake. And he was sixty-seven years old.

II

HIS age sat lightly enough on him; and of his ruin he was not ashamed. He had not been alone to believe in the stability of the Banking Corporation. Men whose judgment in matters of finance was as expert as his seamanship had commended the prudence of his investments, and had themselves lost much money in the great failure. The only difference between him

and them was that he had lost his all. And yet not his all. There
had remained to him from his lost fortune a very pretty little
barque, *Fair Maid,* which he had bought to occupy his leisure
of a retired sailor—'to play with,' as he expressed it himself.

He had formally declared himself tired of the sea the year
preceding his daughter's marriage. But after the young couple
had gone to settle in Melbourne he found out that he could
not make himself happy on shore. He was too much of a
merchant sea captain for mere yachting to satisfy him. He
wanted the illusion of affairs; and his acquisition of the *Fair
Maid* preserved the continuity of his life. He introduced her to
his acquaintances in various ports as 'my last command'.
When he grew too old to be trusted with a ship, he would lay
her up and go ashore to be buried, leaving directions in his
will to have the barque towed out and scuttled decently in
deep water on the day of the funeral. His daughter would not
grudge him the satisfaction of knowing that no stranger
would handle his last command after him. With the fortune
he was able to leave her, the value of a 500-ton barque was
neither here nor there. All this would be said with a jocular
twinkle in his eye: the vigorous old man had too much vitality
for the sentimentalism of regret; and a little wistfully withal,
because he was at home in life, taking a genuine pleasure in its
feelings and its possessions; in the dignity of his reputation
and his wealth, in his love for his daughter, and in his
satisfaction with the ship—the plaything of his lonely leisure.

He had the cabin arranged in accordance with his simple
ideal of comfort at sea. A big bookcase (he was a great reader)
occupied one side of his stateroom; the portrait of his late
wife, a flat bituminous oil painting representing the profile
and one long black ringlet of a young woman, faced his
bedplace. Three chronometers ticked him to sleep and greeted
him on waking with the tiny competition of their beats. He
rose at five every day. The officer of the morning watch,

drinking his early cup of coffee aft by the wheel would hear through the wide orifice of the copper ventilators all the splashings, blowings and splutterings of his captain's toilet. These noises would be followed by a sustained deep murmur of the Lord's Prayer recited in a loud earnest voice. Five minutes afterwards the head and shoulders of Captain Whalley emerged out of the companion hatchway. Invariably he paused for a while on the stairs, looking all round at the horizon; upwards at the trim of the sails; inhaling deep draughts of the fresh air. Only then he would step out on the poop, acknowledging the hand raised to the peak of the cap with a majestic and benign 'Good morning to you.' He walked the deck till eight scrupulously. Sometimes, not above twice a year, he had to use a thick cudgel-like stick on account of a stiffness in the hip—a slight touch of rheumatism, he supposed. Otherwise he knew nothing of the ills of the flesh. At the ringing of the breakfast bell he went below to feed his canaries, wind up the chronometers, and take the head of the table. From there he had before his eyes the big carbon photographs of his daughter, her husband, and two fat-legged babies—his grandchildren—set in black frames into the maplewood bulkheads of the cuddy. After breakfast he dusted the glass over these portraits himself with a cloth, and brushed the oil painting of his wife with a plummet kept suspended from a small brass hook by the side of the heavy gold frame. Then with the door of his stateroom shut, he would sit down on the couch under the portrait to read a chapter out of a thick pocket Bible—her Bible. But on some days he only sat there for half an hour with his finger between the leaves and the closed book resting on his knees. Perhaps he had remembered suddenly how fond of boat-sailing she used to be.

She had been a real shipmate and a true woman, too. It was like an article of faith with him that there never had been, and never could be, a brighter, cheerier home anywhere afloat or ashore than his home under the poop deck of the *Condor*, with the big main cabin all white and gold, garlanded as if for a perpetual festival with an unfading wreath. She had decorated the centre of every panel with a cluster of home flowers. It took her a twelvemonth to go round the cuddy with this labour of love. To him it had remained a marvel of painting, the highest achievement of taste and skill; and as to old Swinburne, his mate, every time he came down to his meals he stood transfixed with admiration before the progress of the work. You could almost smell these roses, he declared, sniffing the faint flavour of turpentine which at that time pervaded the saloon, and (as he confessed afterwards) made him somewhat less hearty than usual in tackling his food. But there was nothing of the sort to interfere with his enjoyment of her singing. 'Mrs Whalley is a regular out-and-out nightingale, sir,' he would pronounce with a judicial air after listening profoundly over the skylight to the very end of the piece. In fine weather, in the second dog watch, the two men could hear her trills and roulades going on to the accompaniment of the piano in the cabin. On the very day they got engaged he had written to London for the instrument; but they had been married for over a year before it reached them, coming out round the Cape. The big case made part of the first direct general cargo landed in Hongkong harbour—an event that to the men who walked the busy quays of to-day seemed as hazily remote as the dark ages of history. But Captain Whalley could in a half-hour of solitude live again all his life, with its romance, its idyll and its sorrow. He had to close her eyes himself. She went away from under the ensign like a sailor's wife, a sailor herself at heart. He had read the service over her, out of her own prayer book without a break in his voice. When he raised his eyes he could see old Swinburne facing him with his cap pressed to his breast, and his rugged, weatherbeaten, impassive face streaming with drops of water like a lump of chipped red granite in a shower. It was all very well for that old sea dog to cry. He had to read on to the end; but after the splash he did not remember much of what happened for the next few days. An elderly sailor of the crew, deft at needlework, put together a mourning frock for the child out of one of her black skirts.

He was not likely to forget; but you cannot dam up life like a sluggish stream. It will break out and flow over a man's troubles, it will close upon a sorrow like the sea upon a dead body, no matter how much love has gone to the bottom. And the world is not bad. People had been very kind to him; especially Mrs Gardner, the wife of the senior partner in Gardner, Patteson & Co., the owners of the *Condor*. It was she who volunteered to look after the little one, and in due course took her to England (something of a journey in those days, even by the overland mail route) with her own girls to finish her education. It was ten years before he saw her again.

As a little child she had never been frightened of bad weather; she would beg to be taken up on deck in the bosom of his oilskin coat to watch the big seas hurling themselves upon the *Condor*. The swirl and crash of the waves seemed to fill her small soul with a breathless delight. 'A good boy spoiled,' he used to say of her in joke. He had named her Ivy because of the sound of the word, and obscurely fascinated by a vague association of ideas. She had twined herself tightly round his heart, and he intended her to cling close to her father as to a tower of strength; forgetting while she was little, that in the nature of things she would probably elect to cling to someone else. But he loved life well enough for even that event to give him a certain satisfaction, apart from his more intimate feeling of loss.

After he had purchased the *Fair Maid* to occupy his loneliness, he hastened to accept a rather unprofitable freight to Australia simply for the opportunity of seeing his daughter in her own home. What made him dissatisfied there was not to see that she clung now to somebody else, but that the prop she had selected seemed on closer examination 'a rather poor stick' even in the matter of health. He disliked his son-in-law's studied civility perhaps more than his method of handling the sum of money he had given Ivy at her marriage. But of his apprehensions he said nothing. Only on the day of his departure, with the hall door open all ready, holding her hands and looking steadily into her eyes, he had said, 'You know, my dear, all I have is for you and the chicks. Mind you write to me openly.' She had answered him by an almost imperceptible movement of her head. She resembled her mother in the colour of her eyes, and in character—and also in this, that she understood him without many words.

Sure enough she had to write; and some of the these made Captain Whalley lift his white eyebrows. For the rest he considered he was reaping the true reward of his life by being thus able to produce on demand whatever was needed. He had not enjoyed himself so much in a way since his wife had died. Characteristically enough his son-in-law's punctuality in failure caused him at a distance to feel a sort of kindness towards the man. The fellow was so perpetually being jammed on a lee shore that to charge it all to his reckless navigation would be manifestly unfair. No, no! He knew well what that meant. It was bad luck. His own had been simply marvellous, but he had seen in his life too many good men—seamen and others—go under with the sheer weight of bad luck not to recognize the fatal signs. For all that, he was cogitating on the best way of tying up very strictly every penny he had to leave, when with a preliminary rumble of rumours (whose first sound reached him in Shanghai as it happened), the shock of the big failure came; and, after passing through the phases of stupor, of incredulity, of indignation, he had to accept the fact that he had nothing to speak of to leave.

Upon that, as if he had only waited for this catastrophe, the unlucky man, away there in Melbourne, gave up his unprofitable game, and sat down—in an invalid's bath chair at that, too. 'He will never walk again,' wrote the wife. For the first time in his life Captain Whalley was a bit staggered.

The *Fair Maid* had to go to work in bitter earnest now. It was no longer a matter of preserving alive the memory of Daredevil Harry Whalley in the Eastern Seas, or of keeping an old man in pocketmoney and clothes, with, perhaps, a bill for a few hundred first-class cigars thrown in at the end of the year. He would have to buckle-to, and keep her going hard on a scant allowance of gilt for the gingerbread scrolls at her stem and stern.

This necessity opened his eyes to the fundamental changes of the world. Of his past only the familiar names remained, here and there, but the things and the men, as he had known them, were gone. The name of Gardner, Patteson & Co. was still displayed on the walls of warehouses by the waterside, on the brass plates and windowpanes in the business quarters of more than one Eastern port, but there was no longer a Gardner or a Patteson in the firm. There was no longer for Captain Whalley an armchair and a welcome in the private office, with a bit of business ready to be put in the way of an old friend, for the sake of bygone services. The husbands of the Gardner girls sat behind the desks in that room where, long after he had left the employ, he had kept his right of entrance in the old man's time. Their ships now had yellow funnels with black tops, and a timetable of appointed routes like a confounded service of tramways. The winds of December and June were all one to them; their captains (excellent young men he doubted not) were, to be sure, familiar with Whalley Island, because of late years the

Government had established a white fixed light on the north end (with a red danger sector over the Condor Reef), but most of them would have been extremely surprised to hear that a flesh-and-blood Whalley still existed—an old man going about the world trying to pick up a cargo here and there for his little barque.

And everywhere it was the same. Departed the men who would have nodded appreciatively at the mention of his name, and would have thought themselves bound in honour to do something for Daredevil Harry Whalley. Departed the opportunities which he would have known how to seize; and gone with them the white-winged flock of clippers that lived in the boisterous uncertain life of the winds, skimming big fortunes out of the foam of the sea. In a world that pared down the profits to an irreducible minimum, in a world that was able to count its disengaged tonnage twice over every day and in which lean charters were snapped up by cable three months in advance, there were no chances of fortune for an individual wandering haphazard with a little barque—hardly indeed any room to exist.

He found it more difficult from year to year. He suffered greatly from the smallness of remittances he was able to send his daughter. Meantime he had given up good cigars, and even in the matter of inferior cheroots limited himself to six a day. He never told her of his difficulties, and she never enlarged upon her struggle to live. Their confidence in each other needed no explanations, and their perfect understanding endured without protestations of gratitude or regret. He would have been shocked if she had taken it into her head to thank him in so many words, but he found it perfectly natural that she should tell him she needed two hundred pounds.

He had come in with the *Fair Maid* in ballast to look for a freight in the *Sofala's* port of registry, and her letter met him there. Its tenor was that it was no use mincing matters. Her only resource was in opening a boarding house, for which the prospects, she judged, were good. Good enough, at any rate, to make her tell him frankly that with two hundred pounds she could make a start. He had torn the envelope open, hastily, on deck, where it was handed to him by the ship chandler's runner, who had brought his mail at the moment of anchoring. For the second time in his life he was appalled, and remained stock-still at the cabin door with the paper trembling between his fingers. Open a boarding house! Two hundred pounds for a start! The only resource! And he did not know where to lay his hands on two hundred pence.

All that night Captain Whalley walked the poop of his anchored ship, as though he had been about to close with the land in thick weather, and uncertain of his position after a run of many gray days without a sight of sun, moon, or stars. The black night twinkled with the guiding lights of seamen and the steady straight lines of lights on shore; and all around the *Fair Maid* the riding lights of ships cast trembling trails upon the water of the roadstead. Captain Whalley saw not a gleam anywhere till the dawn broke and he found out that his clothing was soaked through with the heavy dew.

His ship was awake. He stopped short, stroked his wet beard, and descended the poop ladder backwards, with tired feet. At the sight of him the chief officer, lounging about sleepily on the quarterdeck, remained open-mouthed in the middle of a great early-morning yawn.

'Good morning to you,' pronounced Captain Whalley, solemnly, passing into the cabin. But he checked himself in the doorway, and without looking back, 'By the by,' he said, 'there should be an empty wooden case put away in the lazarette. It has not been broken up—has it?'

The mate shut his mouth, and then asked as if dazed, 'What empty case, sir?'

'A big flat packing case belonging to that painting in my room. Let it be taken up on deck and tell the carpenter to look it over. I may want to use it before long.'

The chief officer did not stir a limb till he had heard the door of the captain's stateroom slam within the cuddy. Then he beckoned aft the second mate with his forefinger to tell him that there was something 'in the wind'.

When the bell rang Captain Whalley's authoritative voice boomed out through a closed door, 'Sit down and don't wait for me.' And his impressed officers took their places, exchanging looks and whispers across the table. What! No breakfast? And after apparently knocking about all night on deck, too! Clearly, there was something in the wind. In the skylight above their heads, bowed earnestly over the plates, three wire cages rocked and rattled to the restless jumping of the hungry canaries; and they could detect the sounds of their 'old man's' deliberate movements within his stateroom. Captain Whalley was methodically winding up the chronometers, dusting the portrait of his late wife, getting a clean white shirt out of the drawers, making himself ready in his punctilious, unhurried manner to go ashore. He could not have swallowed a single mouthful of food that morning. He had made up his mind to sell the *Fair Maid*.

III

JUST at that time the Japanese were casting far and wide for ships of European build, and he had no difficulty in finding a purchaser, a speculator who drove a hard bargain, but paid cash down for the *Fair Maid*, with a view to a profitable resale. Thus it came about that Captain Whalley found himself on a certain afternoon descending the steps of one of the most important post offices of the East with a slip of bluish paper in his hand. This was the receipt of a registered letter enclosing a draft for two hundred pounds, and addressed to Melbourne. Captain Whalley pushed the paper into his waistcoat pocket, took his stick from under his arm, and walked down the street.

It was a recently opened and untidy thoroughfare with rudimentary sidewalks and a soft layer of dust cushioning the whole width of the road. One end touched the slummy street of Chinese shops near the harbour, the other drove straight on, without houses, for a couple of miles, through patches of jungle-like vegetation, to the yard gates of the new Consolidated Docks Company. The crude frontages of the new Government buildings alternated with the blank fencing of vacant plots, and the view of the sky seemed to give an added spaciousness to the broad vista. It was empty and shunned by natives after business hours, as though they had expected to see one of the tigers from the neighbourhood of the New Waterworks on the hill coming at a loping canter down the middle to get a Chinese shopkeeper for supper. Captain Whalley was not dwarfed by the solitude of the grandly planned street. He had too fine a presence for that. He was only a lonely figure walking purposefully, with a great white beard like a pilgrim, and with a thick stick that resembled a weapon. On one side the new Courts of Justice had a low and unadorned portico of squat columns half concealed by a few old trees left in the approach. On the other the pavilion wings of the new Colonial Treasury came out to the line of the street. But Captain Whalley, who had now no ship and no home, remembered in passing that on that very site when he first came out from England there had stood a fishing village, a few mat huts erected on piles between a muddy tidal creek and a miry pathway that went writhing into a tangled wilderness without any docks or waterworks.

No ship—no home. And his poor Ivy away there had no home either. A boarding house is no sort of home though it may get you a living. His feelings were horribly rasped by the idea of the boarding house. In his rank of life he had that truly aristocratic temperament characterized by a scorn of vulgar gentility and by prejudiced views as to the derogatory nature of certain occupations. For his own part he had always preferred sailing merchant ships (which is a straightforward occupation) to buying and selling merchandise of which the essence is to get the better of somebody in a bargain—an undignified trial of wits at best. His father had been Colonel Whalley (retired) of the H.E.I. Company's service, with very slender means besides his pension, but with distinguished connections. He could remember as a boy how frequently waiters at the inns, country tradesmen and small people of that sort, used to 'My lord' the old warrior on the strength of his appearance.

Captain Whalley himself (he would have entered the Navy if his father had not died before he was fourteen) had something of a grand air which would have suited an old and glorious admiral; but he became lost like a straw in the eddy of a brook amongst the swarm of brown and yellow humanity filling a thoroughfare, that by contrast with the vast and empty avenue he had left seemed as narrow as a lane and absolutely riotous with life. The walls of the houses were blue; the shops of the Chinamen yawned like cavernous lairs; heaps of nondescript merchandise overflowed the gloom of the long range of arcades, and the fiery serenity of sunset took the middle of the street from end to end with a glow like the reflection of a fire. It fell on the bright colours and the dark faces of the barefooted crowd, on the pallid yellow backs of the half-naked jostling coolies, on the accoutrements of a tall Sikh trooper with a parted beard and fierce moustaches on sentry before the gate of the police compound. Looming very big above the heads in a red haze of dust, the tightly packed car of the cable tramway navigated cautiously up the human

stream, with the incessant blare of its horn, in the manner of a
steamer groping in a fog.

Captain Whalley emerged like a diver on the other side,
and in the desert shade between the walls of closed
warehouses removed his hat to cool his brow. A certain
disrepute attached to the calling of a landlady of a boarding
house. These women were said to be rapacious,
unscrupulous, untruthful; and though he condemned no class
of his fellow-creatures—God forbid!—these were suspicions
to which it was unseemly that a Whalley should lay herself
open. He had not expostulated with her, however. He was
confident she shared his feelings; he was sorry for her; he
trusted her judgment; he considered it a merciful dispensation
that he could help her once more—but in his aristocratic heart
of hearts he would have found it more easy to reconcile
himself to the idea of her turning seamstress. Vaguely he
remembered reading years ago a touching piece called the
'Song of the Shirt'. It was all very well making songs about
poor women. The granddaughter of Colonel Whalley, the
landlady of a boarding house! Pooh! He replaced his hat,
dived into two pockets, and stopping a moment to apply a
flaring match to the end of a cheap cheroot, blew an
embittered cloud of smoke at a world that could hold such
surprises.

Of one thing he was certain—that she was the own child
of a clever mother. Now he had got over the wrench of parting
with his ship, he perceived clearly that such a step had been
unavoidable. Perhaps he had been growing aware of it all
along with an unconfessed knowledge. But she, far away
there, must have had an intuitive perception of it, with the
pluck to face that truth and the courage to speak out—all the
qualities which had made her mother a woman of such
excellent counsel.

It would have had to come to that in the end! It was

fortunate she had forced his hand. In another year or two it would have been an utterly barren sale. To keep the ship going he had been involving himself deeper every year. He was defenceless before the insidious work of adversity, to whose more open assaults he could present a firm front; like a cliff that stands unmoved the open battering of the sea, with a lofty ignorance of the treacherous backwash undermining its base. As it was, every liability satisfied, her request answered, and owing no man a penny, there remained to him from the proceeds a sum of five hundred pounds put away safely. In addition he had upon his person some forty odd dollars—enough to pay his hotel bill; providing he did not linger too long in the modest bedroom where he had taken refuge.

Scantily furnished, and with a waxed floor, it opened into one of the side verandas. The straggling building of bricks, as airy as a birdcage, resounded with the incessant flapping of rattan screens worried by the wind between the whitewashed square pillars of the seafront. The rooms were lofty, a ripple of sunshine flowed over the ceilings; and the periodical invasions of tourists from some passenger steamer in the harbour flitted through the windswept dusk of the apartments with the tumult of their unfamiliar voices and impermanent presences, like relays of migratory shades condemned to speed headlong round the earth without leaving a trace. The babble of their irruptions ebbed out as suddenly as it had arisen; the draughty corridors and the long chairs of the verandas knew their sightseeing hurry or their prostrate repose no more; and Captain Whalley, substantial and dignified, left well nigh alone in the vast hotel by each lighthearted scurry, felt more and more like a stranded tourist with no aim in view, like a forlorn traveller without a home. In the solitude of his room he smoked thoughtfully, gazing at the two sea chests which held all that he could call his own in this world. A thick roll of charts in a sheath of sailcloth leaned in a corner; the flat packing case containing the portrait in oils and the three carbon photographs had been pushed under the bed. He was tired of discussing terms, of assisting at surveys, of all the routine of the business. What to the other parties was merely the sale of a ship was to him a momentous event involving a radically new view of existence. He knew that after this ship there would be no other; and the hopes of his youth, the exercise of his abilities, every feeling and achievement of his manhood, had been indissolubly connected with ships. He had served ships; he had owned ships; and even the years of his actual retirement from the sea had been made bearable by the idea that he had only to stretch out his hand full of money to get a ship. He had been at liberty to feel as though he were the owner of all the ships in the world. The selling of this one was weary work; but when she passed from him at last, when he signed the last receipt, it was as though all the ships had gone out of the world together, leaving him on the shore of inaccessible oceans with seven hundred pounds in his hands.

Striding firmly, without haste, along the quay, Captain Whalley averted his glances from the familiar roadstead. Two generations of seamen born since his first day at sea stood between him and all these ships at the anchorage. His own was sold, and he had been asking himself, What next?

From the feeling of loneliness, of inward emptiness—and of loss, too, as if his very soul had been taken out of him forcibly—there had sprung at first a desire to start right off and join his daughter. 'Here are the last pence,' he would say to her; 'take them, my dear. And here's your old father: you must take him, too.'

His soul recoiled, as if afraid of what lay hidden at the bottom of this impulse. Give up! Never! When one is thoroughly weary all sorts of nonsense come into one's head.

A pretty gift it would have been for a poor woman—this seven hundred pounds with the incumbrance of a hale old fellow more than likely to last for years and years to come. Was he not as fit to die in harness as any of the youngsters in charge of these anchored ships out yonder? He was as solid now as ever he had been. But as to who would give him work to do, that was another matter. Were he, with his appearance and antecedents, to go about looking for a junior's berth, people, he was afraid, would not take him seriously; or else if he succeeded in impressing them, he would maybe obtain their pity, which would be like stripping yourself naked to be kicked. He was not anxious to give himself away for less than nothing. He had no use for anybody's pity. On the other hand, a command—the only thing he could try for with due regard for common decency—was not likely to be lying in wait for him at the corner of the next street. Commands don't go a-begging nowadays. Ever since he had come ashore to carry out the business of the sale he had kept his ears open, but had heard no hint of one being vacant in the port. And even if there had been one, his successful past itself stood in his way. He had been his own employer too long. The only credential he could produce was the testimony of his whole life. What better recommendation could any one require? But vaguely he felt that the unique document would he looked upon as an archaic curiosity of the Eastern waters, a screed traced in obsolete words—in a half-forgotten language.

IV

REVOLVING these thoughts, he strolled on near the railings of the quay, broad-chested, without a stoop, as though his big shoulders had never felt the burden of the loads that must be carried between the cradle and the grave. No single betraying fold or line of care disfigured the reposeful modelling of his face. It was full and untanned; and the upper part emerged, massively quiet, out of the downward flow of silvery hair, with the striking delicacy of its clear complexion and the powerful width of the forehead. The first cast of his glance fell on you candid and swift, like a boy's; but because of the ragged snowy thatch of the eyebrows the affability of his attention acquired the character of a keen and searching scrutiny. With age he had put on flesh a little, had increased his girth like an old tree presenting no symptoms of decay; and even the opulent, lustrous ripple of white hairs upon his chest seemed an attribute of unquenchable vitality and vigour.

Once rather proud of his great bodily strength, and even of his personal appearance, conscious of his worth, and firm in his rectitude, there had remained to him, like the heritage of departed prosperity, the tranquil bearing of a man who had proved himself fit in every sort of way for the life of his choice. He strode on squarely under the projecting brim of an ancient Panama hat. It had a low crown, a crease through its whole diameter, a narrow black ribbon. Imperishable and a little discoloured, this headgear made it easy to pick him out from afar on thronged wharves and in the busy streets. He had never adopted the comparatively modern fashion of pipeclayed cork helmets. He disliked the form; and he hoped he could manage to keep a cool head to the end of his life without all these contrivances for hygienic ventilation. His hair was cropped close, his linen always of immaculate whiteness; a suit of thin gray flannel, worn threadbare but scrupulously brushed, floated about his burly limbs, adding to his bulk by the looseness of its cut. The years had mellowed the good-humoured, imperturbable audacity of his prime into a temper carelessly serene; and the leisurely tapping of his iron-shod stick accompanied his footfalls with a self-confident sound on the flagstones. It was impossible to connect such a fine presence and this unruffled aspect with the belittling troubles of poverty; the man's whole existence appeared to pass before you, facile and large, in the freedom of means as ample as the clothing of his body.

The irrational dread of having to break into his five hundred pounds for personal expenses in the hotel disturbed the steady poise of his mind. There was no time to lose. The bill was running up. He nourished the hope that this five hundred would perhaps be the means, if everything else failed, of obtaining some work which, keeping his body and soul together (not a matter of great outlay), would enable him to be of use to his daughter. To his mind it was her own money which he employed, as it were, in backing her father and solely for her benefit. Once at work, he would help her with the greater part of his earnings; he was good for many years yet, and this boarding house business, he argued to himself, whatever the prospects, could not be much of a gold mine from the first start. But what work? He was ready to lay hold of anything in an honest way so that it came quickly to his hand; because the five hundred pounds must be preserved intact for eventual use. That was the great point. With the entire five hundred one felt a substance at one's back; but it seemed to him that should he let it dwindle to four-fifty or even four-eighty, all the efficiency would be gone out of the money, as though there were some magic power in the round figure. But what sort of work?

Confronted by that haunting question as by an uneasy ghost, for whom he had no exorcizing förmula, Captain Whalley stopped short on the apex of a small bridge spanning steeply the bed of a canalized creek with granite shores. Moored between the square blocks a seagoing Malay prau floated half hidden under the arch of masonry, with her spars lowered down, without a sound of life on board, and covered from stem to stern with a ridge of palm-leaf mats. He had left behind him the overheated pavements bordered by the stone frontages that, like the sheer face of cliffs, followed the sweep of the quays; and an unconfined spaciousness of orderly and sylvan aspect opened before him its wide plots of rolled grass, like pieces of green carpet smoothly pegged out, its long ranges of trees lined up in colossal porticos of dark shafts roofed with a vault of branches.

Some of these avenues ended at the sea. It was a terraced shore; and beyond, upon the level expanse, profound and glistening like the gaze of a dark blue eye, an oblique band of stippled purple lengthened itself indefinitely through the gap between a couple of verdant twin islets. The masts and spars of a few ships far away, hull down in the outer roads, sprang straight from the water in a fine maze of rosy lines pencilled on the clear shadow of the eastern board. Captain Whalley gave them a long glance. The ship, once his own, was anchored out there. It was staggering to think that it was open to him no longer to take a boat at the jetty and get himself pulled off to her when the evening came. To no ship. Perhaps never more. Before the sale was concluded, and till the purchase money had been paid, he had spent daily some time on board the *Fair Maid*. The money had been paid this very morning, and now, all at once, there was positively no ship that he could go on board of when he liked; no ship that would need his presence in order to do her work—to live. It seemed an incredible state of affairs, something too bizarre to last. And the sea was full of craft of all sorts. There was that prau lying so still swathed in her shroud of sewn palm leaves—she, too, had her indispensable man. They lived through each other, this Malay he had never seen, and this high-sterned thing of no size that seemed to be resting after a long journey. And of all the ships in sight, near and far, each was provided with a man, the man without whom the finest ship is a dead thing, a floating and purposeless log.

After his one glance at the roadstead he went on since there was nothing to turn back for, and the time must be got through somehow. The avenues of big trees ran straight over the Esplanade, cutting each other at diverse; angles, columnar below and luxuriant above. The interlaced boughs high up there seemed to slumber; not a leaf stirred overhead: and the reedy cast-iron lamp posts in the middle of the road, gilt like sceptres diminished in a long perspective, with their globes of white porcelain atop, resembling a barbarous decoration of ostriches' eggs displayed in a row. The flaming sky kindled a tiny crimson spark upon the glistening surface of each glassy shell.

With his chin sunk a little, his hands behind his back, and the end of his stick marking the gravel with a faint wavering line at his heels, Captain Whalley reflected that if a ship without a man was like a body without a soul, a sailor without a ship was of not much more account in this world than an aimless log adrift upon the sea. The log might be sound enough by itself, tough of fibre, and hard to destroy—but what of that! And a sudden sense of irremediable idleness weighted his feet like a great fatigue.

A succession of open carriages came bowling along the newly opened sea road. You could see across the wide grass plots the discs of vibration made by the spokes. The bright domes of the parasols swayed lightly outwards like full-blown blossoms on the rim of a vase; and the quiet sheet of dark blue water, crossed by a bar of purple, made a background for the spinning wheels and the high action of the horses, whilst the turbaned heads of the Indian servants elevated above the line of the sea horizon glided rapidly on the paler blue of the sky. In an open space near the little bridge each turnout trotted smartly in a wide curve away from the sunset; then pulling up sharp, entered the main alley in a long slow-moving file with the great red stillness of the sky at the back. The trunks of mighty trees stood all touched with red on the same side, the air seemed aflame under the high foliage, the very ground under the hoofs of the horses was red. The wheels turned solemnly; one after another the sunshades drooped, folding their colours like gorgeous flowers shutting their petals at the end of the day. In the whole half-mile of human beings no voice uttered a distinct word, only a faint thudding noise went on mingled with slight jingling sounds, and the motionless heads and shoulders of men and women sitting in couples emerged stolidly above the lowered hoods—as if wooden. But one carriage and pair coming late did not join the line.

It fled along in a noiseless roll; but on entering the avenue one of the dark bays snorted, arching his neck and shying against the steel-tipped pole; a flake of foam fell from the bit upon the point of a satiny shoulder, and the dusky face of the coachman leaned forward at once over the hands taking a fresh grip of the reins. It was a long dark green landau, having a dignified and buoyant motion between the sharply curved C-springs, and a sort of strictly official majesty in its supreme elegance. It seemed more roomy than is usual, its horses seemed slightly bigger, the appointments a shade more perfect, the servants perched somewhat higher on the box. The dresses of three women—two young and pretty, and one, handsome, large, of mature age—seemed to fill completely the shallow body of the carriage. The fourth face was that of a man, heavy lidded, distinguished and sallow, with a sombre, thick, iron-grey imperial and moustaches, which somehow had the air of solid appendages. His Excellency—

The rapid motion of that one equipage made all the others appear utterly inferior, blighted, and reduced to crawl painfully at a snail's pace. The landau distanced the whole file in a sort of sustained rush; the features of the occupants whirling out of sight left behind an impression of fixed stares and impassive vacancy; and after it had vanished in full flight as it were, notwithstanding the long line of vehicles hugging the curb at a walk, the whole lofty vista of the avenue seemed to lie open and emptied of life in the enlarged impression of an august solitude.

Captain Whalley had lifted his head to look, and his mind, disturbed in its meditation, turned with wonder (as men's minds will do) to matters of no importance. It struck him that it was to this port, where he had just sold his last ship, that he had come with the very first he had ever owned, and with his head full of a plan for opening a new trade with a distant part of the archipelago. The then governor had given him no end of encouragement. No Excellency he—this Mr Denham—this governor with his jacket off; a man who tended night and day, so to speak, the growing prosperity of the settlement with the self-forgetful devotion of a nurse for a child she loves; a lone bachelor who lived as in a camp with the few servants and his three dogs in what was called then the Government Bungalow: a low-roofed structure on the half-cleared slope of a hill, with a new flagstaff in front and a police orderly on the veranda. He remembered toiling up that hill under a heavy sun for his audience; the unfurnished aspect of the cool shaded room; the long table covered at one end with piles of papers, and with two guns, a brass telescope, a small bottle of oil with a feather stuck in the neck at the other—and the flattering attention given to him by the man in power. It was an undertaking full of risk he had come to expound, but a twenty minutes' talk in the Government Bungalow on the hill had made it go smoothly from the start. And as he was retiring Mr Denham, already seated before the papers, called out after him, 'Next month the *Dido* starts for a cruise that way, and I shall request her captain officially to give you a look in and see how you get on.' The *Dido* was one of the smart frigates on the China station—and five-and-thirty years make a big slice of time. Five-and-thirty years ago an enterprise like his had for the colony enough importance to be looked after by a Queen's ship. A big slice of time. Individuals were of some account then. Men like himself; men, too, like poor Evans, for instance, with his red face, his coal-black whiskers, and his restless eyes, who had set up the first patent slip for repairing small ships, on the edge of the forest, in a lonely bay three miles up the coast. Mr Denham had encouraged that enterprise, too, and yet somehow poor Evans had ended by dying at home deucedly hard up. His son, they said, was squeezing oil out of coconuts for a living on some godforsaken islet of the Indian Ocean; but it was from that patent slip in a lonely wooded bay that had sprung the workshops of the Consolidated Docks Company, with its three graving basins carved out of solid rock, its wharves, its jetties, its electric-light plant, its steam powerhouses—with its gigantic sheer legs, fit to lift the heaviest weight ever carried afloat, and whose head could be seen like the top of a queer white monument peeping over bushy points of land and sandy promontories, as you approached the New Harbour from the west.

There had been a time when men counted: there were not so many carriages in the colony then, though Mr Denham, he fancies, had a buggy. And Captain Whalley seemed to be swept out of the great avenue by the swirl of a mental backwash. He remembered muddy shores, a harbour without quays, the one solitary wooden pier (but that was a public work) jutting out crookedly, the first coal sheds erected on Monkey Point, that caught fire mysteriously and smouldered for days, so that amazed ships came into a roadstead full of sulphurous fog, and the sun hung blood-red at midday. He remembered the things, the faces, and something more besides—like the faint flavour of a cup quaffed to the bottom, like a subtle sparkle of the air that was not to be found in the atmosphere of today.

In this evocation, swift and full of detail like a flash of magnesium light into the niches of a dark memorial hall, Captain Whalley contemplated things once important, the efforts of small men, the growth of a great place, but now robbed of all consequence by the greatness of accomplished facts, by hopes greater still; and they gave him for a moment such an almost physical grip upon time, such a comprehension of our unchangeable feelings, that he stopped short, struck the ground with his stick, and ejaculated mentally, 'What the devil am I doing here!' He seemed lost in a sort of surprise; but he heard his name called out in wheezy tones once, twice—and turned on his heels slowly.

He beheld then, waddling towards him autocratically, a man of an old-fashioned and gouty aspect, with hair as white as his own, but with shaved, florid cheeks, wearing a necktie—almost a neckcloth—whose stiff ends projected far beyond his chin; with round legs, round arms, a round body, a round legs, face—generally producing the effect of his short figure having been distended by means of an air pump as much as the seams of his clothing would stand. This was the Master Attendant of the port. A master attendant is a superior sort of harbour master; a person, out in the East, of some consequence in his sphere; a Government official, a magistrate for the waters of the port, and possessed of vast but ill-defined disciplinary authority over seamen of all classes. This particular Master Attendant was reported to consider it miserably inadequate, on the ground that it did not include the power of life and death. This was a jocular exaggeration. Captain Eliott was fairly satisfied with his position, and nursed no inconsiderable sense of such power as he had. His conceited and tyrannical disposition did not allow him to let it dwindle in his hands for want of use. The uproarious, choleric frankness of his comments on people's character and conduct caused him to be feared at bottom. Though in conversation many pretended not to mind him in the least, others would only smile sourly at the mention of his name, and there were even some who dared to pronounce him 'a meddlesome old ruffian'. But for almost all of them one of Captain Eliott's outbreaks was nearly as distasteful to face as a chance of annihilation.

V

AS SOON as he had come up quite close he said, mouthing in a growl—

'What's this I hear, Whalley? Is it true you're selling the *Fair Maid?*'

Captain Whalley, looking away, said the thing was done—money had been paid that morning; and the other expressed at once his approbation of such an extremely sensible proceeding. He had got out of his trap to stretch his legs, he explained, on his way home to dinner. Sir Frederick looked well at the end of his time. Didn't he?

Captain Whalley could not say; had only noticed the carriage going past.

The Master Attendant, plunging his hands into the pockets of an alpaca jacket inappropriately short and tight for a man of his age and appearance, strutted with a slight limp, and with his head reaching only to the shoulder of Captain Whalley, who walked easily, staring straight before him. They had been good comrades years ago, almost intimates. At the time when Whalley commanded the renowned *Condor*, Eliott had charge of the nearly as famous *Ringdove* for the same owners; and when the appointment of Master Attendant was created, Whalley would have been the only other serious candidate. But Captain Whalley, then in the prime of life, was resolved to serve no one but his own

auspicious Fortune. Far away, tending his hot irons, he was
glad to hear the other had been successful. There was a
worldly suppleness in bluff Ned Eliott that would serve him
well in that sort of official appointment. And they were so
dissimilar at bottom that as they came slowly to the end of the
avenue before the Cathedral, it had never come into
Whalley's head that he might have been in that man's
place—provided for to the end of his days.

The sacred edifice, standing in solemn isolation amongst
the converging avenues of enormous trees, as if to put grave
thoughts of heaven into the hours of ease, presented a closed
Gothic portal to the light and glory of the west. The glass of
the rosace above the ogive glowed like fiery coal in the deep
carvings of a wheel of stone. The two men faced about.

'I'll tell you what they ought to do next, Whalley,'
growled Captain Eliott suddenly.

'Well?'

'They ought to send a real live lord out here when Sir
Frederick's time is up. Eh?'

Captain Whalley perfunctorily did not see why a lord of
the right sort should not do as well as any one else. But this
was not the other's point of view.

'No, no. Place runs itself. Nothing can stop it now. Good
enough for a lord,' he growled in short sentences. 'Look at the
changes in our own time. We need a lord here now. They have
got a lord in Bombay.'

He dined once or twice every year at the Government
House—a many-windowed, arcaded palace upon a hill laid
out in roads and gardens. And lately he had been taking about
a duke in his Master Attendant's steam launch to visit the
harbour improvements. Before that he had 'most obligingly'
gone out in person to pick out a good berth for the ducal
yacht. Afterwards he had an invitation to lunch on board. The
duchess herself lunched with them. A big woman with a red

face. Complexion quite sunburnt. He should think ruined. Very gracious manners. They were going on to Japan. . . .

He ejaculated these details for Captain Whalley's edification, pausing to blow out his cheeks as if with a pent-up sense of importance, and repeatedly protruding his thick lips till the blunt crimson end of his nose seemed to dip into the milk of his moustache. The place ran itself; it was fit for any lord; it gave no trouble except in its Marine department—in its Marine department, he repeated twice, and after a heavy snort began to relate how the other day her Majesty's Consul-General in French Cochin-China had cabled to him—in his official capacity—asking for a qualified man to be sent over to take charge of a Glasgow ship whose master had died in Saigon.

'I sent word of it to the officers' quarters in the Sailors' Home,' he continued, while the limp in his gait seemed to grow more accentuated with the increasing irritation of his voice. 'Place's full of them. Twice as many men as there are berths going in the local trade. All hungry for an easy job. Twice as many—and—What d'you think, Whalley? . . .'

He stopped short; his hands, clenched and thrust deeply downwards, seemed ready to burst the pockets of his jacket. A slight sigh escaped Captain Whalley.

'Hey? You would think they would be falling over each other. Not a bit of it. Frightened to go home. Nice and warm out here to lie about a veranda waiting for a job. I sit and wait in my office. Nobody. What did they suppose? That I was going to sit there like a dummy with the Consul-General's cable before me? Not likely. So I looked up a list of them I keep by me and sent word for Hamilton—the worst loafer of them all—and just made him go. Threatened to instruct the steward of the Sailors' Home to have him turned out neck and crop. He did not think the berth was good enough—if you—please. "I've your little record by me," said I. "You came ashore here eighteen months ago, and you haven't done six months' work since. You are in debt for your board now at the Home, and I suppose you reckon the Marine Office will pay in the end. Eh? So it shall; but if you don't take this chance, away you go to England, assisted passage, by the first homeward steamer that comes along. You are no better than a pauper. We don't want any white paupers here." I scared him. But look at the trouble all this gave me.'

'You would not have had any trouble,' Captain Whalley said almost involuntarily, 'if you had sent for me.'

Captain Elliott was immensely amused; he shook with laughter as he walked. But suddenly he stopped laughing. A vague recollection had crossed his mind. Hadn't he heard it said at the time of the Travancore and Deccan smash that poor Whalley had been cleaned out completely. 'Fellow's hard up, by heavens!' he thought; and at once he cast a sidelong upwards glance at his companion. But Captain Whalley was smiling austerely straight before him, with a carriage of the head inconceivable in a penniless man—and he became reassured. Impossible. Could not have lost everything. That ship had been only a hobby of his. And the reflection that a man who had confessed to receiving that very morning a presumably large sum of money was not likely to spring upon him a demand for a small loan put him entirely at his ease again. Then had come a long pause in their talk, however, and not knowing how to begin again, he growled out soberly, 'We old fellows ought to take a rest now.'

'The best thing for some of us would be to die at the oar,' Captain Whalley said, negligently.

'Come, now. Aren't you a bit tired by this time of the whole show?' muttered the other, sullenly.

'Are you?'

Captain Eliott was. Infernally tired. He only hung on to his berth so long in order to get his pension on the highest scale before he went home. It would be no better than poverty, anyhow; still, it was the only thing between him and the workhouse. And he had a family. Three girls, as Whalley knew. He gave 'Harry, old boy,' to understand that these three girls were a source of the greatest anxiety and worry to him. Enough to drive a man distracted.

'Why? What have they been doing now?' asked Captain Whalley with a sort of amused absent-mindedness.

'Doing! Doing nothing. That's just it. Lawn tennis and silly novels from morning to night . . .'

If one of them at least had been a boy! But all three! And, as ill luck would have it, there did not seem to be any decent young fellows left in the world. When he looked around in the club he saw only a lot of conceited popinjays too selfish to think of making a good woman happy. Extreme indigence stared him in the face with all that crowd to keep at home. He had cherished the idea of building himself a little house in the country—in Surrey—to end his days in, but he was afraid it was out of the question . . . and his staring eyes rolled upwards with such a pathetic anxiety that Captain Whalley charitably nodded down at him, restraining a sort of sickening desire to laugh.

'You must know what it is yourself, Harry. Girls are the very devil for worry and anxiety.'

'Ay! But mine is doing well,' Captain Whalley pronounced slowly, staring to the end of the avenue.

The Master Attendant was glad to hear this. Uncommonly glad. He remembered her well. A pretty girl she was.

Captain Whalley, stepping out carelessly, assented as if in a dream:

'She was pretty.'

The procession of carriages was breaking up.

One after another they left the file to go off at a trot,

animating the vast avenue with their scattered life and movement; but soon the aspect of dignified solitude returned and took possession of the straight wide road. A syce in white stood at the head of a Burmah pony harnessed to a varnished two-wheel cart; and the whole thing waiting by the curb seemed no bigger than a child's toy forgotten under the soaring trees. Captain Eliott waddled up to it and made as if to clamber in, but refrained; and keeping one hand resting easily on the shaft, he changed the conversation from his pension, his daughters, and his poverty back again to the only other topic in the world—the Marine Office, the men and the ships of the port.

He proceeded to give instances of what was expected of him; and his thick voice drowsed in the still air like the obstinate droning of an enormous bumblebee. Captain Whalley did not know what was the force or the weakness that prevented him from saying goodnight and walking away. It was as though he had been too tired to make the effort. How queer. More queer than any of Ned's instances. Or was it that overpowering sense of idleness alone that made him stand there and listen to these stories? Nothing very real had ever troubled Ned Eliott; and gradually he seemed to detect deep in, as if wrapped up in the gross wheezy rumble, something of the clear hearty voice of the young captain of the *Ringdove*. He wondered if he, too, had changed to the same extent; and it seemed to him that the voice of his old chum had not changed so very much—that the man was the same. Not a bad fellow the pleasant, jolly Ned Eliott, friendly, well up to his business—and always a bit of a humbug. He remembered how he used to amuse his poor wife. She could read him like an open book. When the *Condor* and the *Ringdove* happened to be in port together, she would frequently ask him to bring Captain Eliott to dinner. They had not met often since those old days. Not once in five years, perhaps. He regarded from under his white eyebrows this man he could not bring himself to take into his confidence at this juncture; and the other went on with his intimate outpourings, and as remote from his hearer as though he had been talking on a hilltop a mile away.

He was in a bit of a quandary now as to the steamer *Sofala*. Ultimately every hitch in the port came into his hands to undo. They would miss him when he was gone in another eighteen months, and most likely some retired naval officer had been pitchforked into the appointment—a man that would understand nothing and care less. That steamer was a coasting craft having a steady trade connection as far north as Ten-asserim; but the trouble was she could get no captain to take her on her regular trip. Nobody would go in her. He really had no power, of course, to order a man to take a job. It was all very well to stretch a point on the demand of a consul-general, but . . .

'What's the matter with the ship?' Captain Whalley interrupted in measured tones.

'Nothing's the matter. Sound old steamer. Her owner has been in my office this afternoon tearing his hair.'

'Is he a white man?' asked Whalley in an interested voice.

'He calls himself a white man,' answered the Master Attendant scornfully; 'but if so, it's just skin-deep and no more. I told him that to his face too.'

'But who is he, then?'

'He's the chief engineer of her. See *that,* Harry?'

'I see,' Captain Whalley said, thoughtfully. 'The engineer. I see.'

How the fellow came to be a shipowner at the same time was quite a tale. He came out third in a home ship nearly fifteen years ago, Captain Eliott remembered, and got paid off after a bad sort of row both with his skipper and his chief. Anyway, they seemed jolly glad to get rid of him at all costs. Clearly a mutinous sort of chap. Well, he remained out here, a perfect nuisance, everlastingly shipped and unshipped, unable to keep a berth very long; pretty nigh went through every engine room afloat belonging to the colony. Then suddenly, 'What do you think happened, Harry?'

Captain Whalley, who seemed lost in a mental effort as of doing a sum in his head, gave a slight start. He really couldn't imagine. The Master Attendant's voice vibrated dully with hoarse emphasis. The man actually had the luck to win the second great prize in the Manilla lottery. All these engineers and officers of ships took tickets in that gamble. It seemed to be a perfect mania with them all.

Everybody expected now that he would take himself off home with his money, and go to the devil in his own way. Not at all. The *Sofala*, judged too small and not quite modern enough for the sort of trade she was in, could be got for a moderate price from her owners, who had ordered a new steamer from Europe. He rushed in and bought her. This man had never given any signs of that sort of mental intoxication the mere fact of getting hold of a large sum of money may produce—not till he got a ship of his own; but then he went off his balance all at once: came bouncing into the Marine Office on some transfer business, with his hat hanging over his left eye and switching a little cane in his hand, and told each one of the clerks separately that 'Nobody could put him out now. It was his turn. There was no one over him on earth, and there never would be either.' He swaggered and strutted between the desks, talking at the top of his voice, and trembling like a leaf all the while, so that the current business of the office was suspended for the time he was in there, and everybody in the big room stood open-mouthed looking at his antics. Afterwards he could be seen during the hottest hours of the day with his face as red as fire rushing along up and down the quays to look at his ship from different points of view: he seemed inclined to stop every stranger he came across just to let them know 'that there would be no longer any one over him; he had bought a ship; nobody on earth could put him out of his engine room now.'

Good bargain as she was, the price of the *Sofala* took up pretty near all the lottery money. He had left himself no capital to work with. That did not matter so much, for these were the halcyon days of steam coasting trade, before some of the home shipping firms had thought of establishing local fleets to feed their main lines. These, when once organized, took the biggest slices out of that cake, of course; and by and by a squad of confounded German tramps turned up east of Suez Canal and swept up all the crumbs. They prowled on the cheap to and fro along the coast and between the islands, like a lot of sharks in the water ready to snap up anything you let drop. And then the high old times were over for good; for years the *Sofala* had made no more, he judged, than a fair living. Captain Eliott looked upon it as his duty in every way to assist an English ship to hold her own; and it stood to reason that if for want of a captain the *Sofala* began to miss her trips she would very soon lose her trade. There was the quandary. The man was too impracticable. 'Too much of a beggar on horseback from the first,' he explained. 'Seemed to grow worse as the time went on. In the last three years he's run through eleven skippers; he had tried every single man here, outside of the regular lines. I had warned him before that this would not do. And now, of course, no one will look at the *Sofala*. I had one or two men up at my office and talked to them; but, as they said to me, what was the good of taking the berth to lead a regular dog's life for a month and then get the sack at the end of the first trip? The fellow, of course, told me it was all nonsense; there has been a plot hatching for years against him. And now it had come. All the horrid sailors in the port had conspired to bring him to his knees, because he was an engineer.' Captain Eliott emitted a throaty chuckle.

'And the fact is, that if he misses a couple more trips he need never trouble himself to start again. He won't find any cargo in his old trade. There's too much competition nowadays for people to keep their stuff lying about for a ship that does not turn up when she's expected. It's a bad lookout for him. He swears he will shut himself on board and starve to death in his cabin rather than sell her—even if be could find a buyer. And that's not likely in the least. Not even the Japs would give her insured value for her. It isn't like selling sailing ships. Steamers *do* get out of date, besides getting old.'

'He must have laid by a good hit of money though,' observed Captain Whalley, quietly.

The Master Attendant puffed out his purple cheeks to an amazing size.

'Not a stiver, Harry. Not—a—single stiver.' He waited; but as Captain Whalley, stroking his beard slowly, looked down on the ground without a word, he tapped him on the forearm, tiptoed, and said in a hoarse whisper—

'The Manila lottery has been eating him up.'

He frowned a little, nodding in tiny affirmative jerks. They all were going in for it; a third of the wages paid to ships' officers ('in my port,' he snorted) went to Manila. It was a mania. That fellow Massy had been bitten by it like the rest of them from the first; but after winning once he seemed to have persuaded himself he had only to try again to get another big prize. He had taken dozens and scores of tickets for every drawing since. What with this vice and his ignorance of affairs, ever since he had improvidently bought that steamer he had been more or less short of money.

This, in Captain Eliott's opinion, gave an opening for a sensible sailor-man with a few pounds to step in and save that fool from the consequences of his folly. It was his craze to quarrel with his captains. He had had some really good men, too, who would have been too glad to stay if he would only let them. But no. He seemed to think he was no owner unless he was kicking somebody out in the morning and having a row with the new man in the evening. What was wanted for him was a master with a couple of hundred or so to take an interest in the ship on proper conditions. You don't discharge a man for no fault, only because of the fun of telling him to pack up his traps and go ashore, when you know that in that case you are bound to buy back his share. On the other hand, a fellow with an interest in the ship is not likely to throw up his job in a huff about a trifle. He had told Massy that. He had said: 'This won't do, Mr Massy. We are getting very sick of you here in the Marine Office. What you must do now is to try whether you could get a sailor to join you as partner. That seems to be the only way. And that was sound advice, Harry.'

Captain Whalley, leaning on his stick, was perfectly still all over, and his hand, arrested in the act of stroking, grasped his whole beard. And what did the fellow say to that?

The fellow had the audacity to fly out at the Master Attendant. He had received the advice in a most impudent manner. 'I didn't come here to be laughed at,' he had shrieked. 'I appeal to you as an Englishman and a shipowner brought to the verge of ruin by an illegal conspiracy of your beggarly sailors, and all you condescend to do for me is to tell me to go and get a partner!' ... The fellow had presumed to stamp with rage on the floor of the private office. Where was he going to get a partner? Was he being taken for a fool? Not a single one of that contemptible lot ashore at the 'Home' had twopence in his pocket to bless himself with. The very native curs in the bazaar knew that much ... 'And it's true enough, Harry,' rumbled Captain Eliott, judicially. 'They are much more likely one and all to owe money to the Chinamen in Denham Road for the clothes on their backs. "Well," said I, "you make too much noise over it for my taste, Mr Massy. Good morning." He banged the door after him; he dared to bang my door, confound his cheek!'

The head of the Marine department was out of breath with indignation; then recollecting himself as it were, 'I'll end by being late to dinner—yarning with you here . . . wife doesn't like it.'

He clambered ponderously into the trap; leaned out sideways, and only then wondered wheezily what on earth Captain Whalley could have been doing with himself of late. They had had no sight of each other for years and years till the other day when he had seen him unexpectedly in the office. What on earth . . .

Captain Whalley seemed to be smiling to himself in his white beard.

'The earth is big,' he said, vaguely.

The other, as if to test the statement, stared all round from his driving seat. The Esplanade was very quiet; only from afar, from very far, a long way from the seashore, across the stretches of grass, through the long ranges of trees, came faintly the toot-toot-toot of the cable car beginning to roll before the empty peristyle of the Public Library on its three-mile journey to the New Harbour Docks.

'Doesn't seem to be so much room on it,' growled the Master Attendant, 'since these Germans came along shouldering us at every turn. It was not so in our time.'

He fell into deep thought, breathing stertorously, as though he had been taking a nap open-eyed. Perhaps he, too, on his side, had detected in the silent pilgrim-like figure, standing there by the wheel, like an arrested wayfarer, the buried lineaments of the features belonging to the young captain of the *Condor*. Good fellow—Harry Whalley—never very talkative. You never knew what he was up to—a bit too off-hand with people of consequence, and apt to take a wrong view of a fellow's actions. Fact was he had a too good opinion of himself. He would have liked to tell him to get in and drive him home to dinner. But one never knew. Wife would not like it.

'And it's funny to think, Harry,' he went on in a big subdued drone, 'that of all the people on it there seems only you and I left to remember this part of the world as it used to be . . .'

He was ready to indulge in the sweetness of a sentimental mood had it not struck him suddenly that Captain Whalley, unstirring and without a word, seemed to be awaiting something—perhaps expecting . . . He gathered the reins at once and burst out in bluff hearty growls—

'Ha! My dear boy. The men we have known—the ships we've sailed—ay! and the things we've done . . .'

The pony plunged—the syce skipped out of the way. Captain Whalley raised his arm.

'Goodbye.'

VI

THE sun had set. And when, after drilling a deep hole with his stick, he moved from that spot the night had massed its army of shadows under the trees. They filled the eastern ends of the avenue as if only waiting the signal for a general advance upon the open spaces of the world; they were gathering low between the deep stone-faced banks of the canal. The Malay prau, half concealed under the arch of the bridge, had not altered its position a quarter of an inch. For a long time Captain Whalley stared down over the parapet, till at last the floating immobility of that beshrouded thing seemed to grow upon him into something inexplicable and alarming. The twilight abandoned the zenith; its reflected gleams left the world below, and the water of the canal seemed to turn into pitch. Captain Whalley crossed it.

The turning to the right, which was his way to his hotel,

was only a very few steps farther. He stopped again (all the houses of the seafront were shut up, the quayside was deserted, but for one or two figures of natives walking in the distance) and began to reckon the amount of his bill. So many days in the hotel at so many dollars a day. To count the days he used his fingers: plunging one hand into his pocket, he jingled a few silver coins. All right for three days more; and then, unless something turned up, he must break into the five hundred—Ivy's money—invested in her father. It seemed to him that the first meal coming out of that reserve would choke him—for certain. Reason was of no use. It was a matter of feeling. His feelings had never played him false.

He did not turn to the right. He walked on, as if there still had been a ship in the roadstead to which he could get himself pulled off in the evening. Far away, beyond the houses, on the slope of an indigo promontory closing the view of the quays, the slim column of a factory chimney smoked quietly straight up into the clear air. A Chinaman, curled down in the stern of one of the half-dozen sampans floating off the end of the jetty, caught sight of a beckoning hand. He jumped up, rolled his pigtail round his head swiftly, tucked in two rapid movements his wide dark trousers high up his yellow thighs, and by a single, noiseless, finlike stir of the oars, sheered the sampan alongside the steps with the ease and precision of a swimming fish.

'Sofala,' articulated Captain Whalley from above; and the Chinaman, a new emigrant probably, stared upwards with a tense attention as if waiting to see the queer word fall visibly from the white man's lips. 'Sofala,' Captain Whalley repeated; and suddenly his heart failed him. He paused. The shores, the islets, the high ground, the low points, were dark: the horizon had grown sombre; and across the eastern sweep of the shore the white obelisk, marking the landing place of the telegraph cable, stood like a pale ghost on the beach before the dark spread of uneven roofs, intermingled with palms, of the native town. Captain Whalley began again:

'*Sofala*. Savee *So-fa-la*, John?'

This time the Chinaman made out that bizarre sound, and grunted his assent uncouthly, low down in his bare throat. With the first yellow twinkle of a star that appeared like the head of a pin stabbed deep into the smooth, pale, shimmering fabric of the sky, the edge of a keen chill seemed to cleave through the warm air of the earth. At the moment of stepping into the sampan to go and try for the command of the *Sofala*, Captain Whalley shivered a little.

When on his return he landed on the quay again, Venus, like a choice jewel set low on the hem of the sky, cast a faint gold trail behind him upon the roadstead, as level as a floor made of one dark and polished stone. The lofty vaults of the avenues were black—all black overhead—and the porcelain globes on the lamp posts resembled egg-shaped pearls, gigantic and luminous, displayed in a row whose farther end seemed to sink in the distance, down to the level of his knees. He put his hands behind his back. He would now consider calmly the discretion of it before saying the final word tomorrow. His feet scrunched the gravel loudly—the discretion of it. It would have been easier to appraise had there been a workable alternative. The honesty of it was indubitable: he meant well by the fellow; and periodically his shadow leaped up intense by his side on the trunks of the trees, to lengthen itself, oblique and dim, far over the grass—repeating his stride.

The discretion of it. Was there a choice? He seemed already to have lost something of himself; to have given up to a hungry spectre something of his truth and dignity in order to live. But his life was necessary. Let poverty do its worst in exacting its toll of humiliation. It was certain that Ned Eliott had rendered him, without knowing it, a service for which it would have been impossible to ask. He hoped Ned would not think there had been something underhand in his action. He supposed that now when he heard of it he would understand—or perhaps he would only think Whalley an eccentric old fool. What would have been the good of telling him—any more than of blurting the whole tale to that man Massy? Five hundred pounds ready to invest. Let him make the best of that. Let him wonder. You want a captain—I want a ship. That's enough. B-r-r-r. What a disagreeable impression that empty, dark, echoing steamer had made upon him . . .

A laid-up steamer was a dead thing and no mistake; a sailing ship somehow seems always ready to spring into life with the breath of the incorruptible heaven; but a steamer, thought Captain Whalley, with her fires out, without the warm whiffs from below meeting you on her decks, without the hiss of steam, the clangs of iron in her breast—lies there as cold and still and pulseless as a corpse.

In the solitude of the avenue, all black above and lighted below, Captain Whalley, considering the discretion of his course, met, as it were incidentally, the thought of death. He pushed it aside with dislike and contempt. He almost laughed at it; and in the unquenchable vitality of his age only thought with a kind of exultation how little he needed to keep body and soul together. Not a bad investment for the poor woman, this solid carcass of her father. And for the rest—in case of anything—the agreement should be clear: the whole five hundred to be paid back to her integrally within three months. Integrally. Every penny. He was not to lose any of her money whatever else had to go—a little dignity—some of his self-respect. He had never before allowed anybody to remain under any sort of false impression as to himself. Well, let that go—for her sake. After all, he had never said anything misleading—and Captain Whalley felt himself corrupt to the marrow of his bones. He laughed a little with the intimate scorn of his worldly prudence. Clearly, with a fellow of that sort, and in the peculiar relation they were to stand to each other, it would not have done to blurt out everything. He did not like the fellow. He did not like his spells of fawning loquacity and bursts of resentfulness. In the end—a poor devil. He would not have liked to stand in his shoes. Men were not evil, after all. He did not like his sleek hair, his queer way of standing at right angles, with his nose in the air, and glancing along his shoulder at you. No. On the whole, men were not bad—they were only silly or unhappy.

Captain Whalley had finished considering the discretion of that step—and there was the whole long night before him. In the full light his long beard would glisten like a silver breastplate covering his heart; in the spaces between the lamps his burly figure passed less distinct, loomed very big, wandering, and mysterious. No; there was not much real harm in men: and all the time a shadow marched with him, slanting on his left hand—which in the East is a presage of evil.

*

'Can you make out the clump of palms yet, Serang?' asked Captain Whalley from his chair on the bridge of the *Sofala* approaching the bar of Batu Berau.

"No, Tuan. By and by see." The old Malay, in a blue dungaree suit, planted on his bony dark feet under the bridge awning, put his hands behind his back and stared ahead out of the innumerable wrinkles at the corners of his eyes.

Captain Whalley sat still, without lifting his head to look for himself. Three years—thirty-six times. He had made these palms thirty-six times from the southward. They would come into view at the proper time. Thank God, the old ship made her courses and distances trip after trip, as correct as clockwork. At last he murmured again—

'In sight yet?'

'The sun makes a very great glare, Tuan.'

'Watch well, Serang.'

'Ya, Tuan.'

A white man had ascended the ladder from the deck noiselessly, and had listened quietly to this short colloquy. Then he stepped out on the bridge and began to walk from end to end, holding up the long cherry wood stem of a pipe. His black hair lay plastered in long lanky wisps across the bald summit of his head; he had a furrowed brow, a yellow complexion, and a thick shapeless nose. A scanty growth of whisker did not conceal the contour of his jaw. His aspect was of brooding care; and sucking at a curved black mouthpiece, he presented such a heavy overhanging profile that even the Serang could not help reflecting sometimes upon the extreme unloveliness of some white men.

Captain Whalley seemed to brace himself up in his chair, but gave no recognition whatever to his presence. The other puffed jets of smoke; then suddenly—

'I could never understand that new mania of yours of having this Malay here for your shadow, partner.'

Captain Whalley got up from the chair in all his imposing stature and walked across to the binnacle; holding such an unswerving course that the other had to back away hurriedly, and remained as if intimidated, with the pipe trembling in his hand. 'Walk over me now,' he muttered in a sort of astounded and discomfited whisper. Then slowly and distinctly he said—

'I-am-not-dirt.' And then added defiantly, 'As you seem to think.'

The Serang jerked out—

'See the palms now, Tuan.'

Captain Whalley strode forward to the rail; but his eyes,

instead of going straight to the point, with the assured keen glance of a sailor, wandered irresolutely in space, as though he, the discoverer of new routes, had lost his way upon this narrow sea.

Another white man, the mate, came up on the bridge. He was tall, young, lean, with a moustache like a trooper, and something malicious in the eye. He took up a position beside the engineer. Captain Whalley with his back to them, inquired—

'What's on the log?'

'Eighty-five,' answered the mate quickly, and nudged the engineer with his elbow.

Captain Whalley's muscular hands squeezed the iron rail with an extraordinary force; his eyes glared with an enormous effort; he knitted his eyebrows, the perspiration fell from under his hat—and in a faint voice he murmured, 'Steady her, Serang—when she is on the proper bearing.'

The silent Malay stepped back, waited a little, and lifted his arm warningly to the helmsman. The wheel revolved rapidly to meet the swing of the ship. Again the mate nudged the engineer. But Massy turned upon him.

'Mr Sterne,' he said, violently, 'let me tell you—as a shipowner—that you are no better than a confounded fool.'

VII

STERNE went down smirking and apparently not at all disconcerted, but the engineer Massy remained on the bridge, moving about with uneasy self-assertion. Everybody on board was his inferior—everyone without exception. He paid their wages and found them in their food. They ate more of his bread and pocketed more of his money than they were worth; and they had no care in the world, while he alone had to meet all the difficulties of shipowning. When he contemplated his position in all its menacing entirety, it seemed to him that he had been for years the prey of a band of parasites; and for years he had scowled at everybody connected with the *Sofala* except, perhaps, at the Chinese firemen who served to get her along. Their use was manifest: they were an indispensable part of the machinery of which he was the master.

When he passed along his decks he shouldered those he came across brutally; but the Malay deckhands had learned to dodge out of his way. He had to bring himself to tolerate them because of the necessary manual labour of the ship which must be done. He had to struggle and plan and scheme to keep the *Sofala* afloat—and what did he get for it? Not even enough respect. They could not have given him enough of that if all their thoughts and all their actions had been directed to that end. The vanity of possession, the vainglory of power, had passed away by this time, and there remained only the material embarrassments, the fear of losing that position which had turned out not worth having, and an anxiety of thought which no abject subservience of men could repay.

He walked up and down. The bridge was his own after all. He had paid for it; and with the stem of the pipe in his hand he would stop short at times as if to listen with a profound and concentrated attention to the deadened beat of the engines (his own engines) and the slight grinding of the steering chains upon the continuous low wash of water alongside. But for these sounds, the ship might have been lying as still as if moored to a bank, and as silent as if abandoned by every living soul; only the coast, the low coast of mud and mangroves with the three palms in a bunch at the back, grew slowly more distinct in its long straight line; without a single feature to arrest attention. The native passengers of the *Sofala* lay about on mats under the awnings; the smoke of her funnel seemed the only sign of her life and connected with her gliding motion in a mysterious manner.

Captain Whalley on his feet, with a pair of binoculars in his hand and the little Malay Serang at his elbow, like an old giant attended by a wizened pigmy, was taking her over the shallow water of the bar.

This submarine ridge of mud, scoured by the stream out of the soft bottom of the river and heaped up far out on the hard bottom of the sea, was difficult to get over. The alluvial coast having no distinguishing marks, the bearings of the crossing place had to be taken from the shape of the mountains inland. The guidance of a form flattened and uneven at the top like a grinder tooth, and of another smooth, saddle-backed summit, had to be searched for within the great unclouded glare that seemed to shift and float like a dry fiery mist, filling the air, ascending from the water, shrouding the distances, scorching to the eye. In this veil of light the near edge of the shore alone stood out almost coal-black with an opaque and motionless solidity. Thirty miles away the serrated range of the interior stretched across the horizon, its outlines and shades of blue, faint and tremulous like a background painted on airy gossamer on the quivering fabric of an impalpable curtain let down to the plain of alluvial soil; and the openings of the estuary appeared, shining white, like bits of silver let into the square pieces snipped clean and sharp out of the body of the land bordered with mangroves.

On the forepart of the bridge the giant and the pigmy muttered to each other frequently in quiet tones. Behind them Massy stood sideways with an expression of disdain and suspense on his face. His globular eyes were perfectly motionless, and he seemed to have forgotten the long pipe he held in his hand.

On the foredeck below the bridge, steeply roofed with the white slopes of the awnings, a young lascar seaman had clambered outside the rail. He adjusted quickly a broad band of sail canvas under his armpits, and throwing his chest against it, leaned out far over the water. The sleeve of his thin cotton shirt, cut off close to the shoulder, bared his brown arm of full rounded form and with a satiny skin like a woman's. He swung it rigidly with the rotary and menacing action of a slinger: the fourteen-pound weight hurtled circling in the air, then suddenly flew ahead as far as the curve of the bow. The wet thin line swished like scratched silk running through the dark fingers of the man, and the plunge of the lead close to the ship's side made a vanishing silvery scar upon the golden glitter; then after an interval the voice of the young Malay uplifted and long-drawn declared the depth of the water in his own language.

'Tiga stengah,' he cried after each splash and pause, gathering the line busily for another cast. 'Tiga stengah,' which means three fathom and a half. For a mile or so from seaward there was a uniform depth of water right up to the bar. 'Half-three. Half-three. Half-three,'—and his modulated cry, returned leisurely and monotonous, like the repeated call of a bird, seemed to float away in sunshine and disappear in the spacious silence of the empty sea and of a lifeless shore lying open, north and south, east and west, without the stir of a single cloud shadow or the whisper of any other voice.

The owner-engineer of the *Sofala* remained very still behind the two seamen of different race, creed and colour; the European with the time-defying vigour of his old frame, the little Malay, old, too, but slight and shrunken like a withered brown leaf blown by a chance wind under the mighty shadow of the other. Very busy looking forward at the land, they had not a glance to spare; and Massy, glaring at them from behind, seemed to resent their attention to their duty like a personal slight upon himself.

This was unreasonable; but he had lived in his own world of unreasonable resentments for many years. At last, passing his moist palm over the rare lanky wisps of coarse hair on the top of his yellow head, he began to talk slowly.

'A leadsman, you want! I suppose that's your correct mailboat style. Haven't you enough judgment to tell where you are by looking at the land? Why, before I had been a twelvemonth in the trade I was up to that trick—and I am only an engineer. I can point to you from here where the bar is, and I could tell you besides that you are likely as not to stick her in the mud in about five minutes from now; only you would call it interfering, I suppose. And there's that written agreement of ours, that says I mustn't interfere.'

His voice stopped. Captain Whalley, without relaxing the set severity of his features, moved his lips to ask in a quick mumble—

'How near, Serang?'

'Very near now, Tuan,' the Malay muttered, rapidly.

'Dead slow,' said the Captain aloud in a firm tone.

The Serang snatched at the handle of the telegraph.

A gong clanged down below. Massy with a scornful snigger walked off and put his head down the engine room skylight.

'You may expect some rare fooling with the engines, Jack,' he bellowed. The space into which he stared was deep and full of gloom; and the grey gleams of steel down there seemed cool after the intense glare of the sea around the ship. The air, however, came up clammy and hot on his face. A short hoot on which it would have been impossible to put any sort of interpretation came from the bottom cavernously. This was the way in which the second engineer answered his chief.

He was a middle-aged man with an inattentive manner, and apparently wrapped up in such a taciturn concern for his engines that he seemed to have lost the use of speech. When addressed directly his only answer would be a grunt or a hoot, according to the distance. For all the years he had been in the

Sofala he had never been known to exchange as much as a frank good morning with any of his shipmates. He did not seem aware that men came and went in the world; he did not seem to see them at all. Indeed he never recognized his shipmates on shore. At table (the four white men of the *Sofala* messed together) he sat looking into his plate dispassionately, but at the end of the meal would jump up and bolt down below as if a sudden thought had impelled him to rush and see whether somebody had not stolen the engines while he dined. In port at the end of the trip he went ashore regularly, but no one knew where he spent his evenings or in what manner. The local coasting fleet had preserved a wild and incoherent tale of his infatuation for the wife of a sergeant in an Irish infantry regiment. The regiment, however, had done its turn of garrison duty there ages before, and was gone somewhere to the other side of the earth, out of men's knowledge. Twice or perhaps three times in the course of the year he would take too much to drink. On these occasions he returned on board at an earlier hour than usual; ran across the deck balancing himself with his spread arms like a tightrope walker; and locking the door of his cabin, he would converse and argue with himself the livelong night in an amazing variety of tones; storm, sneer and whine with an inexhaustible persistence. Massy in his berth next door, raising himself on his elbow, would discover that his second had remembered the name of every white man that had passed through the *Sofala* for years and years back. He remembered the names of men that had died, that had gone home, that had gone to America: he remembered in his cups the names of men whose connection with the ship had been so short that Massy had almost forgotten its circumstances and could barely recall their faces. The inebriated voice on the other side of the bulkhead commented upon them all with an extraordinary and ingenious venom of scandalous inventions. It seems they had all offended him in

159

some way, and in return he had found them all out. He muttered darkly; he laughed sardonically; he crushed them one after another; but of his chief, Massy, he babbled with an envious and naive admiration. Clever scoundrel! Don't meet the likes of him everyday. Just look at him. Ha! Great! Ship of his own. Wouldn't catch *him* going wrong. No fear—the beast! And Massy, after listening with a gratified smile to these artless tributes to his greatness, would begin to shout, thumping at the bulkhead with both fists

'Shut up, you lunatic! Won't you let me go to sleep, you fool!'

But a half smile of pride lingered on his lips; outside the solitary lascar told off for night duty in harbour, perhaps a youth fresh from a forest village, would stand motionless in the shadows of the deck listening to the endless drunken gabble. His heart would be thumping with breathless awe of white men: the arbitrary and obstinate men who pursue inflexibly their incomprehensible purposes—beings with weird intonations in the voice, moved by unaccountable feelings, actuated by inscrutable motives.

VIII

FOR a while after his second's answering hoot Massy hung over the engine room gloomily. Captain Whalley, who, by the power of five hundred pounds, had kept his command for three years, might have been suspected of never having seen that coast before. He seemed unable to put down his glasses, as though they had been glued under his contracted eyebrows. This settled frown gave to his face an air of invincible and just severity; but his raised elbow trembled slightly, and the perspiration poured from under his hat as if a second sun had suddenly blazed up at the zenith by the side of the ardent still globe already there, in whose blinding white heat the earth whirled and shone like a mote of dust.

From time to time, still holding up his glasses, he raised his other hand to wipe his streaming face. The drops rolled down his cheeks, fell like rain upon the white hairs of his beard, and brusquely, as if guided by an uncontrollable and anxious impulse, his arm reached out to the stand of the engine-room telegraph.

The gong clanged down below. The balanced vibration of the dead-slow speed ceased together with every sound and tremor in the ship, as if the great stillness that reigned upon the coast had stolen in through her sides of iron and taken possession of her innermost recesses. The illusion of perfect immobility seemed to fall upon her from the luminous blue dome without a stain arching over a flat sea without a stir. The faint breeze she had made for herself expired, as if all at once the air had become too thick to budge; even the slight hiss of the water on her stem died out. The narrow, long hull, carrying its way without a ripple, seemed to approach the shoal water of the bar by stealth. The plunge of the lead with the mournful, mechanical cry of the lascar came at longer and longer intervals; and the men on her bridge seemed to hold their breath. The Malay at the helm looked fixedly at the compass card, the Captain and the Serang stared at the coast.

Massy had left the skylight, and, walking flat-footed, had returned softly to the very spot on the bridge he had occupied before. A slow, lingering grin exposed his set of big white teeth: they gleamed evenly in the shade of the awning like the keyboard of a piano in a dusky room.

At last, pretending to talk to himself in excessive astonishment, he said not very loud—

'Stop the engines now. What next, I wonder?' He waited, stooping from the shoulders; his head bowed, his glance oblique. Then raising his voice a shade—

'If I dared make an absurd remark I would say that you

haven't the stomach to.'

But a yelling spirit of excitement, like some frantic soul wandering unsuspected in the vast stillness of the coast, had seized upon the body of the lascar at the lead. The languid monotony of his singsong changed to a swift, sharp clamour. The weight flew after a single whirr, the line whistled, splash followed splash in haste. The water had shoaled, and the man, instead of the drowsy tale of fathoms, was calling out the soundings in feet.

'Fifteen feet. Fifteen, fifteen! Fourteen, fourteen . . .'

Captain Whalley lowered the arm holding the glasses. It descended slowly as if by its own weight; no other part of his towering body stirred; and the swift cries with their eager warning note passed him by as though he had been deaf.

Massy, very still, and turning an attentive ear, had fastened his eyes upon the silvery, close-cropped back of the steady old head. The ship herself seemed to be arrested but for the gradual decrease of depth under her keel.

'Thirteen feet . . . Thirteen! Twelve!' cried the leadsman anxiously below the bridge. And suddenly the barefooted Serang stepped away noiselessly to steal a glance over the side.

Narrow of shoulder, in a suit of faded blue cotton; an old gray felt hat rammed down on his head; with a hollow in the nape of his dark neck, and with his slender limbs, he appeared from the back no bigger than a boy of fourteen. There was a childlike impulsiveness in the curiosity with which he watched the spread of the voluminous, yellowish convolutions rolling up from below to the surface of the blue water like massive clouds driving slowly upwards on the unfathomable sky. He was not startled at the sight in the least. It was not doubt, but the certitude that the keel of the *Sofala* must be stirring the mud now, which made him peep over the side.

His peering eyes, set aslant in a face of the Chinese type, a little old face, immovable, as if carved in old brown oak, had informed him long before that the ship was not headed at the bar properly. Paid off from the *Fair Maid*, together with the rest of the crew, after the completion of the sale, he had hung, in his faded blue suit and floppy gray hat, about the doors of the Harbour Office, till one day, seeing Captain Whalley coming along to get a crew for the *Sofala*, he had put himself quietly in the way, with his bare feet in the dust and an upward mute glance. The eyes of his old commander had fallen on him favourably—it must have been an auspicious day—and in less than half an hour the white men in the 'Ofiss' had written his name on a document as Serang of the fireship *Sofala*. Since that time he had repeatedly looked at that estuary, upon that coast, from this bridge and from this side of the bar. The record of the visual world fell through his eyes upon his unspeculating mind as on a sensitized plate through the lens of a camera. His knowledge was absolute and precise; nevertheless, had he been asked his opinion, and especially if questioned in the downright, alarming manner of white men, he would have displayed the hesitation of ignorance. He was certain of his facts—but such a certitude counted for little against the doubt what answer would be pleasing. Fifty years ago, in a jungle village, and before he was a day old, his father (who died without ever seeing a white face) had had his nativity cast by a man of skill and wisdom in astrology, because in the arrangement of the stars may be read the last word of human destiny. His destiny had been to thrive by the favour of various white men on the sea. He had swept the decks of ships, had tended their helms, had minded their stores, had risen at last to be a Serang; and his placid mind had remained as incapable of penetrating the simplest motives of those he served as they themselves were incapable of detecting through the crust of the earth the secret nature of its heart, which may be fire or may be stone. But he had no doubt whatever that the *Sofala* was out of the proper track for crossing the bar at Batu Berau.

It was a slight error. The ship could not have been more than twice her own length too far to the northward; and a white man at a loss for a cause (since it was impossible to suspect Captain Whalley of blundering ignorance, of want of skill, or of neglect) would have been inclined to doubt the testimony of his senses. It was some such feeling that kept Massy motionless, with his teeth laid bare by an anxious grin. Not so the Serang. He was not troubled by any intellectual mistrust of his senses. If his captain chose to stir the mud it was well. He had known in his life white men indulge in outbreaks equally strange. He was only genuinely interested to see what would come of it. At last, apparently satisfied, he stepped back from the rail.

He had made no sound: Captain Whalley, however, seemed to have observed the movements of his Serang, Holding his head rigidly, he asked with a mere stir of his lips—

'Going ahead still, Serang?'

'Still going a little, Tuan,' answered the Malay. Then added casually, 'She is over.'

The lead confirmed his words; the depth of water increased at every cast, and the soul of excitement departed suddenly from the lascar swung in the canvas belt over the *Sofala*'s side. Captain Whalley ordered the lead in, set the engines ahead without haste, and averting his eyes from the coast, directed the Serang to keep a course for the middle of the entrance.

Massy brought the palm of his hand with a loud smack against his thigh.

'You grazed on the bar. Just look astern and see if you didn't. Look at the track she left. You can see it plainly. Upon my soul, I thought you would! What made you do that? What on earth made you do that? I believe you are trying to scare me.'

He talked slowly, as it were circumspectly, keeping his prominent black eyes on his captain. There was also a slight plaintive note in his rising choler, for, primarily, it was the clear sense of a wrong suffered undeservedly that made him hate the man who, for a beggarly five hundred pounds, claimed a sixth part of the profits under the three years' agreement. Whenever his resentment got the better of the awe the person of Captain Whalley inspired, he would positively whimper with fury.

'You don't know what to invent to plague my life out of me. I would not have thought that a man of your sort would condescend.'

He paused, half hopefully, half timidly, whenever Captain Whalley made the slightest movement in the deckchair, as though expecting to be conciliated by a soft speech or else rushed upon and hunted off the bridge.

'I am puzzled,' he went on again, with the watchful, unsmiling baring of his big teeth. 'I don't know what to think. I do believe you are trying to frighten me. You very nearly planted her on the bar for at least twelve hours, besides getting the engines choked with mud. Ships can't afford to lose twelve hours on a trip nowadays—as you ought to know very well, and do know very well to be sure, only . . .'

His slow volubility, the sideways cranings of his neck, the black glances out of the very corners of his eyes, left Captain Whalley unmoved. He looked at the deck with a severe frown. Massy waited for some little time, then began to threaten plaintively.

'You think you've got me bound hand and foot in that agreement. You think you can torment me in any way you please. Ah! But remember it has another six weeks to run yet. There's time for me to dismiss you before the three years are out. You will do yet something that will give me the chance to dismiss you, and make you wait a twelvemonth for your money before you can take yourself off and pull out your five hundred, and leave me without a.penny to get the new boilers for her. You gloat over that idea—don't you? I do believe you sit here gloating. It's as if I had sold my soul for five hundred pounds to be everlastingly damned in the end . . .'

He paused, without apparent exasperation, then continued evenly

'. . . With the boilers worn out and the survey hanging over my head, Captain Whalley—Captain Whalley, I say, what do you do with your money? You must have stacks of money somewhere—a man like you must. It stands to reason. I am not a fool, you know, Captain Whalley—partner.'

Again he paused, as though he had done for good. He passed his tongue over his lips; gave a backward glance at the Serang conning the ship with quiet whispers and slight signs of the hand. The wash of the propeller sent a swift ripple, crested with dark froth, upon a long flat spit of black slime. The *Sofala* had entered the river; the trail she had stirred up over the bar was a mile astern of her now, out of sight, had disappeared utterly; and the smooth, empty sea along the coast was left behind in the glittering desolation of sunshine. On each side of her, low down, the growth of sombre twisted mangroves covered the semi-liquid banks; and Massy continued in his old tone, with an abrupt start, as if his speech had been ground out of him, like the tune of a music box, by turning a handle.

'Though if anybody ever got the best of me, it is you. I don't mind saying this. I've said it—there! What more can you want? Isn't that enough for your pride, Captain Whalley? You got over me from the first. It's all of a piece, when I look back at it. You allowed me to insert that clause about intemperance without saying anything, only looking very sick when I made a point of it going in black on white. How could I tell what was wrong about you? There's generally something wrong somewhere. And, lo and behold! when you come on board it turns out that you've been in the habit of drinking nothing but water for years and years.'

His dogmatic, reproachful whine stopped. He brooded profoundly, after the manner of crafty and unintelligent men. It seemed inconceivable that Captain Whalley should not laugh at the expression of disgust that overspread the heavy, yellow countenance. But Captain Whalley never raised his eyes—sitting in his armchair, outraged, dignified, and motionless.

'Much good it was to me,' Massy remonstrated, monotonously, 'to insert a clause of dismissal for intemperance against a man who drinks nothing but water. And you looked so upset, too, when I read my draft in the lawyer's office that morning, Captain Whalley—you looked so crestfallen, that I made sure I had gone home on your weak spot. A shipowner can't be too careful as to the sort of skipper he gets. You must have been laughing at me in your sleeve all the blessed time . . . Eh? What are you going to say?'

Captain Whalley had only shuffled his feet slightly. A dull animosity became apparent in Massy's sideways stare.

'But recollect that there are other grounds of dismissal. There's habitual carelessness, amounting to incompetence—there's gross and persistent neglect of duty. I am not quite as big a fool as you try to make me out to be. You have been careless of late—leaving everything to that Serang. Why! I've seen you letting that old fool of a Malay take bearings for you, as if you were too big to attend to your work yourself. And what do you call that silly touch-and-go manner in which you took the ship over the bar just now? You expect me to put up with that.'

Leaning on his elbow against the ladder abaft the bridge,

Sterne, the mate, tried to hear, blinking the while from the distance at the second engineer, who had come up for a moment, and stood in the engine room companion. Wiping his hands on a bunch of cotton waste, he looked about with indifference to the right and left at the river banks slipping astern of the *Sofala* steadily.

Massy turned full at the chair. The character of his whine became again threatening.

'Take care. I may yet dismiss you and freeze to your money for a year. I may. . .'

But before the silent, rigid immobility of the man whose money had come in the nick of time to save him from utter ruin, his voice died out in his throat.

'Not that I want you to go,' he resumed after a silence, and in an absurdly insinuating tone. 'I want nothing better than to be friends and renew the agreement, if you will consent to find another couple of hundred to help with the new boilers, Captain Whalley. I've told you before. She must have new boilers; you know it as well as I do. Have you thought this over?'

He waited. The slender stem of the pipe with its bulky lump of a bowl at the end hung down from his thick lips. It had gone out. Suddenly he took it from between his teeth and wrung his hands slightly.

'Don't you believe me?' He thrust the pipe bowl into the pocket of his shiny black jacket.

'It's like dealing with the devil,' he said. 'Why don't you speak? At first you were so high and mighty with me I hardly dared to creep about my own deck. Now I can't get a word from you. You don't seem to see me at all. What does it mean? Upon my soul, you terrify me with this deaf and dumb trick. What's going on in that head of yours? What are you plotting against me there so hard that you can't say a word? You will never make me believe that you—you—don't know where to lay your hands on a couple of hundred. You have made me curse the day I was born . . .'

'Mr Massy,' said Captain Whalley, suddenly, without stirring.

The engineer started violently.

'If that is so I can only beg you to forgive me.'

'Starboard,' muttered the Serang to the helmsman; and the *Sofala* began to swing round the bend into the second reach.

'Ough!' Massy shuddered. 'You make my blood run cold. What made you come here? What made you come aboard that evening all of a sudden, with your high talk and your money—tempting me? I always wondered what was your motive? You fastened yourself on me to have easy times and grow fat on my life blood, I tell you. Was that it? I believe you are the greatest miser in the world, or else why . . .'

'No. I am only poor,' interrupted Captain Whalley, stonily.

'Steady,' murmured the Serang. Massy turned away with his chin on his shoulder.

'I don't believe it,' he said in his dogmatic tone. Captain Whalley made no movement. 'There you sit like a gorged vulture—exactly like a vulture.'

He embraced the middle of the reach and both the banks in one blank, unseeing, circular glance, and left the bridge slowly.

IX

ON TURNING to descend Massy perceived the head of Sterne the mate loitering, with his sly, confident smile, his red moustaches and blinking eyes, at the foot of the ladder.

Sterne had been a junior in one of the larger shipping concerns before joining the *Sofala*. He had thrown up his berth, he said, 'on general principles'. The promotion in the employ was very slow, he complained, and he thought it was time for him to try and get on a bit in the world. It seemed as though nobody would ever die or leave the firm; they all stuck fast in their berths till they got mildewed; he was tired of waiting; and he feared that when a vacancy did occur the best servants were by no means sure of being treated fairly. Besides, the captain he had to serve under—Captain Provost—was an unaccountable sort of man and had taken a dislike to him for some reason or other. For doing rather more than his bare duty as likely as not. When he had done anything wrong he could take a talking to, like a man; but he expected to be treated like a man, too, and not to be addressed invariably as though he were a dog. He had asked Captain Provost plump and plain to tell him where he was at fault, and Captain Provost, in a most scornful way, had told him that he was a perfect officer, and that if he disliked the way he was being spoken to there was the gangway—he could take himself off ashore at once. But everybody knew what sort of man Captain Provost was. It was no use appealing to the office. Captain Provost had too much influence in the employ. All the same, they had to give him a good character. He made bold to say there was nothing in the world against him, and, as he had happened to hear that the mate of the *Sofala* had been taken to the hospital that morning with a sunstroke, he thought there would be no harm in seeing whether he would not do . . .

He had come to Captain Whalley freshly shaved, red-faced, thin-flanked, throwing out his lean chest; and had recited his little tale with an open and manly assurance. Now and then his eyelids quivered slightly, his hand would steal up to the end of the flaming moustache; his eyebrows were straight, furry, of a chestnut colour, and the directness of his gaze seemed to tremble on the verge of impudence. Captain Whalley had engaged him temporarily; then, the other man having been ordered home by the doctors, he had remained for the next trip, and then the next. He had now attained permanency, and the performance of his duties was marked by an air of serious, single-minded application. Directly he was spoken to, he began to smile attentively, with a great deference expressed in his whole attitude; but there was in the rapid winking which went on all the time something quizzical, as though he had possessed the secret of some universal joke cheating all creation and impenetrable to other mortals.

Grave and smiling, he watched Massy come down step by step; when the chief engineer had reached the deck he swung about, and they found themselves face to face. Matched as to height and utterly dissimilar, they confronted each other as if there had been something between them—something else than the bright strip of sunlight that, falling through the wide lacing of two awnings, cut crosswise the narrow planking of the deck and separated their feet as it were a stream; something profound and subtle and incalculable, like an unexpressed understanding, a secret mistrust, or some sort of fear.

At last Sterne, blinking his deep-set eyes and sticking forward his scraped, clean-cut chin, as crimson as the rest of his face, murmured

'You've seen? He grazed! You've seen?'

Massy, contemptuous, and without raising his yellow, fleshy countenance, replied in the same pitch—

'Maybe. But if it had been you we would have been stuck fast in the mud.'

'Pardon me, Mr Massy. I beg to deny it. Of course a shipowner may say what he jolly well pleases on his own deck. That's all right; but I beg to . . .'

'Get out of my way!'

The other had a slight start, the impulse of suppressed indignation perhaps, but held his ground, Massy's downward glance wandered right and left, as though the deck all round Sterne had been bestrewn with eggs that must not be broken, and he had looked irritably for places where he could set his feet in flight. In the end he, too, did not move, though there was plenty of room to pass on.

'I heard you say up there,' went on the mate, 'and a very just remark it was, too—that there's always something wrong . . .'

'Eavesdropping is what's wrong with *you,* Mr Sterne.'

'Now, if you would only listen to me for a moment, Mr Massy, sir, I could . . .'

'You are a sneak,' interrupted Massy in a great hurry, and even managed to get so far as to repeat, 'a common sneak,' before the mate had broken in argumentatively—

'Now, sir, what is it you want? You want . . .'

'I want—I want,' stammered Massy, infuriated and astonished—'I want? How do you know that I want anything? How dare you? . . . What do you mean? . . . What are you after—you . . .'

'Promotion.' Sterne silenced him with candid bravado. The engineer's round, soft cheeks quivered still, but he said quietly enough—

'You are only worrying my head off,' and Sterne met him with a confident little smile.

'A chap in business I know (well up in the world he is now) used to tell me that this was the proper way. "Always push on to the front," he would say. "Keep yourself well before your boss. Interfere whenever you get a chance. Show him what you know. Worry him into seeing you." That was his advice. Now I know no other boss than you here. You are the owner, and no one else counts for *that* much in my eyes. See, Mr Massy? I want to get on. I make no secret of it that I am one of the sort that means to get on. These are the men to make use of, sir. You haven't arrived at the top of the tree, sir, without finding that out—I daresay.'

'Worry your boss in order to get on,' repeated Massy, as if awestruck by the irreverent originality of the idea. 'I shouldn't wonder if this was just what the Blue Anchor people kicked you out of their employ for. Is that what you call getting on? You shall get on in the same way here if you aren't careful—I can promise you.'

At this Sterne hung his head, thoughtful, perplexed, winking hard at the deck. All his attempts to enter into confidential relations with his owner had led of late to nothing better than these dark threats of dismissal; and a threat of dismissal would check him at once into a hesitating silence as though he were not sure that the proper time for defying it had come. On this occasion he seemed to have lost his tongue for a moment, and Massy, getting in motion, heavily passed him by with an abortive attempt at shouldering. Sterne defeated it by stepping aside. He turned then swiftly, opening his mouth very wide as if to shout something after the engineer, but seemed to think better of it.

Always—as he was ready to confess—on the lookout for an opening to get on, it had become an instinct with him to watch the conduct of his immediate superiors for something 'that one could lay hold of'. It was his belief that no skipper in the world would keep his command for a day if only the owners could be 'made to know'. This romantic and naïve theory had led him into trouble more than once, but he remained incorrigible; and his character was so instinctively disloyal that whenever he joined a ship the intention of ousting his commander out of the berth and taking his place was always present at the back of his head, as a matter of course. It filled the leisure of his waking hours with the reveries of careful plans and compromising discoveries—the dreams of his sleep with images of lucky turns and favourable accidents. Skippers had been known to sicken and die at sea, than which nothing could be better to give a smart mate a chance of showing what he's made of. They also would tumble overboard sometimes: he had heard of one or two such cases. Others again . . . But, as it were constitutionally, he was faithful to the belief that the conduct of no single one of them would stand the test of careful watching by a man who 'knew what's what' and who kept his eyes 'skinned pretty well' all the time.

After he had gained a permanent footing on board the *Sofala* he allowed his perennial hope to rise high. To begin with, it was a great advantage to have an old man for captain: the sort of man besides who in the nature of things was likely to give up the job before long from one cause or another. Sterne was greatly chagrined, however, to notice that he did not seem anyway near being past his work yet. Still, these old men go to pieces all at once sometimes. Then there was the owner-engineer close at hand to be impressed by his zeal and steadiness. Sterne never for a moment doubted the obvious nature of his own merits (he was really an excellent officer); only, nowadays, professional merit alone does not take a man along fast enough. A chap must have some push in him, and must keep his wits at work, too, to help him forward. He made up his mind to inherit the charge of this steamer if it was to be done at all; not indeed estimating the command of the *Sofala* as a very great catch, but for the reason that, out East especially, to make a start is everything, and one command leads to another.

He began by promising himself to behave with great circumspection; Massy's sombre and fantastic humours intimidated him as being outside one's usual sea experience;

but he was quite intelligent enough to realize almost from the first that he was there in the presence of an exceptional situation. His peculiar prying imagination penetrated it quickly; the feeling that there was in it an element which eluded his grasp exasperated his impatience to get on. And so one trip came to an end, then another, and he had begun his third before he saw an opening by which he could step in with any sort of effect. It had all been very queer and very obscure; something had been going on near him, as if separated by a chasm from the common life and the working routine of the ship, which was exactly like the life and the routine of any other coasting steamer of that class.

Then one day he made his discovery.

It came to him after all these weeks of watchful observation and puzzled surmises, suddenly, like the long-sought solution of a riddle that suggests itself to the mind in a flash. Not with the same authority however. Great heavens! Could it be that? And after remaining thunderstruck for a few seconds he tried to shake it off with self-contumely, as though it had been the product of an unhealthy bias toward the Incredible, the Inexplicable, the Unheard-of—the Mad!

This—the illuminating moment—had occurred the trip before, on the return passage. They had just left a place of call on the mainland called Pangu; they were steaming straight out of a bay. To the east a massive headland closed the view, with the tilted edges of the rocky strata showing through its ragged clothing of rank bushes and thorny creepers. The wind had begun to sing in the rigging; the sea along the coast, green and as if swollen a little above the line of the horizon, seemed to pour itself over, time after time, with a slow and thundering fall, into the shadow of the leeward cape; and across the wide opening the nearest of a group of small islands stood enveloped in the hazy yellow light of a breezy sunrise; still farther out the hummocky tops of other islets peeped out motionless above the water of the channels between, scoured tumultuously by the breeze.

The usual track of the *Sofala* both going and returning on every trip led her for a few miles along this reef-infested region. She followed a broad lane of water, dropping astern, one after another, these crumbs of the earth's crust resembling a squadron of dismasted hulks run in disorder upon a foul ground of rocks and shoals. Some of these fragments of land appeared, indeed, no bigger than a stranded ship; others, quite flat, lay awash like anchored rafts, like ponderous, black rafts of stone; several, heavily timbered and round at the base, emerged in squat domes of deep green foliage that shuddered darkly all over to the flying touch of cloud shadows driven by the sudden gusts of the squally season. The thunderstorms of the coast broke frequently over that cluster; it turned then shadowy in its whole extent; it turned more dark, and as if more still in the play of fire; as if more impenetrably silent in the peals of thunder; its blurred shapes vanished dissolving utterly at times in the thick rain—to reappear clear-cut and black in the stormy light against the grey sheet of the cloud—scattered on the slaty round table of the sea. Unscathed by storms, resisting the work of years, unfretted by the strife of the world, there it lay unchanged as on that day, four hundred years ago, when first beheld by Western eyes from the deck of a high-pooped caravel.

It was one of these secluded spots that may be found on the busy sea, as on land you come sometimes upon the clustered houses of a hamlet untouched by men's restlessness, untouched by their need, by their thought, and as if forgotten by time itself. The lives of uncounted generations had passed it by, and the multitudes of sea fowl, urging their way from all the points of the horizon to sleep on the outer rocks of the group, unrolled the converging evolutions of their flight in long, sombre streamers upon the glow of the sky. The palpitating cloud of their wings soared and stooped over the pinnacles of the rocks, over the rocks slender like spires, squat like martello towers; over the pyramidal heaps like fallen ruins, over the lines of bald boulders showing like a wall of stones battered to pieces and scorched by lightning—with the sleepy, clear glimmer of water in every breach. The noise of their continuous and violent screaming filled the air.

This great noise would meet the *Sofala* coming up from Batu Berau; it would meet her on quiet evenings, a pitiless and savage clamour enfeebled by distance, the clamour of seabirds settling to rest, and struggling for a footing at the end of the day. No one noticed it especially on board; it was the voice of their ship's unerring landfall, ending the steady stretch of a hundred miles. She had made good her course, she had run her distance till the punctual islets began to emerge one by one, the points of rocks, the hummocks of earth . . . and the cloud of birds hovered—the restless cloud emitting a strident and cruel uproar, the sound of the familiar scene, the living part of the broken land beneath, of the outspread sea, and of the high sky without a flaw.

But when the *Sofala* happened to close with the land after sunset she would find everything very still there under the mantle of the night. All would be still, dumb, almost invisible—but for the blotting out of the low constellations occulted in turns behind the vague masses of the islets whose true outlines eluded the eye amongst the dark spaces of the heaven; and the ship's three lights, resembling three stars—the red and the green with the white above; her three lights, like three companion stars wandering on the earth, held their unswerving course for the passage at the southern end of the group. Sometimes there were human eyes open to watch them come nearer, travelling smoothly in the sombre void; the eyes of a naked fisherman in his canoe floating over a reef. He thought drowsily: 'Ha! The fireship that once in every moon goes in and comes out of Pangu Bay.' More he did not know of her. And just as he had detected the faint rhythm of the propeller beating the calm water a mile and a half away, the time would come for the *Sofala* to alter her course, the lights would swing off him their triple beam—and disappear.

A few miserable, half-naked families, a sort of outcast tribe of long-haired, lean and wild-eyed people, strove for their living in this lonely wilderness of islets, lying like an abandoned outwork of the land at the gates of the bay. Within the knots and loops of the rocks the water rested more transparent than crystal under their crooked and leaky canoes, scooped out of the trunk of a tree: the forms of the bottom undulated slightly to the dip of a paddle; and the men seemed to hang in the air, they seemed to hang enclosed within the fibres of a dark, sodden log, fishing patiently in a strange, unsteady, pellucid, green air above the shoals.

Their bodies stalked brown and emaciated as if dried up in the sunshine; their lives ran out silently; the homes where they were born, went to rest, and died—flimsy sheds of rushes and coarse grass eked out with a few ragged mats—were hidden out of sight from the open sea. No glow of their household fires ever kindled for a seaman a red spark upon the blind night of the group; and the calms of the coast, the flaming long calms of the equator, the unbreathing, concentrated calms like the deep introspection of a passionate nature, brooded awfully for days and weeks together over the unchangeable inheritance of their children; till at last the stones, hot like live embers, scorched the naked sole, till the water clung warm and sickly and as if thickened about the legs of lean men with girded loins, wading thigh-deep in the pale blaze of the shallows. And it would happen now and then that the *Sofala*, through some delay in one of the ports of call, would heave in sight making for Pangu Bay as late as noonday.

Only a blurring cloud at first, the thin mist of her smoke would arise mysteriously from an empty point on the clear line of sea and sky. The taciturn fishermen within the reefs would extend their lean arms toward the offing; and the brown figures stooping on the tiny beaches, the brown figures of men, women and children grubbing in the sand in search of turtles' eggs, would rise up, crooked elbow aloft and hand over the eyes, to watch this monthly apparition glide straight on, swerve on—and go by. Their ears caught the panting of that ship; their eyes followed her till she passed between the two capes of the mainland going at full speed as though she hoped to make her way unchecked into the very bosom of the earth.

On such days the luminous sea would give no sign of the dangers lurking on both sides of her path. Everything remained still, crushed by the overwhelming power of the light; and the whole group, opaque in the sunshine—the rocks resembling pinnacles, the rocks resembling spires, the rocks resembling ruins; the forms of islets resembling beehives, resembling molehills; the islets recalling the shapes of haystacks, the contours of ivy-clad towers—would stand reflected together upside down in the unwrinkled water, like carved toys of ebony disposed on the silvered plate glass of a mirror.

The first touch of blowing weather would envelop the whole at once in the spume of the windward breakers, as if in a sudden cloud-like burst of steam; and the clear water seemed fairly to boil in all the passages. The provoked sea outlined exactly in a design of angry foam the wide base of the group; the submerged level of broken waste and refuse left over from the building of the coast nearby, projecting its dangerous spurs, all awash, far into the channel, and bristling with wicked long spits often a mile long; with deadly spits made of froth and stones.

And even nothing more than a brisk breeze—as on that morning, the voyage before, when the *Sofala* left Pangu Bay early, and Mr Sterne's discovery was to blossom out like a flower of incredible and evil aspect from the tiny seed of instinctive suspicion—even such a breeze had enough strength to tear the placid mask from the face of the sea. To Sterne, gazing with indifference, it had been like a revelation to behold for the first time the dangers marked by the hissing livid patches on the water as distinctly as on the engraved paper of a chart. It came into his mind that this was the sort of day most favourable for a stranger attempting the passage: a clear day, just windy enough for the sea to break on every ledge, buoying, as it were, the channel plainly to the sight; whereas during a calm you had nothing to depend on but the compass and the practised judgment of your eye. And yet the successive captains of the *Sofala* had had to take her through at night more than once. Nowadays you could not afford to throw away six or seven hours of a steamer's time. That you couldn't. But then use is everything, and with proper care . . . The channel was broad and safe enough; the main point was to hit upon the entrance correctly in the dark—for if a man got himself involved in that stretch of broken water over yonder he would never get out with a whole ship—if he ever got out at all.

This was Sterne's last train of thought independent of the great discovery. He had just seen to the securing of the anchor, and had remained forward idling away a moment or two. The captain was in charge on the bridge. With a slight yawn he had turned away from his survey of the sea and had leaned his shoulders against the fish davit.

These, properly speaking, were the very last moments of ease he was to know on board the *Sofala*. All the instants that came after were to be pregnant with purpose and intolerable with perplexity. No more idle, random thoughts; the discovery would put them on the rack, till sometimes he wished to goodness he had been fool enough not to make it at all. And yet, if his chance to get on rested on the discovery of 'something wrong', he could not have hoped for a greater stroke of luck.

X

THE knowledge was too disturbing, really. There was 'something wrong' with a vengeance, and the moral certitude of it was at first simply frightful to contemplate. Sterne had been looking aft in a mood so idle, that for once he was thinking no harm of anyone. His captain on the bridge presented himself naturally to his sight. How insignificant, how casual was the thought that had started the train of discovery—like an accidental spark that suffices to ignite the charge of a tremendous mine!

Caught under by the breeze, the awnings of the foredeck bellied upwards and collapsed slowly, and above their heavy flapping the grey stuff of Captain Whalley's roomy coat fluttered incessantly around his arms and trunk. He faced the wind in full light, with his great silvery beard blown forcibly against his chest; the eyebrows overhung heavily the shadows whence his glance appeared to be staring ahead piercingly. Sterne could just detect the twin gleam of the whites shifting under the shaggy arches of the brow. At short range these eyes, for all the man's affable manner, seemed to look you through and through. Sterne never could defend himself from that feeling when he had occasion to speak with his captain. He did not like it. What a big heavy man he appeared up there, with that little shrimp of a Serang in close attendance—as was usual in this extraordinary steamer! Confounded absurd custom that. He resented it. Surely the old fellow could have looked after his ship without that loafing native at his elbow. Sterne wriggled his shoulders with disgust. What was it? Indolence or what?

That old skipper must have been growing lazy for years. They all grew lazy out East here (Sterne was very conscious of his own unimpaired activity); they got slack all over. But he towered very erect on the bridge; and quite low by his side, as you see a small child looking over the edge of a table, the battered soft hat and the brown face of the Serang peeped over the white canvas screen of the rail.

No doubt the Malay was standing back, nearer to the wheel; but the great disparity of size in close association amused Sterne like the observation of a bizarre fact in nature. There were as queer fish out of the sea as any in it.

He saw Captain Whalley turn his head quickly to speak to his Serang; the wind whipped the whole white mass of the beard sideways. He would be directing the chap to look at the compass for him, or what not. Of course. Too much trouble to step over and see for himself. Sterne's scorn for that bodily indolence which overtakes white men in the East increased on reflection. Some of them would be utterly lost if they hadn't all these natives at their beck and call; they grew perfectly shameless about it too. He was not of that sort, thank God! It wasn't in him to make himself dependent for his work on any shrivelled-up little Malay like that. As if one could ever trust a silly native for anything in the world! But that fine old man thought differently, it seems. There they were together, never far apart; a pair of them, recalling to the mind an old whale attended by a little pilot fish.

The fancifulness of the comparison made him smile. A whale with an inseparable pilot fish! That's what the old man looked like; for it could not be said he looked like a shark, though Mr Massy had called him that very name. But Mr Massy did not mind what he said in his savage fits. Sterne smiled to himself—and gradually the ideas evoked by the sound, by the imagined shape of the word pilot fish; the ideas of aid, of guidance needed and received, came uppermost in his mind: the word pilot awakened the idea of trust, of dependence, the idea of the welcome, clear-eyed help brought to the seaman groping for the land in the dark; groping blindly in fogs; feeling his way in the thick weather of the gales that, filling the air with a salt mist blown up from the sea, contract the range of sight on all sides to a shrunken horizon that seems within reach of the hand.

A pilot sees better than a stranger, because his local knowledge, like a sharper vision, completes the shapes of things hurriedly glimpsed; penetrates the veils of mist spread over the land by the storms of the sea; defines with certitude the outlines of a coast lying under the pall of fog, the forms of landmarks half buried in a starless night as in a shallow grave. He recognizes because he already knows. It is not to his far-reaching eye but to his more extensive knowledge that the pilot looks for certitudes; for this certitude of the ship's position on which may depend a man's good fame and the peace of his conscience, the justification of the trust deposited in his hands, with his own life too, which is seldom wholly his to throw away, and the humble lives of others rooted in distant affections, perhaps, and made as weighty as the lives of kings by the burden of the awaiting mystery. The pilot's knowledge brings relief and certitude to the commander of a ship; the Serang, however, in his fanciful suggestion of a pilot fish attending a whale, could not in any way be credited with a superior knowledge. Why should he have it? These two men had come on that run together—the white and the brown—on the same day: and of course a white man would learn more in a week than the best native would in a month. He was made to stick to the skipper as though he were of some use—as the pilot fish, they say, is to the whale. But how—it was very marked—how? A pilot fish—a pilot—a ... But if not superior knowledge then ...

Sterne's discovery was made. It was repugnant to his imagination, shocking to his ideas of honesty, shocking to his conception of mankind. This enormity affected one's outlook on what was possible in this world; it was as if for instance the sun had turned blue, throwing a new and sinister light on men and nature. Really in the first moment he had felt sickish, as though he had got a blow below the belt; for a second the very colour of the sea seemed changed—appeared queer to his wandering eye; and he had a passing, unsteady sensation in all his limbs as though the earth had started turning the other way.

A very natural incredulity succeeding this sense of upheaval brought a measure of relief. He had gasped; it was over. But afterwards, during all that day, sudden paroxysms of wonder would come over him in the midst of his occupations. He would stop and shake his head. The revolt of his incredulity had passed away almost as quick as the first emotion of discovery, and for the next twenty-four hours he had no sleep. That would never do. At mealtimes (he took the foot of the table set up for the white men on the bridge) he could not help losing himself in a fascinated contemplation of Captain Whalley opposite. He watched the deliberate upward movements of the arm; the old man put his food to his lips as though he never expected to find any taste in his daily bread, as though he did not know anything about it. He fed himself like a somnambulist. 'It's an awful sight,' thought Sterne; and he watched the long period of mournful; silent immobility, with a big brown hand lying loosely closed by the side of the plate, till he noticed the two engineers to the right and left looking at him in astonishment. He would close his mouth in a hurry then, and lowering his eyes, wink rapidly at his plate. It was awful to see the old chap sitting there: it was even awful to think that with three words he could blow him up sky-high. All he had to do was to raise his voice and pronounce a single short sentence, and yet that simple act seemed as impossible to attempt as moving the sun out of its place in the sky. The old chap could eat in his terrific mechanical way; but Sterne, from mental excitement, could not—not that evening, at any rate.

He had had ample time since to get accustomed to the strain of the meal hours. He would never have believed it. But then use is everything; only the very potency of his success prevented anything resembling elation. He felt like a man who, in his legitimate search for a loaded gun to help him on his way through the world, chances to come upon a torpedo—upon a live torpedo with a shattering charge in its head and a pressure of many atmospheres in its tail. It is the sort of weapon to make its possessor careworn and nervous. He had no mind to be blown up himself; and he could not get rid of the notion that the explosion was bound to damage him too in some way.

This vague apprehension had restrained him at first. He was able now to eat and sleep with that fearful weapon by his side, with the conviction of its power always in his mind. It had not been arrived at by any reflective process; but once the idea had entered his head, the conviction had followed overwhelmingly in a multitude of observed little facts to which before he had given only a languid attention. The abrupt and faltering intonations of the deep voice; the taciturnity put on like an armour; the deliberate, as if guarded, movements; the long immobilities, as if the man he watched had been afraid to disturb the very air: every familiar gesture, every word uttered in his hearing, every sigh overheard, had acquired a special significance, a confirmatory import.

Every day that passed over the *Sofala* appeared to Sterne

simply crammed full with proofs—with incontrovertible proofs. At night, when off duty, he would steal out of his cabin in pyjamas (for more proofs) and stand a full hour, perhaps, on his bare feet below the bridge, as absolutely motionless as the awning stanchion in its deck socket nearby. On the stretches of easy navigation it is not usual for a coasting captain to remain on deck all the time of his watch. The Serang keeps it for him as a matter of custom; in open water, on a straight course, he is usually trusted to look after the ship by himself. But this old man seemed incapable of remaining quietly down below. No doubt he could not sleep. And no wonder. This was also a proof. Suddenly in the silence of the ship panting upon the still, dark sea, Sterne would hear a low voice above him exclaiming nervously—

'Serang!'

'Tuan!'

'You are watching the compass well?'

'Yes, I am watching, Tuan.'

'The ship is making her course?'

'She is, Tuan. Very straight.'

'It is well; and remember, Serang, that the order is that you are to mind the helmsmen and keep a lookout with care, the same as if I were not on deck.'

Then, when the Serang had made his answer, the low tones on the bridge would cease, and everything round Sterne seemed to become more still and more profoundly silent. Slightly chilled and with his back aching a little from long immobility, he would steal away to his room on the port side of the deck. He had long since parted with the last vestige of incredulity; of the original emotions, set into a tumult by the discovery, some trace of the first awe alone remained. Not the awe of the man himself—he could blow him up sky-high with six words—rather it was an awestruck indignation at the reckless perversity of avarice (what else could it be?), at the mad and sombre resolution that for the sake of a few dollars more seemed to set at nought the common rule of conscience and pretended to struggle against the very decree of Providence.

You could not find another man like this one in the whole round world—thank God. There was something devilishly dauntless in the character of such a deception which made you pause.

Other considerations occurring to his prudence had kept him tongue-tied from day to day. It seemed to him now that it would yet have been easier to speak out in the first hour of discovery. He almost regretted not having made a row at once. But then the very monstrosity of the disclosure . . . Why! he could hardly face it himself, let alone pointing it out to somebody else. Moreover, with a desperado of that sort one never knew. The object was not to get him out (that was as well as done already), but to step into his place. Bizarre as the thought seemed he might have shown fight. A fellow up to working such a fraud would have enough cheek for anything; a fellow that, as it were, stood up against God Almighty Himself. He was a horrid marvel—that's what he was: he was perfectly capable of brazening out the affair scandalously till he got him (Sterne) kicked out of the ship and everlastingly damaged his prospects in this part of the East. Yet if you want to get on something must be risked. At times Sterne thought he had been unduly timid of taking action in the past; and what was worse, it had come to this, that in the present he did not seem to know what action to take.

Massy's savage moroseness was too disconcerting. It was an incalculable factor of the situation. You could not tell what there was behind that insulting ferocity. How could one trust such a temper? It did not put Sterne in bodily fear for himself, but it frightened him exceedingly as to his prospects.

Though of course inclined to credit himself with

exceptional powers of observation, he had by now lived too long with his discovery. He had gone on looking at nothing else, till at last one day it occurred to him that the thing was so obvious that no one could miss seeing it. There were four white men in all on board the *Sofala*. Jack, the second engineer, was too dull to notice anything that took place out of his engine room. Remained Massy—the owner, the interested person—nearly going mad with worry. Sterne had heard and seen more than enough on board to know what ailed him; but his exasperation seemed to make him deaf to cautious overtures. If he had only known it, there was the very thing he wanted. But how could you bargain with a man of that sort? It was like going into a tiger's den with a piece of raw meat in your hand. He was as likely as not to rend you for your pains. In fact, he was always threatening to do that very thing, and the urgency of the case, combined with the impossibility of handling it with safety, made Sterne in his watches below toss and mutter open-eyed in his bunk for hours, as though he had been burning with fever.

Occurrences like the crossing of the bar just now were extremely alarming to his prospects. He did not want to be left behind by some swift catastrophe. Massy being on the bridge, the old man had to brace himself up, and make a show, he supposed. But it was getting very bad with him, very bad indeed, now. Even Massy had been emboldened to find fault this time; Sterne, listening at the foot of the ladder, had heard the other's whimpering and artless denunciations. Luckily the beast was very stupid and could not see the why of all this. However, small blame to him; it took a clever man to hit upon the cause. Nevertheless, it was high time to do something. The old man's game could not be kept up for many days more.

'I may yet lose my life at this fooling—let alone my chance,' Sterne mumbled angrily to himself, after the stooping back of the chief engineer had disappeared round the corner of the skylight. Yes, no doubt—he thought; but to blurt out his knowledge would not advance his prospects. On the contrary, it would blast them utterly as likely as not. He dreaded another failure. He had a vague consciousness of not being much liked by his fellows in this part of the world; inexplicably enough, for he had done nothing to them. Envy, he supposed. People were always down on a clever chap who made no bones about his determination to get on. To do your duty and count on the gratitude of that brute Massy would be sheer folly. He was a bad lot. Unmanly! A vicious man! Bad! Bad! A brute! A brute without a spark of anything human about him; without so much as simple curiosity even, or else surely he would have responded in some way to all these hints he had been given . . . Such insensibility was almost mysterious. Massy's state of exasperation seemed to Sterne to have made him stupid beyond the ordinary silliness of shipowners.

Sterne, meditating on the embarrassments of that stupidity, forgot himself completely. His stony, unwinking stare was fixed on the planks of the deck.

The slight quiver agitating the whole fabric of the ship was more perceptible in the silent river, shaded and still like a forest path. The *Sofala,* gliding with an even motion, had passed beyond the coast belt of mud and mangroves. The shores rose higher, in firm, sloping banks, and the forest of big trees came down to the brink. Where the earth had been crumbled by the floods it showed a steep brown cut, denuding a mass of roots intertwined as if wrestling underground; and in the air, the interlaced boughs, bound and loaded with creepers, carried on the struggle for life, mingled their foliage in one solid wall of leaves, with here and there the shape of an enormous dark pillar soaring, or a ragged opening, as if torn by the flight of a cannonball, disclosing the impenetrable gloom within, the secular inviolable shade of the virgin forest. The thump of the engines reverberated regularly like the strokes of a metronome beating the measure of the vast silence, the shadow of the western wall had fallen across the river, and the smoke pouring backwards from the funnel eddied down behind the ship, spread a thin dusky veil over the sombre water, which, checked by the flood-tide, seemed to lie stagnant in the whole straight length of the reaches.

Sterne's body, as if rooted on the spot, trembled slightly from top to toe with the internal vibration of the ship; from under his feet came sometimes a sudden clang of iron, the noisy burst of a shout below; to the right the leaves of the treetops caught the rays of the low sun, and seemed to shine with a golden green light of their own shimmering around the highest boughs which stood out black against a smooth blue sky that seemed to droop over the bed of the river like the roof of a tent. The passengers for Batu Berau, kneeling on the planks, were engaged in rolling their bedding of mats busily; they tied up bundles, they snapped the locks of wooden chests. A pockmarked pedlar of small wares threw his head back to drain into his throat the last drops out of an earthenware bottle before putting it away in a roll of blankets. Knots of travelling traders standing about the deck conversed in low tones; the followers of a small Rajah from down the coast, broad-faced simple young fellows in white drawers and round white cotton caps with their coloured sarongs twisted across their bronze shoulders, squatted on their hams on the hatch, chewing betel with bright red mouths as if they had been tasting blood. Their spears, lying piled up together within the circle of their bare toes, resembled a casual bundle of dry bamboos; a thin, livid Chinaman, with a bulky package wrapped up in leaves already thrust under his arm, gazed ahead eagerly; a wandering King rubbed his teeth with a bit of wood, pouring over the side a bright stream of water out of his lips; the fat Rajah dozed in a shabby deckchair—and at the turn of every bend the two walls of leaves reappeared running parallel along the banks, with their impenetrable solidity fading at the top to a vaporous mistiness of countless slender twigs growing free, of young delicate branches shooting from the topmost limbs of hoary trunks, of feathery heads of climbers like delicate silver sprays standing up without a quiver. There was not a sign of a clearing anywhere; not a trace of human habitation, except when in one place, on the bare end of a low point under an isolated group of slender tree-ferns, the jagged, tangled remnants of an old hut on piles appeared with that peculiar aspect of ruined bamboo walls that look as if smashed with a club. Farther on, half hidden under the drooping bushes, a canoe containing a man and a woman together with a dozen green coconuts in a heap, rocked helplessly after the *Sofala* had passed, like a navigating contrivance of venturesome insects, of travelling ants; while two glassy folds of water streaming away from each bow of the steamer across the whole width of the river ran with her upstream smoothly, fretting their outer ends into a brown whispering tumble of froth against the miry foot of each bank.

'I must,' thought Sterne, 'bring that brute Massy to his bearings. It's getting too absurd in the end. Here's the old man up there buried in his chair—he may just as well be in his grave for all the use he'll ever be in the world—and the Serang's in charge. Because that's what he is. In charge. In the place that's mine by rights. I must bring that savage brute to his bearings. I'll do it at once, too . . .'

When the mate made an abrupt start, a little brown, half-naked boy, with large black eyes, and the string of a written charm round his neck, became panic-struck at once. He dropped the banana he had been munching, and ran to the knee of a grave dark Arab in flowing robes; sitting like a

Biblical figure, incongruously, on a yellow tin trunk corded with a rope of twisted rattan. The father, unmoved, put out his hand to pat the little shaven poll protectingly.

XI

STERNE crossed the deck upon the track of the chief engineer. Jack, the second, retreating backwards down the engine room ladder, and still wiping his hands, treated him to an incomprehensible grin of white teeth out of his grimy hard face; Massy was nowhere to be seen. Sterne scratched at the door softly, then, putting his lips to the rose of the ventilator, said—

'I must speak to you, Mr Massy. Just give me a minute or two.'

'I am busy. Go away from my door.'

'But pray, Mr Massy . . .'

'You go away. D'you hear? Take yourself off altogether—to the other end of the ship—quite away . . .' The voice inside dropped low. 'To the devil.'

Sterne paused; then very quietly—

'It's rather pressing. When do you think you will be at liberty, sir?'

The answer to this was an exasperated 'Never'; and at once Sterne, with a very firm expression of face, turned the handle.

Mr Massy's stateroom—a narrow, one-berth cabin—smelt strongly of soap and presented to view a swept, dusted, unadorned neatness, not so much bare as barren, not so much severe as starved and lacking in humanity, like the ward of a public hospital, or rather (owing to the small size) like the clean retreat of a desperately poor but exemplary person. Not a single photograph frame ornamented the bulkheads; not a single article of clothing, not as much as a spare cap, hung from the brass hooks. All the inside was painted in one plain tint of pale blue; two big sea chests in sailcloth covers and with iron padlocks fitted exactly to the space under the bunk. One glance was enough to embrace all the strip of scrubbed planks within the four unconcealed corners. The absence of the usual settee was striking; the teakwood top of the washing stand seemed hermetically closed, and so was the lid of the writing desk, which protruded from the partition at the foot of the bed-place, containing a mattress as thin as a pancake under a threadbare blanket with a faded red stripe, and a folded mosquito net against the nights spent in harbour. There was not a scrap of paper anywhere in sight, no boots on the floor, no litter of any sort, not a speck of dust anywhere; no traces of pipe ash even, which, in a heavy smoker, was morally revolting like a manifestation of extreme hypocrisy; and the bottom of the old wooden armchair (the only seat there), polished with much use, shone as if its shabbiness had been waxed. The screen of leaves on the bank, passing as if unrolled endlessly in the round opening of the port, sent a wavering network of light and shade into the place.

Sterne, holding the door open with one hand, had thrust in his head and shoulders. At this amazing intrusion Massy, who was doing absolutely nothing, jumped up speechless.

'Don't call names,' murmured Sterne, hurriedly, 'I won't be called names. I think of nothing but your good, Mr Massy.'

A pause as of extreme astonishment followed. They both seemed to have lost their tongues. Then the mate went on with discreet glibness:

'You simply couldn't conceive what's going on on board your ship. It wouldn't enter your head for a moment. You are too good—too—too upright, Mr Massy, to suspect anybody of such a . . . It's enough to make your hair stand on end.'

He watched for the effect: Massy seemed dazed,

uncomprehending. He only passed the palm of his hand on the coal-black wisps plastered across the top of his head. In a tone suddenly changed to confidential audacity Sterne hastened on:

'Remember that there's only six weeks left to run . . .' The other was looking at him stonily . . . 'So anyhow you will require a captain for the ship before long.'

Then only, as if that suggestion had scarified his flesh in the manner of red-hot iron, Massy gave a start and seemed ready to shriek. He contained himself by a great effort.

'Require—a—captain,' he repeated with scathing slowness. 'Who requires a captain? You dare tell me that I need any of you humbugging sailors to run my ship. You and your likes have been fattening on me for years. It would have hurt me less to throw my money overboard. Pam-pe-red us-e-less f-f-f-frauds. The old ship knows as much as the best of you.' He snapped his teeth audibly and growled through them, 'The silly law requires a captain.'

Sterne had taken heart of grace meantime.

'And the silly insurance people as well,' he said, lightly. 'But never mind that. What I want to ask is: Why shouldn't *I* do, sir? I don't say but you could take a steamer about the world as well as any of us sailors. I don't pretend to tell *you* that it is a very great trick . . .' He emitted a short, hollow guffaw, familiarly . . . 'I didn't make the law—but there it is; and I am an active young fellow; I quite hold with your ideas; I know your ways by this time, Mr Massy. I wouldn't try to give myself airs like that—that—er—lazy specimen of an old man up there.'

He put a marked emphasis on the last sentence, to lead Massy away from the track in case . . . but he did not doubt of now holding his success. The chief engineer seemed nonplussed, like a slow man invited to catch hold of a whirligig of some sort.

'What you want, sir, is a chap with no nonsense about him, who would be content to be your sailing master. Quite right too. Well, I am fit for the work as much as that Serang. Because that's what it amounts to. Do you know, sir, that a dam' Malay like a monkey is in charge of your ship—and no one else? Just listen to his feet pit-patting above us on the bridge—real officer in charge. He's taking her up the river while the great man is wallowing in the chair—perhaps asleep; and if he is, that would not make it much worse either—take my word for it.'

He tried to thrust himself farther in. Massy, with lowered forehead, one hand grasping the back of the armchair, did not budge.

'You think, sir, that the man has got you tight in his agreement . . .' Massy raised a heavy snarling face at this . . . 'Well, sir, one can't help hearing of it on board. It's no secret. And it has been the talk on shore for years; fellows have been making bets about it. No, sir! It's *you* who have got him at your mercy. You will say that you can't dismiss him for indolence. Difficult to prove in court, and so on. Why, yes. But if you say the word, sir, I can tell you something about his indolence that will give you the clear right to fire him out on the spot and put me in charge for the rest of this very trip—yes, sir, before we leave Batu Berau—and make him pay a dollar a day for his keep till we get back, if you like. Now, what do you think of that? Come, sir. Say the word. It's really well worth your while, and I am quite ready to take your bare word. A definite statement from you would be as good as a bond.'

His eyes began to shine. He insisted. A simple statement—and he thought to himself that he would manage somehow to stick in his berth as long as it suited him. He would make himself indispensable; the ship had a bad name in her port; it would be easy to scare the fellows off. Massy would have to keep him.

'A definite statement from me would be enough,' Massy repeated, slowly.

'Yes, sir. It would.' Sterne stuck out his chin cheerily and blinked at close quarters with that unconscious impudence which had the power to enrage Massy beyond anything.

The engineer spoke very distinctly:

'Listen well to me, then, Mr Sterne: I wouldn't—d'ye hear?—I wouldn't promise you the value of two pence for anything *you* can tell me.'

He struck Sterne's arm away with a smart blow and catching hold of the handle pulled the door to. The terrific slam darkened the cabin instantaneously to his eyes as if after the flash of an explosion. At once he dropped into the chair. 'Oh, no! You don't!' he whispered faintly.

The ship had in that place to shave the bank so close that the gigantic wall of leaves came gliding like a shutter against the port; the darkness of the primeval forest seemed to flow into that bare cabin with the odour of rotting leaves, of sodden soil—the strong muddy smell of the living earth steaming uncovered after the passing of a deluge. The bushes swished loudly alongside; above there was a series of crackling sounds, with a sharp rain of small, broken branches falling on the bridge; a creeper with a great rustle snapped on the head of a boat davit, and a long, luxuriant green twig actually whipped in and out of the open port, leaving behind a few torn leaves that remained suddenly at rest on Mr Massy's blanket. Then, the ship sheering out in the stream, the light began to return, but did not augment beyond a subdued clearness; for the sun was very low already, and the river, wending its sinuous course through a multitude of secular trees as if at the bottom of a precipitous gorge, had been already invaded by a deepening gloom—the swift precursor of the night.

'Oh, no, you don't!' murmured the engineer again. His lips trembled almost imperceptibly; his hands, too, a little; and to calm himself he opened the writing desk, spread out a sheet of thin greyish paper covered with a mass of printed figures and began to scan them attentively for the twentieth time this trip at least.

With his elbows propped, his head between his hands, he seemed to lose himself in the study of an abstruse problem in mathematics. It was the list of the winning numbers from the last drawing of the great lottery which had been the one inspiring fact of so many years of his existence. The conception of a life deprived of that periodical sheet of paper had slipped away from him entirely, as another man, according to his nature, would not have been able to conceive a world without fresh air, without activity, or without affection. A great pile of flimsy sheets had been growing for years in his desk, while the *Sofala*, driven by the faithful Jack, wore out her boilers in tramping up and down the Straits, from cape to cape, from river to river, from bay to bay; accumulating by that hard labour of an overworked, starved ship the blackened mass of these documents. Massy kept them under lock and key like a treasure. There was in them, as in the experience of life, the fascination of hope, the excitement of a half-penetrated mystery, the longing of a half-satisfied desire.

For days together, on a trip, he would shut himself up in his berth with them; the thump of the toiling engines pulsated in his ear; and he would weary his brain poring over the rows of disconnected figures, bewildering by their senseless sequence, resembling the hazards of destiny itself. He nourished a conviction that there must be some logic lurking somewhere in the results of chance. He thought he had seen its very form. His head swam; his limbs ached; he puffed at his pipe mechanically; a contemplative stupor would soothe the fretfulness of his temper, like the passive bodily quietude procured by a drug, while the intellect remains tensely on the stretch. Nine, nine, nought, four, two. He made a note. The next winning number of the great prize was forty-seven thousand and five. These numbers of course would have to be avoided in the future when writing to Manila for the tickets. He mumbled, pencil in hand . . . 'and five. Hm . . . hm.' He wetted his finger: the papers rustled. Ha! But what's this? Three years ago, in the September drawing; it was number nine, nought, four, two that took the first prize. Most remarkable. There was a hint there of a definite rule! He was afraid of missing some recondite principle in the overwhelming wealth of his material. What could it be? And for half an hour he would remain dead still, bent low over the desk, without twitching a muscle. At his back the whole berth would be thick with a heavy body of smoke, as if a bomb had burst in there, unnoticed, unheard.

At last he would lock up the desk with the decision of unshaken confidence, jump up and go out. He would walk swiftly back and forth on that part of the foredeck which was kept clear of the lumber and of the bodies of the native passengers. They were a great nuisance, but they were also a source of profit that could not be disdained. He needed every penny of profit the *Sofala* could make. Little enough it was, in all conscience! The incertitude of chance gave him no concern, since he had somehow arrived at the conviction that, in the course of years, every number was bound to have its winning turn. It was simply a matter of time and of taking as many tickets as he could afford for every drawing. He generally took rather more; all the earnings of the ship went that way, and also the wages he allowed himself as chief engineer. It was the wages he paid to others that he begrudged with a reasoned and at the same time a passionate regret. He scowled at the lascars with their deck brooms, at the quartermasters rubbing the brass rails with greasy rags; he was eager to shake his fist and roar abuse in bad Malay at the poor carpenter—a timid, sickly, opium-fuddled Chinaman, in loose blue drawers for all costume, who invariably dropped his tools and fled below, with streaming tail and shaking all over, before the fury of that 'devil'. But it was when he raised up his eyes to the bridge where one of these sailor frauds was always planted by law in charge of his ship that he felt almost dizzy with rage. He abominated them all; it was an old feud, from the time he first went to sea, an unlicked cub with a great opinion of himself, in the engine room. The slights that had been put upon him. The persecutions he had suffered at the hands of shippers—of absolute nobodies in a steamship after all. And now that he had risen to be a ship-owner they were still a plague to him: he had absolutely to pay away precious money to the conceited useless loafers. As if a fully qualified engineer—who was the owner as well—were not fit to be trusted with the whole charge of a ship. Well, he made it pretty warm for them; but it was a poor consolation. He had come in time to hate the ship, too, for the repairs she required, for the coal bills he had to pay, for the poor beggarly freights she earned. He would clench his hand as he walked and hit the rail a sudden blow, viciously, as though she could be made to feel pain. And yet he could not do without her; he needed her; he must hang on to her tooth and nail to keep his head above water till the expected flood of fortune came sweeping up and landed him safely on the high shore of his ambition.

It was now to do nothing, nothing whatever, and have plenty of money to do it on. He had tasted of power, the highest form of it his limited experience was aware of—the power of ship-owning. What a deception! Vanity of vanities! He wondered at his folly. He had thrown away the substance for the shadow. Of the gratification of wealth he did not know enough to excite his imagination with any visions of luxury. How could he—the child of a drunken boiler-maker—going straight from the workshop into the engine room of a north-country collier! But the notion of the absolute idleness of wealth he could very well conceive. He revelled in it, to forget his present troubles; he imagined himself walking about the streets of Hull (he knew their gutters well as a boy) with his pockets full of sovereigns. He would buy himself a house; his married sisters, their husbands, his old workshop chums, would render him infinite homage. There would be nothing to think of. His word would be law. He had been out of work for a long time before he won his prize, and he remembered how Carlo Mariani (commonly known as Paunchy Charley), the Maltese hotel keeper at the slummy end of Denham Street, had cringed joyfully before him in the evening, when the news had come. Poor Charley though he made his living by ministering to various abject vices, gave credit for the food to many a piece of white wreckage. He was naïvely overjoyed at the idea of his old bills being paid, and he reckoned confidently on a spell of festivities in the cavernous grogshop downstairs. Massy remembered the curious, respectful looks of the 'trashy' white men in the place. His heart had swelled within him. Massy had left Charley's infamous den directly he had realized the possibilities open to him, with his nose in the air. Afterwards the memory of these adulations was a great sadness.

This was the true power of money—and no trouble with it, nor any thinking required either. He thought with difficulty and felt vividly; to his blunt brain the problems offered by any ordered scheme of life seemed in their cruel toughness to have been put in his way by the obvious malevolence of men. As a ship-owner everyone had conspired to make him a nobody. How could he have been such a fool as to purchase that accursed ship? He had been abominably swindled; there was no end to this swindling, and as the difficulties of his improvident ambition gathered thicker round him, he really came to hate everybody he had ever come in contact with. A temper naturally irritable and an amazing sensitiveness to the claims of his own personality had ended by making of life for him a sort of inferno—a place where his lost soul had been given up to the torment of savage brooding.

But he had never hated any one so much as that old man who turned up one evening to save him from an utter disaster—from the conspiracy of the wretched sailors. He seemed to have fallen on board from the sky. His footsteps echoed on the empty steamer, and the strange deep-toned voice on deck repeating interrogatively the words, 'Mr Massy, Mr Massy there?' had been startling like a wonder. And coming up from the depths of the cold engine room, where he had been pottering dismally with a candle amongst the enormous shadows, thrown on all sides by the skeleton limbs of machinery, Massy had been struck dumb by astonishment in the presence of that imposing old man with a beard like a silver plate, towering in the dusk rendered lurid by the expiring flames of sunset.

'Want to see me on business? What business? I am doing no business. Can't you see that this ship is laid up?' Massy had turned at bay before the pursuing irony of his disaster. Afterwards he could not believe his ears. What was that old fellow getting at? Things don't happen that way. It was a dream. He would presently wake up and find the man vanished like a shape of mist. The gravity, the dignity, the firm and courteous tone of that athletic old stranger impressed Massy. He was almost afraid. But it was no dream. Five hundreds pounds are no dream. At once he became suspicious. What did it mean? Of course it was an offer to catch hold of for dear life. But what could there be behind?

Before they had parted, after appointing a meeting in a solicitor's office early on the morrow, Massy was asking himself, What is his motive? He spent the night in hammering out the clauses of the agreement—a unique instrument of its sort whose tenor got bruited abroad somehow and became the talk and wonder of the port.

Massy's object had been to secure for himself as many ways as possible of getting rid of his partner without being called upon at once to pay back his share. Captain Whalley's efforts were directed to making the money secure. Was it not Ivy's money—a part of her fortune whose only other asset was the time-defying body of her old father? Sure of his forbearance in the strength of his love for her, he accepted, with stately serenity, Massy's stupidly cunning paragraphs against his incompetence, his dishonesty, his drunkenness, for the sake of other stringent stipulations. At the end of three years he was at liberty to withdraw from the partnership, taking his money with him. Provision was made for forming a fund to pay him off. But if he left the *Sofala* before the term, from whatever cause (barring death), Massy was to have a whole year for paying. 'Illness?' the lawyer had suggested: a young man fresh from Europe and not overburdened with business, who was rather amused. Massy began to whine unctuously, 'How could he be expected . . . ?'

'Let that go,' Captain Whalley had said with superb confidence in his body. 'Acts of God,' he added. In the midst of life we are in death, but he trusted his Maker with a still greater fearlessness—his Maker who knew his thoughts, his human affections, and his motives. His Creator knew what use he was making of his health—how much he wanted it . . . 'I trust my first illness will be my last. I've never been ill that I can remember,' he had remarked. 'Let it go.'

But at this early stage he had already awakened Massy's hostility by refusing to make it six hundred instead of five. 'I cannot do that,' was all he had said, simply, but with so much decision that Massy desisted at once from pressing the point, but had thought to himself, Can't! Old curmudgeon. *Won't!* He must have lots of money, but he would like to get hold of a soft berth and the sixth part of my profits for nothing if he only could.

And during these years Massy's dislike grew under the restraint of something resembling fear. The simplicity of that man appeared dangerous. Of late he had changed, however, had appeared less formidable and with a lessened vigour of life, as though he had received a secret wound. But still he remained incomprehensible in his simplicity, fearlessness and rectitude. And when Massy learned that he meant to leave him at the end of the time, to leave him confronted with the problem of the boilers, his dislike blazed up secretly into hate.

It had made him so clear-eyed that for a long time now Mr Sterne could have told him nothing he did not know. He had much ado in trying to terrorize that mean sneak into silence; he wanted to deal alone with the situation; and—incredible as it might have appeared to Mr Sterne—he had not yet given up the desire and the hope of inducing that hated old man to stay. Why! there was nothing else to do, unless he were to abandon his chances of fortune. But now, suddenly, since the crossing of the bar at Batu Berau things seemed to be coming rapidly to a point. It disquieted him so much that the study of the winning numbers failed to soothe his agitation; and the twilight in the cabin deepened, very sombre.

He put the list away, muttering once more, 'Oh, no, my boy, you don't. Not if I know it.' He did not mean the blinking, eavesdropping humbug to force his action. He took his head again into his hands; his immobility confined in the darkness of this shut-up little place seemed to make him a thing apart infinitely removed from the stir and the sounds of the deck.

He heard them: the passengers were beginning to jabber

excitedly; somebody dragged a heavy box past his door. He heard Captain Whalley's voice above—

'Stations, Mr Sterne.' And the answer from somewhere on deck forward—

'Ay, ay, sir.'

'We shall moor head upstream this time; the ebb has made.'

'Head upstream, sir.'

'You will see to it, Mr Sterne.'

The answer was covered by the autocratic clang of the engine room gong. The propeller went on beating slowly: one, two, three; one, two three—with pauses as if hesitating on the turn. The gong clanged time after time, and the water churned this way and that by the blades was making a great noisy commotion alongside. Mr Massy did not move. A shore light on the other bank, a quarter of a mile across the river, drifted, no bigger than a tiny star, passing slowly athwart the circle of the port. Voices from Mr Van Wyk's jetty answered the hails from the ship; ropes were thrown and missed and thrown again; the swaying flame of a torch carried in a large sampan coming to fetch away in state the Rajah from down the coast cast a sudden ruddy glare into his cabin, over his very person. Mr Massy did not move. After a few last ponderous turns the engines stopped, and the prolonged clanging of the gong signified that the captain had done with them. A great number of boats and canoes of all sizes boarded the off-side of the *Sofala*. Then after a time the tumult of splashing, of cries, of shuffling feet, of packages dropped with a thump, the noise of the native passengers going away, subsided slowly. On the shore, a voice, cultivated, slightly authoritative, poke very close alongside—

'Brought any mail for me this time?'

'Yes, Mr Van Wyk.' This was from Sterne, answering over the rail in a tone of respectful cordiality. 'Shall I bring it up to you?'

But the voice asked again—

'Where's the captain?'

'Still on the bridge, I believe. He hasn't left his chair. Shall I . . .'

The voice interrupted negligently—

'I will come on board.'

'Mr Van Wyk,' Sterne suddenly broke out with an eager effort, "will you do me the favour . . .' The mate walked away quickly towards the gangway.

A silence fell. Mr Massy in the dark did not move. He did not move even when he heard slow shuffling footsteps pass his cabin lazily. He contented himself to bellow out through the closed door

'You—Jack!'

The footsteps came back without haste; the door handle rattled, and the second engineer appeared in the opening, shadowy in the sheen of the skylight at his back, with his face apparently as black as the rest of his figure.

'We have been very long coming up this time,' Mr Massy growled, without changing his attitude.

'What do you expect with half the boiler tubes plugged up for leaks,' the second defended himself loquaciously.

'None of your lip,' said Massy.

'None of your rotten boilers—I say,' retorted his faithful subordinate without animation, huskily.

.'Go down there and carry a head of steam on them yourself—if you dare. I don't.'

'You aren't worth your salt then,' Massy said. The other made a faint noise which resembled a laugh but might have been a snarl.

'Better go slow than stop the ship altogether,' he admonished his admired superior. Mr Massy moved at last. He turned in his chair, and grinding his teeth—

'Dam' you and the ship! I wish she were at the bottom of the sea. Then you would have to starve.'

The trusty second engineer closed the door gently.

Massy listened. Instead of passing on to the bathroom where he should have gone to clean himself, the second entered his cabin, which was next door. Mr Massy jumped up and waited. Suddenly he heard the lock snap in there. He rushed out and gave a violent kick to the door.

'I believe you are locking yourself up to get drunk,' he shouted.

A muffled answer came after a while.

'My own time.'

'If you take to boozing on the trip I'll fire you out,' Massy cried.

An obstinate silence followed that threat. Massy moved away, perplexed. On the bank two figures at appeared, approaching the gangway. He heard a voice tinged with contempt

'I would rather doubt your word. But I shall certainly speak to him of this.'

The other voice, Sterne's, said with a sort of regretful formality

'Thanks. That's all I want. I must do my duty.' Mr Massy was surprised. A short, dapper figure leaped lightly on the deck and nearly bounded into him where he stood beyond the circle of light from the gangway lamp. When it had passed towards the bridge, after exchanging a hurried 'Good evening', Massy said surlily to Sterne, who followed with slow steps—

'What is it you're making up to Mr Van Wyk for now?'

'Far from it, Mr Massy. I am not good enough for Mr Van Wyk. Neither are you, sir, in his opinion, I am afraid. Captain Whalley is, it seems. He's gone to ask him to dine up at the house this evening.'

Then he murmured to himself darkly—
'I hope he will like it.'

XII

MR VAN WYK, the white man of Batu Berau, an ex-naval officer who, for reasons best known to himself, had thrown away the promise of a brilliant career to become the pioneer of tobacco-planting on that remote part of the coast, had learned to like Captain Whalley. The appearance of the new skipper had attracted his attention. Nothing more unlike all the diverse types he had seen succeeding each other on the bridge of the *Sofala* could be imagined.

At that time Batu Berau was not what it has become since: the centre of a prosperous tobacco-growing district, a tropically suburban-looking little settlement of bungalows in one long street shaded with two rows of trees, embowered by the flowering and trim luxuriance of the gardens, with a three-mile-long carriage road for the afternoon drives and a first-class Resident with a fat, cheery wife to lead the society of married estate managers and unmarried young fellows in the service of the big companies.

All this prosperity was not yet; and Mr Van Wyk prospered alone on the left bank on his deep clearing carved out of the forest, which came down above and below to the water's edge. His lonely bungalow faced across the river the houses of the Sultan, a restless and melancholy old ruler who had done with love and war, for whom life no longer held any savour (except of evil forebodings) and time never had any value. He was afraid of death, and hoped he would die before the white man were ready to take his country from him. He crossed the river frequently (with never less than ten boats crammed full of people), in the wistful hope of extracting some information on the subject from his own white man.

There was a certain chair on the veranda he always took; the dignitaries of the court squatted on the rugs and skins between the furniture; the inferior people remained below on the grass plot between the house and the river in rows three or four deep all along the front. Not seldom the visit began at daybreak. Mr Van Wyk tolerated these inroads. He would nod out of his bedroom window, toothbrush or razor in hand, or pass through the throng of courtiers in his bathing robe. He appeared and disappeared humming a tune, polished his nails with attention, rubbed his shaved face with eau de Cologne, drank his early tea, went out to see his coolies at work; returned, looked through some papers on his desk, read a page or two in a book or sat before his cottage piano leaning back on the stool, his arms extended, fingers on the keys, his body swaying slightly from side to side. When absolutely forced to speak, he gave evasive, vaguely soothing answers out of pure compassion; the same feeling perhaps made him so lavishly hospitable with the aerated drinks that more than once he left himself without soda-water for a whole week. That old man had granted him as much land as he cared to have cleared: it was neither more nor less than a fortune.

Whether it was fortune or seclusion from his kind that Mr Van Wyk sought, he could not have pitched upon a better place. Even the mailboats of the subsidized company calling on the veriest clusters of palm-thatched hovels along the coast steamed past the mouth of Batu Berau river far away in the offing. The contract was old: perhaps in a few years' time, when it had expired, Batu Berau would be included in the service; meantime all Mr Van Dyk's mail was addressed to Malacca, whence his agent sent it across once a month by the *Sofala*. It followed that whenever Massy had run short of money (through taking too many lottery tickets), or got into a difficulty about a skipper, Mr Van Wyk was deprived of his letters and newspapers. In so far he had a personal interest in

the fortunes of the *Sofala*. Though he considered himself a
hermit (and for no passing whim evidently, since he had stood
eight years of it already), he liked to know what went on in the
world.

Handy on the veranda upon a walnut *étagére* (it had
come last year by the *Sofala*—everything came by the *Sofala*)
there lay, piled up under bronze weights, a pile of *The Times*
weekly edition, the large sheets of the *Rotterdam Courant*,
the *Graphic* in its worldwide green wrappers, an illustrated
Dutch publication without a cover, the numbers of a German
magazine with covers of the 'Bismarck malade' colour. There
were also parcels of new music—though the piano (it had
come years ago by the *Sofala)* in the damp atmosphere of the
forests was generally out of tune. It was vexing to be cut off
from everything for sixty days at a stretch sometimes, without
any means of knowing what was the matter. And when the
Sofala reappeared Mr Van Wyk would descend the steps of
the veranda and stroll over the grass plot in front of his house,
down to the waterside, with a frown on his white brow.

'You've been laid up after an accident, I presume.' He
addressed the bridge, but before anybody could answer
Massy was sure to have already scrambled ashore over the rail
and pushed in, squeezing the palms of his hands together,
bowing his sleek head as if gummed all over the top with black
threads and tapes. And he would be so enraged at the
necessity of having to offer such an explanation that his
moaning would be positively pitiful, while all the time he tried
to compose his big lips into a smile.

'No, Mr Van Wyk. You would not believe it. I couldn't
get one of those wretches to take the ship out. Not a single one
of the lazy beasts could be induced, and the law, you know,
Mr Van Wyk . . .'

He moaned at great length apologetically; the words
conspiracy, plot, envy, came out prominently, whined with

greater energy. Mr Van Wyk, examining with a faint grimace his polished fingernails, would say, 'H'm. Very unfortunate', and turn his back on him.

Fastidious, clever, slightly sceptical, accustomed to the best society (he had held a much-envied shore appointment at the Ministry of Marine for a year preceding his retreat from his profession and from Europe), he possessed a latent warmth of feeling and a capacity for sympathy which were concealed by a sort of haughty, arbitrary indifference of manner arising from his early training; and by a something an enemy might have called foppish, in his aspect—like a distorted echo of past elegancies. He managed to keep an almost military discipline amongst the coolies of the estate he had dragged into the light of day out of the tangle and shadows of the jungle; and the white shirt he put on every evening with its stiff glossy front and high collar looked as if he had meant to preserve the decent ceremony of evening dress, but had wound a thick crimson sash above his hips as a concession to the wilderness, once his adversary, now his vanquished companion. Moreover, it was a hygienic precaution. Worn wide open in front, a short jacket of some airy silken stuff floated from his shoulders. His fluffy, fair hair, thin at the top, curled slightly at the sides; a carefully arranged moustache, an ungarnished forehead, the gleam of low patent shoes peeping under the wide bottom of trousers cut straight from the same stuff as the gossamer coat, completed a figure recalling, with its sash, a pirate chief of romance, and at the same time the elegance of a slightly bald dandy indulging, in seclusion, a taste for unorthodox costume.

It was his evening get-up. The proper time for the *Sofala* to arrive at Batu Berau was an hour before sunset, and he looked picturesque, and somehow quite correct, too, walking at the water's edge on the background of grass slope crowned with a low, long bungalow with an immensely steep roof of palm thatch, and clad to the eaves in flowering creepers. While the *Sofala* was being made fast he strolled in the shade of the few trees left near the landing place, waiting till he could go on board. Her white men were not of his kind. The old Sultan (though his wistful invasions were a nuisance) was really much more acceptable to his fastidious taste. But still they were white; the periodical visits of the ship made a break in the well-filled sameness of the day without disturbing his privacy. Moreover, they were necessary from a business point of view; and through a strain of preciseness in his nature he was irritated when she failed to appear at the appointed time.

The cause of the irregularity was too absurd, and Massy, in his opinion, was a contemptible idiot. The first time the *Sofala* reappeared under the new agreement swinging out of the bend below, after he had almost given up all hope of ever seeing her again, he felt so angry that he did not go down at once to the landing place. His servants had come running to him with the news, and he had dragged a chair close against the front rail of the veranda, spread his elbows out, rested his chin on his hands, and went on glaring at her fixedly while she was being made fast opposite his house. He could make out easily all the white faces on board. Who on earth was that kind of patriarch they had got there on the bridge now?

At last he sprang up and walked down the gravel path. It was a fact that the very gravel for his paths had been imported by the *Sofala*. Exasperated out of his quiet superciliousness, without looking at any one right or left, he accosted Massy straightway in so determined a manner that the engineer, taken aback, began to stammer unintelligibly. Nothing could be heard but the words: 'Mr Van Wyk. Indeed, Mr Van Wyk . . . For the future, Mr Van Wyk'—and by the suffusion of blood Massy's vast bilious face acquired an unnatural orange tint, out of which the disconcerted coal-black eyes shone in an extraordinary manner.

'Nonsense. I am tired of this. I wonder you have the impudence to come alongside my jetty as if I had it made for your convenience alone.'

Massy tried to protest earnestly. Mr Van Wyk was very angry. He had a good mind to ask that German firm—those people in Malacca—what was their name?—boats with green funnels. They would be only too glad of the opening to put one of their small steamers on the run. Yes; Schnitzler, Jacob Schnitzler, would in a moment. Yes. He had decided to write without delay.

In his agitation Massy caught up his falling pipe.

'You don't mean it, sir!' he shrieked.

'You shouldn't mismanage your business in this ridiculous manner.'

Mr Van Wyk turned on his heel. The other three whites on the bridge had not stirred during the scene. Massy walked hastily from side to side, puffed out his cheeks, suffocated.

'Stuck-up Dutchman!'

And he moaned out feverishly a long tale of griefs. The efforts he had made for all these years to please that man. This was the return you got for it, heh? Pretty. Write to Schnitzler—let in the green-funnel boats—get an old Hamburg Jew to ruin him. No, really he could laugh . . . He laughed sobbing . . . Ha! ha! ha! And make him carry the letter in his own ship presumably.

He stumbled across a grating and swore. He would not hesitate to fling the Dutchman's correspondence overboard—the whole confounded bundle. He had never, never made any charge for that accommodation. But Captain Whalley, his new partner, would not let him probably; besides, it would be only putting off the evil day. For his own part he would make a hole in the water rather than look on tamely at the green funnels overrunning his trade.

He raved aloud. The China boys hung back with the dishes at the foot of the ladder. He yelled from the bridge down at the deck, 'Aren't we going to have any chow this evening at all?' then turned violently to Captain Whalley, who waited, grave and patient, at the head of the table, smoothing his beard in silence now and then with a forbearing gesture.

'You don't seem to care what happens to me. Don't you see that this affects your interests as much as mine? It's no joking matter.'

He took the foot of the table growling between his teeth.

'Unless you have a few thousands put away somewhere. I haven't.'

Mr Van Wyk dined in his thoroughly lit-up bungalow, putting a point of splendour in the night of his clearing above the dark bank of the river. Afterwards he sat down to his piano, and in a pause he became aware of slow footsteps passing on the path along the front. A plank or two creaked under a heavy tread; he swung half round on the music stool, listening with his fingertips at rest on the keyboard. His little terrier barked violently, backing in from the verandah. A deep voice apologized gravely 'for this intrusion'. He walked out quickly.

At the head of the steps the patriarchal figure, who was the new captain of the *Sofala* apparently (he had seen a round dozen of them, but not one of that sort), towered without advancing. The little dog barked unceasingly, till a flick of Mr Van Wyk's handkerchief made him spring aside into silence. Captain Whalley, opening the matter, was met by a punctiliously polite but determined opposition.

They carried on their discussion standing where they had come face to face. Mr Van Wyk observed his visitor with attention. Then at last, as if forced out of his reserve—

'I am surprised that you should intercede for such a

confounded fool.'

This outbreak was almost complimentary, as if its meaning had been, 'That such a man as you should intercede!' Captain Whalley let it pass by without flinching. One would have thought he had heard nothing. He simply went on to state that he was personally interested in putting things straight between them. Personally . . .

But Mr Van Wyk, really carried away by his disgust with Massy, became very incisive—

'Indeed—if I am to be frank with you—his whole character does not seem to me particularly estimable or trustworthy . . .'

Captain Whalley, always straight, seemed to grow an inch taller and broader, as if the girth of his chest had suddenly expanded under his beard.

'My dear sir, you don't think I came here to discuss a man with whom I am—I am—h'm—closely associated.'

A sort of solemn silence lasted for a moment. He was not used to asking favours, but the importance he attached to this affair had made him willing to try . . . Mr Van Wyk, favourably impressed, and suddenly mollified by a desire to laugh, interrupted—

'That's all right if you make it a personal matter; but you can do no less than sit down and smoke a cigar with me.'

A slight pause, then Captain Whalley stepped forward heavily. As to the regularity of the service, for the future he made himself responsible for it; and his name was Whalley—perhaps to a sailor (he was speaking to a sailor, was he not?) not altogether unfamiliar. There was a lighthouse now, on an island. Maybe Mr Van Wyk himself . . .

'Oh, yes. Oh, indeed.' Mr Van Wyk caught on at once. He indicated a chair. How very interesting. For his own part he had seen some service in the last Acheen War, but had never been so far East. Whalley Island? Of course. Now that was very interesting. What changes his guest must have seen since.

'I can look further back even—on a whole half-century.'

Captain Whalley expanded a bit. The flavour of a good cigar (it was a weakness) had gone straight to his heart, also the civility of that young man. There was something in that accidental contact of which he had been starved in his years of struggle.

The front wall retreating made a square recess furnished like a room. A lamp with a milky glass shade, suspended below the slope of the high roof at the end of a slender brass chain, threw a bright round of light upon a little table bearing an open book and an ivory paperknife. And, in the translucent shadows beyond, other tables could be seen, a number of easy chairs of various shapes, with a great profusion of skin rugs strewn on the teakwood planking all over the veranda. The flowering creepers scented the air. Their foliage clipped out between the uprights made as if several frames of thick, unstirring leaves reflecting the lamplight in a green glow. Through the opening at his elbow Captain Whalley could see the gangway lantern of the *Sofala* burning dim by the shore, the shadowy masses of the town beyond the open lustrous darkness of the river, and, as if hung along the straight edge of the projecting eaves, a narrow black strip of the night sky full of stars—resplendent. The famous cigar in hand he had a moment of complacency.

'A trifle. Somebody must lead the way. I just showed that the thing could be done; but you men brought up to the use of steam cannot conceive the vast importance of my bit of venturesomeness to the Eastern trade of the time. Why, that new route reduced the average time of a southern passage by eleven days for more than half the year. Eleven days! It's on record. But the remarkable thing—speaking to a sailor—I should say was . . .'

He talked well, without egotism, professionally. The powerful voice, produced without effort, filled the bungalow even into the empty rooms with a deep and limpid resonance, seemed to make a stillness outside; and Mr Van Wyk was surprised by the serene quality of its tone, like the perfection of manly gentleness. Nursing one small foot, in a silk sock and a patent leather shoe, on his knee, he was immensely entertained. It was as if nobody could talk like this now, and the over-shadowed eyes, the flowing white beard, the big frame, the serenity, the whole temper of the man, were an amazing survival from the prehistoric times of the world coming up to him out of the sea.

Captain Whalley had been also the pioneer of the early trade in the Gulf of Pe-tchi-li. He even found occasion to mention that he had buried his 'dear wife' there six-and-twenty years ago. Mr Van Wyk, impassive, could not help speculating in his mind swiftly as to the sort of woman that would mate with such a man. Did they make an adventurous and well-matched pair? No. Very possibly she had been small, frail, no doubt very feminine—or most likely commonplace with domestic instincts, utterly insignificant. But Captain Whalley was no garrulous bore, and shaking his head as if to dissipate the momentary gloom that had settled on his handsome old face, he alluded conversationally to Mr Van Wyk's solitude.

Mr Van Wyk affirmed that sometimes he had more company than he wanted. He mentioned smilingly some of the peculiarities of his intercourse with 'my Sultan'. He made his visits in force. Those people damaged his grass plot in front (it was not easy to obtain some approach to a lawn in the tropics), and the other day had broken down some rare bushes he had planted over there. And Captain Whalley remembered immediately that, in 'forty-seven, the then Sultan, 'this man's grandfather', had been notorious as a great protector of the piratical fleets of praus from farther East. They had a safe refuge in the river at Batu Berau. He financed more especially a Balinini chief called Haji Daman. Captain Whalley, nodding significantly his bushy white eyebrows, had very good reason to know something of that. The world had progressed since that time.

Mr Van Wyk demurred with unexpected acrimony. Progressed in what, he wanted to know.

Why, in knowledge of truth, in decency, in justice, in order—in honesty, too, since men harmed each other mostly from ignorance. It was, Captain Whalley concluded quaintly, more pleasant to live in.

Mr Van Wyk whimsically would not admit that Mr Massy, for instance, was more pleasant naturally than the Balinini pirates.

The river had not gained much by the change. They were in their way every bit as honest. Massy was less ferocious than Haji Daman no doubt, but . . .

'And what about you, my good sir?' Captain Whalley laughed a deep soft laugh. '*You* are an improvement, surely.'

He continued in a vein of pleasantry. A good cigar was better than a knock on the head—the sort of welcome he would have found on this river forty or fifty years ago. Then leaning forward slightly, he became earnestly serious. It seems as if, outside their own sea-gipsy tribes, these rovers had hated all mankind with an incomprehensible, bloodthirsty hatred. Meantime their depredations had been stopped, and what was the consequence? The new generation was orderly, peaceable, settled in prosperous villages. He could speak from personal knowledge. And even the few survivors of that time—old men now—had changed so much, that it would have been unkind to remember against them that they had ever slit a throat in their lives. He had one especially in his mind's eye: a dignified, venerable headman of a certain large coast village about sixty miles sou'west of Tampasuk. It did one's heart good to see him—to hear that man speak. He might have been a ferocious savage once. What men wanted was to be checked by superior intelligence, by superior knowledge, by superior force too—yes, by force held in trust from God and sanctified by its use in accordance with His declared will. Captain Whalley believed a disposition for good existed in every man, even if the world were not a very happy place as a whole. In the wisdom of men he had not so much confidence.

The disposition had to be helped up pretty sharply sometimes, he admitted. They might be silly, wrong-headed, unhappy; but naturally evil—no. There was at bottom a complete harmlessness at least . . .

'Is there?' Mr Van Wyk snapped acrimoniously. Captain Whalley laughed at the interjection, in the good humour of large, tolerating certitude. He could look back at half a century, he pointed out. The smoke oozed placidly through the white hairs hiding his kindly lips.

'At all events,' he resumed after a pause, 'I am glad that they've had no time to do you much harm as yet.'

This allusion to his comparative youthfulness did not offend Mr Van Wyk, who got up and wriggled his shoulders with an enigmatic half-smile. They walked out together amicably into the starry night towards the riverside. Their footsteps resounded unequally on the dark path. At the shore end of the gangway the lantern, hung low to the handrail, threw a vivid light on the white legs and the big black feet of Mr Massy waiting about anxiously. From the waist upwards he remained shadowy, with a row of buttons gleaming up to the vague outline of his chin.

'You may thank Captain Whalley for this,' Mr Van Wyk said, curtly, to him before turning away.

The lamps on the veranda flung three long squares of

light between the uprights far over the grass. A bat flitted before his face like a circling flake of velvety blackness. Along the jasmine hedge the night air seemed heavy with the fall of perfumed dew; flowerbeds bordered the path; the clipped bushes uprose in dark, rounded clumps here and there before the house; the dense foliage of creepers filtered the sheen of the lamplight within in a soft glow all along the front; and everything near and far stood still in a great immobility, in a great sweetness.

Mr Van Wyk (a few years before he had had occasion to imagine himself treated more badly than anybody alive had ever been by a woman) felt for Captain Whalley's optimistic views the disdain of a man who had once been credulous himself. His disgust with the world (the woman for a time had filled it for him completely) had taken the form of activity in retirement, because, though capable of great depth of feeling, he was energetic and essentially practical. But there was in that uncommon old sailor, drifting on the outskirts of his busy solitude, something that fascinated his scepticism. His very simplicity (amusing enough) was like a delicate refinement of an upright character. The striking dignity of manner could be nothing else, in a man reduced to such a humble position, but the expression of something essentially noble in the character. With all his trust in mankind he was no fool; the serenity of his temper at the end of so many years, since it could not obviously have been appeased by success, wore an air of profound wisdom. Mr Van Wyk was amused at it sometimes. Even the very physical traits of the old captain of the *Sofala,* his powerful frame, his reposeful mien, his intelligent, handsome face, the big limbs, the benign courtesy, the touch of rugged severity in the shaggy eyebrows, made up a seductive personality. Mr Van Wyk disliked littleness of every kind but there was nothing small about that man, and in the exemplary regularity of many trips an intimacy had grown up between them, a warm feeling at bottom under a kindly stateliness of forms agreeable to his fastidiousness.

They kept their respective opinions on all worldly matters. His other convictions Captain Whalley never intruded. The difference of their ages was like another bond between them. Once, when twitted with the uncharitableness of his youth, Mr Van Wyk, running his eye over the vast proportions of his interlocutor, retorted in friendly banter—

'Oh. You'll come to my way of thinking yet. You'll have plenty of time. Don't call yourself old: you look good for a round hundred.'

But he could not help his stinging incisiveness, and though moderating it by an almost affectionate smile, he added—

'And by then you will probably consent to die from sheer disgust.'

Captain Whalley, smiling too, shook his head. 'God forbid!'

He thought that perhaps on the whole he deserved something better than to die in such sentiments. The time of course would have to come, and he trusted to his Maker to provide a manner of going out of which he need not be ashamed. For the rest he hoped he would live to a hundred if need be; other men had been known; it would be no miracle. He expected no miracles.

The pronounced, argumentative tone caused Mr Van Wyk to raise his head and look at him steadily. Captain Whalley was gazing fixedly with a rapt expression, as though he had seen his Creator's favourable decree written in mysterious characters on the wall. He kept perfectly motionless for a few seconds, then got his vast bulk on to his feet so impetuously that Mr Van Wyk was startled.

He struck first a heavy blow on his inflated chest; and, throwing out horizontally a big arm that remained steady, extended in the air like the limb of a tree on a windless day

'Not a pain or an ache there. Can you see this shake in the least?'

His voice was low, in an awesome, confident contrast with the headlong emphasis of his movements. He sat down abruptly.

'This isn't to boast of it, you know. I am nothing,' he said in his effortless strong voice that seemed to come out as naturally as a river flows. He picked up the stump of the cigar he had laid aside, and added peacefully, with a slight nod, 'As it happens, my life is necessary; it isn't my own, it isn't—God knows.'

He did not say much for the rest of the evening, but several times Mr Van Wyk detected a faint smile of assurance flitting under the heavy moustache.

Later on Captain Whalley would now and then consent to dine 'at the house'. He could even be induced to drink a glass of wine. 'Don't think I'm afraid of it, my good sir,' he explained. 'There was a very good reason why I should give it up.'

On another occasion, leaning back at ease, he remarked, 'You have treated me most—most humanely, my dear Mr Van Wyk, from the very first.'

'You'll admit there was some merit,' Mr Van Wyk hinted, slily. 'An associate of that excellent Massy. . . . Well, well, my dear captain, I won't say a word against him.'

'It would be no use your saying anything against him,' Captain Whalley affirmed a little moodily. 'As I've told you before, my life—my work, is necessary, not for myself alone. I can't choose . . .' He paused, turned the glass before him right round.

'I have an only child—a daughter.'

The ample downward sweep of his arm over the table seemed to suggest a small girl at a vast distance. 'I hope to see her once more before I die. Meantime it's enough to know that she has me sound and solid, thank God. You can't understand how one feels. Bone of my bone, flesh of my flesh; the very image of my poor wife. Well, she . . .'

Again he paused, then pronounced stoically the words, 'She has a hard struggle.'

And his head fell on his breast, his eyebrows remained knitted, as by an effort of meditation. But generally his mind seemed steeped in the serenity of boundless trust in a higher power. Mr Van Wyk wondered sometimes how much of it was due to the splendid vitality of the man, to the bodily vigour which seems to impart something of its force to the soul. But he had learned to like him very much.

XIII

THIS was the reason why Mr Sterne's confidential communication, delivered hurriedly on the shore alongside the dark silent ship, had disturbed his equanimity. It was the most incomprehensible and unexpected thing that could happen; and the perturbation of his spirit was so great that, forgetting all about his letters, he ran rapidly up the bridge ladder.

The portable table was being put together for dinner to the left of the wheel by two pig-tailed 'boys', who as usual snarled at each other over the job, while another, a doleful, burly, very yellow Chinaman, resembling Mr Massy, waited apathetically with the cloth over his arm and a pile of thick dinner plates against his chest. A common cabin lamp with its globe missing, brought up from below, had been hooked to the wooden framework of the awning; the side screens had been lowered all round; Captain Whalley, filling the depths of the wicker chair, seemed to sit benumbed in a canvas tent crudely lighted, and used for the storing of nautical objects; a shabby steering wheel, a battered brass binnacle on a stout mahogany stand, two dingy lifebuoys, an old cork fender lying in a corner, dilapidated deck lockers with loops of tin rope instead of door handles.

He shook off the appearance of numbness to return Mr Van Wyk's unusually brisk greeting, but relapsed directly afterwards. To accept a pressing invitation to dinner 'up at the house' cost him another very visible physical effort. Mr Van Wyk, perplexed, folded his arms, and leaning back against the rail, with his little, black, shiny feet well out, examined him covertly.

'I've noticed of late that you are not quite yourself, old friend.'

He put an affectionate gentleness into the last two words. The real intimacy of their intercourse had never been so vividly expressed before.

'Tut, tut, tut!'

The wicker chair creaked heavily.

'Irritable,' commented Mr Van Wyk to himself; and aloud, 'I'll expect to see you in half an hour, then,' he said, negligently, moving off.

'In half an hour,' Captain Whalley's rigid silvery head repeated behind him as if out of a trance.

Amidships, below, two voices, close against the engine room, could be heard answering each other—one angry and slow; the other alert.

'I tell you the beast has locked himself in to get drunk.'

'Can't help it now, Mr Massy. After all, a man has a right to shut himself up in his cabin in his time.'

'Not to get drunk.'

'I heard him swear that the worry with the boilers was enough to drive any man to drink,' Sterne said, maliciously.

Massy hissed out something about bursting the door in. Mr Van Wyk, to avoid them, crossed in the dark to the other side of the deserted deck. The planking of the little wharf rattled faintly under his hasty feet.

'Mr Van Wyk! Mr Van Wyk!'

He walked on; somebody was running on the path. 'You've forgotten to get your mail.'

Sterne, holding a bundle of papers in his hand, caught up with him.

'Oh, thanks.'

But as the other continued at his elbow, Mr Van Wyk stopped short. The overhanging eaves, descending low upon the lighted front of the bungalow, threw their black straight-edged shadow into the great body of the night on that side. Everything was very still. A tinkle of cutlery and a slight jingle of glasses were heard. Mr Van Wyk's servants were laying the table for two on the verandah.

'I am afraid you give me no credit whatever for my good intentions in the matter I've spoken to you about,' said Sterne.

'I simply don't understand you.'

'Captain Whalley is a very audacious man, but he will understand that his game is up. That's all that anybody need ever know of it from me. Believe me, I am very considerate in this, but duty is duty. I don't want to make a fuss. All I ask you, as his friend, is to tell him from me that the game's up. That will be sufficient.'

Mr Van Wyk felt a loathsome dismay at this queer privilege of friendship. He would not demean himself by asking for the slightest explanation; to drive the other away with contumely he did not think prudent—as yet, at any rate. So much assurance staggered him. Who could tell what there could be in it, he thought. His regard for Captain Whalley had the tenacity of a disinterested sentiment, and his practical instinct coming to his aid, he concealed his scorn.

'I gather, then, that this is something grave.'

'Very grave,' Sterne assented, solemnly, delighted at

having produced an effect at last. He was ready to add some effusive protestations of regret at the unavoidable necessity, but Mr Van Wyk cut him short—very civilly, however.

Once on the veranda Mr Van Wyk put his hands in his pockets, and, straddling his legs, stared down at a black panther skin lying on the floor before a rocking chair. 'It looks as if the fellow had not the pluck to play his own precious game openly,' he thought.

This was true enough. In the face of Massy's last rebuff Sterne dared not declare his knowledge. His object was simply to get charge of the steamer and keep it for some time. Massy would never forgive him for forcing himself on; but if Captain Whalley left the ship of his own accord, the command would devolve upon him for the rest of the trip; so he hit upon the brilliant idea of scaring the old man away. A vague menace, a mere hint, would be enough in such a brazen case; and, with a strange admixture of compassion, he thought that Batu Berau was a very good place for throwing up the sponge. The skipper could go ashore quietly and stay with that Dutchman of his. Weren't these two as thick as thieves together? And on reflection he seemed to see that there was a way to work the whole thing through that great friend of the old man's. This was another brilliant idea. He had an inborn preference for circuitous methods. In this particular case he desired to remain in the background as much as possible, to avoid exasperating Massy needlessly. No fuss! Let it all happen naturally.

Mr Van Wyk all through the dinner was conscious of a sense of isolation that invades sometimes the closeness of human intercourse. Captain Whalley failed lamentably and obviously in his attempts to eat something. He seemed overcome by a strange absentmindedness. His hand would hover irresolutely, as if left without guidance by a preoccupied mind. Mr Van Wyk had heard him coming up from a long way off in the profound stillness of the riverside, and had noticed the irresolute character of the footfalls. The toe of his boot had struck the bottom stair as though he had come along mooning with his head in the air right up to the steps of the veranda. Had the captain of the *Sofala* been another sort of man he would have suspected the work of age there. But one glance at him was enough. Time—after, indeed, marking him for its own—had given him up to his usefulness, in which his simple faith would see a proof of Divine mercy. 'How could I contrive to warn him?' Mr Van Wyk wondered, as if Captain Whalley had been miles and miles away, out of sight and earshot of all evil. He was sickened by an immense disgust of Sterne. To even mention his threat to a man like Whalley would be positively indecent. There was something more vile and insulting in its hint than in a definite charge of crime—the debasing taint of blackmailing. 'What could any one bring against him?' he asked himself. This was a limpid personality. 'And for what object?' The Power that man trusted had thought fit to leave him nothing on earth that envy could lay hold of, except a bare crust of bread.

'Won't you try some of this?' he asked, pushing a dish slightly. Suddenly it occurred to Mr Van Wyk that Sterne might possibly be coveting the command of the *Sofala*. His cynicism was quite startled by what looked like a proof that no man may count himself safe from his kind unless in the very abyss of misery. An intrigue of that sort was hardly worth troubling about, he judged; but still, with such a fool as Massy to deal with, Whalley ought to and must be warned.

At this moment Captain Whalley, bolt upright, the deep cavities of the eyes overhung by a bushy frown, and one large brown hand resting on each side of his empty plate, spoke across the tablecloth abruptly—

'Mr Van Wyk, you've always treated me with the most

humane consideration.'

'My dear captain, you make too much of the simple fact that I am not a savage.' Mr Van Wyk, utterly revolted by the thought of Sterne's obscure attempt, raised his voice incisively, as if the mate had been hiding somewhere within earshot. 'Any consideration I have been able to show was no more than the rightful due of a character I've learned to regard by this time with an esteem that nothing can shake.'

A slight ring of glass made him lift his eyes from the slice of pineapple he was cutting into small pieces on his plate. In changing his position Captain Whalley had contrived to upset an empty tumbler.

Without looking that way, leaning sideways on his elbow, his other hand shading his brow, he groped shadily for it, then desisted. Van Wyk stared blankly, as if something momentous had happened all at once. He did not know why he should feel so startled; but he forgot Sterne utterly for the moment.

'Why, what's the matter?'

And Captain Whalley, his face half-averted, in a deadened, agitated voice, muttered—

'Esteem!'

'And I may add something more,' Mr Van Wyk, very steady-eyed, pronounced slowly.

'Hold! Enough!' Captain Whalley did not change his attitude or raise his voice. 'Say no more! I can make you no return. I am too poor even for that now. Your esteem is worth having. You are not a man that would stoop to deceive the poorest sort of devil on earth, or make a ship unseaworthy every time he takes her to sea.'

Mr Van Wyk, leaning forward, his face gone pink all over, with the starched table napkin over his knees, was inclined to mistrust his senses, his power of comprehension, the sanity of his guest.

'Where? Why? In the name of God!—What's this? What ship? I don't understand who . . .'

'Then, in the name of God, it is I! A ship's unseaworthy when her captain can't see. I am going blind.'

Mr Van Wyk made a slight movement, and sat very still afterwards for a few seconds; then, with the thought of Sterne's 'The game's up', he ducked under the table to pick up the napkin which had slipped off his knees. This was the game that was up. And at the same time the muffled voice of Captain Whalley passed over him

'I've deceived them all. Nobody knows.'

He emerged flushed to the eyes. Captain Whalley, motionless under the full blaze of the lamp, shaded his face with his hand.

'And you had that courage?'

'Call it by what name you like. But you are a humane man—a-a-gentleman, Mr Van Wyk. You may have asked me what I had done with my conscience.'

He seemed to muse, profoundly silent, very still in his mournful pose.

'I began to tamper with it in my pride. You begin to see a lot of things when you are going blind. I could not be frank with an old chum even. I was not frank with Massy—no, not altogether. I knew he took me for a wealthy sailor fool, and I let him. I wanted to keep up my importance—because there was poor Ivy away there—my daughter. What did I want to trade on his misery for? I did trade on it—for her. And now, what mercy could I expect from him? He would trade on mine if he knew it. He would hunt the old fraud out, and stick to the money for a year. Ivy's money. And I haven't kept a penny for myself. How am I going to live for a year. A year! In a year there will be no sun in the sky for her father.'

His deep voice came out, awfully veiled, as though he had been overwhelmed by the earth of a landslide and talking of the thoughts that haunt the dead in their graves. A cold shudder ran down Mr Van Wyk's back.

'And how long is it since you have . . . ?' he began.

'It was a long time before I could bring myself to believe in this-this visitation.' Captain Whalley spoke with gloomy patience from under his hand.

He had not thought he had deserved it. He had begun by deceiving himself from day to day, from week to week. He had the Serang at hand there—an old servant. It came on gradually, and when he could no longer deceive himself . . .

His voice died out.almost.

'Rather than give her up I set myself to deceive you all.'

'It's incredible,' whispered Mr Van Wyk. Captain Whalley's appalling murmur flowed on.

'Not even the sign of God's anger could make me forget her. How could I forsake my child, feeling my vigour all the time—the blood warm within me? Warm as yours. It seems to me that, like the blinded Samson, I would find the strength to shake down a temple upon my head. She's a struggling woman—my own child that we used to pray over together, my poor wife and I. Do you remember that day I as well as told you that I believed God would let me live to a hundred for her sake? What sin is there in loving your child? Do you see it? I was ready for her sake to live for ever. I half believed I would. I've been praying for death since. Ha! Presumptuous man—you wanted to live . . .'

A tremendous, shuddering upheaval of that big frame, shaken by a gasping sob, set the glasses jingling all over the table, seemed to make the whole house tremble to the roof-tree. And Mr Van Wyk, whose feeling of outraged love had been translated into a form of struggle with nature, understood very well that, for that man whose whole life had been conditioned by action, there could exist no other expression for all the emotions; that, to voluntarily cease venturing, doing, enduring, for his child's sake, would have been exactly like plucking his warm love for her out of his living heart. Something too monstrous, too impossible, even to conceive.

Captain Whalley had not changed his attitude, that seemed to express something of shame, sorrow, and defiance.

'I have even deceived you. If it had not been for that word "esteem". These are not the words for me. I would have lied to you. Haven't I lied to you? Weren't you going to trust your property on board this very trip?'

'I have a floating yearly policy,' Mr Van Wyk said almost unwittingly, and was amazed at the sudden cooping up of a commercial detail.

'The ship is unseaworthy, I tell you. The policy would be invalid if it were known . . .'

'We shall share the guilt, then.'

'Nothing could make mine less,' said Captain Whalley.

He had not dared to consult a doctor; the man would have perhaps asked who he was, what he was doing; Massy might have heard something. He had lived on without any help, human or divine. The very prayers stuck in his throat. What was there to pray for? And death seemed as far as ever. Once he got into his cabin he dared not come out again; when he sat down he dared not get up; he dared not raise his eyes to anybody's face, he felt reluctant to look upon the sea or up to the sky. The world was fading before his great fear of giving himself away. The old ship was his last friend; he was not afraid of her; he knew every inch of her deck; but at her too he hardly dared to look, for fear of finding he could see less than the day before. A great incertitude enveloped him. The horizon was gone; the sky mingled darkly with the sea. Who was this figure standing over yonder? What was this thing lying down there? And a frightful doubt of the reality of what He could see made even the remnant of sight that remained to him an added torment, a pitfall always open for his miserable pretence. He was afraid to stumble inexcusably over something—to say a fatal Yes or No to a question. The hand of God was upon him, but it could not tear him away from his child. And, as if in a nightmare of humiliation, every featureless man seemed an enemy.

He let his hand fall heavily on the table. Mr Van Wyk, arms down, chin on breast, with a gleam of white teeth pressing on the lower lip, meditated on Sterne's 'The game's up'.

'The Serang of course does not know.'

'Nobody,' said Captain Whalley, with assurance.

'Ah, yes. Nobody. Very well. Can you keep it up to the end of the trip? That is the last under the agreement with Massy.'

Captain Whalley got up and stood erect, very stately, with the great white beard lying like a silver breastplate over the awful secret of his heart. Yes; that was the only hope there was for him of ever seeing her again, of securing the money, the last he could do for her, before he crept away somewhere—useless, a burden, a reproach to himself. His voice faltered.

'Think of it! Never see her any more: the only human being besides myself now on earth that can remember my wife. She's just like her mother. Lucky the poor woman is where there are no tears shed over those they loved on earth and that remain to pray not to be led into temptation—because, I suppose, the blessed know the secret of grace in God's dealings with His created children.'

He swayed a little, said with austere dignity—

'I don't. I know only the child He has given me.' And he began to walk. Mr Van Wyk, jumping up, saw the full meaning of the rigid head, the hesitating feet, the vaguely extended hand. His heart was beating fast; he moved a chair aside, and instinctively advanced as if to offer his arm. But Captain Whalley passed him by, making for the stairs quite straight.

'He could not see me at all out of his line,' Van Wyk thought, with a sort of awe. Then going to the head of the stairs, he asked a little tremulously—

'What is it like—like a mist—like . . .' Captain Whalley, halfway down, stopped, and turned round undismayed to answer:

'It is as if the light were ebbing out of the world. Have you ever watched the ebbing sea on an open stretch of sands withdrawing farther and farther away from you? It is like this—only there will be no flood to follow. Never. It is as if the sun were growing smaller, the stars going out one by one. There can't be many left that I can see by this. But I haven't had the courage to look of late . . .' He must have been able to make out Mr Van Wyk, because he checked him by an authoritative gesture and a stoical—

'I can get about alone yet.'

It was as if he had taken his line, and would accept no help from men, after having been cast out, like a presumptuous Titan from his heaven. Mr Van Wyk, arrested, seemed to count the footsteps right out of earshot. He walked between the tables, tapping smartly with his heels, took up a paperknife, dropped it after a vague glance along the blade; then happening upon the piano, struck a few chords, standing up before the keyboard with an attentive poise of the head like a piano-tuner; closing it, he pivoted on his heels brusquely, avoided the little terrier sleeping trustfully on crossed forepaws, came upon the stairs next, and, as though he had lost his balance on the top step, ran down headlong out of the house. His servants, beginning to clear the table, heard him mutter to himself (evil words no doubt) down there, and then after a pause go away with a strolling gait in the direction of the wharf.

The bulwarks of the *Sofala* lying alongside the bank made a low, black wall on the undulating contour of the shore. Two masts and a funnel uprose from behind it with a great rake, as if about to fall; a solid, square elevation in the middle bore the ghostly shapes of white boats, the curves of davits, lines of rail and stanchions, all confused and mingling darkly everywhere; but low down, amidships, a single lighted port stared out on the night, perfectly round, like a small, full moon, whose yellow beam caught a patch of wet mud, the edge of trodden grass, two turns of heavy cable wound round the foot of a thick wooden post in the ground.

Mr Van Wyk, peering alongside, heard a muzzy boastful voice apparently jeering at a person called Prendergast. It mouthed abuse thickly, choked; then pronounced very distinctly the word 'Murphy', and chuckled. Glass tinkled tremulously. All these sounds came from the lighted port. Mr Van Wyk hesitated, stooped; it was impossible to look through unless he went down into the mud.

'Sterne—of course. Look at him blink. Look at him! Sterne, Whalley, Massy. Massy, Whalley, Sterne. But Massy's the best. You can't come over him. He would just love to see you starve.'

Mr Van Wyk moved away, made out farther forward a shadowy head stuck out from under the awnings as if on the watch, and spoke quietly in Malay, 'Is the mate asleep?'

'No. Here, at your service.'

In a moment Sterne appeared, walking as noiselessly as a cat on the wharf.

'It's so jolly dark, and I had no idea you would be down tonight.'

'What's this horrible raving?' asked Mr Van Wyk, as if to explain the cause of a shudder that ran over him audibly.

'Jack's broken out on a drunk. That's our second. It's his

233

way. He will be right enough by tomorrow afternoon, only Mr Massy will keep on worrying up and down the deck. We had better get away.'

He muttered suggestively of a talk 'up at the house'. He had long desired to effect an entrance there, but Mr Van Wyk nonchalantly demurred; it would not, he feared, be quite prudent perhaps; and the opaque black shadow under one of the two big trees left at the landing place swallowed them up, impenetrably dense by the side of the wide river, that seemed to spin into threads of glitter the light of a few big stars dropped here and there upon its outspread and flowing stillness.

'The situation is grave beyond doubt,' Mr Van Wyk said. Ghost-like in their white clothes they could not distinguish each other's features, and their feet made no sound on the soft earth. A sort of purring was heard. Mr Sterne felt gratified by such a beginning.

'I thought, Mr Van Wyk, a gentleman of your sort would see at once how awkwardly I was situated.'

'Yes, very. Obviously his health is bad. Perhaps he's breaking up. I see, and he himself is well aware—I assume I am speaking to a man of sense—he is well aware that his legs are giving out.'

'His legs—ah!' Mr Sterne was disconcerted, and then turned sulky. 'You may call it his legs if you like; what I want to know is whether he intends to clear out quietly. That's a good one, too! His legs! Pooh!'

'Why, yes. Only look at the way he walks,' Van Wyk took him up in a perfectly cool and undoubting tone. 'The question, however, is whether your sense of duty does not carry you too far from your true interest. After all, I, too, could do something to serve you. You know who I am.'

'Everybody along the Straits has heard of you, sir.'

Mr Van Wyk presumed that this meant something

favourable. Sterne had a soft laugh at this pleasantry. He should think so! To the opening statement, that the partnership agreement was to expire at the end of this very trip, he gave an attentive assent. He was aware. One heard of nothing else on board all the blessed day long. As to Massy, it was no secret that he was in a jolly deep hole with these worn-out boilers. He would have to borrow somewhere a couple of hundred first of all to pay off the captain; and then he would have to raise money on mortgage upon the ship for the new boilers—that is, if he could find a lender at all. At best it meant loss of time, a break in the trade, short earnings for the year—and there was always the danger of having his connection filched away from him by the Germans. It was whispered about that he had already tried two firms. Neither would have anything to do with him. Ship too old, and the man too well known in the place . . . Mr Sterne's final rapid winking remained buried in the deep darkness sibilating with his whispers.

· 'Supposing, then, he got the loan,' Mr Van Wyk resumed in a deliberate undertone, 'on your own showing he's more than likely to get a mortgagee's man thrust upon him as captain. For my part, I know that I would make that very stipulation myself if I had to find the money. And as a matter of fact I am thinking of doing so. It would be worth my while in many ways. Do you see how this would bear on the case under discussion?'

'Thank you, sir. I am sure you couldn't get anybody that would care more for your interests.'

'Well, it suits my interest that Captain Whalley should finish his time. I shall probably take a passage with you down the Straits. If that can be done, I'll be on the spot when all these changes take place, and in a position to look after *your* interests.'

'Mr Van Wyk, I want nothing better. I am sure I am

infinitely . . .'

'I take it, then, that this may be done without any trouble.'

'Well, sir, what risk there is can't be helped; but (speaking to you as my employer now) the thing is more safe than it looks. If anybody had told me of it I wouldn't have believed it, but I have been looking on myself. That old Serang has been trained up to the game. There's nothing the matter with his—his limbs, sir. He's got used to do things on his own in a remarkable way. And let me tell you, sir, that Captain Whalley, poor man, is by no means useless. Fact. Let me explain to you, sir. He stiffens up that old monkey of a Malay, who knows well enough what to do. Why, he must have kept captain's watches in all sorts of country ships off and on for the last five-and-twenty years. These natives, sir, as long as they have a white man close at the back, will go on doing the right thing most surprisingly well—even if left quite to themselves. Only the white man must be of the sort to put starch into them, and the captain is just the one for that. Why, sir, he has drilled him so well that now he needs hardly speak at all. I have seen that little wrinkled ape made to take the ship out of Pangu Bay on a blowy morning and on all through the islands; take her out first-rate, sir, dodging under the old man's elbow, and in such quiet style that you could not have told for the life of you which of the two was doing the work up there. That's where our poor friend would be still of use to the ship even if—if—he could no longer lift a foot, sir. Providing the Serang does not know that there's anything wrong.'

'He doesn't.'

'Naturally not. Quite beyond his apprehension. They aren't capable of finding out anything about us, sir.'

'You seem to be a shrewd man,' said Mr Van Wyk in a choked mutter, as though he were feeling sick.

'You'll find me a good enough servant, sir.'

Mr Sterne hoped now for a handshake at least, but unexpectedly with a 'What's this? Better not to be seen together', Mr Van Wyk's white shape wavered, and instantly seemed to melt away in the black air under the roof of boughs. The mate was startled. Yes. There was that faint thumping clatter.

He stole out silently from under the shade. The lighted porthole shone from afar. His head swam with the intoxication of sudden success. What a thing it was to have a gentleman to deal with! He crept aboard, and there was something weird in the shadowy stretch of empty decks, echoing with shouts and blows proceeding from a darker part amidships. Mr Massy was raging before the door of the berth; the drunken voice within flowed on undisturbed in the violent racket of kicks.

'Shut up! Put your light out and turn in, you confounded swilling pig—you! D'you hear me, you beast?'

The kicking stopped, and in the pause the muzzy oracular voice announced from within—

'Ah! Massy, now—that's another thing. Massy's deep.'

'Who's that aft there? You, Sterne? He'll drink himself into a fit of horrors.' The chief engineer appeared vague and big at the corner of the engine room skylight.

'He will be good enough for duty tomorrow. I would let him be, Mr Massy.'

Sterne slipped away into his berth, and at once had to sit down. His head swam with exultation. He got into his bunk as if in a dream. A feeling of profound peace, of pacific joy, came over him. On deck all was quiet.

Mr Massy, with his ear against the door of Jack's cabin, listened critically to a deep, stertorous breathing within. This was a dead-drunk sleep. The bout was over: tranquillized on that score, he too went in, and with slow wriggles got out of his old tweed jacket. It was a garment with many pockets, which he used to put on at odd times of the day, being subject to sudden chilly fits, and when he felt it warmed he would take it off and hang it about anywhere all over the ship. It would be seen swinging on belaying pins, thrown over the heads of winches, suspended on people's very door handles for that matter. Was he not the owner? But his favourite place was a hook on a wooden awning stanchion on the bridge, almost against the binnacle. He had even in the early days more than one tussle on that point with Captain Whalley, who desired the bridge to be kept tidy. He had been overawed then. Of late, though, he had been able to defy his partner with impunity. Captain Whalley never seemed to notice anything now. As to the Malays, in their awe of that scowling man not one of the crew would dream of laying a hand on the thing, no matter where or what it swung from.

With an unexpectedness which made Mr Massy jump and drop the coat at his feet, there came from the next berth the crash and thud of a headlong, jingling, clattering fall. The faithful Jack must have dropped to sleep suddenly as he sat at his revels, and now had gone over chair and all, breaking, as it seemed by the sound, every single glass and bottle in the place. After the terrific smash all was still for a time in there, as though he had killed himself on the spot. Mr Massy held his breath. At last a sleepy, uneasy groaning sigh was exhaled slowly on the other side of the bulkhead.

'I hope to goodness he's too drunk to wake up now,' muttered Mr Massy.

The sound of a softly knowing laugh nearly drove him to despair. He swore violently under his breath. The fool would keep him awake all night now for certain. He cursed his luck. He wanted to forget his maddening troubles in sleep sometimes. He could detect no movements. Without apparently making the slightest attempt to get up, Jack went on sniggering to himself where he lay; then began to speak, where he had left off as it were—

'Massy! I love the dirty rascal. He would like to see his poor old Jack starve—but just you look where he has climbed to . . .' He hiccupped in a superior, leisurely manner . . . 'Ship-owning it with the best. A lottery ticket you want. Ha! ha! I will give you lottery tickets, my boy. Let the old ship sink and the old chum starve—that's right. He don't go wrong—Massy don't. Not he. He's a genius—that man is. That's the way to win your money. Ship and chum must go.'

'The silly fool has taken it to heart,' muttered Massy to himself. And, listening with a softened expression of face for any slight sign of returning drowsiness, he was discouraged profoundly by a burst of laughter full of joyful irony.

'Would like to see her at the bottom of the sea! Oh, you clever, clever devil! Wish her sunk, eh? I should think you would, my boy; the damned old thing and all your troubles with her. Rake in the insurance money—turn your back on your old chum—all's well—gentleman again.'

A grim stillness had come over Massy's face. Only his big black eyes rolled uneasily. The raving fool. And yet it was all true. Yes. Lottery tickets, too. All true. What? Beginning again? He wished he wouldn't . . .

But it was even so. The imaginative drunkard on the other side of the bulkhead shook off the death-like stillness that after his last words had fallen on the dark ship moored to a silent shore.

'Don't you dare to say anything against George Massy, Esquire. When he's tired of waiting he will do away with her. Look out! Down she goes—chum and all. He'll know how to . . .'

The voice hesitated, weary, dreamy, lost, as if dying away in a vast open space.

'. . . Find a trick that will work. He's up to it—never fear . . .'

239

He must have been very drunk, for at last the heavy sleep gripped him with the suddenness of a magic spell, and the last word lengthened itself into an interminable, noisy, indrawn snore. And then even the snoring stopped, and all was still.

But it seemed as though Mr Massy had suddenly come to doubt the efficacy of sleep as against a man's troubles; or perhaps he had found the relief he needed in the stillness of a calm contemplation that may contain the vivid thoughts of wealth, of a stroke of luck of long idleness, and may bring before you the imagined form of every desire; for, turning about and throwing his arms over the edge of his bunk, he stood there with his feet on his favourite old coat, looking out through the round port into the night over the river. Sometimes a breath of wind would enter and touch his face, a cool breath charged with the damp, fresh feel from a vast body of water. A glimmer here and there was all he could see of it; and once he might after all suppose he had dozed off, since there appeared before his vision, unexpectedly and connected with no dream, a row of flaming and gigantic figures—three nought seven one two—making up a number such as you may see on a lottery ticket. And then all at once the port was no longer black: it was pearly grey, framing a shore crowded with houses, thatched roof beyond thatched roof, walls of mats and bamboo, gables of carved teak timber. Rows of dwellings raised on a forest of piles lined the steely bank of the river, brimful and still, with the tide on the turn. This was Batu Berau—and the day had come.

Mr Massy shook himself, put on the tweed coat, and, shivering nervously as if from some great shock, made a note of the number. A fortunate, rare hint that. Yes; but to pursue fortune one wanted money—ready cash.

Then he went out and prepared to descend into the engine room. Several small jobs had to be seen to, and Jack was lying dead drunk on the floor of his cabin, with the door locked at that. His gorge rose at the thought of work. Ay! But if you wanted to do nothing you had to get first a good bit of money. A ship won't save you. True, all true. He was tired of waiting for some chance that would rid him at last of that ship that had turned out a curse on his life.

XIV

THE deep, interminable hoot of the steam whistle had, in its grave, vibrating note, something intolerable which sent a slight shudder down Mr Van Wyk's back. It was the early afternoon; the *Sofala* was leaving Batu Berau for Pangu, the next place of call. She swung in the stream, scantily attended by a few canoes, and, gliding on the broad river, became lost to view from the Van Wyk bungalow.

Its owner had not gone this time to see her off. Generally he came down to the wharf, exchanged a few words with the bridge while she cast off, and waved his hand to Captain Whalley at the last moment. This day he did not even go as far as the balustrade of the veranda. 'He couldn't see me if I did,' he said to himself. 'I wonder whether he can make out the house at all.' And this thought somehow made him feel more alone than he had ever felt for all these years. What was it? Six or seven? Seven. A long time.

He sat on the veranda with a closed book on his knee, and, as it were, looked out upon his solitude, as if the fact of Captain Whalley's blindness had opened his eyes to his own. There were many sorts of heartaches and troubles, and there was no place where they could not find a man out. And he felt ashamed, as though he had for six years behaved like a peevish boy.

His thought followed the *Sofala* on her way. On the spur of the moment he had acted impulsively, turning to the thing most pressing. And what else could he have done? Later on he should see. It seemed necessary that he should come out into the world, for a time at least. He had money—something could be arranged; he would grudge no time, no trouble, no loss of his solitude. It weighed on him now—and Captain Whalley appeared to him as he had sat shading his eyes, as if, being deceived in the trust of his faith, he were beyond all the good and evil that can be wrought by the hands of men.

Mr Van Wyk's thoughts followed the *Sofala* down the river, winding about through the belt of the coast forest, between the buttressed shafts of the big trees, through the mangrove strip, and over the bar. The ship crossed it easily in broad daylight, piloted, as it happened, by Mr Sterne, who took the watch from four to six, and then went below to hug himself with delight at the prospect of being virtually employed by a rich man—like Mr Van Wyk. He could not see how any hitch could occur now. He did not seem able to get over the feeling of being 'fixed up at last'. From six to eight, in the course of duty, the Serang looked alone after the ship. She had a clear road before her now till about three in the morning, when she would close with the Pangu group. At eight Mr Sterne came out cheerily to take charge again till midnight. At ten he was still chirruping and humming to himself on the bridge, and about that time Mr Van Wyk's thought abandoned the *Sofala*. Mr Van Wyk had fallen asleep at last.

Massy, blocking the engine-room companion, jerked himself into his tweed jacket surlily, while the second waited with a scowl.

'Oh. You came out! You sot! Well, what have you got to say for yourself?'

He had been in charge of the engines till then. A sombre fury darkened his mind: a hot anger against the ship, against the facts of life, against the men for their cheating, against himself, too—because of an inward tremor in his heart.

An incomprehensible growl answered him.

'What? Can't you open your mouth now? You yelp out your infernal rot loud enough when you are drunk. What do you mean by abusing people in that way?—You old useless boozer, you!'

'Can't help it. Don't remember anything about it. You shouldn't listen.'

'You dare to tell me! What do you mean by going on a drunk like this?'

'Don't ask me. Sick of the dam' boilers—you would be. Sick of life.'

'I wish you were dead, then. You've made me sick of you. Don't you remember the uproar you made last night? You miserable old soaker!'

'No; I don't. Don't want to. Drink is drink.'

'I wonder what prevents me from kicking you out. What do you want here?'

'Relieve you. You've been long enough down there, George.'

'Don't you George me—you tippling old rascal. You! If I were to die tomorrow you would starve. Remember that. Say Mr Massy.'

'Mr Massy,' repeated the other, stolidly. Dishevelled, with dull bloodshot eyes, a snuffy, grimy shirt, greasy trousers, naked feet thrust into ragged slippers, he bolted in head down directly Massy had made way for him.

The chief engineer looked around. The deck was empty as far as the taffrail. All the native passengers had left in Batu Berau this time, and no others had joined. The dial of the patent log tinkled periodically in the dark at the end of the ship. It was a dead calm, and, under the clouded sky, through the still air that seemed to cling warm, with a seaweed smell, to her slim hull, on a sea of sombre grey and unwrinkled, the ship moved on an even keel, as if floating detached in empty space. But Mr Massy slapped his forehead, tottered a little, and caught hold of a belaying pin at the foot of the mast.

'I shall go mad,' he muttered, walking across the deck unsteadily. A shovel was scraping loose coal down below—a fire door clanged. Sterne on the bridge began whistling a new tune.

Captain Whalley, sitting on the couch, awake and fully dressed, heard the door of his cabin open. He did not move in the least, waiting to recognize the voice, with an appalling strain of prudence.

A bulkhead lamp blazed on the white paint, the crimson plush, the brown varnish of mahogany tops. The white wood packing case under the bed-place had remained unopened for three years now, as though Captain Whalley had felt that, after the *Fair Maid* was gone, there could be no abiding-place on earth for his affections. His hands rested on his knees; his handsome head with big eyebrows presented a rigid profile to the doorway. The expected voice spoke out at last.

'Once more, then. What am I to call you?'

Ha! Massy. Again. The weariness of it crushed his heart—and the pain of shame was almost more than he could bear without crying out,

'Well. Is it to be "partner" still?'

'You don't know what you ask.'

'I know what I want . . .'

Massy stepped in and closed the door.

'. . . And I am going to have a try for it with you once more.'

His whine was half persuasive, half menacing.

'For it's no manner of use to tell me that you are poor. You don't spend anything on yourself, that's true enough; but there's another name for that. You think you are going to have what you want out of me for three years, and then cast me off without hearing what I think of you. You think I would

244

have submitted to your airs if I had known you had only a beggarly five hundred pounds in the world. You ought to have told me.'

'Perhaps,' said Captain Whalley, bowing his head. 'And yet it has saved you . . .' Massy laughed scornfully. 'I have told you often enough since.'

'And I don't believe you now. When I think how I let you lord it over my ship! Do you remember how you used to bullyrag me about my coat and *your* bridge? It was in his way. *His* bridge! "And I won't be a party to this—and I couldn't think of doing that." Honest man. And now it all comes out. "I am poor, and I can't. I have only this five hundred in the world."'

He contemplated the immobility of Captain Whalley, that seemed to present an inconquerable obstacle in his path. His face took a mournful cast.

'You are a hard man.'

'Enough,' said Captain Whalley, turning upon him. 'You shall get nothing from me, because I have nothing of mine to give away now.'

'Tell that to the marines!'

Mr Massy, going out, looked back once; then the door closed, and Captain Whalley, alone, sat as still as before. He had nothing of his own—even his own past of honour, of truth, of just pride, was gone. All his spotless life had fallen into the abyss. He had said his last goodbye to it. But what belonged to *her,* that he meant to save. Only a little money. He would take it to her in his own hands—this last gift of a man that had lasted too long. And an immense and fierce impulse, the very passion of paternity, flamed up with all the unquenched vigour of his worthless life in a desire to see her face.

Just across the deck Massy had gone straight to his cabin, struck a light, and hunted up the note of the dreamed number whose figures had flamed up also with the fierceness of another passion. He must contrive somehow not to miss a drawing. That number meant something. But what expedient could he contrive to keep himself going?

'Wretched miser!' he mumbled.

If Mr Sterne could at no time have told him anything new about his partner, he could have told Mr Sterne that another use could be made of a man's affliction than just to kick him out, and thus defer the term of a difficult payment for a year. To keep the secret of the affliction and induce him to stay was a better move. If without means, he would be anxious to remain; and that settled the question of refunding him his share. He did not know exactly how much Captain Whalley was disabled; but if it so happened that he put the ship ashore somewhere for good and all, it was not the owner's fault—was it? He was not obliged to know that there was anything wrong. But probably nobody would raise such a point, and the ship was fully insured. He had had enough self-restraint to pay up the premiums. But this was not all. He could not believe Captain Whalley to be so confoundedly destitute as not to have some more money put away somewhere. If he, Massy, could get hold of it, that would pay for the boilers, and everything went on as before. And if she got lost in the end, so much the better. He hated her: he loathed the troubles that took his mind off the chances of fortune. He wished her at the bottom of the sea, and the insurance money in his pocket. And as, baffled, he left Captain Whalley's cabin, he enveloped in the same hatred the ship with the worn-out boilers and the man with the dimmed eyes.

And our conduct after all is so much a matter of outside suggestion, that had it not been for his Jack's drunken gabble he would have there and then had it out with this miserable man, who would neither help, nor stay, nor yet lose the ship.

The old fraud! He longed to kick him out. But he restrained himself. Time enough for that—when he liked. There was a fearful new thought put into his head. Wasn't he up to it after all? How that beast Jack had raved! 'Find a safe trick to get rid of her.' Well, Jack was not so far wrong. A very clever trick had occurred to him. Ay! But what of the risk?

A feeling of pride—the pride of superiority to common prejudices—crept into his breast, made his heart beat fast, his mouth turn dry. Not everybody would dare; but he was Massy, and he was up to it!

Six bells were struck on deck. Eleven! He drank a glass of water, and sat down for ten minutes or so to calm himself. Then he got out of his chest a small bull's-eye lantern of his own and lit it.

Almost opposite his berth, across the narrow passage under the bridge, there was, in the iron deck structure covering the stokehold fiddle and the boiler space, a storeroom with iron sides, iron roof, iron-plated floor, too, on account of the heat below. All sorts of rubbish was shot there: it had a mound of scrap iron in a corner; rows of empty oil cans; sacks of cotton waste, with a heap of charcoal, a deck forge, fragments of an old hencoop, winch-covers all in rags, remnants of lamps, and a brown felt hat, discarded by a man dead now (of a fever on the Brazil coast), who had been once mate of the *Sofala*, had remained for years jammed forcibly behind a length of burst copper pipe, flung at some time or other out of the engine room. A complete and impervious blackness pervaded that Capharnaum of forgotten things. A small shaft of light from Mr Massy's bull's-eye fell slanting right through it.

His coat was unbuttoned; he shot the bolt of the door (there was no other opening), and, squatting before the scrap heap, began to pack his pockets with pieces of iron. He packed them carefully, as if the rusty nuts, the broken bolts, the links of cargo chain, had been so much gold he had that one chance to carry away. He packed his side pockets till they bulged, the breast pocket, the pockets inside. He turned over the pieces. Some he rejected. A small mist of powdered rust began to rise about his busy hands. Mr Massy knew something of the scientific basis of his clever trick. If you want to deflect the magnetic needle of a ship's compass, soft iron is the best; likewise many small pieces in the pockets of a jacket would have more effect than a few large ones, because in that way you obtain a greater amount of surface for weight in your iron, and it's surface that tells.

He slipped out swiftly—two strides sufficed—and in his cabin he perceived that his hands were all red—red with rust. It disconcerted him, as though he had found them covered with blood; he looked himself over hastily. Why, his trousers, too! He had been rubbing his rusty palms on his legs.

He tore off the waistband button in his haste, brushed his coat, washed his hands. Then the air of guilt left him, and he sat down to wait.

He sat bolt upright and weighted with iron in his chair. He had a hard, lumpy bulk against each hip, felt the scrappy iron in his pockets touch his ribs at every breath, the downward drag of all these pounds hanging upon his shoulders. He looked very dull, too, sitting idle there, and his yellow face, with motionless black eyes, had something passive and sad in its quietness.

When he heard eight bells struck above his head, he rose and made ready to go out. His movements seemed aimless, his lower lip had dropped a little, his eyes roamed about the cabin, and the tremendous tension of his will had robbed them of every vestige of intelligence.

With the last stroke of the bell the Serang appeared noise-lessly on the bridge to relieve the mate. Sterne overflowed with good nature, since he had nothing more to desire.

'Got your eyes well open yet, Serang? It's middling dark; I'll wait till you get your sight properly.'

The old Malay murmured, looked up with his worn eyes, sidled away into the light of the binnacle, and, clasping his hands behind his back, fixed his eyes on the compass card.

'You'll have to keep a good lookout ahead for land, about half past three. It's fairly clear, though. You have looked in on the captain as you came along—eh? He knows the time? Well, then, I am off.'

At the foot of the ladder he stood aside for the captain. He watched him go up with an even, certain tread, and remained thoughtful for a moment. 'It's funny,' he said to himself, 'but you can never tell whether that man has seen you or not. He might have heard me breathe this time.'

He was a wonderful man when all was said and done. They said he had had a name in his day. Mr Sterne could well believe it; and he concluded serenely that Captain Whalley must be able to see people more or less—as himself just now, for instance—but not being certain of anybody, had to keep up that unnoticing silence of manner for fear of giving himself away. Mr Sterne was a shrewd guesser.

This necessity of every moment brought home to Captain Whalley's heart the humiliation of his falsehood. He had drifted into it from paternal love, from incredulity, from boundless trust in divine justice meted out to men's feelings on this earth. He would give his poor Ivy the benefit of another month's work; perhaps the affliction was only temporary. Surely God would not rob his child of his power to help, and cast him naked into a night without end. He had caught at every hope; and when the evidence of his misfortune was stronger than hope, he tried not to believe the manifest thing.

In vain. In the steadily darkening universe a sinister clearness fell upon his ideas. In the illuminating moments of suffering he saw life, men, all things, the whole earth with all her burden of created nature, as he had never seen them before.

Sometimes he was seized with a sudden vertigo and an overwhelming terror; and then the image of his daughter appeared. Her, too, he had never seen so clearly before. Was it possible that he should ever be unable to do anything whatever for her? Nothing. And not see her any more? Never.

Why? The punishment was too great for a little presumption, for a little pride. And at last he came to cling to his deception with a fierce determination to carry it out to the end, to save her money intact, and behold her once more with his own eyes. Afterwards—what? The idea of suicide was revolting to the vigour of his manhood. He had prayed for death till the prayers had stuck in his throat. All the days of his life he had prayed, for daily bread, and not to be led into temptation, in a childlike humility of spirit. Did words mean anything? Whence did the gift of speech come? The violent beating of his heart reverberated in his head—seemed to shake his brain to pieces.

He sat down heavily in the deck chair to keep the pretence of his watch. The night was dark. All the nights were dark now.

'Serang,' he said, half aloud.

'Ada, Tuan. I am here.'

'There are clouds on the sky?'

'There are, Tuan.'

'Let her be steered straight. North.'

'She is going north, Tuan.'

The Serang stepped back. Captain Whalley recognized Massy's footfalls on the bridge.

The engineer walked over to port and returned, passing behind the chair several times. Captain Whalley detected an unusual character as of prudent care in this prowling. The near presence of that man brought with it always a recrudescence of moral suffering for Captain Whalley. It was not remorse. After all, he had done nothing but good to the poor devil. There was also a sense of danger—the necessity of a greater care.

Massy stopped and said—

'So you still say you must go?'

'I must indeed.'

'And you couldn't at least leave the money for a term of years?'

'Impossible.'

'Can't trust it with me without your care, eh?'

Captain Whalley remained silent. Massy sighed deeply over the back of the chair.

'It would just do to save me,' he said in a tremulous voice.

'I've saved you once.'

The chief engineer took off his coat with careful movements, and proceeded to feel for the brass hook screwed into the wooden stanchion. For this purpose he placed himself right in front of the binnacle, thus hiding completely the compass card from the quartermaster at the wheel. 'Tuan!' the lascar at last murmured softly, meaning to let the white man know that he could not see to steer.

Mr Massy had accomplished his purpose. The coat was hanging from the nail, within six inches of the binnacle. And directly he had stepped aside the quartermaster, a middle-aged, pockmarked Sumatra Malay, almost as dark as a negro, perceived with amazement that in that short time, in this smooth water, with no wind at all, the ship had gone swinging far out of her course. He had never known her get away like this before. With a slight grunt of astonishment he turned the wheel hastily to bring her head back north, which was the course. The grinding of the steering chains, the chiding murmurs of the Serang, who had come over to the wheel, made a slight stir, which attracted Captain Whalley's anxious attention. He said, 'Take better care.' Then everything settled to the usual quiet on the bridge. Mr Massy had disappeared.

But the iron in the pockets of the coat had done its work; and the *Sofala,* heading north by the compass made untrue by this simple device, was no longer making a safe course for Pangu Bay.

The hiss of water parted by her stem, the throb of her engines, all the sounds of her faithful and laborious life, went on uninterrupted in the great calm of the sea joining on all sides the motionless layer of cloud over the sky. A gentle stillness as vast as the world seemed to wait upon her path, enveloping her lovingly in a supreme caress. Mr Massy thought there could be no better night for an arranged shipwreck.

Run up high and dry on one of the reefs east of Pangu—wait for daylight—hole in the bottom—out boats—Pangu Bay same evening. That's about it. As soon as she touched he would hasten on the bridge, get hold of the coat (nobody would notice in the dark) and shake it upside down over the side, or even fling it into the sea. A detail. Who could guess? Coat been seen hanging there from that hook hundreds of times. Nevertheless, when he sat down on the lower step of the bridge ladder his knees knocked together a little. The waiting part was the worst of it. At times he would begin to pant quickly, as though he had been running, and then breathe largely, swelling with the intimate sense of a mastered fate. Now and then he would hear the shuffle of the Serang's bare feet up there: quiet, low voices would exchange a few words, and lapse almost at once into silence . . .

'Tell me directly you see any land, Serang.'

'Yes, Tuan. Not yet.'

'No, not yet,' Captain Whalley would agree.

The ship had been the best friend of his decline. He had sent all the money he had made by and in the *Sofala* to his daughter. His thought lingered on the name. How often he and his wife had talked over the cot of the child in the big stern cabin of the *Condor;* she would grow up, she would marry, she would love them, they would live near her and look at her happiness—it would go on without end. Well, his wife was dead, to the child he had given all he had to give; he wished he could come near her, see her, see her face once, live in the sound of her voice, that could make the darkness of the living grave ready for him supportable. He had been starved of love too long. He imagined her tenderness.

The Serang had been peering forward, and now and then glancing at the chair. He fidgeted restlessly, and suddenly burst out close to Captain Whalley—

'Tuan, do you see anything of the land?'

The alarmed voice brought Captain Whalley to his feet at once. He! See! And at the question, the curse of his blindness seemed to fall on him with a hundredfold force.

'What's the time?' he cried.

'Half-past three, Tuan.'

'We are close. You *must* see. Look, I say. Look.' Mr Massy, awakened by the sudden sound of talking from a short doze on the lowest step, wondered why he was there. Ah! A faintness came over him. It is one thing to sow the seed of an accident and another to see the monstrous fruit hanging over your head ready to fall in the sound of agitated voice. 'There's no danger,' he muttered thickly to himself.

The horror of incertitude had seized upon Captain Whalley, the miserable mistrust of men, of things—of the very earth. He had steered that very course thirty-six times by the same compass—if anything was certain in this world it was its absolute, unerring correctness. Then what had happened? Did the Serang lie? Why lie? Why? Was he going blind, too?

'Is there a mist? Look low on the water. Low down, I say.'

'Tuan, there's no mist. See for yourself.'

Captain Whalley steadied the trembling of his limbs by an effort. Should he stop the engines at once and give himself away? A gust of irresolution swayed all sorts of bizarre notions in his mind. The unusual had come, and he was not fit to deal with it. In this passage of inexpressible anguish he saw her face—the face of a young girl—with an amazing strength of illusion. No, he must not give himself away after having gone so far for her sake. 'You steered the course? You made it? Speak the truth.'

'Ya, Tuan. On the course now. Look.'

Captain Whalley strode to the binnacle, which to him made such a dim spot of light in an infinity of shapeless shadow. By bending his face right down to the glass he had been able before . . .

Having to stoop so low, he put out, instinctively, his arm to where he knew there was a stanchion to steady himself against. His hand closed on something that was not wood but cloth. The slight pull adding to the weight, the loop broke, and Mr Massy's coat falling, struck the deck heavily with a dull thump accompanied by a lot of clicks.

'What's this?'

Captain Whalley fell on his knees, with groping hands extended in a frank gesture of blindness. They trembled, these hands feeling for the truth. He saw it. Iron near the compass. Wrong course. Wreck her! His ship. Oh, no. Not that.

'Jump and stop her!' he roared out in a voice not his own.

He ran himself—hands forward, a blind man, and while the clanging of the gong echoed still all over the ship, she seemed to butt full tilt into the side of a mountain.

It was low water along the north side of the strait. Mr Massy had not reckoned on that. Instead of running aground for half her length, the *Sofala* butted the sheer ridge of a stone reef which would have been awash, at high water. This made the shock absolutely terrific. Everybody in the ship that was standing was thrown down headlong: the shaken rigging made a great rattling to the very trucks. All the lights went out; several chain guys, snapping, clattered against the funnel; there were crashes, pings of parted wire rope, splintering sounds, loud cracks; the masthead lamp flew over the bows, and all the doors about the deck began to bang heavily. Then, after having hit, she rebounded, hit the second time the very same spot like a battering ram. This completed the havoc: the funnel, with all the guys gone, fell over with a hollow sound of thunder, smashing the wheel to bits, crushing the frame of the awnings, breaking the lockers, filling the bridge with a mass of broken wood. Captain Whalley picked himself up and stood knee-deep in wreckage, torn, bleeding, knowing the nature of the danger he had escaped mostly by the sound, and holding Mr Massy's coat in his arms.

By this time Sterne (he had been flung out of his bunk) had set the engines astern. They worked for a few turns, then a voice bawled out, 'Get out of the damned engine room, Jack!'—and they stopped; but the ship had gone clear of the reef and lay still, with a heavy cloud of steam issuing from the broken deck pipes, and vanishing in wispy shapes into the night. Notwithstanding the suddenness of the disaster there was no shouting, as if the very violence of the shock had half-stunned the shadowy lot of people swaying here and there about her decks. The voice of the Serang pronounced distinctly above the confused murmurs

'No bottom.' He had heaved the lead.

Mr Sterne cried out next in a strained pitch—

'Where the devil has she got to? Where are we?' Captain Whalley replied in a calm bass—

'Amongst the reefs to the eastward.'

'You know it, sir? Then she will never get out again.'

'She will be gone in five minutes. Boats, Sterne. Even one will save you all in this calm.'

The Chinaman stokers went in a disorderly rush for the port boats. Nobody tried to check them. The Malays, after a moment of confusion, became quiet, and Mr Sterne showed a good countenance. Captain Whalley had not moved. His thoughts were darker than this night in which he had lost his first ship.

'He made me lose a ship.'

Another tall figure standing before him amongst the litter of the smash on the bridge whispered insanely—

'Say nothing of it.'

Massy stumbled closer. Captain Whalley heard the chattering of his teeth.

'I have the coat.'

'Throw it down and come along,' urged the chattering voice. 'B-b-b-b-boat!'

'You will get five years for this.'

Mr Massy had lost his voice. His speech was mere dry rustling in his throat.

'Have mercy!'

'Had you any when you made me lose my ship Mr Massy, you shall get five years for this!'

'I wanted money? Money! My own money! I will give you some money. Make half of it. You love money yourself.'

'There's a justice . . .'

Massy made an awful effort, and in a strange, half-choked utterance—

'You blind devil! It's you that drove me to it.'

Captain Whalley, hugging the coat to his breast, made no sound. The light had ebbed for ever from the world—let everything go. But this man should not escape scot-free.

Sterne's voice commanded—

'Lower away!'

The blocks rattled.

'Now then,' he cried, 'over with you. This way. You, Jack, here. Mr Massy! Mr Massy! Captain! Quick, sir! Let's get—'

'I shall go to prison for trying to cheat the insurance, but you'll get exposed; you, honest man, who has been cheating me. You are poor. Aren't you? You've nothing but the five hundred pounds. Well, you have nothing at all now. The ship's lost, and the insurance won't be paid.'

Captain Whalley did not move. True! Ivy's money. Gone in this wreck. Again he had a flash of insight. He was indeed at the end of his tether.

Urgent voices cried out together alongside. Massy did not seem able to tear himself away from the bridge. He chattered and hissed despairingly

'Give it up to me! Give it up!'

'No,' said Captain Whalley; 'I could not give it up. You had better go. Don't wait, man, if you want to live. She's settling down by the head fast. No; I shall keep it, but I shall stay on board.'

Massy did not seem to understand; but the love of life, awakened suddenly, drove him away from the bridge. Captain Whalley laid the coat down, and stumbled amongst the heaps of wreckage to the side.

'Is Mr Massy with you?' he called out into the night.

Sterne from the boat shouted—

'Yes; we've got him. Come along, sir. It's madness to stay longer.'

Captain Whalley felt along the rail carefully, and, without a word, cast off the painter. They were expecting him still down there. They were waiting, till a voice suddenly exclaimed—

'We are adrift! Shove off!'

'Captain Whalley! Leap! . . . Pull up a little . . . Leap! You can swim.'

In that old heart, in that vigorous body, there was, that nothing should be wanting, a horror of death that apparently could not be overcome by the horror of blindness. But after all, for Ivy he had carried his point, walking in his darkness to the very verge of a crime. God had not listened to his prayers. The light had finished ebbing out of the world; not a glimmer. It was a dark waste; but it was unseemly that a Whalley who had gone so far to carry a point should continue to live. He must pay the price.

'Leap as far as you can, sir; we will pick you up.'

They did not hear him answer. But their shouting seemed to remind him of something. He groped his way back, and sought for Mr Massy's coat. He could swim indeed; people sucked down by the whirlpool of a sinking ship do come up sometimes to the surface, and it was unseemly that a Whalley, who had made up his mind to die, should be beguiled by chance into a struggle. He would put all these pieces of iron into his own pockets.

They, looking from the boat, saw the *Sofala*, a black mass upon a black sea, lying still at an appalling cant. No sound came from her. Then, with a great bizarre shuffling noise, as if the boilers had broken through the bulkheads, and with a faint muffled detonation, where the ship had been there appeared for a moment something standing upright and narrow, like a rock out of the sea. Then that, too, disappeared.

When the *Sofala* failed to come back to Batu Berau at the proper time, Mr Van Wyk understood at once that he would never see her any more. But he did not know what had happened till some weeks afterwards, when, in a native craft lent him by his Sultan, he had made his way to the *Sofala's* port of registry, where already her existence and the official inquiry into her loss were beginning to be forgotten.

It had not been a very remarkable or interesting case, except for the fact that the captain had gone down with his sinking ship. It was the only life lost; and Mr Van Wyk would not have been able to learn any details had it not been for Sterne, whom he met one day on the quay near the bridge over the creek, almost on the very spot where Captain Whalley, to preserve his daughter's five hundred pounds intact, had turned to get a sampan which would take him on board the *Sofala*.

From afar Mr Van Wyk saw Sterne blink straight at him and raise his hand to his hat. They drew into the shade of a building (it was a bank), and the mate related how the boats with the crew got into Pangu Bay about six hours after the accident, and how they had lived for a fortnight in a state of destitution before they found an opportunity to get away from that beastly place. The inquiry had exonerated everybody from all blame. The loss of the ship was put down to an unusual set of the current. Indeed, it could not have been anything else: there was no other way to account for the ship being set seven miles to the eastward of her position during the middle watch.

'A piece of bad luck for me, sir.'

Sterne passed his tongue on his lips and glanced aside. 'I lost the advantage of being employed by you, sir. I can never be sorry enough. But here it is: one man's poison, another man's meat. This could not have been handier for Mr Massy if he had arranged that ship wreck himself. The most timely total loss I've ever heard of.'

'What became of that Massy?' asked Mr Van Wyk.

'He, sir? Ha! ha! He would keep on telling me that he meant to buy another ship; but as soon as he had the money in his pocket he cleared out for Manila by mailboat early in the morning. I gave him chase right aboard, and he told me then he was going to make his fortune dead sure in Manila. I could go to the devil for all he cared. And yet he as good as promised to give me the command if I didn't talk too much.'

'You never said anything . . .' Mr Van Wyk began.

'Not I, sir. Why should I? I mean to get on, but the dead aren't in my way,' said Sterne. His eyelids were beating rapidly, then drooped for an instant. 'Besides, sir, it would have been an awkward business. You made me hold my tongue just a bit too long.'

'Do you know how it was that Captain Whalley remained on board? Did he really refuse to leave? Come now! Or was it perhaps an accidental . . .?'

'Nothing!' Sterne interrupted with energy. 'I tell you I yelled for him to leap overboard. He simply must have cast off the painter of the boat himself. We all yelled to him—that is, Jack and I. He wouldn't even answer us. The ship was as silent as a grave to the last. Then the boilers fetched away, and down she went. Accident! Not it! The game was up, sir, I tell you.'

This was all that Sterne had to say.

Mr Van Wyk had been of course made the guest of the club for a fortnight, and it was there that he met the lawyer in whose office had been signed the agreement between Massy and Captain Whalley.

'Extraordinary old man,' he said. 'He came into my office from nowhere in particular as you may say, with his five hundred pounds to invest, and that engineer fellow following him anxiously. And now he is gone out a little inexplicably, just as he came. I could never understand him quite. There was no mystery at all about that Massy, eh? I wonder whether Whalley refused to leave the ship. It would have been foolish. He was blameless, as the court found.'

Mr Van Wyk had known him well, he said, and he could not believe in suicide. Such an act would not have been in character with what he knew of the man.

'It is my opinion, too,' the lawyer agreed. The general theory was that the captain had remained too long on board trying to save something of importance. Perhaps the chart which would clear him, or else something of value in his cabin. The painter of the boat had come adrift of itself, it was supposed. However, strange to say, some little time before that voyage poor Whalley had called in his office and had left with him a sealed envelope addressed to his daughter, to be forwarded to her in case of his death. Still it was nothing very unusual, especially in a man of his age. Mr Van Wyk shook his head. Captain Whalley looked good for a hundred years.

'Perfectly true,' assented the lawyer. 'The old fellow looked as though he had come into the world full grown and with that long beard. I could never, somehow, imagine him either younger or older—don't you know. There was a sense of physical power about that man, too. And perhaps that was the secret of that something peculiar in his person which struck everybody who came in contact with him. He looked indestructible by any ordinary means that put an end to the rest of us. His deliberate, stately courtesy of manner was full of significance. It was as though he were certain of having plenty of time for everything. Yes, there was something indestructible about him; and the way he talked sometimes you might have thought he believed it himself. When he called on me last with that letter he wanted me to take charge of, he was not depressed at all. Perhaps a shade more deliberate in his talk and manner. Not depressed in the least. Had he a presentiment, I wonder? Perhaps! Still it seems a miserable end for such a striking figure.'

'Oh, yes! It was a miserable end,' Mr Van Wyk said, with so much fervour that the lawyer looked up at him curiously; and afterwards, after parting with him, he remarked to an acquaintance—

'Queer person that Dutch tobacco planter from Batu Berau. Know anything of him?'

'Heaps of money,' answered the bank manager. 'I hear he's going home by the next mail to form a company to take over his estates. Another tobacco district thrown open. He's wise, I think. These good times won't last for ever.'

In the southern hemisphere Captain Whalley's daughter had no presentiment of evil when she opened the envelope addressed to her in the lawyer's handwriting. She had received it in the afternoon; all the boarders had gone out, her boys were at school, her husband sat upstairs in his big armchair with a book, thin-faced, wrapped up in rugs to the waist. The house was still, and the greyness of a cloudy day lay against the panes of the windows.

In a shabby dining room, where a faint cold smell of dishes lingered all the year round, sitting at the end of a long table surrounded by many chairs pushed in with their backs close against the edge of the perpetually laid tablecloth, she read the opening sentences: 'Most profound regret—painful duty—your father is no more—in accordance with his instructions—fatal casualty—consolation—no blame attached to his memory . . .'

Her face was thin, her temples a little sunk under the smoother bands of black hair, her lips remained resolutely compressed, while her dark eyes grew larger, till at last, with a low cry, she stood up, and instantly stooped to pick up another envelope which had slipped off her knees on to the floor.

She tore it open, snatched out the enclosure . . . 'My dearest child,' it said, 'I am writing this while I am able yet to write legibly. I am trying hard to save for you all the money that is left; I have only kept it to serve you better. It is yours. It shall not be lost; it shall not be touched. There's five hundred pounds. Of what I have earned I have kept nothing back till now. For the future, if I live, I must keep back some—a little—to bring me to you. I must come to you. I must see you once more.

'It is hard to believe that you will ever look on these lines. God seems to have forgotten me. I want to see you—and yet death would be a greater favour. If you ever read these words, I charge you to begin by thanking a God merciful at last, for I shall be dead then, and it will be well. My dear, I am at the end of my tether.'

The next paragraph began with the words: 'My sight is going . . .'

She read no more that day. The hand holding up the paper to her eyes fell slowly, and her slender figure in a plain black dress walked rigidly to the window. Her eyes were dry; no cry of sorrow or whisper of thanks went up to heaven from her lips. Life had been too hard, for all the efforts of his love. It had silenced her emotions. But for the first time in all these years its sting had departed, the carking care of poverty, the meanness of a hard struggle for bread. Even the image of her husband and of her children seemed to glide away from her into the gray twilight; it was her father's face alone that she saw, as though he had come to see her, always quiet and big, as she had seen him last, but with something more august and tender in his aspect.

She slipped his folded letter between the two buttons of her plain black bodice, and leaning her forehead against a windowpane remained there till dusk, perfectly motionless, giving him all the time she could spare. Gone! Was it possible? My God, was it possible? The blow had come softened by the spaces of the earth, by the years of absence. There had been whole days when she had not thought of him at all—had no time. But she had loved him, she felt she had loved him after all.

Because of the Dollars

I

WHILE we were hanging about near the water's edge, as sailors idling ashore will do (it was in the open space before the Harbour Office of a great Eastern port), a man came towards us from the 'front' of business houses, aiming obliquely at the landing steps. He attracted my attention because in the movement of figures in white drill suits on the pavement from which he stepped, his costume, the usual tunic and trousers, being made of light grey flannel, made him noticeable.

I had time to observe him. He was stout, but he was not grotesque. His face was round and smooth, his complexion very fair. On his nearer approach I saw a little moustache made all the fairer by a good many white hairs. And he had, for a stout man, quite a good chin. In passing us he exchanged nods with the friend I was with and smiled.

My friend was Hollis, the fellow who had so many adventures and had known so many queer people in that part of the (more or less) gorgeous East in the days of his youth. He said: 'That's a good man. I don't mean good in the sense of smart or skilful in his trade. I mean a really *good* man.'

I turned round at once to look at the phenomenon. The 'really *good* man' had a very broad back. I saw him signal a sampan to come alongside, get into it, and go off in the direction of a cluster of local steamers anchored close inshore.

I said: 'He's a seaman, isn't he?'

'Yes. Commands that biggish dark-green steamer: *Sissie*-Glasgow. He has never commanded anything else but the *Sissie*-Glasgow, only it wasn't always the same *Sissie*. The first he had was about half the length of this one, and we used to tell poor Davidson that she was a size too small for him. Even at that time Davidson had bulk. We warned him he would get callosities on his shoulders and elbows because of

267

the tight fit of his command. And Davidson could well afford
the smiles he gave us for our chaff. He made lots of money in
her. She belonged to a portly Chinaman resembling a
mandarin in a picture book, with goggles and thin drooping
moustaches, and as dignified as only a Celestial knows how to
be.

'The best of Chinamen as employers is that they have
such gentlemanly instincts. Once they become convinced that
you are a straight man, they give you their unbounded
confidence. You simply can't do wrong, then. And they are
pretty quick judges of character, too. Davidson's Chinaman
was the first to find out his worth, on some theoretical
principle. One day in his counting house, before several white
men he was heard to declare: "Captain Davidson is a good
man." And that settled it. After that you couldn't tell if it was
Davidson who belonged to the Chinaman or the Chinaman
who belonged to Davidson. It was he who, shortly before he
died, ordered in Glasgow the new *Sissie* for Davidson to
command.'

We walked into the shade of the Harbour Office and
leaned our elbows on the parapet of the quay.

'She was really meant to comfort poor Davidson,'
continued Hollis. 'Can you fancy anything more naïvely
touching than this old mandarin spending several thousand
pounds to console his white man? Well, there she is. The old
mandarin's sons have inherited her, and Davidson with her;
and he commands her; and what with his salary and trading
privileges he makes a lot of money; and everything is as
before; and Davidson even smiles—you have seen it? Well,
the smile's the only thing which isn't as before.'

'Tell me, Hollis,' I asked, 'what do you mean by good in
this connection?'

'Well, there are men who are born good just as others are
born witty. What I mean is his nature. No simpler, more

scrupulously delicate soul had ever lived in such a—a—comfortable envelope. How we used to laugh at Davidson's fine scruples! In short, he's thoroughly humane, and I don't imagine there can be much of any other sort of goodness that counts on this earth. And as he's that with a shade of particular refinement, I may well call him a *"really good man"*.'

I knew from old that Hollis was a firm believer in the final value of shades. And I said: 'I see'—because I really did see Hollis's Davidson in the sympathetic stout man who had passed us a little while before. But I remembered that at the very moment he smiled his placid face appeared veiled in melancholy—a sort of spiritual shadow. I went on.

'Who on earth has paid him off for being so fine by spoiling his smile?'

'That's quite a story, and I will tell it to you if you like. Confound it! It's quite a surprising one, too. Surprising in every way, but mostly in the way it knocked over poor Davidson—and apparently only because he is such a good sort. He was telling me all about it only a few days ago. He said that when he saw these four fellows with their heads in a bunch over the table, he at once didn't like it. He didn't like it at all. You mustn't suppose that Davidson is a soft fool. These men—

'But I had better begin at the beginning. We must go back to the first time the old dollars had been called in by our Government in exchange for a new issue. Just about the time when I left these parts to go home for a long stay. Every trader in the islands was thinking of getting his old dollars sent up here in time, and the demand for empty French wine cases—you know the dozen of vermouth or claret size—was something unprecedented. The custom was to pack the dollars in little bags of a hundred each. I don't know how many bags each case would hold. A good lot. Pretty tidy sums must have been moving afloat just then. But let us get away from here. Won't do to stay in the sun. Where could we—? I know! Let us go to those tiffin rooms over there.'

We moved over accordingly. Our appearance in the long empty room at that early hour caused visible consternation amongst the China boys. But Hollis led the way to one of the tables between the windows screened by rattan blinds. A brilliant half-light trembled on the ceiling, on the whitewashed walls, bathed the multitude of vacant chairs and tables in a peculiar, stealthy glow.

'All right. We will get something to eat when it's ready,' he said, waving the anxious Chinaman waiter aside. He took his temples touched with grey between his hands, leaning over the table to bring his face, his dark, keen eyes, closer to mine.

'Davidson then was commanding the steamer *Sissie*—the little one which we used to chaff him about. He ran her alone, with only the Malay serang for a deck officer. The nearest approach to another white man on board of her was the engineer, a Portuguese half-caste, as thin as a lath and quite a youngster at that. For all practical purposes Davidson was managing that command of his single-handed; and of course this was known in the port. I am telling you of it because the fact had its influence on the developments you shall hear of presently.

'His steamer, being so small, could go up tiny creeks and into shallow bays and through reefs and over sandbanks, collecting produce, where no other vessel but a native craft would think of venturing. It is a paying game, often. Davidson was known to visit in her places that no one else could find and that hardly anybody had ever heard of.

'The old dollars being called in, Davidson's Chinaman thought that the *Sissie* would be just the thing to collect them from small traders in the less frequented parts of the Archipelago. It's a good business. Such cases of dollars are dumped aft in the ship's lazarette, and you get good freight for very little trouble and space.

'Davidson, too, thought it was a good idea; and together they made up a list of his calls on his next trip. Then Davidson (he had naturally the chart of his voyages in his head) remarked that on his way back he might look in at a certain settlement up a mere creek, where a poor sort of white man lived in a native village. Davidson pointed out to his Chinaman that the fellow was certain to have some rattans to ship.

'"Probably enough to fill her forward," said Davidson. "And that'll be better than bringing her back with empty holds. A day more or less doesn't matter."

'This was sound talk, and the Chinaman owner could not but agree. But if it hadn't been sound it would have been just the same. Davidson did what he liked. He was a man that could do no wrong. However, this suggestion of his was not merely a business matter. There was in it a touch of Davidsonian kindness. For you must know that the man could not have continued to live quietly up that creek if it had not been for Davidson's willingness to call there from time to time. And Davidson's Chinaman knew this perfectly well, too. So he only smiled his dignified bland smile, and said: "All right, Captain. You do what you like."

'I will explain presently how this connection between Davidson and that fellow came about. Now I want to tell you about the part of this affair which happened here—the preliminaries of it.

'You know as well as I do that these tiffin rooms where we are sitting now have been in existence for many years. Well, next day about twelve o'clock, Davidson dropped in here to get something to eat.

'And here comes the only moment in this story where accident—mere accident—plays a part. If Davidson had gone

271

home that day for tiffin, there would be now, after twelve years or more, nothing changed in his kindly, placid smile.

'But he came in here; and perhaps it was sitting at this very table that he remarked to a friend of mine that his next trip was to be a dollar-collecting trip. He added, laughing, that his wife was making rather a fuss about it. She had begged him to stay ashore and get somebody else to take his place for a voyage. She thought there was some danger on account of the dollars. He told her, he said, that there were no Java sea pirates nowadays except in boys' books. He had laughed at her fears, but he was very sorry, too; for when she took any notion in her head it was impossible to argue her out of it. She would be worrying herself all the time he was away. Well, he couldn't help it. There was no one ashore fit to take his place for the trip.

'This friend of mine and I went home together in the same mailboat, and he mentioned that conversation one evening in the Red Sea while we were talking over the things and people we had just left, with more or less regret.

'I can't say that Davidson occupied a very prominent place. Moral excellence seldom does. He was quietly appreciated by those who knew him well; but his more obvious distinction consisted in this, that he was married. Ours, as you remember, was a bachelor crowd; in spirit anyhow, if not absolutely in fact. There might have been a few wives in existence, but if so they were invisible, distant, never alluded to. For what would have been the good? Davidson alone was visibly married.

'Being married suited him exactly. It fitted him so well that the wildest of us did not resent the fact when it was disclosed. Directly he had felt his feet out here, Davidson sent for his wife. She came out (from West Australia) in the *Somerset,* under the care of Captain Ritchie—you know, Monkey-face Ritchie—who couldn't praise enough her sweetness, her gentleness, and her charm. She seemed to be the heaven-born mate for Davidson. She found on arrival a very pretty bungalow on the hill, ready for her and the little girl they had. Very soon he got for her a two-wheeled trap and a Burmah pony, and she used to drive down of an evening to pick up Davidson, on the quay. When Davidson, beaming, got into the trap, it would become very full all at once.

'We used to admire Mrs Davidson from a distance. It was a girlish head out of a keepsake. From a distance. We had not many opportunities for a closer view, because she did not care to give them to us. We would have been glad to drop in at the Davidson bungalow, but we were made to feel somehow that we were not very welcome there. Not that she ever said anything ungracious. She never had much to say for herself. I was perhaps the one who saw most of the Davidsons at home. What I noticed under the superficial aspect of vapid sweetness was her convex, obstinate forehead, and her small, red, pretty, ungenerous mouth. But then I am an observer with strong prejudices. Most of us were fetched by her white, swanlike neck, by that drooping, innocent profile. There was a lot of latent devotion to Davidson's wife hereabouts, at that time, I can tell you. But my idea was that she repaid it by a profound suspicion of the sort of men we were; a mistrust which extended—I fancied—to her very husband at times. And I thought then she was jealous of him in a way; though there were no women that she could be jealous about. She had no women's society. It's difficult for a shipmaster's wife unless there are other shipmasters' wives about, and there were none here then. I know that the dock manager's wife called on her; but that was all. The fellows here formed the opinion that Mrs Davidson was a meek, shy, little thing. She looked it, I must say. And this opinion was so universal that the friend I have been telling you of remembered his conversation with Davidson simply because of the statement about Davidson's wife. He even wondered to me: "Fancy Mrs Davidson making a fuss to that extent. She didn't seem to me the sort of woman that would know how to make a fuss about anything."

'I wondered, too—but not so much. That bumpy forehead—eh? I had always suspected her of being silly. And I observed that Davidson must have been vexed by this display of wifely anxiety.

'My friend said: "No. He seemed rather touched and distressed. There really was no one he could ask to relieve him; mainly because he intended to make a call in some godforsaken creek, to look up a fellow of the name of Bamtz who apparently had settled there."

'And again my friend wondered. "Tell me," he cried, "what connection can there be between Davidson and such a creature as Bamtz?"

'I don't remember now what answer I made. A sufficient one could have been given in two words: "Davidson's goodness". *That* never boggled at unworthiness if there was the slightest reason for compassion. I don't want you to think that Davidson had no discrimination at all. Bamtz could not have imposed on him. Moreover, everybody knew what Bamtz was. He was a loafer with a beard. When I think of Bamtz, the first thing I see is that long black beard and a lot of propitiatory wrinkles at the corners of two little eyes. There was no such beard from here to Polynesia, where a beard is a valuable property in itself. Bamtz's beard was valuable to him in another way. You know how impressed Orientals are by a fine beard. Years and years ago, I remember, the grave Abdullah, the great trader of Sambir, unable to repress signs of astonishment and admiration at the first sight of that imposing beard. And it's very well known that Bamtz lived on Abdullah off and on for several years. It was a unique beard, and so was the bearer of the same. A unique loafer. He made a fine art of it, or rather a sort of craft and mystery. One can understand a fellow living by cadging and small swindles in towns, in large communities of people; but Bamtz managed to do that trick in the wilderness, to loaf on the outskirts of the virgin forest.

'He understood how to ingratiate himself with the natives. He would arrive in some settlement up a river, make a present of a cheap carbine or a pair of shoddy binoculars, or something of that sort, to the Rajah, or the headman, or the principal trader; and on the strength of that gift, ask for a house, posing mysteriously as a very special trader. He would spin them no end of yarns, live on the fat of the land for a while, and then do some mean swindle or other—or else they would get tired of him and ask him to quit. And he would go off meekly with an air of injured innocence. Funny life. Yet, he never got hurt somehow. I've heard of the Rajah of Dongala giving him fifty dollars' worth of trade goods and paying his passage in a prau only to get rid of him. Fact. And observe that nothing prevented the old fellow having Bamtz's throat cut and the carcase thrown into deep water outside the reefs; for who on earth would have inquired after Bamtz?

'He had been known to loaf up and down the wilderness as far north as the Gulf of Tonkin. Neither did he disdain a spell of civilization from time to time. And it was while loafing and cadging in Saigon, bearded and dignified (he gave himself out there as a bookkeeper), that he came across Laughing Anne.

'The less said of her early history the better, but something must be said. We may safely suppose there was very little heart left in her famous laugh when Bamtz spoke first to her in some low cafe. She was stranded in Saigon with precious little money and in great trouble about a kid she had, a boy of five or six.

'A fellow I just remember, whom they called Pearler

Harry, brought her out first into these parts—from Australia, I believe. He brought her out and then dropped her, and she remained knocking about here and there, known to most of us by sight, at any rate. Everybody in the Archipelago had heard of Laughing Anne. She had really a pleasant silvery laugh always at her disposal, so to speak, but it wasn't enough apparently to make her fortune. The poor creature was ready to stick to any half-decent man if he would only let her, but she always got dropped, as it might have been expected.

'She had been left in Saigon by the skipper of a German ship with whom she had been going up and down the China coast as far as Vladivostok for near upon two years. The German said to her: "This is all over, *mein Taubchen*. I am going home now to get married to the girl I got engaged to before coming out here." And Anne said: "All right, I'm ready to go. We part friends, don't we?"

'She was always anxious to part friends. The German told her that of course they were parting friends. He looked rather glum at the moment of parting. She laughed and went ashore.

'But it was no laughing matter for her. She had some notion that this would be her last chance. What frightened her most was the future of her child. She had left her boy in Saigon before going off with the German, in the care of an elderly French couple. The husband was a doorkeeper in some Government office, but his time was up, and they were returning to France. She had to take the boy back from them; and after she had got him back, she did not like to part with him any more.

'That was the situation when she and Bamtz got acquainted casually. She could not have had any illusions about that fellow. To pick up with Bamtz was coming down pretty low in the world, even from a material point of view. She had always been decent, in her way; whereas Bamtz was, not to mince words, an abject sort of creature. On the other hand, that bearded loafer, who looked much more like a pirate than a bookkeeper, was not a brute. He was gentle—rather—even in his cups. And then, despair, like misfortune, makes us acquainted with strange bedfellows. For she may well have despaired. She was no longer young—you know.

'On the man's side this conjunction is more difficult to explain, perhaps. One thing, however, must be said of Bamtz; he had always kept clear of native women. As one can't suspect him of moral delicacy, I surmise that it must have been from prudence. And he, too, was no longer young. There were many white hairs in his valuable black beard by then. He may have simply longed for some kind of companionship in his queer, degraded existence. Whatever their motives, they vanished from Saigon together. And of course nobody cared what had become of them.

'Six months later Davidson came into the Mirrah Settlement. It was the very first time he had been up that creek, where no European vessel had ever been seen before. A Javanese passenger he had on board offered him fifty dollars to call in there—it must have been some very particular business—and Davidson consented to try. Fifty dollars, he told me, were neither here nor there; but he was curious to see the place, and the little *Sissie* could go anywhere where there was water enough to float a soup plate.

'Davidson landed his Javanese plutocrat, and, as he had to wait a couple of hours for the tide, he went ashore himself to stretch his legs.

'It was a small settlement. Some sixty houses, most of them built on piles over the river, the rest scattered in the long grass; the usual pathway at the back; the forest hemming in the clearing and smothering what there might have been of air into a dead, hot stagnation.

'All the population was on the river-bank staring silently, as Malays will do, at the *Sissie* anchored in the stream. She was almost as wonderful to them as an angel's visit. Many of the old people had only heard vaguely of fireships, and not many of the younger generation had seen one. On the back path Davidson strolled into perfect solitude. But he became aware of a bad smell and concluded he would go no farther.

'While he stood wiping his forehead, he heard from somewhere the exclamation: "My God! It's Davy!"

'Davidson's lower jaw, as he expressed it, came unhooked at the crying of this excited voice. Davy was the name used by the associates of his young days; he hadn't heard it for many years. He stared about with his mouth open and saw a white woman issue from the long grass in which a small hut stood buried nearly up to the roof.

'Try to imagine the shock: in that wild place that you couldn't find on a map, and more squalid than the most poverty-stricken Malay settlement had a right to be, this European woman coming swishing out of the long grass in a fanciful tea-gown thing, dingy pink satin, with a long train and frayed lace trimmings; her eyes like black coals in a pasty-white face. Davidson thought that he was asleep, that he was delirious. From the offensive village mudhole (it was what Davidson had sniffed just before) a couple of filthy buffaloes uprose with loud snorts and lumbered off crashing through the bushes, panic-struck by this apparition.

'The woman came forward, her arms extended and laid her hands on Davidson's shoulders, exclaiming: "Why! You have hardly changed at all. The same good Davy." And she laughed a little wildly.

'This sound was to Davidson like a galvanic shock to a corpse. He started in every muscle. "Laughing Anne," he said in an awestruck voice.

'"All that's left of her, Davy. All that's left of her."

'Davidson looked up at the sky; but there was to be seen no balloon from which she could have fallen on that spot. When he brought his distracted gaze down, it rested on a child holding on with a brown little paw to the pink satin gown. He had run out of the grass after her. Had Davidson seen a real hobgoblin his eyes could not have bulged more than at this small boy in a dirty white blouse and ragged knickers. He had a round head of tight chestnut curls, very sunburnt legs, a freckled face, and merry eyes. Admonished by his mother to greet the gentleman, he finished off Davidson by addressing him in French.

'"Bonjour."

'Davidson, overcome, looked up at the woman in silence. She sent the child back to the hut, and when he had disappeared in the grass, she turned to Davidson, tried to speak, but after getting out the words, "That's my Tony", burst into a long fit of crying. She had to lean on Davidson's shoulder. He, distressed in the goodness of his heart, stood rooted to the spot where she had come upon him.

'What a meeting, eh? Bamtz had sent her out to see what white man it was who had landed. And she had recognized him from that time when Davidson, who had been pearling himself in his youth, had been associating with Harry the Pearler and others, the quietest of a rather rowdy set.

'Before Davidson retraced his steps to go on board the steamer, he had heard much of Laughing Anne's story, and had even had an interview, on the path, with Bamtz himself. She ran back to the hut to fetch him, and he came out lounging, with his hands in his pockets, with the detached, casual manner under which he concealed his propensity to cringe. Ya-a-as-as. He thought he would settle here permanently—with her. This with a nod at Laughing Anne, who stood by, a haggard, tragically anxious figure, her black hair hanging over her shoulders.

279

'"No more paint and dyes for me, Davy," she struck in, "if only you will do what he wants you to do. You know that I was always ready to stand by my men—if they had only let me."

'Davidson had no doubt of her earnestness. It was of Bamtz's good faith that he was not at all sure. Bamtz wanted Davidson to promise to call at Mirrah more or less regularly. He thought he saw an opening to do business with rattans there, if only he could depend on some craft to bring out trading goods and take away his produce.

'"I have a few dollars to make a start on. The people are all right."

'He had come there, where he was not known, in a native prau, and had managed, with his sedate manner and the exactly right kind of yarn he knew how to tell to the natives, to ingratiate himself with the chief man. "The Orang Kaya has given me that empty house there to live in as long as I will stay," added Bamtz.

'"Do it, Davy," cried the woman suddenly. "Think of that poor kid."

'"Seen him? Cute little customer," said the reformed loafer in such a tone of interest as to surprise Davidson into a kindly glance.

'"I certainly can do it," he declared. He thought of at first making some stipulation as to Bamtz behaving decently to the woman, but his exaggerated delicacy and also the conviction that such a fellow's promises were worth nothing restrained him. Anne went a little distance down the path with him talking anxiously.

'"It's for the kid. How could I have kept him with me if I had to knock about in towns? Here he will never know that his mother was a painted woman. And this Bamtz likes him. He's real fond of him. I suppose I ought to thank God for that."

'Davidson shuddered at any human creature being brought so low as to have to thank God for the favours or affection of a Bamtz.

'"And do you think that you can make out to live here?" he asked gently.

'"Can't I? You know I have always stuck to men through thick and thin till they had enough of me. And now look at me! But inside I am as I always was. I have acted on the square to them all one after another. Only they do get tired somehow. Oh, Davy! Harry ought not to have cast me off. It was he that led me astray."

'Davidson mentioned to her that Harry the Pearler had been dead now for some years. Perhaps she had heard?

'She made a sign that she had heard; and walked by the side of Davidson in silence nearly to the bank. Then she told him that her meeting with him had brought back the old times to her mind. She had not cried for years. She was not a crying woman either. It was hearing herself called Laughing Anne that had started her sobbing like a fool. Harry was the only man she had loved. The others—

'She shrugged her shoulders. But she prided herself on her loyalty to the successive partners of her dismal adventures. She had never played any tricks in her life. She was a pal worth having. But men did get tired. They did not understand women. She supposed it had to be.

'Davidson was attempting a veiled warning as to Bamtz, but she interrupted him. She knew what men were. She knew what this man was like. But he had taken wonderfully to the kid. And Davidson desisted willingly, saying to himself that surely poor Laughing Anne could have no illusions by this time. She wrung his hand hard at parting.

'"It's for the kid, Davy—it's for the kid. Isn't he a bright little chap?"

II

'ALL this happened about two years before the day when Davidson, sitting in this very room, talked to my friend. You will see presently how this room can get full. Every seat'll be occupied, and as you notice the tables are set close, so that the backs of the chairs are almost touching. There is also a good deal of noisy talk here about one o'clock.

'I don't suppose Davidson was talking very loudly; but very likely he had to raise his voice across the table to my friend. And here accident, mere accident, put in its work by providing a pair of fine ears close behind Davidson's chair. It was ten to one against the owner of the same having enough change in his pockets to get his tiffin here. But he had. Most likely had rooked somebody of a few dollars at cards overnight. He was a bright creature of the name of Fector, a spare, short, jumpy fellow with a rod face and muddy eyes. He described himself as a journalist as certain kind of women give themselves out as actresses in the dock of a police court.

'He used to introduce himself to strangers as a man with a mission to track out abuses and fight them whenever found. He would also hint that he was a martyr. And it's a fact that he had been kicked, horsewhipped, imprisoned, and hounded with ignominy out of pretty well every place between Ceylon and Shanghai, for a professional blackmailer.

'I suppose, in that trade, you've got to have active wits and sharp ears. It's not likely that he overheard every word Davidson said about his dollar-collecting trip, but he heard enough to set his wits at work.

'He let Davidson go out, and then hastened away down to the native slums to a sort of lodging house kept in partnership by the usual sort of Portuguese and a very disreputable Chinaman. Macao Hotel, it was called, but it was mostly a gambling den that one used to warn fellows against. Perhaps you remember?

'There, the evening before, Fector had met a precious couple, a partnership even more queer than the Portuguese and the Chinaman. One of the two was Niclaus—you know. Why! the fellow with a Tartar moustache and a yellow complexion, like a Mongolian, only that his eyes were set straight and his face was not so flat. One couldn't tell what breed he was. A nondescript beggar. From a certain angle you would think a very bilious white man. And I daresay he was. He owned a Malay prau and called himself The Nakhoda, as one would say: The Captain. Aha! Now you remember. He couldn't, apparently, speak any other European language than English, but he flew the Dutch flag on his prau.

'The other was the Frenchman without hands. Yes. The very same we used to know in '79 in Sydney, keeping a little tobacco shop at the lower end of George Street. You remember the huge carcass hunched up behind the counter, the big white face and the long black hair brushed back off a high forehead like a bard's. He was always trying to roll cigarettes on his knee with his stumps, telling endless yarns of Polynesia and whining and cursing in turn about *"mon malheur"*. His hands had been blown away by a dynamite cartridge while fishing in some lagoon. This accident, I believe, had made him more wicked than before, which is saying a good deal.

'He was always talking about "resuming his activities", some day, whatever they were, if he could only get an intelligent companion. It was evident that the little shop was no field for his activities, and the sickly woman with her face tied up, who used to look in sometimes through the back door, was no companion for him.

'And, true enough, he vanished from Sydney before long, after some trouble with the excise fellows about his stock. Goods stolen out of a warehouse or something similar. He left the woman behind, but he must have secured some sort of companion—he could not have shifted for himself; but whom he went away with, and where, and what other companions he might have picked up afterwards, it is impossible to make the remotest guess about.

'Why exactly he came this way I can't tell. Towards the end of my time here we began to hear talk of a maimed Frenchman who had been seen here and there. But no one knew then that he had foregathered with Niclaus and lived in his prau. I daresay he put Niclaus up to a thing or two. Anyhow, it was a partnership. Niclaus was somewhat afraid of the Frenchman on account of his tempers, which were awful. He looked then like a devil; but a man without hands, unable to load or handle a weapon, can at best go for one only with his teeth. From that danger Niclaus felt certain he could always defend himself.

'The couple were alone together loafing in the common room of that infamous hotel when Fector turned up. After some beating about the bush, for he was doubtful how far he could trust these two, he repeated what he had overheard in the tiffin rooms.

'His tale did not have much success till he came to mention the creek and Bamtz's name. Niclaus, sailing about like a native in a prau, was, in his own words, "familiar with the locality". The huge Frenchman, walking up and down the room with his stumps in the pockets of his jacket, stopped short in surprise. "*Comment? Bamtz! Bamtz!*"

'He had run across him several times in his life. He exclaimed: "*Bamtz! Mais je ne connais que ça!*" And he applied such a contemptuously indecent epithet to Bamtz that when, later, he alluded to him as "*une chiffe*" (a mere rag) it sounded quite complimentary. "We can do with him what we like," he asserted confidently. "Oh, yes. Certainly we must hasten to pay a visit to that—(another awful descriptive epithet.quite unfit for repetition). Devil take me if we don't pull off a coup that will set us all up for a long time.

'He saw all that lot of dollars melted into bars and disposed of somewhere on the China coast. Of the escape after the coup he never doubted. There was Niclaus's prau to manage that in.

'In his enthusiasm he pulled his stumps out of his pockets and waved them about. Then, catching sight of them, as it were, he held them in front of his eyes, cursing and blaspheming and bewailing his misfortune and his helplessness, till Niclaus quieted him down.

'But it was his mind that planned out the affair and it was his spirit which carried the other two on. Neither of them was of the bold buccaneer type; and Fector, especially, had never in his adventurous life used other weapons than slander and lies.

'That very evening they departed on a visit to Bamtz in Niclaus's prau, which had been lying, emptied of her cargo of cocoanuts, for a day or two under the canal bridge. They must have crossed the bows of the anchored *Sissie,* and no doubt looked at her with interest as the scene of their future exploit, the great haul, *le grand* coup!

'Davidson's wife, to his great surprise, sulked with him for several days before he left. I don't know whether it occurred to him that, for all her angelic profile, she was a very stupidly obstinate girl. She didn't like the tropics. He had brought her out there, where she had no friends, and now, she said, he was becoming inconsiderate. She had a presentiment of some misfortune, and notwithstanding Davidson's painstaking explanations, she could not see why her presentiments were to be disregarded. On the very last evening before Davidson went away she asked him in a suspicious manner:

'"Why is it that you are so anxious to go this time?"

'"I am not anxious," protested the good Davidson. "I simply can't help myself. There's no one else to go in my place."

'"Oh! There's no one," she said, turning away slowly.

'She was so distant with him that evening that Davidson from a sense of delicacy made up his mind to say goodbye to her at once and go and sleep on board. He felt very miserable and, strangely enough, more on his own account than on account of his wife. She seemed to him much more offended than grieved.

'Three weeks later, having collected a good many cases of old dollars (they were stowed aft in the lazarette with an iron bar and a padlock securing the hatch under his cabin table), yes, with a bigger lot than he had expected to collect, he found himself homeward bound and off the entrance of the creek where Bamtz lived and even, in a sense, flourished.

'It was so late in the day that Davidson actually hesitated whether he should not pass by this time. He had no regard for Bamtz, who was a degraded but not a really unhappy man. His pity for Laughing Anne was no more than her case deserved. But his goodness was of a particularly delicate sort. He realized how these people were dependent on him, and how they would feel their dependence (if he failed to turn up) through a long month of anxious waiting. Prompted by his sensitive humanity, Davidson, in the gathering dusk, turned the *Sissie's* head towards the hardly discernible coast, and navigated her safely through a maze of shallow patches. But by the time he got to the mouth of the creek the night had come.

'The narrow waterway lay like a black cutting through the forest. And as there were always grounded snags in the channel which it would be impossible to make out, Davidson very prudently turned the *Sissie* round, and with only enough steam on the boilers to give her a touch ahead if necessary, let her drift up stern first with the tide, silent and invisible in the impenetrable darkness and in the dumb stillness.

'It was a long job, and when at the end of two hours Davidson thought he must be up to the clearing, the settlement slept already, the whole land of forests and rivers was asleep.

'Davidson, seeing a solitary light in the massed darkness of the shore, knew that it was burning in Bamtz's house. This was unexpected at this time of the night, but convenient as a guide. By a turn of the screw and a touch of the helm he sheered the *Sissie* alongside Bamtz's wharf—a miserable structure of a dozen piles and a few planks, of which the ex-vagabond was very proud. A couple of kalashes jumped down on it, took a turn with the ropes thrown to them round the posts, and the *Sissie* came to rest without a single loud word or the slightest noise. And just in time too, for the tide turned even before she was properly moored.

'Davidson had something to eat, and then, coming on deck for a last look round, noticed that the light was still burning in the house.

'This was very unusual, but since they were awake so late, Davidson thought that he would go up to say that he was in a hurry to be off and to ask that what rattans there were in store should be sent on board with the first sign of dawn.

'He stepped carefully over the shaky planks, not being anxious to get a sprained ankle, and picked his way across the waste ground to the foot of the house ladder. The house was but a glorified hut on piles, unfenced and lonely.

'Like many a stout man, Davidson is very light-footed. He climbed the seven steps or so, stepped across the bamboo platform quietly, but what he saw through the doorway stopped him short.

'Four men were sitting by the light of a solitary candle.

There was a bottle, a jug and glasses on the table, but they were not engaged in drinking. Two packs of cards were lying there too, but they were not preparing to play. They were talking together in whispers, and remained quite unaware of him. He himself was too astonished to make a sound for some time. The world was still, except for the sibilation of the whispering heads bunched together over the table.

'And Davidson, as I have quoted him to you before, didn't like it. He didn't like it at all.

'The situation ended with a scream proceeding from the dark, interior part of the room. "O Davy! You've given me a turn."

'Davidson made out beyond the table Anne's very pale face. She laughed a little hysterically, out of the deep shadows between the gloomy mat walls. "Ha! ha! ha!"

'The four heads sprang apart at the first sound, and four pairs of eyes became fixed stonily on Davidson. The woman came forward, having little more on her than a loose chintz wrapper and straw slippers on her bare feet. Her head was tied up Malay fashion in a red handkerchief, with a mass of loose hair hanging under it behind. Her professional, gay, European feathers had literally dropped off her in the course of these two years, but a long necklace of amber beads hung round her uncovered neck. It was the only ornament she had left; Bamtz had sold all her poor-enough trinkets during the flight from Saigon—when their association began.

'She came forward, past the table, into the light, with her usual groping gesture of extended arms, as though her soul—poor thing!—had gone blind long ago, her white cheeks hollow, her eyes darkly wild, distracted, as Davidson thought. She came on swiftly, grabbed him by the arm, dragged him in. "It's heaven itself that sends you tonight. My Tony's so bad—come and see him. Come along—do!"

'Davidson submitted. The only one of the men to move was Bamtz, who made as if to get up but dropped back in his chair again. Davidson in passing heard him mutter confusedly something that sounded like "poor little beggar".

'The child, lying very flushed in a miserable cot knocked up out of gin cases, stared at Davidson with wide, drowsy eyes. It was a bad bout of fever clearly. But while Davidson was promising to go on board and fetch some medicines, and generally trying to say reassuring things, he could not help being struck by the extraordinary manner of the woman standing by his side. Gazing with despairing expression down at the cot, she would suddenly throw a quick, startled glance at Davidson and then towards the other room.

'"Yes, my poor girl," he whispered, interpreting her distraction in his own way, though he had nothing precise in his mind. "I'm afraid this bodes no good to you. How is it they are here?"

'She seized his forearm and breathed out forcibly: "No good to me! Oh, no! But what about you! They are after the dollars you have on board."

'Davidson let out an astonished "How do they know there are any dollars?"

'She clapped her hands lightly in distress. "So it's true! You have them on board? Then look out for yourself."

'They stood gazing down at the boy in the cot, aware that they might be observed from the other room.

'We must get him to perspire as soon as possible,' said Davidson in his ordinary voice. "You'll have to give him hot drink of some kind. I will go on board and bring you a spirit kettle amongst other things." And he added under his breath: "Do they actual mean murder?"

'She made no sign, she had returned to her desolate contemplation of the boy. Davidson thought she had not heard him even, when with an unchanged expression she spoke under her breath.

'"The Frenchman would, in a minute. The others shirk it—unless you resist. He's a devil. He keeps them going.

Without him they would have done nothing but talk. I've got chummy with him. What can you do when you are with a man like the fellow I am with now. Bamtz is terrified of them, and they know it. He's in it from funk. Oh, Davy! Take your ship away—quick!"

'"Too late," said Davidson. "She's on the mud already."

'"If the kid hadn't been in this state I would have run off with him—to you—into the woods—anywhere. Oh, Davy! Will he die?" she cried aloud suddenly.

'Davidson met three men in the doorway. They made way for him without actually daring to face his glance. But Bamtz was the only one who looked down with an air of guilt. The big Frenchman had remained lolling in his chair; he kept his stumps in his pockets and addressed Davidson.

'"Isn't it unfortunate about that child! The distress of that woman there upsets me, but I am of no use in the world. I couldn't smooth the sick pillow of my dearest friend. I have no hands. Would you mind sticking one of those cigarettes there into the mouth of a poor, harmless cripple? My nerves want soothing—upon my honour, they do."

'Davidson complied with his naturally kind smile. As his outward placidity becomes only more pronounced if possible, the more reason there is for excitement; and as Davidson's eyes, when his wits are hard at work get very still and as if sleepy, the huge Frenchman might have been justified in concluding that the man there was a mere sheep—a sheep ready for slaughter. With a "*merci bien*" he uplifted his huge carcass to reach the light of the candle with his cigarette, and Davidson left the house.

'Going down to the ship and returning, he had time to consider his position. At first he was inclined to believe that these men (Niclaus—the white Nakhoda—was the only one he knew by sight before, besides Bamtz) were not of the stamp to proceed to extremities. This was partly the reason why he never attempted to take any measures on board. His pacific kalashes were not to be thought of as against white men. His wretched engineer would have had a fit from fright at the mere idea of any sort of combat. Davidson knew that he would have to depend on himself in this affair if it ever came off.

'Davidson underestimated naturally the driving power of the Frenchman's character and the force of the actuating motive. To that man so hopelessly crippled these dollars were an enormous opportunity. With his share of the robbery he would open another shop in Vladivostok, Haï-phong, Manila—somewhere far away.

'Neither did it occur to Davidson, who is a man of courage, if ever there was one, that his psychology was not known to the world at large, and that to this particular lot of ruffians, who judged him by his appearance, he appeared an unsuspicious, inoffensive, soft creature, as he passed again through the room, his hands full of various objects and parcels destined for the sick boy.

'All the four were sitting again round the table, Bamtz not having the pluck to open his mouth, it was Niclaus who, as a collective voice, called out to him thickly to come out soon and join in a drink.

'"I think I'll have to stay some little time in there to help her look after the boy," Davidson answered without stopping.

'This was a good thing to say to allay a possible suspicion. And, as it was, Davidson felt he must not stay very long.

'He sat down on an old empty nail keg near the improvised cot and looked at the child; while Laughing Anne, moving to and fro, preparing the hot drink, giving it to the boy in spoonfuls, or stopping to gaze motionless at the flushed face, whispered disjointed bits of information. She had succeeded in making friends with that French devil. Davy would understand that she knew how to make herself pleasant to a man.

'And Davidson nodded without looking at her.

'The big beast had got to be quite confidential with her. She held his cards for him when they were having a game. Bamtz! Oh! Bamtz in his funk was only too glad to see the Frenchman humoured. And the Frenchman had come to believe that she was a woman who didn't care what she did. That's how it came about they got to talk before her openly. For a long time she could not make out what game they were up to. The new arrivals, not expecting to find a woman with Bamtz, had been very startled and annoyed at first, she explained.

'She busied herself in attending to the boy; and nobody looking into that room would have seen anything suspicious in those two people exchanging murmurs by the sickbed.

'"But now they think I am a better man than Bamtz ever was," she said with a faint laugh.

'The child moaned. She went down on her knees , and, bending low, contemplated him mournfully. Then raising her head, she asked Davidson whether he thought the child would get better. Davidson was sure of it. She murmured sadly: "Poor kid. There's nothing in life for such as he. Not a dog's chance. But I couldn't let him go, Davy! I couldn't."

'Davidson felt a profound pity for the child. She laid her hand on his knee and whispered an earnest warning against the Frenchman. Davy must never let him come to close quarters. Naturally Davidson wanted to know the reason, for a man without hands did not strike him as very formidable under any circumstances.

'"Mind you don't let him—that's all," she insisted anxiously, hesitated, and then confessed that the Frenchman had got her away from the others that afternoon and had ordered her to tie a seven-pound iron weight (out of the set of weights Bamtz used in business) to his right stump. She had to do it for him. She had been afraid of his savage temper. Bamtz was such a craven, and neither of the other men would have cared what happened to her. The Frenchman, however, with many awful threats had warned her not to let the others know what she had done for him. Afterwards he had been trying to cajole her. He had promised her that if she stood by him faithfully in this business he would take her with him to Haï-phong or some other place. A poor cripple needed somebody to take care of him—always.

'Davidson asked her again if they really meant mischief. It was, he told me, the hardest thing to believe he had run up against, as yet, in his life. Anne nodded. The Frenchman's heart was set on this robbery. Davy might expect them, about midnight, creeping on board his ship, to steal anyhow—to murder, perhaps. Her voice sounded weary, and her eyes remained fastened on her child.

'And still Davidson could not accept it somehow; his contempt for these men was too great.

'"Look here, Davy," she said. "I'll go outside with them when they start, and it will be hard luck if I don't find something to laugh at. They are used to that from me. Laugh or cry—what's the odds. You will be able to hear me on board on this quiet night. Dark it is too. Oh! it's dark, Davy!—it's dark!"

'"Don't you run any risks," said Davidson. Presently he called her attention to the boy, who, less flushed now, had dropped into a sound sleep. "Look. He'll be all right."

'She made as if to snatch the child up to her breast, but restrained herself. Davidson prepared to go. She whispered hurriedly:

'"Mind, Davy! I've told them that you generally sleep aft in the hammock under the awning over the cabin. They have been asking me about your ways and about your ship, too. I told them all I knew. I had to keep in with them. And Bamtz would have told them if I hadn't—you understand?"

'He made a friendly sign and went·out. The men about the table (except Bamtz) looked at him. This time it was Fector who spoke. "Won't you join us in a quiet game, Captain?"

'Davidson said that now the child was better he thought he would go on board and turn in. Fector was the only one of the four whom he had, so to speak, never seen, for he had had a good look at the Frenchman already. He observed Fector's muddy eyes, his mean, bitter mouth. Davidson's contempt for these men rose in his gorge, while his placid smile, his gentle tones and general air of innocence put heart into them. They exchanged meaning glances.

'"We shall be sitting late over the cards," Fector said in his harsh, low voice.

'"Don't make more noise than you can help."

'"Oh! We are a quiet lot. And if the invalid shouldn't be so well, she will be sure to send one of us down to call you, so that you may play the doctor again. So don't shoot at sight."

'"He isn't a shooting man," struck in Niclaus.

'"I never shoot before making sure there's a reason for it—at any rate," said Davidson.

'Bamtz let out a sickly snigger. The Frenchman alone got up to make a bow to Davidson's careless nod. His stumps were stuck immovably in his pocket, Davidson understood now the reason.

'He went down to the ship. His wits were working actively, and he was thoroughly angry. He smiled, he says (it must have been the first grim smile of his life), at the thought of the seven-pound weight lashed to the end of the Frenchman's stump. The ruffian had taken that precaution in case of a quarrel that might arise over the division of the spoil.

A man with an unsuspected power to deal killing blows could take his own part in a sudden scrimmage round a heap of money, even against adversaries armed with revolvers, especially if he himself started the row.

'"He's ready to face any of his friends with that thing. But he will have no use for it. There will be no occasion to quarrel about these dollars here," thought Davidson, getting on board quietly. He never paused to look if there was anybody about the decks. As a matter of fact, most of his crew were on shore, and the rest slept, stowed away in dark corners.

'He had his plan, and he went to work methodically.

'He fetched a lot of clothing from below and disposed it in his hammock in such a way as to distend it to the shape of a human body; then he threw over all the light cotton sheet he used to draw over himself when sleeping on deck. Having done this, he loaded his two revolvers and clambered into one of the boats the *Sissie* carried right aft, swung out on their davits. Then he waited.

'And again the doubt of such a thing happening to him crept into his mind. He was almost ashamed of this ridiculous vigil in a boat. He became bored, and then he became drowsy. The stillness of the black universe wearied him. There was not even the lapping of the water to keep him company, for the tide was out and the *Sissie* was lying on soft mud. Suddenly in the breathless, soundless, hot night an argus pheasant screamed in the woods across the stream. Davidson started violently, all his senses on the alert at once.

'The candle was still burning in the house. Everything was quiet again, but Davidson felt drowsy no longer. An uneasy premonition of evil oppressed him.

'"Surely I am not afraid," he argued with himself.

'The silence was like a seal on his ears, and his nervous inward impatience grew intolerable. He commanded himself to keep still. But all the same he was just going to jump out of the boat when a faint ripple on the immensity of silence, a mere tremor in the air, the ghost of a silvery laugh, reached his ears.

'Illusion!

'He kept very still. He had no difficulty now in emulating the stillness of the mouse—a grimly determined mouse. But he could not shake off that premonition of evil unrelated to the mere danger of the situation. Nothing happened. It had been an illusion!

'A curiosity came to him to learn how they would go to work. He wondered and wondered, till the whole thing seemed more absurd than ever.

'He had left the hanging lamp in the cabin burning as usual. It was part of his plan that everything should be as usual. Suddenly in the dim glow of the skylight panes a bulky shadow came up the ladder without a sound, made two steps towards the hammock (it hung right over the skylight), and stood motionless. The Frenchman!

'The minutes began to slip away. Davidson guessed that the Frenchman's part (the poor cripple) was to watch his (Davidson's) slumbers while the others were no doubt in the cabin busy forcing off the lazarette hatch.

'What was the course they meant to pursue once they got hold of the silver (there were ten cases, and each could be carried easily by two men) nobody can tell now. But so far, Davidson was right. They were in the cabin. He expected to hear the sounds of breaking-in every moment. But the fact was that one of them (perhaps Fector, who had stolen papers out of desks in his time) knew how to pick a lock, and apparently was provided with the tools. Thus while Davidson expected every moment to hear them begin down there, they had the bar off already and two cases actually up in the cabin out of the lazarette.

'In the diffused faint glow of the skylight the Frenchman

moved no more than a statue. Davidson could have shot him with the greatest ease—but he was not homicidally inclined. Moreover, he wanted to make sure before opening fire that the others had gone to work. Not hearing the sounds he expected to hear, he felt uncertain whether they all were on board yet.

'While he listened, the Frenchman, whose immobility might have but cloaked an internal struggle, moved forward a pace, then another. Davidson, entranced, watched him advance one leg, withdraw his right stump, the armed one, out of his pocket, and swinging his body to put greater force into the blow, bring the seven-pound weight down on the hammock where the head of the sleeper ought to have been.

'Davidson admitted to me that his hair stirred at the roots then. But for Anne, his unsuspecting head would have been there. The Frenchman's surprise must have been simply overwhelming. He staggered away from the lightly swinging hammock, and before Davidson could make a movement he had vanished, bounding down the ladder to warn and alarm the other fellows.

'Davidson sprang instantly out of the boat, threw up the skylight flap, and had a glimpse of the men down there crouching round the hatch. They looked up scared, and at that moment the Frenchman outside the door bellowed out *"Trahison—trahison!"* They bolted out of the cabin, falling over each other and swearing awfully. The shot Davidson let off down the skylight had hit no one; but he ran to the edge of the cabin top and at once opened fire at the dark shapes rushing about the deck. These shots were returned, and a rapid fusillade burst out, reports and flashes, Davidson dodging behind a ventilator and pulling the trigger till his revolver clicked, and then throwing it down to take the other in his right hand.

'He had been hearing in the din the Frenchman's

infuriated yells "*Tuez-le*! *Tuez-le*!" above the fierce cursing of the others. But though they fired at him they were only thinking of clearing out. In the flashes of the last shots Davidson saw them scrambling over the rail. That he had hit more than one he was certain. Two different voices had cried out in pain. But apparently none of them were disabled.

'Davidson leaned against the bulwark reloading his revolver without haste. He had not the slightest apprehension of their coming back. On the other hand, he had no intention of pursuing them on shore in the dark. What they were doing he had no idea. Looking to their hurts probably. Not very far from the bank the invisible Frenchman was blaspheming and cursing his associates, his luck, and all the world. He ceased; then with a sudden, vengeful yell, "It's that woman!—it's that woman that has sold us", was heard running off in the night.

'Davidson caught his breath in a sudden pang of remorse. He perceived with dismay that the stratagem of his defence had given Anne away. He did not hesitate a moment. It was for him to save her now. He leaped ashore. But even as he landed on the wharf he heard a shrill shriek which pierced his very soul.

'The light was still burning in the house. Davidson, revolver in hand, was making for it when another shriek, away to his left, made him change his direction.

'He changed his direction—but very soon he stopped. It was then that he hesitated in cruel perplexity. He guessed what had happened. The woman had managed to escape from the house in some way, and now was being chased in the open by the infuriated Frenchman. He trusted she would try to run on board for protection.

'All was still around Davidson. Whether she had run on board or not, this silence meant that the Frenchman had lost her in the dark.

'Davidson, relieved, but still very anxious, turned

towards the riverside. He had not made two steps in that direction when another shriek burst out behind him, again close to the house.

'His belief that the Frenchman had lost sight of the poor woman was right enough. Then had come that period of silence. But the horrible ruffian had not given up his murderous purpose. He reasoned that she would try to steal back to her child, and went to lie in wait for her near the house.

'It must have been something like that. As she entered the light falling about the house ladder, he had rushed at her too soon, impatient for vengeance. She had let out that second scream of mortal fear when she caught sight of him, and turned to run for life again.

'This time she was making for the river, but not in a straight line. Her shrieks circled about Davidson. He turned on his heels, following the horrible trail of sound in the darkness. He wanted to shout "This way, Anne! I am here!" but he couldn't. At the horror of this chase, more ghastly in his imagination than if he could have seen it, the perspiration broke out on his forehead, while his throat was as dry as tinder. A last supreme scream was cut short suddenly.

'The silence which ensued was even more dreadful. Davidson felt sick. He tore his feet from the spot and walked straight before him, gripping the revolver and peering into the obscurity fearfully. Suddenly a bulky shape sprang from the ground within a few yards of him and bounded away. Instinctively he fired at it, started to run in pursuit, and stumbled against something soft which threw him down headlong.

'Even as he pitched forward on his head he knew it could be nothing else but Laughing Anne's body. He picked himself up and, remaining on his knees, tried to lift her in his arms. He felt her so limp that he gave it up. She was lying on her face, her long hair scattered on the ground. Some of it was wet. Davidson, feeling about her head, came to a place where the crushed bone gave way under his fingers. But even before that discovery he knew that she was dead. The pursuing Frenchman had flung her down with a kick from behind, and, squatting on her back, was battering in her skull with the weight she herself had fastened to his stump, when the totally unexpected Davidson loomed up in the night and scared him away.

'Davidson, kneeling by the side of that woman done so miserably to death, was overcome by remorse. She had died for him. His manhood was as if stunned. For the first time he felt afraid. He might have been pounded upon in the dark at any moment by the murderer of Laughing Anne. He confesses to the impulse of creeping away from that pitiful corpse on his hands and knees to the refuge of the ship. He even says that he actually began to do so . . .

'One can hardly picture to oneself Davidson crawling away on all fours from the murdered woman—Davidson unmanned and crushed by the idea that she had died for him in a sense. But he could not have gone very far. What stopped him was the thought of the boy, Laughing Anne's child, that (Davidson remembered her very words) would not have a dog's chance.

'This life the woman had left behind her appeared to Davidson's conscience in the light of a sacred trust. He assumed an erect attitude and, quaking inwardly still, turned about and walked towards the house.

'For all his tremors he was very determined, but that smashed skull had affected his imagination, and he felt very defenceless in the darkness in which he seemed to hear faintly now here, now there, the prowling footsteps of the murderer without hands. But he never faltered in his purpose. He got away with the boy safely after all. The house he found empty.

A profound silence encompassed him all the time, except once, just as he got down the ladder with Tony in his arms, when a faint groan reached his ears. It seemed to come from the pitch-black space between the posts on which the house was built, but he did not stop to investigate.

'It's no use telling you in detail how Davidson got on board with the burden Anne's miserably cruel fate had thrust into his arms; how next morning his scared crew, after observing from a distance the state of affairs on board, rejoined with alacrity; how Davidson went ashore and, aided by his engineer (still half-dead with fright), rolled up Laughing Anne's body in a cotton sheet and brought it on board for burial at sea later. While busy with this pious task, Davidson, glancing about, perceived a huge heap of white clothes huddled up against the cornerpost of the house. That it was the Frenchman lying there he could not doubt. Taking it in connection with the dismal groan he had heard in the night, Davidson is pretty sure that his random shot gave a mortal hurt to the murderer of poor Anne.

'As to the others, Davidson never set eyes on a single one of them. Whether they had concealed themselves in the scared settlement, or bolted into the forest, or were hiding on board Niclaus's prau, which could be seen lying on the mud a hundred yards or so higher up the creek, the fact is that they vanished; and Davidson did not trouble his head about them. He lost no time in getting out of the creek directly the *Sissie* floated. After steaming some twenty miles clear of the coast, he (in his own words) "committed the body to the deep". He did everything himself. He weighted her down with a few fire bars, he read the service, he lifted the plank, he was the only mourner. And while he was rendering these last services to the dead, the desolation of that life and the atrocious wretchedness of its end cried aloud to his compassion, whispered to him in tones of self-reproach.

'He ought to have handled the warning she had given him in another way. He was convinced now that a simple display of watchfulness would have been enough to restrain that vile and cowardly crew. But the fact was that he had not quite believed that anything would be attempted.

'The body of Laughing Anne having been "committed to the deep" some twenty miles south-south-west from Cape Selatan, the task before Davidson was to commit Laughing Anne's child to the care of his wife. And there poor, good Davidson made a fatal move. He didn't want to tell her the whole awful story, since it involved the knowledge of the danger from which he, Davidson, had escaped. And this, too, after he had been laughing at her unreasonable fears only a short time before.

'"I thought that if I told her everything," Davidson explained to me, "she would never have a moment's peace while I was away on my trips."

'He simply stated that the boy was an orphan, the child of some people to whom he, Davidson, was under the greatest obligation, and that he felt morally bound to look after him. Some day he would tell her more, he said, and meantime he trusted in the goodness and warmth of her heart, in her woman's natural compassion.

'He did not know that her heart was about the size of a parched pea, and had the proportional amount of warmth; and that her faculty of compassion was mainly directed to herself. He was only startled and disappointed at the air of cold surprise and the suspicious look with which she received his imperfect tale. But she did not say much. She never had much to say. She was a fool of the silent, hopeless kind.

'What story Davidson's crew thought fit to set afloat in Malay town is neither here nor there. Davidson himself took some of his friends into his confidence, besides giving the full story officially to the Harbour Master.

'The Harbour Master was considerably astonished. He didn't think, however, that a formal complaint should be made to the Dutch Government. They would probably do nothing in the end, after a lot of trouble and correspondence. The robbery had not come off, after all. Those vagabonds could be trusted to go to the devil in their own way. No amount of fuss would bring the poor woman to life again, and the actual murderer had been done justice to by a chance shot from Davidson. Better let the matter drop.

'This was good common sense. But he was impressed.

'"Sounds a terrible affair, Captain Davidson."

'"Aye, terrible enough," agreed the remorseful Davidson. But the most terrible thing for him, though he didn't know it then, was that his wife's silly brain was slowly coming to the conclusion that Tony was Davidson's child, and that he had invented that lame story to introduce him into her pure home in defiance of decency, of virtue—of her most sacred feelings.

'Davidson was aware of some constraint in his domestic relations. But at the best of times she was not demonstrative; and perhaps that very coldness was part of her charm in the placid Davidson's eyes. Women are loved for all sorts of reasons and even for characteristics which one would think repellent. She was watching him and nursing her suspicions.

'Then, one day, Monkey-face Ritchie called on that sweet, shy Mrs Davidson. She had come out under his care, and he considered himself a privileged person—her oldest friend in the tropics. He posed for a great admirer of hers. He was always a great chatterer. He had got hold of the story rather vaguely, and he started chattering on that subject, thinking she knew all about it. And in due course he let out something about Laughing Anne.

'"Laughing Anne," says Mrs Davidson with a start. "What's that?"

303

'Ritchie plunged into circumlocution at once, but she very soon stopped him. "Is that creature dead?" she asks.

'"I believe so," stammered Ritchie. "Your husband says so."

'"But you don't know for certain?"

'"No! How could I, Mrs Davidson!'

'"That's all I wanted to know," says she, and goes out of the room.

'When Davidson came home she was ready to go for him, not with common voluble indignation, but as if trickling a stream of cold clear water down his back. She talked of his base intrigue with a vile woman, of being made a fool of, of the insult to her dignity.

'Davidson begged her to listen to him and told her all the story, thinking that it would move a heart of stone. He tried to make her understand his remorse. She heard him to the end, said "Indeed!" and turned her back on him.

'"Don't you believe me?" he asked, appalled.

'She didn't say yes or no. All she said was, "Send that brat away at once."

'"I can't throw him out into the street," cried Davidson. "You don't mean it."

'"I don't care. There are charitable institutions for such children, I suppose."

'"That I will never do," said Davidson.

'"Very well. That's enough for me."

'Davidson's home after this was like a silent, frozen hell for him. A stupid woman with a sense of grievance is worse than an unchained devil. He sent the boy to the White Fathers in Malacca. This was not a very expensive sort of education, but she could not forgive him for not casting the offensive child away utterly. She worked up her sense of her wifely wrongs and of her injured purity to such a pitch that one day, when poor Davidson was pleading with her to be reasonable and not to make an impossible existence for them both, she turned on him in a chill passion and told him that his very sight was odious to her.

'Davidson, with his scrupulous delicacy of feeling, was not the man to assert his rights over a woman who could not bear the sight of him. He bowed his head; and shortly afterwards arranged for her to go back to her parents. That was exactly what she wanted in her outraged dignity. And then she had always disliked the tropics and had detested secretly the people she had to live amongst as Davidson's wife. She took her pure, sensitive, mean little soul away to Fremantle or somewhere in that direction. And of course the little girl went away with her too. What could poor Davidson had done with a little girl on his hands, even if she had consented to leave her with him—which is unthinkable.

'This is the story that has spoiled Davidson's smile for him—which perhaps it wouldn't have done so thoroughly had he been less of a good fellow.'

Hollis ceased. But before we rose from the table I asked him if he knew what had become of Laughing Anne's boy.

He counted carefully the change handed him by the Chinaman waiter, and raised his head.

'Oh! that's the finishing touch. He was a bright, taking little chap, as you know, and the Fathers took very special pains in his bringing up. Davidson expected in his heart to have some comfort out of him. In his placid way he's a man who needs affection. Well, Tony has grown into a fine youth—but there you are! He wants to be a priest; his one dream is to be a missionary. The Fathers assure Davidson that it is a serious vocation. They tell him he has a special disposition for mission work, too. So Laughing Anne's boy will lead a saintly life in China somewhere; he may even become a martyr; but poor Davidson is left out in the cold. He will have to go downhill without a single human affection near him because of these old dollars.'

The Secret Sharer

I

ON MY right hand there were lines of fishing-stakes resembling a mysterious system of half-submerged bamboo fences, incomprehensible in its division of the domain of tropical fishes, and crazy of aspect as if abandoned forever by some nomad tribe of fishermen now gone to the other end of the ocean; for there was no sign of human habitation as far as the eye could reach. To the left a group of barren islets, suggesting ruins of stone walls, towers and blockhouses, had its foundations set in a blue sea that itself looked solid, so still and stable did it lie below my feet; even the track of light from the westering sun shone smoothly, without that animated glitter which tells of an imperceptible ripple. And when I turned my head to take a parting glance at the tug which had just left us anchored outside the bar, I saw the straight line of the flat shore joined to the stable sea, edge to edge, with a perfect and unmarked closeness, in one levelled floor half brown, half blue under the enormous dome of the sky. Corresponding in their insignificance to the islets of the sea, two small clumps of trees, one on each side of the only fault in the impeccable joint, marked the mouth of the river Meinam we had just left on the first preparatory stage of our homeward journey; and, far back on the inland level, a larger and loftier mass, the grove surrounding the great Paknam pagoda, was the only thing on which the eye could rest from the vain task of exploring the monotonous sweep of the horizon. Here and there gleams as of a few scattered pieces of silver marked the windings of the great river; and on the nearest of them, just within the bar, the tug steaming right into the land became lost to my sight, hull and funnel and masts, as though the impassive earth had swallowed her up without an effort, without a tremor. My eye followed the light cloud of her smoke, now here, now there, above the plain, according to the devious curves of the stream, but always fainter and farther away, till I lost it at last behind the mitre-shaped hill of the great pagoda. And then I was left alone with my ship, anchored at the head of the Gulf of Siam.

She floated at the starting point of a long journey, very still in an immense stillness, the shadows of her spars flung far to the eastward by the setting sun. At that moment I was alone on her decks. There was not a sound in her—and around us nothing moved, nothing lived, not a canoe on the water; not a bird in the air, not a cloud in the sky. In this breathless pause at the threshold of a long passage we seemed to be measuring our fitness for a long and arduous enterprise, the appointed task of both our existences to be carried out, far from all human eyes, with only sky and sea for spectators and for judges.

There must have been some glare in the air to interfere with one's sight, because it was only just before the sun left us that my roaming eyes made out beyond the highest ridge of the principal islet of the group something which did away with the solemnity of perfect solitude. The tide of darkness flowed on swiftly; and with tropical suddenness a swarm of stars came out above the shadowy earth, while I lingered yet, my hand resting lightly on my ship's rail as if on the shoulder of a trusted friend. But, with all that multitude of celestial bodies staring down at one, the comfort of quiet communion with her was gone for good. And there were also disturbing sounds by this time—voices, footsteps forward; the steward flitted along the main deck, a busily ministering spirit; a handbell tinkled urgently under the poop deck . . .

I found my two officers waiting for me near the supper table, in the lighted cuddy. We sat down at once, and as I helped the chief mate, I said: 'Are you aware that there is a ship anchored inside the islands? I saw her mastheads above the ridge as the sun went down.'

He raised sharply his simple face, overcharged by a terrible growth of whisker, and emitted his usual ejaculations: 'Bless my soul, sir! You don't say so!'

My second mate was a round-cheeked, silent young man, grave beyond his years, I thought; but as our eyes happened to meet I detected a slight quiver on his lips. I looked down at once. It was not my part to encourage sneering on board my ship. It must be said, too, that I knew very little of my officers. In consequence of certain events of no particular significance, except to myself, I had been appointed to the command only a fortnight before. Neither did I know much of the hands forward. All these people had been together for eighteen months or so, and my position was that of the only stranger on board. I mention this because it has some bearing on what is to follow. But what I felt most was my being a stranger to the ship; and if all the truth must be told, I was somewhat of a stranger to myself. The youngest man on board (barring the second mate), and untried as yet by a position of the fullest responsibility, I was willing to take the adequacy of the others for granted. They had simply to be equal to their tasks; but I wondered how far I should turn out faithful to that ideal conception of one's own personality every man sets up for himself secretly.

Meantime the chief mate, with an almost visible effect of collaboration on the part of his round eyes and frightful whiskers, was trying to evolve a theory of the anchored ship. His dominant trait was to take all things into earnest consideration. He was of a painstaking turn of mind. As he used to say, he 'liked to account to himself' for practically everything that came in his way, down to a miserable scorpion he had found in his cabin a week before. The why and the wherefore of that scorpion—how it got on board and came to select his room rather than the pantry (which was a dark place and more what a scorpion would be partial to), and how on earth it managed to drown itself in the inkwell of his writing-desk—had exercised him infinitely. The ship within the islands was much more easily accounted for; and just as we were about to rise from table he made his pronouncement. She was, he doubted not, a ship from home lately arrived. Probably she drew too much water to cross the bar except at the top of spring tides. Therefore she went into that natural harbour to wait for a few days in preference to remaining in an open roadstead.

'That's so,' confirmed the second mate, suddenly, in his slightly hoarse voice. 'She draws over twenty feet. She's the Liverpool ship *Sephora* with a cargo of coal. Hundred and twenty-three days from Cardiff.'

We looked at him in surprise.

'The tugboat skipper told me when he came on board for your letters, sir,' explained the young man. 'He expects to take her up the river the day after tomorrow.'

After thus overwhelming us with the extent of his information he slipped out of the cabin. The mate observed regretfully that he 'could not account for that young fellow's whims'. What prevented him telling us all about it at once, he wanted to know.

I detained him as he was making a move. For the last two days the crew had had plenty of hard work, and the night before they had had very little sleep. I felt painfully that I—a stranger—was doing something unusual when I directed him to let all hands turn in without setting an anchor-watch. I proposed to keep on deck myself till one o'clock or thereabouts. I would get the second mate to relieve me at that hour.

'He will turn out the cook and the steward at four,' I concluded, 'and then give you a call. Of course at the slightest sign of any sort of wind we'll have the hands up and make a start at once.'

He concealed his astonishment. 'Very well, sir.' Outside the cuddy he put his head in the second mate's door to inform him of my unheard-of caprice to take a five hours' anchor watch on myself. I heard the other raise his voice incredulously—'What? The captain himself?' Then a few more murmurs, a door closed, then another. A few moments later I went on deck.

My strangeness, which had made me sleepless, had prompted that unconventional arrangement, as if I had expected in those solitary hours of the night to get on terms with the ship of which I knew nothing, manned by men of whom I knew very little more. Fast alongside a wharf, littered like any ship in port with a tangle of unrelated things, invaded by unrelated shore people, I had hardly seen her yet properly. Now, as she lay cleared for sea, the stretch of her main deck seemed to me very fine under the stars. Very fine, very roomy for her size, and very inviting. I descended the poop and paced the waist, my mind picturing to myself the coming passage through the Malay archipelago, down the Indian Ocean, and up the Atlantic. All its phases were familiar enough to me, every characteristic, all the alternatives which were likely to face me on the high seas—everything!—except the novel responsibility of command. But I took heart from the reasonable thought that the ship was like other ships, the men like other men, and that the sea was not likely to keep any special surprises expressly for my discomfiture.

Arrived at that comforting conclusion, I bethought myself of a cigar and went below to get it. All was still down there. Everybody at the after end of the ship was sleeping profoundly. I came out again on the quarterdeck, agreeably at ease in my sleeping suit on that warm breathless night, barefooted, a glowing cigar in my teeth, and, going forward, I was met by the profound silence of the fore end of the ship. Only as I passed the door of the forecastle I heard a deep, quiet, trustful sigh of some sleeper inside. And suddenly I rejoiced in the great security of the sea as compared with the unrest of the land, in my choice of that untempted life presenting no disquieting problems, invested with an elementary moral beauty by the absolute straightforwardness of its appeal and by the singleness of its purpose.

The riding light in the fore rigging burned with a clear, untroubled, as if symbolic, flame, confident and bright in the mysterious shades of the night. Passing on my way aft along the other side of the ship, I observed that the rope side ladder, put over, no doubt, for the master of the tug when he came to fetch away our letters, had not been hauled in as it should have been. I became annoyed at this, for exactitude in small matters is the very soul of discipline. Then I reflected that I had myself peremptorily dismissed my officers from duty, and by my own act had prevented the anchor watch being formally set and things properly attended to. I asked myself whether it was wise ever to interfere with the established routine of duties even from the kindest of motives. My action might have made me appear eccentric. Goodness only knew how that absurdly whiskered mate would 'account' for my conduct, and what the whole ship thought of that informality of their new captain. I was vexed with myself.

Not from compunction certainly, but, as it were mechanically, I proceeded to get the ladder in myself. Now a side ladder of that sort is a light affair and comes in easily, yet my vigorous tug, which should have brought it flying on board, merely recoiled upon my body in a totally unexpected jerk. What the devil! . . . I was so astounded by the immovableness of that ladder that I remained stock-still, trying to account for it to myself like that imbecile mate of mine. In the end, of course, I put my head over the rail.

The side of the ship made an opaque belt of shadow on the darkling glassy shimmer of the sea. But I saw at once something elongated and pale floating very close to the ladder. Before I could form a guess a faint flash of phosphorescent light, which seemed to issue suddenly from the naked body of a man, flickered in the sleeping water with the elusive, silent play of summer lightning in a night sky. With a gasp I saw revealed to my stare a pair of feet, the long legs, a broad livid back immersed right up to the neck in a greenish cadaverous glow. One hand, awash, clutched the bottom rung of the ladder. He was complete but for the head. A headless corpse! The cigar dropped out of my gaping mouth with a tiny plop and a short hiss quite audible in the absolute stillness of all things under heaven. At that I suppose he raised up his face, a dimly pale oval in the shadow of the ship's side. But even then I could only barely make out down there the shape of his black-haired head. However, it was enough for the horrid, frost-bound sensation which had gripped me about the chest to pass off. The moment of vain exclamations was past, too. I only climbed on the spare spar and leaned over the rail as far as I could, to bring my eyes nearer to that mystery floating alongside.

As he hung by the ladder, like a resting swimmer, the sea lightning played about his limbs at every stir; and he appeared in it ghastly, silvery, fish-like. He remained as mute as a fish, too. He made no motion to get out of the water, either. It was inconceivable that he should not attempt to come on board, and strangely troubling to suspect that perhaps he did not want to. And my first words were prompted by just that troubled incertitude.

'What's the matter?' I asked in my ordinary tone, speaking down to the face upturned exactly under mine.

'Cramp,' it answered, no louder. Then slightly anxious, 'I say, no need to call anyone.'

'I was not going to,' I said.

'Are you alone on deck?'

'Yes.'

I had somehow the impression that he was on the point of letting go the ladder to swim away beyond my ken—mysterious as he came. But, for the moment, this being appearing as if he had risen from the bottom of the sea (it was certainly the nearest land to the ship) wanted only to know the time. I told him. And he, down there, tentatively: 'I suppose your captain's turned in?'

'I am sure he isn't,' I said.

He seemed to struggle with himself, for I heard something like the low, bitter murmur of doubt. 'What's the good?' His next words came out with a hesitating effort.

'Look here, my man. Could you call him out quietly?' I thought the time had come to declare myself.

'I am the captain.'

I heard a 'By Jove!' whispered at the level of the water. The phosphorescence flashed in the swirl of the water all about his limbs, his other hand seized the ladder.

'My name's Leggatt.'

The voice was calm and resolute. A good voice. The self possession of that man had somehow induced a corresponding state in myself. It was very quietly that I remarked: 'You must be a good swimmer.'

'Yes. I've been in the water practically since nine o'clock. The question for me now is whether I am to let go this ladder and go on swimming till I sink from exhaustion, or—to come on board here.'

I felt this was no mere formula of desperate speech, but a real alternative in the view of a strong soul. I should have gathered from this that he was young; indeed, it is only the young who are ever confronted by such clear issues. But at the time it was pure intuition on my part. A mysterious communication was established already between us two—in the face of that silent, darkened tropical sea. I was young, too;

young enough to make no comment. The man in the water began suddenly to climb up the ladder, and I hastened away from the rail to fetch some clothes.

Before entering the cabin I stood still, listening in the lobby at the foot of the stairs. A faint snore came through the closed door of the chief mate's room. The second mate's door was on the hook, but the darkness in there was absolutely soundless. He, too, was young and could sleep like a stone. Remained the steward, but he was not likely to wake up before he was called. I got a sleeping suit out of my room and, coming back on deck, saw the naked man from the sea sitting on the main hatch, glimmering white in the darkness, his elbows on his knees and his head in his hands. In a moment he had concealed his damp body in a sleeping suit of the same grey-stripe pattern as the one I was wearing and followed me like my double on the poop. Together we moved right aft, barefooted, silent.

'What is it?' I asked in a deadened voice, taking the lighted lamp out of the binnacle, and raising it to his face.

'An ugly business.'

He had rather regular features; a good mouth; light eyes under somewhat heavy, dark eyebrows; a smooth, square forehead; no growth on his cheeks; a small, brown moustache, and a well-shaped, round chin. His expression was concentrated, meditative, under the inspecting light of the lamp I held up to his face; such as a man thinking hard in solitude might wear. My sleeping suit was just right for his size. A well-knit young fellow of twenty-five at most. He caught his lower lip with the edge of white, even teeth.

'Yes,' I said, replacing the lamp in the binnacle. The warm, heavy tropical night closed upon his head again.

'There's a ship over there,' he murmured.

'Yes, I know. The *Sephora*. Did you know of us?'

'Hadn't the slightest idea. I am the mate of her—' He

paused and corrected himself. 'I should say I was.'

'Aha! Something wrong?'

'Yes. Very wrong indeed. I've killed a man.'

'What do you mean? Just now?'

'No, on the passage. Weeks ago. Thirty-nine south. When I say a man—'

'Fit of temper,' I suggested, confidently.

The shadowy, dark head, like mine, seemed to nod imperceptibly above the ghostly grey of my sleeping suit. It was, in the night, as though I had been faced by my own reflection in the depths of a sombre and immense mirror.

'A pretty thing to have to own up to for a Conway boy,' murmured my double, distinctly.

'You're a Conway boy?'

'I am,' he said, as if startled. Then, slowly . . . 'Perhaps you too—'

It was so; but being a couple of years older I had left before he joined. After a quick interchange of dates a silence fell; and I thought suddenly of my absurd mate with his terrific whiskers and the 'Bless my soul—you don't say so' type of intellect.

My double gave me an inkling of his thoughts by saying: 'My father's a parson in Norfolk. Do you see me before a judge and jury on that charge? For myself I can't see the necessity. There are fellows that an angel from heaven—And I am not that. He was one of the creatures that are just simmering all the time with a silly sort wickedness. Miserable devils that have no business to live at all. He wouldn't do his duty and wouldn't let anybody else do theirs. But what's the good of talking! You know well enough the sort of conditioned snarling cur—'

He appealed to me as if our experiences had been as identical as our clothes. And I knew well enough the pestiferous danger of such character where there are no means of legal repression. And I knew well enough also that my double there was no homicidal ruffian. I did not think of asking him for details, and he told me the story roughly in brusque, disconnected sentences. I needed no more. I saw it all going on as though I were myself inside that other sleeping suit.

'It happened while we were setting a reefed foresail, at dusk. Reefed foresail! You understand the sort of weather. The only sail we had left to keep the ship running; so you may guess what it had been like for days. Anxious sort of job, that. He gave me some of his cursed insolence at the sheet. I tell you I was overdone with this terrific weather that seemed to have no end to it. Terrific, I tell you—and a deep ship. I believe the fellow himself was half crazed with funk. It was no time for gentlemanly reproof, so I turned round and felled him like an ox. He was soon up and at me. We closed just as an awful sea made for the ship. All hands saw it coming and took to the rigging, but I had him by the throat, and went on shaking him like a rat, the men above us yelling, "Look out! Look out!" Then a crash as if the sky had fallen on my head. They say that for over ten minutes hardly anything was to be seen of the ship—just the three masts and a bit of the forecastle head and of the poop all awash driving along in a smother of foam. It was a miracle that they found us, jammed together behind the forebits. It's clear that I meant business, because I was holding him by the throat still when they picked us up. He was black in the face. It was too much for them. It seems they rushed us aft together, gripped as we were, screaming "Murder!" like a lot of lunatics, and broke into the cuddy. And the ship running for her life, touch and go all the time, any minute her last in a sea fit to turn your hair grey only a-looking at it. I understand that the skipper, too, started raving like the rest of them. The man had been deprived of sleep for more than a week, and to have this sprung on him at the height of a furious

319

gale nearly drove him out of his mind. I wonder they didn't fling me overboard after getting the carcass of their precious shipmate out of my fingers. They had rather a job to separate us, I've been told. A sufficiently fierce story to make an old judge and a respectable jury sit up a bit. The first thing I heard when I came to myself was the maddening howling of that endless gale, and on that the voice of the old man. He was hanging on to my bunk, staring into my face out of his sou'wester.

'"Mr Leggatt, you have killed a man. You can act no longer as chief mate of this ship."'

His care to subdue his voice made it sound monotonous. He rested a hand on the end of the skylight to steady himself with, and all that time did not stir a limb, so far as I could see. 'Nice little tale for a quiet tea party,' he concluded in the same tone.

One of my hands, too, rested on the end of the skylight; neither did I stir a limb, so far as I knew. We stood less than a foot from each other. It occurred to me that if old 'Bless my soul—you don't say so' were to put his head up the companion and catch sight of us, he would think he was seeing double, or imagine himself come upon a scene of weird witchcraft; the strange captain having a quiet confabulation by the wheel with his own grey ghost. I became very much concerned to prevent anything of the sort. I heard the other's soothing undertone.

'My father's a parson in Norfolk,' it said. Evidently he had forgotten he had told me this important fact before. Truly a nice little tale.

'You had better slip down into my stateroom now,' I said, moving off stealthily. My double followed my movements; our bare feet made no sound; I let him in, closed the door with care, and, after giving a call to the second mate, returned on deck for my relief.

'Not much sign of any wind yet,' I remarked when he approached.

'No, sir. Not much,' he assented, sleepily, in his hoarse voice, with just enough deference, no more, and barely suppressing a yawn.

'Well, that's all you have to look out for. You have got your orders.'

'Yes, sir.'

I paced a turn or two on the poop and saw him take up his position face forward with his elbow in the ratlines of the mizzen-rigging before I went below. The mate's faint snoring was still going on peacefully. The cuddy lamp was burning over the table on which stood a vase with flowers, a polite attention from the ship's provision merchant—the last flowers we should see for the next three months at the very least. Two bunches of bananas hung from the beam symmetrically, one on each side of the rudder-casing. Everything was as before in the ship—except that two of her captain's sleeping suits were simultaneously in use, one motionless in the cuddy, the other keeping very still in the captain's stateroom.

It must be explained here that my cabin had the form of the capital letter L, the door being within the angle and opening into the short part of the letter. A couch was to the left, the bed-place to the right; my writing desk and the chronometers' table faced the door. But anyone opening it, unless he stepped right inside, had no view of what I call the long (or vertical) part of the letter. It contained some lockers surmounted by a bookcase; and a few clothes, a thick jacket or two, caps, oilskin coat, and suchlike, hung on hooks. There was at the bottom of that part a door opening into my bathroom, which could be entered also directly from the saloon. But that way was never used.

The mysterious arrival had discovered the advantage of

this particular shape. Entering my room, lighted strongly by a big bulkhead lamp swung on gimbals above my writing desk, I did not see him anywhere till he stepped out quietly from behind the coats hung in the recessed part.

'I heard somebody moving about, and went in there at once,' he whispered.

I, too, spoke under my breath.

'Nobody is likely to come in here without knocking and getting permission.'

He nodded. His face was thin and the sunburn faded, as though he had been ill. And no wonder. He had been, I heard presently, kept under arrest in his cabin for nearly nine weeks. But there was nothing sickly in his eyes or in his expression. He was not a bit like me, really; yet, as we stood leaning over my bed-place, whispering side by side, with our dark heads together and our backs to the door, anybody bold enough to open it stealthily would have been treated to the uncanny sight of a double captain busy talking in whispers with his other self.

'But all this doesn't tell me how you came to hang on to our side ladder,' I enquired, in the hardly audible murmurs we used, after he had told me something more of the proceedings on board the *Sephora* once the bad weather was over.

'When we sighted Java Head I had had time to think all those matters out several times over. I had six weeks of doing nothing else, and with only an hour or so every evening for a tramp on the quarterdeck.'

He whispered, his arms folded on the side of my bed-place, staring through the open port. And I could imagine perfectly the manner of this thinking out—a stubborn if not a steadfast operation; something of which I should have been perfectly incapable.

'I reckoned it would be dark before we closed with the land,' he continued, so low that I had to strain my hearing, near as we were to each other, shoulder touching shoulder almost. 'So I asked to speak to the old man. He always seemed very sick when he came to see me—as if he could not look me in the face. You know, that foresail saved the ship. She was too deep to have run long under bare poles. And it was I that managed to set it for him. Anyway, he came. When I had him in my cabin—he stood by the door looking at me as if I had the halter round my neck already—I asked him right away to leave my cabin door unlocked at night while the ship was going through Sunda Straits. There would be the Java coast within two or three miles, off Angier Point. I wanted nothing more. I've had a prize for swimming—my second year in the Conway.'

'I can believe it,' I breathed out.

'God only knows why they locked me in every night. To see some of their faces you'd have thought they were afraid I'd go about at night strangling people. Am I a murdering brute? Do I look it? By Jove, if I had been he wouldn't have trusted himself like that into my room. You'll say I might have chucked him aside and bolted out, there and then—it was dark already. Well, no. And for the same reason I wouldn't think of trying to smash the door. There would have been a rush to stop me at the noise, and I did not mean to get into a confounded scrimmage. Somebody else might have got killed—for I would not have broken out only to get chucked back, and I did not want any more of that work. He refused, looking more sick than ever. He was afraid of the men, and also of that old second mate of his who had been sailing with him for years a grey-headed old humbug; and his steward, too, had been with him devil knows how long—seventeen years or more—a dogmatic sort of loafer who hated me like poison, just because I was the chief mate. No chief mate ever made more than one voyage in the *Sephora*, you know. Those two old chaps ran the ship. Devil only knows what the skipper wasn't afraid of (all his nerve went to pieces altogether in that hellish spell of bad weather we had)—of what the law would do to him—of his wife, perhaps. Oh, yes! She's on board. Though I don't think she would have .meddled. She would have been only too glad to have me out of the ship in any way. The "brand of Cain" business, don't you see. That's all right. I was ready enough to go off wandering on the face of the earth and that was price enough to pay for an Abel of that sort. Anyhow, he wouldn't listen to me. "This thing must take its course. I represent the law here." He was shaking like a leaf. "So you won't?" "No!" "Then I hope you will be able to sleep on that," I said, and turned my back on him. "I wonder that *you* can," cries he, and locks the door.

'Well, after that, I couldn't. Not very well. That was three weeks ago We have had a slow passage through the Java Sea; drifted about Carimata for ten days. When we anchored here they thought, I suppose, it was all right. The nearest land (and that's five miles) is the ship's destination; the consul would soon set about catching me; and there would have been no object in bolting to these islets there. I don't suppose there's a drop of water on them. I don't know how it was, but tonight that steward, after bringing me my supper, went out to let me eat it, and left the door unlocked. And I ate it—all there was, too. After I had finished I strolled out on the quarterdeck. I don't know that I meant to do anything. A breath of fresh air was all I wanted, I believe. Then a sudden temptation came over me. I kicked off my slippers and was in the water before I had made up my mind fairly. Somebody heard the splash and they raised an awful hullabaloo. "He's gone! Lower the boats! He's committed suicide! No, he's swimming." Certainly I was swimming. It's not so easy for a swimmer like me to commit suicide by drowning. I landed on the nearest islet before the boat left the ship's side. I heard them pulling about in the dark, hailing, and so on, but after a bit they gave up. Everything quieted down and the anchorage became as still as death. I sat down on a stone and began to think. I felt certain they would start searching for me at daylight. There was no place to hide on those stony things—and if there had been, what would have been the good? But now I was clear of that ship, I was not going back. So after a while I took off all my clothes, tied them up in a bundle with a stone inside, and dropped them in the deep water on the outer side of that islet. That was suicide enough for me. Let them think what they liked, but I didn't mean to drown myself. I meant to swim till I sank—but that's not the same thing. I struck out for another of these little islands, and it was from that one that I first saw your riding light. Something to swim for. I went on easily, and on the way I came upon a flat rock a foot or two above water. In the daytime, I dare say, you might make it out with a glass from your poop. I scrambled up on it and rested myself for a bit. Then I made another start. That last spell must have been over a mile.'

His whisper was getting fainter and fainter, and all the time he stared straight out through the porthole, in which there was not even a star to be seen. I had not interrupted him. There was something that made comment impossible in his narrative, or perhaps in himself; a sort of feeling, a quality, which I can't find a name for. And when he ceased, all I found was a futile whisper: 'So you swam for our light?'

'Yes—straight for it. It was something to swim for. I couldn't see any stars low down because the coast was in the way, and I couldn't see the land, either. The water was like glass. One might have been swimming in a confounded thousand-feet-deep cistern with no place for scrambling out anywhere; but what I didn't like was the notion of swimming round and round like a crazed bullock before I gave out; and as I didn't mean to go back . . . No. Do you see me being hauled back, stark naked, off one of these little islands by the scruff of the neck and fighting like a wild beast? Somebody would have got killed for certain, and I did not want any of that. So I went on. Then your ladder—'

'Why didn't you hail the ship?' I asked, a little louder.

He touched my shoulder lightly. Lazy footsteps came right over our heads and stopped. The second mate had crossed from the other side of the poop and might have been hanging over the rail, for all we knew.

'He couldn't hear us talking—could he?' My double breathed into my very ear, anxiously.

His anxiety was an answer, a sufficient answer, to the question I had put to him. An answer containing all the difficulty of that situation. I closed the porthole quietly, to make sure. A louder word might have been overheard.

'Who's that?' he whispered then.

'My second mate. But I don't know much more of the fellow than you do.'

And I told him a little about myself. I had been appointed to take charge while I least expected anything of the sort, not quite a fortnight ago. I didn't know either the ship or the people. Hadn't had the time in port to look about me or size anybody up. And as to the crew, all they knew was that I was appointed to take the ship home. For the rest, I was almost as much of a stranger on board as himself, I said. And at the moment I felt it most acutely. I felt that it would take very little to make me a suspect person in the eyes of the ship's company.

He had turned about meantime; and we, the two strangers in the ship, faced each other in identical attitudes.

'Your ladder—' he murmured; after a silence. 'Who'd have thought of finding a ladder hanging over at night in a ship anchored out here! I felt just then a very unpleasant faintness. After the life I've been leading for nine weeks, anybody would have got out of condition. I wasn't capable of swimming round as far as your rudder chains. And, lo and behold! There was a ladder to get hold of. After I gripped it I said to myself, "What's the good?" When I saw a man's head looking over I thought I would swim away presently and leave him shouting—in whatever language it was. I didn't mind being looked at. I—I liked it. And then you speaking to me so quietly—as if you had expected me—made me hold on a little longer. It had been a confounded lonely time—I don't mean while swimming. I was glad to talk a little to somebody that didn't belong to the *Sephora*. As to asking for the captain, that was a mere impulse. It could have been no use, with all the ship knowing about me and the other people pretty certain to be round here in the morning. I don't know—I wanted to be seen, to talk with somebody, before I went on. I don't know what I would have said . . . "Fine night, isn't it?" or something of the sort.'

'Do you think they will be round here presently?' I asked with some incredulity.

'Quite likely,' he said, faintly.

He looked extremely haggard all of a sudden. His head rolled on his shoulders.

'H'm. We shall see then. Meantime get into that bed,' I whispered. 'Want help? There.'

It was a rather high bed-place with a set of drawers underneath. This amazing swimmer really needed the lift I gave him by seizing his leg. He tumbled in, rolled over on his back, and flung one arm across his eyes. And then, with his face nearly hidden, he must have looked exactly as I used to look in that bed. I gazed upon my other self for a while before drawing across carefully the two green serge curtains which ran on a brass rod. I thought for a moment of pinning them together for greater safety, but I sat down on the couch, and once there I felt unwilling to rise and hunt for a pin. I would do it in a moment. I was extremely tired, in a peculiarly

327

intimate way, by the strain of stealthiness, by the effort of whispering and the general secrecy of this excitement. It was three o'clock by now and I had been on my feet since nine, but I was not sleepy; I could not have gone to sleep. I sat there, fagged out, looking at the curtains, trying to clear my mind of the confused sensation of being in two places at once, and greatly bothered by an exasperating knocking in my head. It was a relief to discover suddenly that it was not in my head at all, but on the outside of the door. Before I could collect myself the words 'Come in' were out of my mouth, and the steward entered with a tray, bringing in my morning coffee. I had slept, after all, and I was so frightened that I shouted, 'This way! I am here, steward,' as though he had been miles away. He put down the tray on the table next the couch and only then said, very quietly, 'I can see you are here, sir.' I felt him give me a keen look, but I dared not meet his eyes just then. He must have wondered why I had drawn the curtains of my bed before going to sleep on the couch. He went out, hooking the door open as usual.

I heard the crew washing decks above me. I knew I would have been told at once if there had been any wind. Calm, I thought, and I was doubly vexed. Indeed, I felt dual more than ever. The steward reappeared suddenly in the doorway. I jumped up from the couch so quickly that he gave a start.

'What do you want here?'

'Close your port, sir—they are washing decks.'

'It is closed,' I said, reddening.

'Very well, sir.' But he did not move from the doorway and returned my stare in an extraordinary, equivocal manner for a time. Then his eyes wavered, all his expression changed, and in a voice unusually gentle, almost coaxingly: 'May I come in to take the empty cup away, sir?'

'Of course!' I turned my back on him while he popped in and out. Then I unhooked and closed the door and even

328

pushed the bolt. This sort of thing could not go on very long. The cabin was as hot as an oven, too. I took a peep at my double, and discovered that he had not moved, his arm was still over his eyes; but his chest heaved; his hair was wet; his chin glistened with perspiration. I reached over him and opened the port.

'I must show myself on deck,' I reflected.

Of course, theoretically, I could do what I liked, with no one to say nay to me within the whole circle of the horizon; but to lock my cabin door and take the key away I did not dare. Directly I put my head out of the companion I saw the group of my two officers, the second mate barefooted, the chief mate in long India-rubber boots, near the break of the poop, and the steward half way down the poop ladder talking to them eagerly. He happened to catch sight of me and dived, the second ran down on the main deck shouting some order or other, and the chief mate came to meet me, touching his cap.

There was a sort of curiosity in his eye that I did not like. I don't know whether the steward had told them that I was 'queer' only, or downright drunk, but I know the man meant to have a good look at me. I watched him coming with a smile which, as he got into point-blank range, took effect and froze his very whiskers. I did not give him time to open his lips.

'Square the yards by lifts and braces before the hands go to breakfast.'

It was the first particular order I had given on board that ship; and I stayed on deck to see it executed, too. I had felt the need of asserting myself without loss of time. That sneering young cub got taken down a peg or two on that occasion, and I also seized the opportunity of having a good look at the face of every foremast man as they filed past me to go to the after braces. At breakfast time, eating nothing myself, I presided with such frigid dignity that the two mates were only too glad to escape from the cabin as soon as decency permitted; and all the time the dual working of my mind distracted me almost to the point of insanity. I was constantly watching myself, my secret self, as dependent on my actions as my own personality, sleeping in that bed, behind that door which faced me as I sat at the head of the table. It was very much like being mad, only it was worse because one was aware of it.

I had to shake him for a solid minute, but when at last he opened his eyes it was in the full possession of his senses, with an enquiring look. 'All's well so far,' I whispered. 'Now you must vanish into the bathroom.'

He did so, as noiseless as a ghost, and I then rang for the steward, and facing him boldly, directed him to tidy up my stateroom while I was having my bath—'and be quick about it'. As my tone admitted of no excuses, he said, 'Yes, sir,' and ran off to fetch his dustpan and brushes. I took a bath and did most of my dressing, splashing, and whistling softly for the steward's edification, while the secret sharer of my life stood drawn up bolt upright in that little space, his face looking very sunken in daylight, his eyelids lowered under the stern, dark line of his eyebrows drawn together by a slight frown.

When I left him there to go back to my room the steward was finishing dusting. I sent for the mate and engaged him in some insignificant conversation. It was, as it were, trifling with the terrific character of his whiskers; but my object was to give him an opportunity for a good look at my cabin. And then I could at last shut, with a clear conscience, the door of my stateroom and get my double back into the recessed part. There was nothing else for it. He had to sit still on a small folding stool, half smothered by the heavy coats hanging there. We listened to the steward going into the bathroom out of the saloon filling the water bottles there, scrubbing the bath, setting things to rights, whisk, bang, clatter—out again into the saloon—turn the key—click. Such was my scheme for keeping my second self invisible. Nothing better could be contrived under the circumstances. And there we sat; I at my writing desk ready to appear busy with some papers, he behind me, out of sight of the door. It would not have been prudent to talk in daytime; and I could not have stood the excitement of that queer sense of whispering to myself. Now and then, glancing over my shoulder, I saw him far back there, sitting rigidly on the low stool, his bare feet close together, his arms folded, his head hanging on his breast—and perfectly still. Anybody would have taken him for me.

I was fascinated by it myself. Every moment I had to glance over my shoulder. I was looking at him when a voice outside the door said: 'Beg pardon, sir.'

'Well . . . !' I kept my eyes on him, and so, when the voice outside the door announced, 'There's a ship's boat coming our way, sir;' I saw him give a start—the first movement he had made for hours. But he did not raise his bowed head.

'All right. Get the ladder over.'

I hesitated. Should I whisper something to him? But what? His immobility seemed never to have been disturbed. What could I tell him he did not know already . . . ? Finally I went on deck.

II

THE skipper of the *Sephora* had thin red whiskers all round his face, and the sort of complexion that goes with hair of that colour; also the particular, rather smeary shade of blue in the eyes. He was not exactly a showy figure; his shoulders were high, his stature but middling—one leg slightly more bandy than the other. He shook hands, looking vaguely around. A spiritless tenacity was his main characteristic, I judged. I behaved with a politeness which seemed to disconcert him. Perhaps he was shy. He mumbled to me as if he were ashamed of what he was saying; gave his name (it was something like

Archbold—but at this distance of years I am hardly sure), his ship's name, and a few other particulars of that sort, in the manner of a criminal making a reluctant and doleful confession. He had had terrible weather on the passage out—terrible—terrible—wife aboard, too.

By this time we were seated in the cabin and the steward brought in a tray with a bottle and glasses. 'Thanks! No.' Never took liquor. Would have some water, though. He drank two tumblerfuls. Terrible thirsty work. Ever since daylight had been exploring the islands round his ship.

'What was that for—fun?' I asked, with an appearance of polite interest.

'No!' He sighed. 'Painful duty.'

As he persisted in his mumbling and I wanted my double to hear every word, I hit upon the notion of informing him that I regretted to say I was hard of hearing.

'Such a young man, too!' he nodded, keeping his smeary blue, unintelligent eyes fastened upon me. What was the cause of it—some disease? he enquired, without the least sympathy and as if he thought that, if so, I'd got no more than I deserved.

'Yes; disease,' I admitted in a cheerful tone which seemed to shock him. But my point was gained, because he had to raise his voice to give me his tale. It is not worth while to record that version. It was just over two months since all this had happened, and he had thought so much about it that he seemed completely muddled as to its bearings, but still immensely impressed.

'What would you think of such a thing happening on board your own ship? I've had the *Sephora* for these fifteen years. I am a well-known shipmaster.'

He was densely distressed—and perhaps I should have sympathized with him if I had been able to detach my mental vision from the unsuspected sharer of my cabin as though he were my second self. There he was on the other side of the bulkhead, four or five feet from us, no more, as we sat in the saloon. I looked politely at Captain Archbold (if that was his name), but it was the other I saw, in a grey sleeping suit, seated on a low stool, his bare feet close together, his arms folded, and every word said between us falling into the ears of his dark head bowed on his chest.

'I have been at sea now, man and boy, for seven-and-thirty years, and I've never heard of such a thing happening in an English ship. And that it should be my ship. Wife on board, too.'

I was hardly listening to him.

'Don't you think,' I said, 'that the heavy sea which, you told me, came aboard just then might have killed the man? I have seen the sheer weight of a sea kill a man very neatly, by simply breaking his neck.'

'Good God!' he uttered, impressively, fixing his smeary blue eyes on me. 'The sea! No man killed by the sea ever looked like that.' He seemed positively scandalized at my suggestion. And as I gazed at him, certainly not prepared for anything original on his part, he advanced his head close to mine and thrust his tongue out at me so suddenly that I couldn't help starting back.

After scoring over my calmness in this graphic way he nodded wisely. If I had seen the sight, he assured me, I would never forget it as long as I lived. The weather was too bad to give the corpse a proper sea burial. So next day at dawn they took it up on the poop, covering its face with a bit of bunting; he read a short prayer, and then, just as it was, in its oilskins and long boots, they launched it amongst those mountainous seas that seemed ready every moment to swallow up the ship herself and the terrified lives on board of her.

'That reefed foresail saved you,' I threw in.

'Under God—it did,' he exclaimed fervently. 'It was by a special mercy, I firmly believe, that it stood some of those hurricane squalls.'

'It was the setting of that sail which—' I began.

'God's own hand in it,' he interrupted me. 'Nothing less could have done it. I don't mind telling you that I hardly dared give the order. It seemed impossible that we could touch anything without losing it, and then our last hope would have been gone.'

The terror of that gale was on him yet. I let him go on for a bit, then said, casually—as if returning to a minor subject: 'You were very anxious to give up your mate to the shore people, I believe?'

He was. To the law. His obscure tenacity on that point had in it something incomprehensible and a little awful; something, as it were, mystical, quite apart from his anxiety that he should not be suspected of 'countenancing any doings of that sort'. Seven-and-thirty virtuous years at sea, of which over twenty of immaculate command, and the last fifteen in the *Sephora*, seemed to have laid him under some pitiless obligation.

'And you know,' he went on, groping shamefacedly amongst his feelings, 'I did not engage that young fellow. His people had some interest with my owners. I was in a way forced to take him on. He looked very smart, very gentlemanly, and all that. But do you know—I never liked him, somehow. I am a plain man. You see, he wasn't exactly the sort for the chief mate of a ship like the *Sephora*.'

I had become so connected in thoughts and impressions with the secret sharer of my cabin that I felt as if I, personally, were being given to understand that I, too, was not the sort that would have done for the chief mate of a ship like the *Sephora*. I had no doubt of it in my mind.

'Not at all the style of man. You understand,' he insisted, superfluously, looking hard at me.

I smiled urbanely. He seemed at a loss for a while.

'I suppose I must report a suicide.'

'Beg pardon?'

'Sui-cide! That's what I'll have to write to my owners directly I get in.'

'Unless you manage to recover him before tomorrow,' I assented, dispassionately, '. . . I mean, alive.'

He mumbled something which I really did not catch, and I turned my ear to him in a puzzled manner.

He fairly bawled: 'The land—I say, the mainland is at least seven miles off my anchorage.'

'About that.'

My lack of excitement, of curiosity, of surprise, of any sort of pronounced interest, began to arouse his distrust. But except for the felicitous pretence of deafness I had not tried to pretend anything. I had felt utterly incapable of playing the part of ignorance properly, and therefore was afraid to try. It is also certain that he had brought some readymade suspicions with him, and that he viewed my politeness as a strange and unnatural phenomenon. And yet how else could I have received him? Not heartily! That was impossible for psychological reasons, which I need not state here. My only object was to keep off his enquiries. Surlily? Yes, but surliness might have provoked a point-blank question. From its novelty to him and from its nature, punctilious courtesy was the manner best calculated to restrain the man. But there was the danger of his breaking through my defence bluntly. I could not, I think have met him by a direct lie, also for psychological (not moral) reasons. If he had only known how afraid I was of his putting my feeling of identity with the other to the test! But, strangely enough (I thought of it only afterward), I believe that he was not a little disconcerted by the reverse side of that weird situation, by something in me that reminded him of the man he was seeking—suggested a mysterious similitude to the young fellow he had distrusted and disliked from the first.

However that might have been, the silence was not very prolonged. He took another oblique step.

'I reckon I had no more than a two-mile pull to your ship. Not a bit more.'

'And quite enough, too, in this awful heat,' I said.

Another pause full of mistrust followed. Necessity, they say, is mother of invention, but fear, too, is not barren of ingenious suggestions. And I was afraid he would ask me point-blank for news of my other self.

'Nice little saloon, isn't it?' I remarked, as if noticing for the first time the way his eyes roamed from one closed door to the other. 'And very well fitted out, too. Here, for instance,' I continued, reaching over the back of my seat negligently and flinging the door open, 'is my bathroom.'

He made an eager movement, but hardly gave it a glance. I got up, shut the door of the bathroom, and invited him to have a look round, as if I were very proud of my accommodation. He had to rise and be shown round, but he went through the business without any raptures whatever.

'And now we'll have a look at my stateroom,' I declared, in a voice as loud as I dared to make it, crossing the cabin to the starboard side with purposely heavy steps.

He followed me in and gazed around. My intelligent double had vanished. I played my part.

'Very convenient—isn't it?'

'Very nice. Very comf . . .' He didn't finish, and went out brusquely as if to escape from some unrighteous wiles of mine. But it was not to be. I had been too frightened not to feel vengeful; I felt I had him on the run, and I meant to keep him on the run. My polite insistence must have had something menacing in it, because he gave in suddenly. And I did not let him off a single item: mate's room, pantry, storerooms, the very sail-locker which was also under the poop—he had to look into them all. When at last I showed him out on the quarterdeck he drew a long, spiritless sigh, and mumbled dismally that he must really be going back to his ship now. I desired my mate, who had joined us, to see to the captain's boat.

The man of whiskers gave a blast on the whistle which he used to wear hanging round his neck, and yelled, '*Sephoras* away!' My double down there in my cabin must have heard, and certainly could not feel more relieved than I. Four fellows came running out from somewhere forward and went over the side, while my own men, appearing on deck too, lined the rail. I escorted my visitor to the gangway ceremoniously, and nearly overdid it. He was a tenacious beast. On the very ladder he lingered, and in that unique, guiltily conscientious manner of sticking to the point: 'I say . . . you . . . you don't think that—'

I covered his voice loudly: 'Certainly not . . . I am delighted. Goodbye.'

I had an idea of what he meant to say, and just saved myself by the privilege of defective hearing. He was too shaken generally to insist, but my mate, close witness of that parting, looked mystified and his face took on a thoughtful cast. As I did not want to appear as if I wished to avoid all communication with my officers, he had the opportunity to address me.

'Seems a very nice man. His boat's crew told our chaps a very extraordinary story, if what I am told by the steward is true. I suppose you had it from the captain, sir?'

'Yes. I had a story from the captain.'

'A very horrible affair—isn't it, sir?'

'It is.'

'Beats all these tales we hear about murders in Yankee ships.'

'I don't think it beats them. I don't think it resembles

them in the least.'

'Bless my soul—you don't say so! But of course I've no acquaintance whatever with American ships, not I, so I couldn't go against your knowledge. It's horrible enough for me . . . But the queerest part is that those fellows seemed to have some idea the man was hidden aboard here. They had really. Did you ever hear of such a thing?'

'Preposterous—isn't it?'

We were walking to and fro athwart the quarterdeck. No one of the crew forward could be seen (the day was Sunday), and the mate pursued: 'There was some little dispute about it. Our chaps took offence. "As if we would harbour a thing like that," they said. "Wouldn't you like to look for him in our coal-hole?" Quite a tiff. But they made it up in the end. I suppose he did drown himself. Don't you, sir?'

'I don't suppose anything.'

'You have no doubt in the matter, sir?'

'None whatever.'

I left him suddenly. I felt I was producing a bad impression, but with my double down there it was most trying to be on deck. And it was almost as trying to be below. Altogether a nerve-trying situation. But on the whole I felt less torn in two when I was with him. There was no one in the whole ship whom I dared take into my confidence. Since the hands had got to know his story, it would have been impossible to pass him off for anyone else, and an accidental discovery was to be dreaded now more than ever . . .

The steward being engaged in laying the table for dinner, we could talk only with our eyes when I first went down. Later in the afternoon we had a cautious try at whispering. The Sunday quietness of the ship was against us; the stillness of air and water around her was against us in the elements, the men were against us—everything was against us in our secret partnership; time itself—for this could not go on forever. The very trust in Providence was, I suppose, denied to his guilt. Shall I confess that this thought cast me down very much? And as to the chapter of accidents which counts for so much in the book of success, I could only hope that it was closed. For what favourable accident could be expected?

'Did you hear everything?' were my first words as soon as we took up our position side by side, leaning over my bed-place.

He had. And the proof of it was his earnest whisper, 'The man told you he hardly dared to give the order.'

I understood the reference to be to that saving foresail. 'Yes. He was afraid of it being lost in the setting.'

'I assure you he never gave the order. He may think he did, but he never gave it. He stood there with me on the break of the poop after the main topsail blew away, and whimpered about our last hope—positively whimpered about it and nothing else—and the night coming on! To hear one's skipper go on like that in such weather was enough to drive any fellow out of his mind. It worked me up into a sort of desperation. I just took it into my own hands and went away from him, boiling, and—But what's the use telling you? *You* know! . . . Do you think that if I had not been pretty fierce with them I should have got the men to do anything? Not it! The bo's'n perhaps? Perhaps! It wasn't a heavy sea—it was a sea gone mad! I suppose the end of the world will be something like that; and a man may have the heart to see it coming once and be done with it—but to have to face it day after day I don't blame anybody. I was precious little better than the rest. Only—I was an officer of that old coal waggon, anyhow—'

'I quite understand,' I conveyed that sincere assurance into his ear. He was out of breath with whispering; I could hear him pant slightly. It was all very simple. The same strung-up force which had given twenty-four men a chance, at least, for their lives, had, in a sort of recoil, crushed an unworthy mutinous existence.

But I had no leisure to weigh the merits of the matter—footsteps in the saloon, a heavy knock. 'There's enough wind to get under way with, sir.' Here was the call of a new claim upon my thoughts and even upon my feelings.

'Turn the hands up,' I cried through the door. 'I'll be on deck directly.'

I was going out to make the acquaintance of my ship. Before I left the cabin our eyes met—the eyes of the only two strangers on board. I pointed to the recessed part where the little camp stool awaited him and laid my finger on my lips. He made a gesture—somewhat vague—a little mysterious, accompanied by a faint smile, as if of regret.

This is not the place to enlarge upon the sensations of a man who feels for the first time a ship move under his feet to his own independent word. In my case they were not unalloyed. I was not wholly alone with my command; for there was that stranger in my cabin. Or rather, I was not completely and wholly with her. Part of me was absent. That mental feeling of being in two places at once affected me physically as if the mood of secrecy had penetrated my very soul. Before an hour had elapsed since the ship had begun to move, having occasion to ask the mate (he stood by my side) to take a compass bearing of the Pagoda, I caught myself reaching up to his ear in whispers. I say I caught myself, but enough had escaped to startle the man. I can't describe it otherwise than by saying that he shied. A grave, preoccupied manner, as though he were in possession of some perplexing intelligence, did not leave him henceforth. A little later I moved away from the rail to look at the compass with such a stealthy gait that the helmsman noticed it—and I could not help noticing the unusual roundness of his eyes. These are trifling instances, though it's to no commander's advantage to be suspected of ludicrous eccentricities. But I was also more seriously affected. There are to a seaman certain words, gestures, that should in given conditions come as naturally, as instinctively as the winking of a menaced eye. A certain order should spring on to his lips without thinking; a certain sign should get itself made, so to speak, without reflection. But all unconscious alertness had abandoned me. I had to make an effort of will to recall myself back (from the cabin) to the conditions of the moment. I felt that I was appearing an irresolute commander to those people who were watching me more or less critically.

And, besides, there were the scares. On the second day out, for instance, coming off the deck in the afternoon (I had straw slippers on my bare feet) I stopped at the open pantry door and spoke to the steward. He was doing something there with his back to me. At the sound of my voice he nearly jumped out of his skin, as the saying is, and incidentally broke a cup.

'What on earth's the matter with you?' I asked, astonished.

He was extremely confused. 'Beg your pardon, sir. I made sure you were in your cabin.'

'You see I wasn't.'

'No, sir. I could have sworn I had heard you moving in there not a moment ago. It's most extraordinary . . . very sorry, sir.'

I passed on with an inward shudder. I was so identified with my secret double that I did not even mention the fact in those scanty, fearful whispers we exchanged. I suppose he had made some slight noise of some kind or other. It would have been miraculous if he hadn't at one time or another. And yet, haggard as he appeared, he looked always perfectly self controlled, more than calm—almost invulnerable. On my suggestion he remained almost entirely in the bathroom, which, upon the whole, was the safest place. There could be really no shadow of an excuse for anyone ever wanting to go in there, once the steward had done with it. It was a very tiny place. Sometimes he reclined on the floor, his legs bent, his head sustained on one elbow. At others I would find him on the camp stool, sitting in his grey sleeping suit and with his cropped dark hair like a patient, unmoved convict. At night I would smuggle him into my bed-place, and we would whisper together, with the regular footfalls of the officer of the watch passing and repassing over our heads. It was an infinitely miserable time. It was lucky that some tins of fine preserves were stowed in a locker in my stateroom; hard bread I could always get hold of; and so he lived on stewed chicken, pâté de foie gras, asparagus, cooked oysters, sardines, on all sorts of abominable sham delicacies out of tins. My early morning coffee he always drank; and it was all I dared do for him in that respect.

Every day there was the horrible manoeuvring to go through so that my room and then the bathroom should be done in the usual way. I came to hate the sight of the steward, to abhor the voice of that harmless man. I felt that it was he who would bring on the disaster of discovery. It hung like a sword over our heads.

The fourth day out, I think (we were then working down the east side of the Gulf of Siam, tack for tack, in light winds and smooth water)—the fourth day, I say, of this miserable juggling with the unavoidable, as we sat at our evening meal, that man, whose slightest movement I dreaded, after putting down the dishes ran up on deck busily. This could not be dangerous. Presently he came down again; and then it appeared that he had remembered a coat of mine which I had thrown over a rail to dry after having been wetted in a shower which had passed over the ship in the afternoon. Sitting stolidly at the head of the table I became terrified at the sight of the garment on his arm. Of course he made for my door.

There was no time to lose.

'Steward,' I thundered. My nerves were so shaken that I could not govern my voice and conceal my agitation. This was the sort of thing that made my terrifically whiskered mate tap his forehead with his forefinger. I had detected him using that gesture while talking on deck with a confidential air to the carpenter. It was too far to hear a word, but I had no doubt that this pantomime could only refer to the strange new captain.

'Yes, sir,' the pale-faced steward turned resignedly to me. It was this maddening course of being shouted at, checked without rhyme or reason, arbitrarily chased out of my cabin, suddenly called into it, sent flying out of his pantry on incomprehensible errands, that accounted for the growing wretchedness of his expression.

'Where are you going with that coat?'

'To your room, sir.'

'Is there another shower coming?'

'I'm sure I don't know, sir. Shall I go up again and see, sir?'

'No! Never mind.'

My object was attained, as of course my other self in there would have heard everything that passed. During this interlude my two officers never raised their eyes off their respective plates; but the lip of that confounded cub, the second mate, quivered visibly.

I expected the steward to hook my coat on and come out at once. He was very slow about it; but I dominated my nervousness sufficiently not to shout after him. Suddenly I became aware (it could be heard plainly enough) that the fellow for some reason or other was opening the door of the bathroom. It was the end. The place was literally not big enough to swing a cat in. My voice died in my throat and I went stony all over. I expected to hear a yell of surprise and terror, and made a movement, but had not the strength to get on my legs. Everything remained still. Had my second self taken the poor wretch by the throat? I don't know what I would have done next moment if I had not seen the steward come out of my room, close the door, and then stand quietly by the sideboard.

'Saved,' I thought. 'But, no! Lost! Gone! He was gone!'

I laid my knife and fork down and leaned back in my chair. My head swam. After a while, when sufficiently recovered to speak in a steady voice, I instructed my mate to put the ship round at eight o'clock himself.

'I won't come on deck,' I went on. 'I think I'll turn in, and unless the wind shifts I don't want to be disturbed before midnight. I feel a bit seedy.'

'You did look middling bad a little while ago,' the chief mate remarked without showing any great concern.

They both went out, and I stared at the steward clearing the table. There was nothing to be read on that wretched man's face. But why did he avoid my eyes, I asked myself. Then I thought I should like to hear the sound of his voice.

'Steward!'

'Sir!' Startled as usual.

'Where did you hang up that coat?'

'In the bathroom, sir.' The usual anxious tone. 'It's not quite dry yet, sir.'

For some time longer I sat in the cuddy. Had my double vanished as he had come? But of his coming there was an explanation, whereas his disappearance would be inexplicable . . . I went slowly into my dark room, shut the door, lighted the lamp, and for a time dared not turn round. When at last I did I saw him standing bolt upright in the narrow recessed part. It would not be true to say I had a shock, but an irresistible doubt of his bodily existence flitted through my mind. Can it be, I asked myself, that he is not visible to other eyes than mine? It was like being haunted. Motionless, with a grave face, he raised his hands slightly at me in a gesture which meant clearly, 'Heavens! what a narrow escape!' Narrow indeed. I think I had come creeping quietly as near insanity as any man who has not actually gone over the border. That gesture restrained me, so to speak.

The mate with the terrific whiskers was now putting the ship on the other tack. In the moment of profound silence which follows upon the hands going to their stations I heard on the poop his raised voice:

'Hard alee!' and the distant shout of the order repeated on the main deck. The sails, in that light breeze, made but a faint fluttering noise. It ceased. The ship was coming round slowly; I held my breath in the renewed stillness of expectation; one wouldn't have thought that there was a single living soul on her decks. A sudden brisk shout, 'Mainsail haul!' broke the spell, and in the noisy cries and rush overhead of the men running away with the main brace, we two, down in my cabin, came together in our usual position by the bed-place.

He did not wait for my question. 'I heard him fumbling here and just managed to squat myself down in the bath,' he whispered to me. 'The fellow only opened the door and put his arm in to hang the coat up. All the same—'

'I never thought of that,' I whispered back, even more appalled than before at the closeness of the shave, and marvelling at that something unyielding in his character which was carrying him through so finely. There was no agitation in his whisper. Whoever was being driven distracted, it was not he. He was sane. And the proof of his sanity was continued when he took up the whispering again.

'It would never do for me to come to life again.'

It was something that a ghost might have said. But what he was alluding to was his old captain's reluctant admission of the theory of suicide. It would obviously serve his turn—if I had understood at all the view which seemed to govern the unalterable purpose of his action.

'You must maroon me as soon as ever you can get amongst these islands off the Cambodje shore,' he went on.

'Maroon you! We are not living in a boy's adventure tale,' I protested. His scornful whispering took me up.

'We aren't indeed! There's nothing of a boy's tale in this. But there's nothing else for it. I want no more. You don't suppose I am afraid of what can be done to me? Prison or gallows or whatever they may please. But you don't see me coming back to explain such things to an old fellow in a wig and twelve respectable tradesmen, do you? What can they know whether I am guilty or not—or of *what* I am guilty, either? That's my affair. What does the Bible say? "Driven off the face of the earth." Very well. I am off the face of the earth now. As I came at night so I shall go.'

'Impossible!' I murmured. 'You can't.'

'Can't? . . . Not naked like a soul on the Day of Judgment. I shall freeze on to this sleeping suit. The Last Day is not yet—and . . . you have understood thoroughly. Didn't you?'

I felt suddenly ashamed of myself. I may say truly that I understood and my hesitation in letting that man swim away from my ship's side had been a mere sham sentiment, a sort of cowardice.

'It can't be done now till next night,' I breathed out. 'The ship is on the offshore tack and the wind may fail us.'

'As long as I know that you understand,' he whispered. 'But of course you do. It's a great satisfaction to have got somebody to understand. You seem to have been there on purpose.' And in the same whisper, as if we two whenever we talked had to say things to each other which were not fit for the world to hear, he added, 'It's very wonderful.'

We remained side by side talking in our secret way—but

sometimes silent or just exchanging a whispered word or two at long intervals. And as usual he stared through the port. A breath of wind came now and again into our faces. The ship might have been moored in dock, so gently and on an even keel she slipped through the water, that did not murmur even at our passage, shadowy and silent like a phantom sea.

At midnight I went on deck, and to my mate's great surprise put the ship round on the other tack. His terrible whiskers flitted round me in silent criticism. I certainly should not have done it if it had been only a question of getting out of that sleepy gulf as quickly as possible. I believe he told the second mate, who relieved him, that it was a great want of judgment. The other only yawned. That intolerable cub shuffled about so sleepily and lolled against the rails in such a slack, improper fashion that I came down on him sharply.

'Aren't you properly awake yet?'

'Yes, sir! I am awake.'

'Well, then, be good enough to hold yourself as if you were. And keep a lookout. If there's any current we'll be closing with some islands before daylight.'

The east side of the gulf is fringed with islands, some solitary, others in groups. On the blue background of the high coast they seem to float on silvery patches of calm water, arid and grey, or dark green and rounded like clumps of evergreen bushes, with the larger ones, a mile or two long, showing the outlines of ridges, ribs of grey rock under the dank mantle of matted leafage. Unknown to trade, to travel, almost to geography, the manner of life they harbour is an unsolved secret. There must be villages—settlements of fishermen at least—on the largest of them, and some communication with the world is probably kept up by native craft. But all that forenoon, as we headed for them, fanned along by the faintest of breezes, I saw no sign of man or canoe in the field of the telescope I kept on pointing at the scattered group.

At noon I gave no orders for a change of course, and the mate's whiskers became much concerned and seemed to be offering themselves unduly to my notice.

At last I said: 'I am going to stand right in. Quite in—as far as I can take her.'

The stare of extreme surprise imparted an air of ferocity also to his eyes, and he looked truly terrific for a moment.

'We're not doing well in the middle of the gulf,' I continued, casually. 'I am going to look for the land breezes tonight.'

'Bless my soul! Do you mean, sir, in the dark amongst the lot of all them islands and reefs and shoals?'

'Well—if there are any regular land breezes at all on this coast one must get close inshore to find them, mustn't one?'

'Bless my soul!' he exclaimed again under his breath. All that afternoon he wore a dreamy, contemplative appearance which in him was a mark of perplexity. After dinner I went into my stateroom as if I meant to take some rest. There we two bent our dark heads over a half unrolled chart lying on my bed.

'There,' I said. 'It's got to be Koh-ring. I've been looking at it ever since sunrise. It has got two hills and a low point. It must be inhabited. And on the coast opposite there is what looks like the mouth of a biggish river—with some town, no doubt, not far up. It's the best chance for you that I can see.'

'Anything. Koh-ring let it be.'

He looked thoughtfully at the chart as if surveying chances and distances from a lofty height—and following with his eyes his own figure wandering on the blank land of Cochin-China, and then passing off that piece of paper clean out of sight into uncharted regions. And it was as if the ship had two captains to plan her course for her. I had been so worried and restless running up and down that I had not had the patience to dress that day. I had remained in my sleeping suit, with straw slippers and a soft floppy hat. The closeness of the heat in the gulf had been most oppressive, and the crew were used to see me wandering in that airy attire.

'She will clear the south point as she heads now,' I whispered into his ear. 'Goodness only knows when, though, but certainly after dark. I'll edge her in to half a mile, as far as I may be able to judge in the dark—'

'Be careful,' he murmured, warningly—and I realized suddenly that all my future, the only future for which I was fit, would perhaps go irretrievably to pieces in any mishap to my first command.

I could not stop a moment longer in the room. I motioned him to get out of sight and made my way on the poop. That unplayful cub had the watch. I walked up and down for a while thinking things out, then beckoned him over.

'Send a couple of hands to open the two quarterdeck ports,' I said, mildly.

He actually had the impudence, or else so forgot himself in his wonder at such an incomprehensible order, as to repeat: 'Open the quarterdeck ports! What for, sir?'

'The only reason you need concern yourself about is because I tell you to do so. Have them open wide and fastened properly.'

He reddened and went off, but I believe made some jeering remark to the carpenter as to the sensible practice of ventilating a ship's quarterdeck. I know he popped into the mate's cabin to impart the fact to him because the whiskers came on deck, as it were by chance, and stole glances at me from below—for signs of lunacy or drunkenness, I suppose.

A little before supper, feeling more restless than ever, I rejoined, for a moment, my second self. And to find him sitting so quietly was surprising, like something against nature, inhuman.

I developed my plan in a hurried whisper.

'I shall stand in as close as I dare and then put her round. I shall presently find means to smuggle you out of here into the sail-locker, which communicates with the lobby. But there is an opening, a sort of square for hauling the sails out, which gives straight on the quarterdeck and which is never closed in fine weather, so as to give air to the sails. When the ship's way is deadened in stays and all the hands are aft at the main braces you shall have a clear road to slip out and get overboard through the open quarterdeck port. I've had them both fastened up. Use a rope's end to lower yourself into the water so as to avoid a splash—you know. It could be heard and cause some beastly complication.'

He kept silent for a while, then whispered, 'I understand.'

'I won't be there to see you go,' I began with an effort. 'The rest . . . I only hope I have understood, too.'

'You have. From first to last'—and for the first time there seemed to be a faltering, something strained in his whisper. He caught hold of my arm, but the ringing of the supper bell made me start. He didn't, though; he only released his grip.

After supper I didn't come below again till well past eight o'clock. The faint, steady breeze was loaded with dew; and the wet, darkened sails held all there was of propelling power in it. The night, clear and starry, sparkled darkly, and the opaque, lightless patches shifting slowly against the low stars were the drifting islets. On the port bow there was a big one more distant and shadowily imposing by the great space of sky it eclipsed.

On opening the door I had a back view of my very own self looking at a chart. He had come out of the recess and was standing near the table.

'Quite dark enough,' I whispered.

He stepped back and leaned against my bed with a level, quiet glance. I sat on the couch. We had nothing to say to each other. Over our heads the officer of the watch moved here and there. Then I heard him move quickly. I knew what that meant. He was making for the companion; and presently his voice was outside my door.

'We are drawing in pretty fast, sir. Land looks rather close.'

'Very well,' I answered. 'I am coming on deck directly.'

I waited till he was gone out of the cuddy, then rose. My double moved too. The time had come to exchange our last whispers, for neither of us was ever to hear each other's natural voice.

'Look here!' I opened a drawer and took out three sovereigns. 'Take this, anyhow. I've got six and I'd give you the lot, only I must keep a little money to buy some fruit and vegetables for the crew from native boats as we go through Sunda Straits.'

He shook his head.

'Take it,' I urged him, whispering desperately. 'No one can tell what—'

He smiled and slapped meaningly the only pocket of the sleeping jacket. It was not safe, certainly. But I produced a large old silk handkerchief of mine, and tying the three pieces of gold in a corner, pressed it on him. He was touched, I suppose, because he took it at last and tied it quickly round his waist under the jacket, on his bare skin.

Our eyes met; several seconds elapsed, till, our glances still mingled, I extended my hand and turned the lamp out. Then I passed through the cuddy, leaving the door of my room wide open . . . 'Steward!'

He was still lingering in the pantry in the greatness of his zeal, giving a rub-up to a plated cruet stand the last thing before going to bed. Being careful not to wake up the mate, whose room was opposite, I spoke in an undertone.

He looked round anxiously. 'Sir!'

'Can you get me a little hot water from the galley?'

'I am afraid, sir, the galley fire's been out for some time now.'

'Go and see.'

He fled up the stairs.

'Now,' I whispered, loudly, into the saloon—too loudly, perhaps, but I was afraid I couldn't make a sound. He was by my side in an instant—the double captain slipped past the stairs—through a tiny dark passage . . . a sliding door. We were in the sail-locker, scrambling on our knees over the sails. A sudden thought struck me. I saw myself wandering barefooted, bareheaded, the sun beating on my dark poll. I snatched off my floppy hat and tried hurriedly in the dark to ram it on my other self. He dodged and fended off silently. I wonder what he thought had come to me before he understood and suddenly desisted. Our hands met gropingly, lingered united in a steady, motionless clasp for a second . . . No word was breathed by either of us when they separated.

I was standing quietly by the pantry door when the steward returned. 'Sorry, sir. Kettle barely warm. Shall I light the spirit lamp?'

'Never mind.'

I came out on deck slowly. It was now a matter of conscience to shave the land as close as possible—for now he must go overboard whenever the ship was put in stays. Must! There could be no going back for him. After a moment I walked over to leeward and my heart flew into my mouth at the nearness of the land on the bow. Under any other circumstances I would not have held on a minute longer. The second mate had followed me anxiously.

I looked on till I felt I could command my voice. 'She will weather,' I said then in a quiet tone.

'Are you going to try that, sir?' he stammered out incredulously.

I took no notice of him and raised my tone just enough to

be heard by the helmsman.

'Keep her good full.'

'Good full, sir.'

The wind fanned my cheek, the sails slept, the world was silent. The strain of watching the dark loom of the land grow bigger and denser was too much for me. I had shut my eyes—because the ship must go closer. She must! The stillness was intolerable. Were we standing still?

When I opened my eyes the second view started my heart with a thump. The black southern hill of Koh-ring seemed to hang right over the ship like a towering fragment of the everlasting night. On that enormous mass of blackness there was not a gleam to be seen, not a sound to be heard. It was gliding irresistibly toward us and yet seemed already within reach of the hand. I saw the vague figures of the watch grouped in the waist, gazing in awed silence.

'Are you going on, sir?' enquired an unsteady voice at my elbow. I ignored it. I had to go on.

'Keep her full. Don't check her way. That won't do now,' I said, warningly.

'I can't see the sails very well,' the helmsman answered me, in strange, quavering tones.

Was she close enough? Already she was, I won't say in the shadow of the land, but in the very blackness of it, already swallowed up as it were, gone too close to be recalled, gone from me altogether.

'Give the mate a call,' I said to the young man who stood at my elbow as still as death. 'And turn all hands up.'

My tone had a borrowed loudness reverberated from the height of the land. Several voices cried out together: 'We are all on deck, sir.'

Then stillness again, with the great shadow gliding closer, towering higher, without a light, without a sound. Such a hush had fallen on the ship that she might have been a bark of the dead floating in slowly under the very gate of Erebus.

'My God! Where are we?'

It was the mate moaning at my elbow. He was thunderstruck, and as it were deprived of the moral support of his whiskers. He clapped his hands and absolutely cried out, 'Lost!'

'Be quiet,' I said, sternly.

He lowered his tone, but I saw the shadowy gesture of his despair. 'What are we doing here?'

'Looking for the land wind.'

He made as if to tear his hair, and addressed me recklessly.

'She will never get out. You have done it, sir. I knew it'd end in something like this. She will never weather, and you are too close now to stay. She'll drift ashore before she's round. O my God!'

I caught his arm as he was raising it to batter his poor devoted head, and shook it violently.

'She's ashore already,' he wailed, trying to tear himself away.

'Is she? . . . Keep good full there!'

'Good full, sir,' cried the helmsman in a frightened, thin, childlike voice.

I hadn't let go the mate's arm and went on shaking it. 'Ready about, do you hear? You go forward'—shake— 'and stop there'—shake—'and hold your noise'—shake— 'and see these head sheets properly overhauled'—shake, shake— shake.

And all the time I dared not look toward the land lest my heart should fail me. I released my grip at last and he ran forward as if fleeing for dear life.

I wondered what my double there in the sail-locker thought of this commotion. He was able to hear everything—and perhaps he was able to understand why, on my conscience, it had to be thus close—no less. My first order 'Hard alee!' re-echoed ominously under the towering shadow of Koh-ring as if I had shouted in a mountain gorge. And then I watched the land intently. In that smooth water and light wind it was impossible to feel the ship coming to. No! I could not feel her. And my second self was making now ready to slip out and lower himself overboard. Perhaps he was gone already . . . ?

The great black mass brooding over our very mastheads began to pivot away from the ship's side silently. And now I forgot the secret stranger ready to depart, and remembered only that I was a total stranger to the ship. I did not know her. Would she do it? How was she to be handled?

I swung the main yard and waited helplessly. She was perhaps stopped, and her very fate hung in the balance, with the black mass of Koh-ring like the gate of the everlasting night towering over her taffrail. What would she do now? Had she way on her yet? I stepped to the side swiftly, and on the shadowy water I could see nothing except a faint phosphorescent flash revealing the glassy smoothness of the sleeping surface. It was impossible to tell—and I had not learned yet the feel of my ship. Was she moving? What I needed was something easily seen, a piece of paper, which I could throw overboard and watch. I had nothing on me. To run down for it I didn't dare. There was no time. All at once my strained, yearning stare distinguished a white object floating within a yard of the ship's side. White on the black water. A phosphorescent flash passed under it. What was that thing? . . . I recognized my own floppy hat. It must have fallen off his head . . . and he didn't bother. Now I had what I wanted—the saving mark for my eyes. But I hardly thought of my other self, now gone from the ship, to be hidden forever from all friendly faces, to be a fugitive and a vagabond on the earth, with no brand of the curse on his sane forehead to stay a slaying hand . . . too proud to explain.

And I watched the hat—the expression of my sudden pity for his mere flesh. It had been meant to save his homeless head from the dangers of the sun. And now—behold—it was saving the ship, by serving me for a mark to help out the ignorance of my strangeness. Ha! It was drifting forward, warning me just in time that the ship had gathered sternway.

'Shift the helm,' I said in a low voice to the seaman standing still like a statue.

The man's eyes glistened wildly in the binnacle light as he jumped round to the other side and spun round the wheel.

I walked to the break of the poop. On the overshadowed deck all hands stood by the forebraces waiting for my order. The stars ahead seemed to be gliding from right to left. And all was so still in the world that I heard the quiet remark 'She's round' passed in a tone of intense relief between two seamen.

'Let go and haul.'

The foreyards ran round with a great noise, amidst cheery cries. And now the frightful whiskers made themselves heard giving various orders. Already the ship was drawing ahead. And I was alone with her. Nothing! No one in the world should stand now between us, throwing a shadow on the way of silent knowledge and mute affection, the perfect communion of a seaman with his first command.

Walking to the taffrail, I was in time to make out, on the very edge of a darkness thrown by a towering black mass like the very gateway of Erebus—yes, I was in time to catch an evanescent glimpse of my white hat left behind to mark the spot where the secret sharer of my cabin and of my thoughts, as though he were my second self, had lowered himself into the water to take his punishment: a free man, a proud swimmer striking out for a new destiny.